"Then let me put it more clearly, Manuel." She spoke in that same quiet voice. "The two women who were murdered were killed in exactly the same way as two of Armando Bacalao's victims more than fifty years ago. Bacalao's bones were removed from his grave. We both know what that means, don't we, Manuel."

The old woman paused and looked hard at him. "Well, let that rest for the moment. Why don't you tell me about the black moon, Manuel?" She smiled as if challenging him.

For long seconds Manuel simply stared at her. His hatred was sudden, intense and exploded from him like a hot raging wind. . . .

BLACK MOON

Alison Drake

BALLANTINE BOOKS • NEW YORK

Library of Congress Catalog Card Number: 89-90946

ISBN 0-345-35780-9

Manufactured in the United States of America

First Edition: September 1989

For Rob

"The detective and his criminal wear versions of the same mask."

—Jane Roberts

"Convictions are more dangerous enemies of truth than lies."

—Friedrich Nietzsche

THE APPRENTICE
May 12

Ortega was proud of the knife.

He'd had it made in Miami of the finest steel, according to the specifications his *padrino* had given him. It was exactly seven inches long, no more than two inches wide at any part, and quite sharp. It had been his first test, proof of his sincerity, his dedication, and he'd spent a long time polishing it to a high sheen. Now, when the light inside the car struck it, the blade gleamed. He touched his fingertip to the razor edge.

"Perfect, no?"

Padrino smiled. "Show me how perfect, Manuel."

Ortega pressed his finger down against the blade, moved it back and forth. Blood bubbled and oozed from the cut. "See?" He held out his finger.

"Rub it on the sides of the blade."

He did. The blood streaked on the steel, red against silver, and seemed to pulse and throb, beckoning, whispering of promises to be kept. *Padrino* took the knife, slipped it inside the leather sheath, and switched off the light. He didn't open the door, didn't move at all.

The dark crept in, rubbing up against them, a dog in heat. The car's clock ticked loudly in the silence. Ortega counted the seconds and listened to the sounds in the woods and sucked on his bloody finger, waiting for *Padrino's* next command. This, too, was part of the lesson. An apprentice had to cultivate patience, to know when to wait, when to act, when to remain still and centered. It was a difficult lesson; Ortega hated to wait.

"Help me with the bike," *Padrino* said finally, opening the door and stepping outside.

Ortega exited quickly, shoes sinking into a bed of pine needles. The dark smelled sweet, of pine and spring and impending rain. A breeze dried the perspiration on his face. It had begun.

Padrino unlocked the trunk and he and Ortega pulled out the bicycle. They checked the tires, the light on the handlebars, the brakes. *Padrino* wrapped the knife in a jacket and put it in the rear basket. "Time check, Manuel."

"Half past two."

"Same here. I'll arrive at three sharp. Make sure the door isn't locked and that she's in the kitchen."

"I know what to do."

Padrino heard the annoyance in his voice and chuckled. It was a low, husky sound, unpleasant. "Just making sure. What happens after I arrive?"

Ortega told him, repeating the plan step by step.

"Good, Manuel. You have an excellent memory."

He beamed.

"Now move."

Ortega got back in the car and rolled down the window. His finger throbbed a little where he'd cut it, and he sucked on it as he started the engine. He didn't turn on the headlights until he was on the road, and only then did he glance in the rearview mirror. The bike was nowhere in sight.

Thunder rumbled in the distance: the voice of Changó, who ruled fire, thunder, lightning. An excellent sign, Ortega thought.

The little bungalow was less than a mile away, on a dead-end dirt road, set back among pines, brush, nicely hidden. It was such an ideal place, Ortega knew it had been divinely selected, that Ikú was clearing the path for them, facilitating things.

He stopped behind Rikki's VW Rabbit. The porch light was on; she had waited up for him. Something small and sharp plucked at his heart as he walked to the door, and he hesitated before his hand touched the knob. *It's necessary*, he reminded himself. The way to power was not an easy road. There were rules to observe. Details to be carried out. Sacrifices to be made for the higher vision.

An apprentice must obey and prove worthy: *Padrino* had told him this repeatedly.

Ortega's hand turned the knob, and he stepped into the tiny kitchen.

He smelled baked apples and coffee. Music drifted from one of the other rooms: Sergio Mendez. Brazil. One of Rikki's fantasies. She appeared in the doorway, dark hair pulled away from her face with barrettes, exposing the long lines of her neck. She was wearing tight khaki slacks, spiked heels, a plain cotton blouse, and the red and black beads he had given her. Her face was scrubbed clean of makeup; her cheeks glowed.

"I didn't think you were coming," she said, fixing a hand to her shapely hip.

"I told you I would."

"Hmm. You've told me lots of things, Manuel. Not all of them true."

"*Mi amor*, please. I don't want to argue. I am here, no?" He moved toward her, into the scent of her perfume, and kissed her.

Her lips were unyielding; her hand remained on her hip, and the other arm hung at her side. He hated her a little for that.

"Don't be angry." He touched the sides of her mouth, moving it into a smile, and she laughed and slapped his hand away.

"Okay, okay. C'mon, let's have some apple pie and coffee."

"Whose place is this?" he asked.

"A friend's. She's away for awhile. I'm watering her plants."

Her high heels clicked against the tile floor as she walked over to the stove. Ortega turned, watching her from the back. Nice, very nice. Dancing had kept her in excellent shape. Her legs were long, slender, and solid, her buttocks were firm, her waist narrow. Ikú would be pleased.

They had apple pie and coffee at the butcher-block table, night owls who kept to their own schedule. She understood the nature of darkness, as he did.

Ortega glanced surreptitiously at his watch, checking the time. He asked for a second piece of pie, even though he didn't want it, and for a refill on the coffee, even though the first cup was already pumping through him. Speeding up his heart. Making him sweat.

Rikki chatted. He nodded. Murmured something now and then. Looked at the time again.

At exactly 2:55, he polished off the last of his pie and helped her clear the table. He rinsed the dishes, thoroughly scrubbing everything he'd touched. When he turned off the porch light, he used a piece of Kleenex. He made sure the door was unlocked.

"How about a glass of wine?" she asked.

"Sure." He came up behind her as she stood at the refrigerator and nuzzled her neck. "We'll take it into the bedroom with us."

"Hmm." She leaned back against him, trusting, blind.

He knew he would be one of the primary suspects later. But this too was part of his test as an apprentice, one of the ways in which he demonstrated his trust in Ikú, his belief in the god's protection of those who served him. He would also have an alibi. After all, he lived in the world of men as fully as he did in the world of sorcery, and he had to exhibit the ability to bridge the two.

He turned her around, kissing her, softening her up, then danced with her, swaying to the music, and she laughed. Ortega loved the sound of it, so American, so coy. He kept her back to the door now as it opened, as *Padrino* slipped inside, the unsheathed knife at his side, parallel to his body.

He smiled.

Ortega's heart beat a little faster. Everything was working perfectly, just as they'd planned. *Padrino* moved closer. Closer. And then something went wrong. The music stopped. Rikki stepped away from him. Said she would change the record, put on something more romantic, and why didn't he grab the wine and—

Her head suddenly whipped around. "What're you . . ." Then she saw his knife and she screamed as she lurched for the door to the living room. Ortega grabbed her, clamped a hand over her mouth, pinned her arms behind her. She struggled, screamed into his hand, kicked, bit, and he yelled, *"Just do it!"*

Padrino sank the blade into her solar plexus. Rikki gasped and went limp in Ortega's arms. He kept holding her as the blade tore upward in precisely the way the ritual required. This part was important, Ortega knew it was. But he couldn't help feeling sickened when her limbs twitched and she expelled one last rasp of air. Bloody spittle splattered *Padrino*'s face seconds before he pulled the knife out.

"Let her go, Manuel."

She crumpled to the floor at Ortega's feet. Her hair had slipped loose from the clips that had held it. Her shoes had come off. For a moment or two, his heart ached for her. He wanted to brush the strands of hair from her cheeks, her forehead, wanted to pick her up, hold her, rock her, comfort her.

But *Padrino* was saying something, and when Ortega glanced up, the man's eyes were hard stones that burned at the center. *Mad eyes*, Ortega thought.

"Don't ever tell me what to do again, Manuel."

"You were just *standing* there. I couldn't hold her much longer."

He ignored the remark and pulled out a pair of latex gloves identical to the ones he wore. "Put these on. You know what to do now. I'll get the keys to her car."

He held out the knife, the perfect knife, and Ortega took it and did what had to be done.

It was drizzling when Ortega carried her outside in a garbage bag and slid her into the back of her VW Rabbit. *Padrino* fastened the bike to the luggage rack on top of it. "I'll meet you in the woods."

"Okay."

He started toward his own car, but *Padrino* caught his arm. "You did real well, Manuel. But we're not finished yet."

"I understand."

"You're all right?"

"Yes."

"You're sure?"

"Positive."

But it was a lie. The moment the Rabbit was out of sight, Ortega stopped his car, threw open the door, and stumbled out. He fell to his knees and vomited in the road. His head swirled with the smell of Rikki's blood. The scent of her perfume clung to his shirt. He felt the imprint of her mouth against his.

The rain came down harder, drops kissing the back of his neck. He rocked onto his heels and raised his head, eyes turning toward the sky. Thunder rumbled. Lightning scorched a trail through the dark. The rain cooled his burning cheeks but didn't wash away the stink of her blood. He moved his hands through the dirt, faster and faster as he wept, as he sobbed. He rubbed the dirt on his arms and neck and face, trying to scrub the smell away.

He collapsed, sprawled in the dirt like a dog, and the rain poured down, drenching his clothes, chilling him to the bone.

After a time, he didn't know how long, he smelled only the rain and the earth and his own sorrow. Until now, he didn't know that sorrow had a smell, but it did, and it was worse than the stink of blood, of death.

He lifted himself up, climbed into his car and drove toward the woods, shivering, teeth chattering, his head throbbing. The ritual had to be completed.

It was necessary.

And the worst was yet to come.

IKÚ
May 17–19

1

The Zodiac raft slipped through the dark waters, in and out of moonlight, barely making a sound. The thick mangroves on either side blocked whatever breeze there was, leaving the air warm and still, a vacuum the mosquitos had rapidly filled. They buzzed around Aline's head, biting wherever her skin was exposed, then swooped low into the raft and feasted on the rest of her, piercing her jeans, her socks, her windbreaker. They persevered despite repeated sprays of insect repellent.

"I'm about to gag on that stuff," said Simon Martell, who was sitting behind her.

"Damn thing's empty." She rattled the can and set it on the floor. "You have any?"

"Nope. They don't bite me."

"Must be your bad blood, Si."

"It's vitamin B. Mosquitos hate the taste of vitamin B."

"Sure."

"It's like moonshine to a Scotch drinker."

"Right."

"Are we almost there, Al?"

"Bernie said that when we see the ceiba, it's another ten minutes, and we just passed the ceiba."

"I thought this was supposed to be close to the lagoon."

"*Close* means something different to Bernie."

He sighed and grumbled, worse than a kid on a car trip.

"No griping allowed, Si. *I'm* doing *you* the favor, remember? You're the one who's going to prosecute this guy, not me. Hell, he wasn't even my arrest."

"Okay, okay. Sorry. You're right. I appreciate this, really. Dinner's on me when we get back."

"I'll hold you to it," she said.

Martell laughed. "Don't I know it."

The raft hugged the shore now. Sawgrass scraped against its sides as they passed, and the rich, sweet fragrance of the glades scented the warm air, a smell of brine and unimagined lushness. Night sounds swelled inside the dark behind the trees, inside the brush and sawgrass: frogs, crickets, the occasional hoot of an owl, fish leaping from the waters and splashing down again.

At any time of day, you felt like an intruder here, she thought. But it was especially true at night, when the wilderness seemed stronger somehow, ubiquitous, a force that would crush you if you made the wrong move, entered a place where you were not wanted, if you got careless. Aline paddled a little faster.

The raft slipped under low-hanging branches that snapped back in her face and poked at her windbreaker, forcing her to duck. She thought of snakes, alligators, bats, and knew it was exactly what Martell had intended when he'd directed the raft toward shore. She could feel him smile in the dark.

"You're playing mean, Si."

He laughed, then guided the raft away from the shore and out into the channel again.

They were in the wilderness preserve at the northeast side of Tango Key, in the small part of it that was a mangrove swamp. It definitely wasn't her idea of a fun place to be, especially at night, but the cause was worthy. Martell, one of Tango County's prosecutors, had been assigned an animal cruelty case involving pit bull fights. He needed additional testimony from the old trapper who'd snitched on the pair of brothers who'd run the racket until a month ago, when they'd been busted. The trapper lived out here in the sticks, in a shack Martell called a 'hooch,' that had no electricity and no phone.

It would've been easier to get in on an airboat, but the only two the Tango P.D. owned were in the garage being repaired. So they'd flown in, with a detour first to Key West for a bowl of conch chowder at Captain Tony's. Aline had landed the seaplane in a lagoon about a mile from here, and they'd inflated the raft and set out into the dark like a couple of amateur explorers.

They rounded the jut of land and cut to the left. The channel twisted for a quarter of a mile, then dead-ended at a hooch that was exactly what Bernie had described. Stilts, driftwood, a tin roof covered by thatch, a pair of windows lit up by lanterns. It looked like something you'd find on the Amazon.

A dog appeared in the glow of the windows, its furious barks resounding for miles in the stillness. Aline welcomed the noise; it was something from her world.

A second later, a tall man brandishing a rifle was silhouetted in the doorway. "Hush up, Gator," he said to the dog, and the animal immediately stopped barking and sat back, panting. "You's trespassing."

"It's Simon Martell, Mr. Griber."

"Who?"

"The county prosecutor."

"Kinda late for house calls, ain't it, counselor?"

"You don't have a phone. Mind if we come up?"

"We?"

"Claudia Bernelli's partner is with me."

"She don't got a name?"

"Detective Scott," said Aline.

"Where's Bernelli?"

"Out of town for the weekend," Aline replied.

"Uh-huh. Well, come on up. Stop at the top of the ladder and let Gator smell you. He don't cotton to strangers."

Griber kept a tight hold on the dog's collar as they climbed the ladder, but it didn't discourage Gator's low, menacing growls as he sniffed at their shoes, their legs, and bared his teeth. Griber, in fact, seemed to be enjoying the show. A smile creased his leathery face and made his gray mustache quiver. When the dog had determined they weren't a threat and licked Aline's hand, Griber patted him on the head and said, "Good, boy, good," as if he'd performed some monumental feat. Then the four of them traipsed into the hooch like old friends, Griber chattering about the weather, Gator whimpering and begging for attention.

The place was basic, and that was being kind. There were two rooms—one to sleep in, one to eat in—but the furniture was comfortable, and the screen kept out the mosquitos. Small blessings.

"Folks want anything to drink? Got whiskey and some cold soft drinks."

"Whiskey," said Martell.

"A Coke," said Aline.

Griber opened the gas-powered fridge, an antique if she'd

ever seen one. He pulled out a can of Coke and set it on the table with two shot glasses and a bottle of unlabeled whiskey. He was a husky man with tattoos on his thick arms, white hair pulled back into a ponytail, and a scraggly beard that he scratched at as he settled down. "So whatcha need, counselor?"

"More detail on what you saw the night the Vicker brothers were fighting the pit bulls."

"Shee-it. I already done gave that to Bernelli."

"She just took your statement, Mr. Griber. I've got to build a case that'll stick. You mind if I record this?"

"Yeah, I mind. But I mind more if those Vicker boys end up back out here, fucking things up."

So he talked into Martell's recorder and Aline sat back, listening, stroking Gator, sipping her Coke, watching Martell doing what he did best: pulling information from the unlikeliest of people.

He was in his early forties, with dark hair that was going gray, just like his mustache, and deep creases at the corners of his black eyes, testimony that his real love was the sea. At just under six feet, he was lean but not thin, pleasant-looking but not handsome, bright but not arrogant. He was also good-natured about the ribbing he'd taken from cops and other attorneys about having to prosecute this case, a low-priority shit case if there ever was one, and she liked him enormously for that. But not enough to become just one more woman in his life.

And there were a number of women.

For the last two months, though, Martell had been showering her with attention, and she wasn't immune to it. She liked being courted. Romantic dinners, ferry trips to Key West to poke around the shops like a tourist, sailing to Palm Key on Martell's sloop, long, hot hours in the sun. But he was interested in an affair, and she was not.

Lately, in fact, she seemed to be surrounded by events and people whose interests and expectations didn't coincide with hers. Ryan Kincaid, for instance.

Two weeks ago he'd returned from a six-month trip to the Orient, expecting to pick up where they'd left off, and was surprised when she'd told him she no longer felt the same about things. Much of their three-plus years together had been spent apart, with Kincaid in some far-flung corner of the world, satisfying a nomadic itch that seemed to worsen as he got older,

and her here on Tango, feeling like a whaler's widow. The lifestyle no longer appealed to her, even though Kincaid did.

Choices.

When you were pushing forty, you had to start making
choices. She was finding it a difficult thing to do.

". . . And while you're at it, you oughta be tracking down
the fools who's killing the panthers," Griber was saying.

"How do you know someone's killing panthers?" Aline
asked.

"Found a carcass." Griber knocked back a slug of whiskey,
then refilled his shot glass and Martell's. "Couple, three weeks
ago, I guess it was, I come. Come across a carcass out in the
groves where I trap. Just a young thing. Skin hadn't been taken,
though. Normally, poachers like the skins."

No one knew exactly how many panthers there were on Tango.
She'd heard estimates as low as two and as high as six. A few
years back a group of zoologists from the University of Miami
had attempted to capture and tag the panthers. But the program
had been disbanded after several months because the cats had
eluded every trap the zoologists had set. Such programs had
enjoyed more success on the mainland, where the statewide es-
timate of the panther population stood around thirty, with their
numbers decreasing yearly as their breeding grounds were consumed by developers. And poachers.

"How do you know it was a poacher? Maybe the panther was
injured and some other animal killed it," said Martell.

"Not likely." Griber shook his head and wiped the back of
his hand across his mouth. "Her heart was cut out."

"Jesus," Aline said.

"Jesus got nuthin' to do with it."

Martell shut off his recorder, put it back into his knapsack,
and changed the subject. "Is there an easier way to get in touch
with you, Mr. Griber?"

"Shortwave." He stabbed a thumb over his shoulder at a
radio perched on top of a bookcase. "I keep it on most nights
between seven and midnight. I make it into town 'bout once a
month."

"Shortwave it is, then." Martell polished off his whiskey,
stood and offered his hand. "Thanks for your time."

"Sure thing." Griber looked at Aline. "You tell Bernelli I
asked after her, huh?" When he grinned, his teeth lined up in
his mouth like a yellow picket fence. "She's one nice-looking

woman, and if she ever got a mind to leave that doctor she's
married to, you tell her she's welcome here.''

Aline smiled. "I'll pass that along, Mr. Griber."

"I can see it now," Martell said when they were in the raft.
"Bernie living out here, miles from a shopping center. She'd
die of withdrawal in a matter of days."

"She's not *that* bad. She's—"

"—worse," Martell finished, and they both laughed.

The trip back to the plane seemed faster. Even though Martell
swore he wasn't buzzed from the whiskey, she knew he was.
His laughter was a shade too loud, his stories were punctuated
by long pauses, as though he'd momentarily forgotten what he
was going to say, and he kept touching her, rocking the raft
every time he did. When the plane wouldn't start, he had a tough
time keeping the flashlight steady as she peered under the cowling, trying to figure out what was wrong.

"What's the verdict?" he asked after a bit.

"Wet plugs, I think, from when we landed. There must be a
leak in the cowling."

"So what do we do now?" He was gripping the door with
one hand and the flashlight with the other as he balanced himself
on the pontoon. "Radio for help? Go back to Griber's?"

"Wait until the plugs dry."

"How long's that take?"

"I don't know. It depends on how wet they are."

"Will it take all night?"

"It could."

"This is sounding better all the time."

Aline laughed and pulled her head out from under the cowling. He was grinning like a kid who'd done something he was
terribly proud of, and she barely repressed an urge to pat him
on the head. "Talk about transparent."

"At least I'm honest." He freed one hand by tucking the
flashlight under his arm, and slid his fingers into her hair, gently
easing off the elastic band that kept it bound in a loose ponytail.
It streamed over her shoulders. "There. You should wear your
hair loose all the time, Aline."

"It's too hot."

"That's sounds like a step in the right direction."

She laughed again and touched her palm to the side of his
face. In the moonlight, the webs at the corners of his eyes dis-

appeared and the gray in his hair seemed to shine. "You're buzzed," she said.

"So what," he replied, and kissed her.

The plane rocked on its pontoons. The night sounds rose and fell around them. Aline drew back. "Let's see if I can find an extra set of plugs."

"Let's not."

"C'mon, Si. I don't want to spend the night out here."

"Because of Kincaid?"

"Because this isn't my idea of a great spot to camp."

He cupped her chin in his hand, his expression so utterly serious he looked for a moment like a different man, a man she didn't know well, a man she had only met. But when he spoke, it was in that same jesting tone that characterized him. "I'm a good loser, Aline. I want you to remember that."

"I'm sure you'll remind me every opportunity you get, Si."

He smiled, and so did she, then a breeze skipped across the lagoon, chilling her, and she nudged him in the ribs. "C'mon, it's cool out here. Let's go share a chocolate bar or something while I look through the tools. I think there might be an extra set of plugs in there."

"A chocolate bar," he repeated. "That isn't exactly what I had in mind. But what the hell."

He clasped her hand and they inched back along the pontoon, into the cabin. The breeze whistled along the edge of the door when it closed, and the seaplane swayed on the surface of the lagoon, a water dancer dreaming of flight, open skies, home.

Aline found spare plugs in the dusty tool kit in the back. But it took her more than an hour to change them, what with the dark and the balancing act on the pontoon and the fact that she'd never done it before. She'd watched it being done, but that wasn't quite the same as doing it herself. Once they were in, she had no idea whether she'd calibrated them correctly or if the plugs had even been the problem to begin with.

She scooted behind the wheel and leaned toward the open passenger door. Martell was balanced on the pontoon, squeezing the air from the raft. "You almost finished?" she asked.

"Yeah. But if the plane doesn't start, we may need the raft. Maybe I shouldn't deflate it yet."

"If we need it, we've got the bicycle pump."

She flicked on the master switch and radios. The seaplane

belonged to the police department and was outfitted with top-of-the-line navigational gear—and a police radio, which squawked the second she turned it on. "Come in, please," said the station's dispatcher. "Calling November Bravo two six."

"Hey, that's us," Martell said.

"Yeah."

He poked his head into the cabin. "Aren't you going to answer?"

"I don't know." The only reason the dispatcher would track her down on her night off was because something had happened and Bernie was out of town and everyone else was tied up. Never mind that the real problem was a grossly understaffed department that hadn't managed to keep up with the rapid population growth on the island. Never mind that she was going to answer the call and resent it for the rest of the night. The point was that she needed a vacation, a new profession, a different job. Once again, other people's interests did not coincide with hers.

"This is November Bravo two six," she said. "What's up, Penny?"

"Al, I've been trying to reach you for the last half hour. We've got a Code One and the chief's already on his way. How soon can you get back here? Over."

"If the plane starts, we can be at the airport in fifteen minutes. Over."

"Call me when you get there and I'll give you directions. Over and out."

"Shit." She heard the cargo door shut. "Is the raft in?"

"Yup." Martell sidestepped his way along the pontoon, slid into the passenger seat, and closed the door. "Isn't Code One a . . ."

"Yeah. Homicide."

Tango Key measured eleven miles at its longest point and seven at its widest. Its shape was vaguely that of a cat's head—a cat with some proportion problems, Aline thought. Ears too widely set, a rounded jaw, a face that was too long.

They were crossing between the cat's ears now, headed south. One ear was occupied by Pirate's Cove, the exclusive development on the island with its $2 million marina, and the other was nothing but wilderness, part of the same preserve where old man Griber lived. The cat's mouth fell around Tango, the main town to the south, and its nose and whiskers marked the beginning of the hills and the location of the airport.

Their destination lay in a culvert between two hills just north of the airport—a man-made lake owned by Tango Power and Light. Prime fishing spot and home base to a dozen seaplanes. At night, its perimeter was lit by pale blue lights, but even without them, landing wouldn't have been a problem: the moon was bright.

As the pontoons struck the lake's surface, water sprayed the windshield, covering it until she pulled back on the throttle. She taxied to the dock and Martell hopped out to tie down the plane and remove the raft. She shut off the equipment and the master switch. The plane died with a whine, a sigh, a shudder; it probably wasn't too different from the way the human body wound down as it died.

Morbid thought.

Ten minutes later she stepped out of a phone booth near the parking lot and Martell looked a question at her, brows lifting.

"A body was found in a dumpster on the boardwalk," she said.

He made a face. "Christ. Tango's sounding more like Miami all the time."

"This one smells like a repeater," she said as they hurried toward the parking lot.

"What makes you think so?"

"Just a hunch."

"I can't prosecute on hunches, Aline."

She hooked her arm through his. "You won't have to."

"Rain check on dinner?" They stopped at her Honda.

"You bet."

"What's your preference?"

"Surprise me."

"Okay." He grinned, rocked toward her, kissed her lightly. "I'll call."

On her way down through the hills, Martell's white Camaro roared past her. The horn hit a high note before the car blurred, a white angel on urgent business. Like drinks at the Pink Moose with one of his standby honeys, she thought, and wondered if she could ticket him after the fact for speeding.

2

Kincaid weaved his way through the TGIF crowd on the upper deck of the Pink Moose. He was balancing a pitcher of beer, two glasses, and a bowl of popcorn above his head so that if he was jostled, nothing would spill. This absurd college student posture was probably as good a metaphor as any for his present circumstances. *Maintain a delicate equilibrium, move slowly and deliberately and keep your eyes open, and maybe you'll get where you're going.* In his life, however, as opposed to the metaphor, there were problems with this line of thought, namely money.

Or more specifically, the lack of it.

He set the beer and popcorn down on a table near the rear of the deck, where Ferret was poring over racing forms. "I'm telling you, Ryan, this solar eclipse we're going to have in June is already doing weird shit to the races. You place a bet now and you can't lose. I've got a couple of looking-goods on the races at Calder tomorrow night, and five hundred would bring a pretty return."

"I need more than a looking-good. I can't afford to lose five hundred bucks."

"Oh, c'mon." Ferret glanced up, his lips drawing away from his teeth in that strange smile that completed his resemblance to the rodent he was nicknamed after. He peered at Kincaid over the rim of his Ben Franklin glasses. "Five hundred is chicken shit for you."

Kincaid folded his six-foot-four frame into a chair meant for a man half as tall. "That was in my other life, Ferret."

"Yeah? Which life was that? The one where you were Marc Anthony and Aline was Queen Cleo?"

He laughed. "Not quite that far back."

"That's it? That's your answer?" exclaimed Ferret. "This must be serious. You get mugged or something in the Orient and lose everything you had or what, Ryan?"

"Yeah, more or less." Only he wasn't just talking money. He'd returned to find that his old life wasn't waiting around like it had in the past. The local businesses for whom he'd done grunt work that paid well—mostly background checks—had found another private eye who was "more available." Translation: more dependable. In the circles that counted in his business, his name had been retired. And then there was Aline, who'd hadn't exactly welcomed him back with open arms, and who, in his absence, had been seeing a prosecutor.

On top of it, the IRS had billed him for over ten grand in back taxes, and since he wasn't in the country to respond to their first three letters, they had impounded his plane and frozen his accounts. Fortunately, he was paranoid by nature and several years ago had put his house in Ferret's name and had buried some cash in his backyard. Cash, he thought, that might last him two months if he was frugal.

Ferret listened to Kincaid's tax woes with rapt attention, then reached into his pocket and pulled out a wad of money. "Two grand, Ryan. I'll put it on Catch-Me-If-You-Can. Right now, she's running fifty to one odds, which will probably go down somewhat before tomorrow night. My sources say she's going to win, but I'll put five hundred each on second and third place and a grand on first. If we get anything out of this, we split. If we lose, it's my loss."

"Since when are you in social services, Ferret?"

"I'm collecting good karma." He reached into his windbreaker and pulled out a paperback entitled, *The Karmic Wheel*. "Sweet Pea lent me this." Sweet Pea was Aline. "I've decided my karma is suffering from gross neglect, Ryan, and you're going to be my redemption. Now do we have a deal or not?"

"Since your soul's at stake, how can I refuse?"

Ferret grinned. "Good. Two grand on Catch-Me. Where's Sweet Pea tonight, anyway?"

"Probably out with her pal Martell."

"Nope." Ferret tilted his head toward the crowd. "He's right over there."

Martell was working the crowd, a drink in hand, and despite

the casual clothes, looked like what he was, a successful attorney, a yuppie on the rise. Not Aline's type at all.

"I don't know what the hell she sees in him," Kincaid grumbled.

"Oh, that's easy."

"It can't be his nauseating charm."

"Nope."

"Or his wit."

"Nope."

"Then what?"

"He's got a future."

"A future. Yeah. Pimping for justice and the American way. Some future."

"Is that jealousy I hear, Ryan?"

"I didn't like the man any better even before Al started seeing him."

"He's not my favorite character, either. But look at it from Aline's point of view. He's got a *stable* income, if he runs for county judge next year he'll probably win, and he isn't gone six months out of the year."

"I'm not gone for six months of the year, either. This is the first long trip I've taken since—"

"You're missing the point, Ryan. Sweet Pea's thirty-eight years old. She's starting to fuss and fret about things women always fuss and fret about when they're pushing forty. Home, husband, kids, a dead-end job . . ."

"Bullshit."

Ferret sat back, palms turned up. "Hey, don't take my word for it. Ask her yourself."

Kincaid pointed out that Aline was the one who hadn't wanted to get married.

The little man smoothed a hand over his slick, black hair and rolled his eyes as if to say Kincaid was hopelessly obtuse. "Listen, I'm no expert on women, and I'm sure as hell no expert on marriage, Ryan. But I know how Sweet Pea is. She figures why should she be married to someone who's going to be gone half the year? Okay, so maybe she can take a month off here, a month off there, and the two of you travel together, but hey, for that, why be married at all?"

He didn't get a chance to reply, because Martell materialized at their table, smiling, patting Kincaid on the shoulder like they were old buddies, shaking Ferret's hand, asking how Kincaid's trip was. "The South Pacific, right? Isn't that where you were?"

"The Orient."

"Well, I was close. I knew it was over there somewhere." He waved vaguely off to his left, as though the Orient lay a few miles offshore in the Gulf of Mexico. Then, still smiling, he pulled out a chair and sat down. He glanced at the racing forms. "Any good bets, Ferret?"

"Nope." Ferret stacked the forms and pushed them off to the side. "Not a goddamn thing."

"Either of you heard anything about the homicide?"

"*Which* homicide?" asked Ferret. "You've got to be more specific than that, Simon. Are we talking one of your old cases or a new case? Or maybe someone else's case? No, probably not someone else's case."

Martell ignored the implication that he was interested only in those things that directly concerned him and got on with the real reason he'd strolled over: the call that had come in over the radio while he and Aline had been out in the swamp earlier. He didn't ease into it; he leaped, just like he did in court.

No wonder defense attorneys hated like hell to come up against the man in court, Kincaid thought. But the grapevine said he'd lost his last two big cases and was now on the outs with the powers in the D.A.'s office. The animal cruelty case was probably a not-so-subtle hint that if he didn't shape up, he was out. But even that shouldn't have caused Martell undue concern. There were any number of firms on the island that would hire him in a minute, and in private practice, he could easily earn three times the money he was making now.

But maybe money wasn't one of Martell's high priorities. Kincaid wasn't sure *what* Martell's priorities were, and that bothered him more than anything else, especially where Aline was concerned.

"Where'd the homicide happen?" Kincaid asked.

"Over on the boardwalk somewhere. A woman's body was found in a dumpster."

Ferret shook his head. "Terrific. A dumpster. Real class, yes siree." He looked at Kincaid. "Let's go check it out."

Kincaid wasn't in the mood for a homicide scene. But the idea of shooting the breeze with Martell, who didn't look like he was in any hurry to shove off, didn't appeal to him, either.

The lesser of two evils, he thought, like voting in last year's presidential election.

When the Tango boardwalk was built in 1836, it was only a mile long and belonged to the Flamingo, the first hotel on the island. Both the boardwalk and the hotel were destroyed in a hurricane ten years later. The Flamingo was rebuilt farther inland and the boardwalk was reconstructed on pilings and extended another three miles.

By the turn of the century, cafes and bars had sprung up along its perimeter. Many of them were washed away with two miles of boardwalk in 1909, when a powerful storm slammed into the Keys. Although Key West, twelve miles to the east, sustained most of the damage during that storm—four hundred buildings destroyed and two people killed—Tango hadn't escaped unscathed. Three dozen buildings in the downtown area were badly damaged by torrential rains, and landslides in the hills had destroyed two farms, killing livestock and five people.

In 1948, two years before the bridge was built between Tango and Key West, the boardwalk was demolished again during a storm packing 140-mile-per-hour winds. After that, it was rebuilt on concrete pilings that were at least a foot thick and reinforced by steel. All new buildings along its four-mile stretch were constructed of reinforced concrete, equipped with storm shutters, and triple-strength cypress doors. These were the only structures that remained standing after Hurricane Donna hit the Keys in 1960, causing more than ten million dollars damage on the island.

Kincaid was a teenager when Donna had struck. He remembered how cars had poured off the island, jammed on the bridge to Key West, and streamed into the hills. He remembered his folks had argued about how long it would take to reach the Upper Keys before the storm struck. There was only one road out and hundreds of cars were already on it. They'd finally opted to stay with relatives in the hills, near where the airport stood today. Traffic was so tangled on the old two-lane road it had taken them almost an hour to get there. He remembered the howling of the wind, the driving fury of the rain, the power blackout, and how they'd huddled around the tiny transistor for news.

Today, this same boardwalk was a bustling place of shops and bars and restaurants. It wasn't an eyesore yet. But if Tango kept growing the way it had for the last several years, Kincaid would lay odds that it would rival Atlantic City for tackiness by the mid 1990s.

He swung the Saab into the municipal lot at the east end of the boardwalk, where the sodium vapor lights painted everything a sickly orange. There were three cops, an ambulance, a couple of vehicles from the Skeleton Crew. The alley between a restaurant and a strip joint called Platinum's had been cordoned off, and the usual crowd of gawkers had gathered.

"They smell blood a mile away," Ferret remarked as they got out of the car.

"They're probably thinking the same about us."

"I'm the first to admit I've got numerous faults, Ryan, but blood lust isn't among them. This is strictly business. I've had good luck in the past picking up tips at crime scenes."

Ferret: the island's information broker.

They stopped at the edge of the crowd. Ferret, who was nearly a foot shorter than Kincaid, looked up at him. "I can't see a goddamn thing. What's going on?"

"The usual stuff."

"You're a big help. I'll meet you back by the car." He weaseled his way into the crowd and quickly vanished.

Kincaid remained where he was, scanning the area for a familiar face. Radios squawked, the crowd of gawkers murmured, rookies hurried back and forth, as busy as ants, several men were carefully removing garbage from the dumpster where the body had been found. He spotted the chief of police, Gene Frederick, talking to a woman with a nest of dyed blond hair who was wearing pink leotards and a sequined shirt that fell to her hips. One of the strippers from Platinum's, he guessed.

"You're the giant in the crowd, Kincaid."

He didn't have to look around to connect the voice with a face. But he was glad he did. She looked good. Aline's cinnamon-colored hair was loose, the way he liked it best, curling over her shoulders and halfway down the back of her denim jumpsuit. Her blue eyes were pinched at the corners, as though she hadn't been sleeping well, but her smile was quick and surprisingly warm.

"Hi, Al."

"Hi, yourself. What're you doing here anyway?"

"News gets around."

"The grapevine's never been *this* fast before."

"I ran into Martell at the Pink Moose. He said a woman was found in a dumpster."

"Oh."

Silence: it floated in the night air like a glob of fat in water. He was tempted to make a snide remark about her getting stuck in the lagoon with Martell, but knew she was expecting him to say something, that she had braced herself for it, so he didn't.

When she realized he was keeping his opinions to himself, she said, "Her name's Rikki Baker. She was a dancer at Platinum's. A wino found her in the dumpster. Bill thinks she'd been there awhile." Bill Prentiss was the coroner.

"How long?"

She drew her eyes back to him. "Four or five days, maybe as long as six. The wino says he'd been smelling something bad the last couple days. Garbage pickup here is twice a week, Mondays and Thursdays, but they missed yesterday. So she's been here at least since Monday after the pickup."

"No one from Platinum's reported her missing?"

"She was on vacation. According to her"—Aline nodded toward the blonde in the pink leotards—"Rikki was supposed to be in Miami auditioning for some part in a movie that's going to be filmed up there."

"Any leads?"

"One. Blondie over there says Rikki had been seeing a Cuban for a couple of months. He owns a *botánica* downtown."

A *botánica* was a Hispanic religious goods store and implied something that probably spelled trouble. "The guy's a *santero*?"

"I don't know. But that seems like a reasonable assumption."

"Is there anything in the way she was killed that could tie her death to *santería*?"

"Maybe." Aline touched his arm, her fingers soft and cool against his skin. "Come take a look."

They walked over to the ambulance and she opened the rear doors. The body bag rested on a stretcher, and she pulled it out. The stench was bad and got worse as she unzipped the bag and peeled it down to the woman's waist. Her dark hair spilled out, fanning across the upper part of the stretcher. Her face was swollen, misshapen, discolored from deterioration. Even in the ambulance's dim light, he could see the white thing inching along her lower lip and didn't have to look closer to know what it was. A maggot. And where there was one, there were sure to be more. He knocked it off with a snap of his wrist.

"This is what I wanted you to see," Aline said, and pulled Rikki's arm free of the body bag.

Kincaid's gut went soft and queasy. The woman's fingers were gone, cut off at the knuckles, so that her hand resembled a kind of crude club. Clean cuts, precise, almost surgical. No protruding tendons. No bones sticking out. No ragged flesh. A machete? A sharp, heavy knife? *Why the fingers?*

"The left hand's the same," Aline said.

He looked at the blood that stained her slacks and blouse at the waist. "Shot or stabbed?"

"Stabbed. Bill says he'll try to have something for me tomorrow, so we'll know more then."

Kincaid fingered the black and red beads around the woman's neck. They were strung on thin thread which would've broken if she'd struggled hard. But all the beads were in place and her clothes weren't torn, so rape was unlikely. He said as much and Aline nodded.

"She might've known the killer. It would fit with the stats."

Aline's assumption annoyed him. Just because the statistics said the majority of homicide victims these days knew their killers didn't mean it applied in this case. She was talking about murder as if it could always be broken down into neat little categories with labels, as though it were an event separate from the person who carried it out. She seemed to have forgotten that unless you understood the mind behind a homicide, facts and statistics weren't worth a damn.

"It's just as possible she was surprised by someone she'd never seen before, and didn't have a chance to struggle."

"So you've been a guest lecturer at the FBI lately, Ryan?"

"I'm just saying you may be jumping to conclusions."

She folded her arms at her waist, stubborn now. "What I'm jumping for, Ryan, are theories, okay? The chief ran her name and she doesn't have a record. But we can't get any information from the Feds until Monday, and it'd be nice to have her prints on file just in case. But we can't get a set of prints because we don't have her fingers. Forensics is going to have to lift prints from her apartment. That means we have *no* leads except this *botánica* guy. So I'm looking for theories, Ryan, that's all. And you know how I get when I'm frustrated, and right now I'm frustrated."

He knew, all right. "Then here's a theory, Al. I'm pretty sure those beads she's wearing are connected to *santería*. Red and black are the colors of an *orisha* named Elegguá. He opens doorways to opportunities, and she was supposedly going to be trying out for a part in a movie, so Elegguá would be the god whose help she needed. Regardless of what the Cuban boyfriend did or didn't do, I'd sure as hell ask him about Rikki and Elegguá."

Aline looked at him like he'd just dropped in from another planet. "You're sure about that Elegguá stuff?"

"I'm part Cuban," he said, zipping up the bag and pushing the stretcher back inside the ambulance. "Didn't you know?"

"Yeah, and I'm a Masai tribeswoman." She shut the ambulance doors and leaned against them. "Would you go with me tomorrow? When I talk to this guy?"

"Why?"

Impatience weighted her sigh. "Because your Spanish is better than mine, Ryan. Because you know more about *santería* than I do. Why do you think?"

He would've preferred an answer more along the lines of *I enjoy your company* or *I like to be with you,* but when you were scraping bottom, you couldn't be picky.

"Okay, sure, I'll go with you."

"I'll talk to the chief and get the department to pay you as a consultant on the case, Ryan."

She knows about the IRS. She couldn't have found out from Ferret, who hadn't known until this evening, so it had to be Prentiss, in whom Kincaid had confided, and who had probably told Bernelli, who had told Aline. A fine, tight circle.

"Just for going to the *botánica* with you?" he laughed. "Things aren't *that* desperate, Al."

"No, I mean on the *case*, Ryan, not just for one lousy visit to a *botánica*."

"I'm no expert on *santería*, Aline."

"What about that trip to Haiti when you—"

"That involved voodoo, not *santería*."

"Oh. Yeah. Well. There're similarities."

"Some." They walked away from the ambulance. "But there're a lot of differences, too."

"How about that case in Miami when—"

"Luck."

"But that thing in the jar that used to sit on your mantel . . ."

"That's a perfect example of my ignorance."

The corners of her mouth slid down; it was her *Don't give me a hard time* expression. "Let me put it this way, then. If you run across something you don't know about, can you find someone who'll fill in the gaps?"

"Probably."

Aline smiled, resting her case. "Good. Let's talk to Gene."

"You talk to Gene and give me Rikki's address. I'll meet you over there in an hour. I've got to find Ferret and give him a ride back to his car."

"What's Ferret doing here?"

Unable to resist a dig, he said, "He wanted to get away from Martell," then walked off to find Ferret.

The interior of Platinum's was cold, smoky, and loud. Its four levels were lit by pale blue neon that splashed across the empty, sunken stage at the front and grew progressively dimmer with each ascending tier until the uppermost was practically dark. Booths and tables on every level were sectioned off by Japanese screens for privacy. The jukebox was turned up full blast.

Kincaid found Ferret at the bar on the upper level, deep in conversation with the bartender. He claimed the stool next to him and ordered a Perrier and lime.

"Any tips?" he asked when the bartender walked off to get his Perrier.

"Not much yet, but I'm working on it. Everyone describes her as 'real nice, but private.' The bartender's my best bet. He's worked here for eight years, and he and I have done some business together. I'll have something for you by tomorrow. You leaving?"

"I'm going to meet Al at Rikki Baker's. You want a ride back to your car?"

"No, I'll get a ride later. Listen, Ryan. There is one thing." And he told Kincaid about the dead woman's interest in *santería*.

"I heard. Find out what you can about whatever men she was seeing."

"Right." Ferret started to say something else, but the bartender returned with Kincaid's Perrier and resumed his conversation with Ferret. Horses and jai alai. By the end of the night, Ferret would have the man betting his week's paycheck on one or the other or both.

Kincaid nursed his Perrier and decided to hang around long enough to see the next act. He kept thinking about the *santería* angle, testing it against what he knew about the religion. It had been around in this country, he supposed, since the first Cubans had settled here. But no one had heard much about it until a hundred thousand Cubans had poured into South Florida during the Mariel boatlift in 1980, and changed the face of the peninsula forever.

It had originated in Nigeria, with the Yoruba people. When they were brought to the New World as slaves, the Spanish tried to convert them to Catholicism. The result was a gradual merging of certain Catholic saints with the Yoruba gods and the birth of *santería*—the worship of saints, called *orishas*. The religion was steeped in mysticism, secrecy, and rituals, and bore some resemblance to voodoo in its use of animal sacrifices, effigies, and homeopathic magic.

By some estimates, there were as many as a hundred million believers in *santería* and its sister religions like *shangó* in Trinidad, voodoo, and *macumba* in Brazil. He suspected the actual figure was much smaller. But then again, it was hard to tell for sure because so many believers and practitioners didn't talk about it. That would make it tough to track down leads.

But the biggest obstacle in this case, he knew, would be convincing people like Chief Frederick that *santería* was more than mystical mumbo jumbo. His approach to the diverse ethnic population on Tango was strictly practical: if you spoke their language and understood something about their culture, they might be more cooperative in an investigation. Beyond that, their beliefs didn't matter.

But Kincaid knew better.

And he'd learned the hard way, during a missing-persons case in Miami six years ago when *santería* had nearly killed him. He knew, and just in case he were ever inclined to forget, the four-inch scar on his stomach was there to remind him.

The music started.

The lights dimmed.

The pretty blonde who'd been wearing the pink leotards strutted out onto the stage to thundering applause. Her silvery outfit shimmered, hugging her in all the right places. Her hair was loose, thick, wild—hair that begged to be touched. Rikki Baker's friend, he thought. A lead.

"Ferret." He nudged the little man. "Ask your buddy what the blonde's name is."

Without missing a beat, Ferret said, "Starr with a double *r*, Ryan, like Brenda the intrepid reporter from the Sunday funnies. Starr Abbott. Got it?"

"Got it."

A drumbeat rolled, then settled into a strange and steady rhythm. It seemed that the scar on his stomach burned bright and hot for a few seconds, as if responding to the primal beat, the pulse of some ancient world.

3

The word had come down from the Skeleton Crew who had searched Rikki Baker's apartment: she hadn't been killed at home. But that much had been obvious to Aline when she and Kincaid had stepped inside. It didn't feel like a place where someone had died. The air was too still and the rooms too tidy, too clean, too perfect, as if they'd been preserved under glass.

The apartment, located in a refurbished Art Deco building north of the city park, was comfortable but not lavish, and furnished mostly in wicker and rattan. It was the sort of apartment that might belong to a young, sensible businesswoman who saved fifteen percent of her earnings, didn't cheat on her taxes, ate the right foods, exercised regularly. A woman in a TV ad.

The rent, the landlord had told her, ran six hundred a month and was always paid promptly on the first of the month. It was well within what Rikki could afford. Dancers at Platinum's, the personnel manager had said, earned excellent money—about three thousand a month, plus another five hundred to a thousand a month in tips. So on forty to fifty grand a year, Rikki Baker had carved out a nice little niche for herself.

Throughout the apartment, mixed in with the possessions of this "sensible" woman, was evidence of what she hoped to become. Posters of Broadway musicals. Magazine photos of dancers like Leslie Caron, Juliette Prowse, a younger Shirley MacLaine. A corkboard on the wall in the spare bedroom was a wishboard of photos and magazine pictures of things Rikki wanted. A new car. A house with a yard. A garden. A part in a movie. A man she would trust. A man she could love. A man who would love her. A baby. To be happy.

"Al, come in here a second. I think you should see this stuff," Kincaid called.

The sound of his voice was a kind of reverse déjà vu, an echo of the old days. Before Orient and After, she thought, his trip as a well-marked juncture in her own life. After all, if she'd decided to take a leave of absence from her job and accompany him, she might be living on a junk in Hong Kong harbor right now instead of excavating the secrets of a dead woman's life.

She walked into the master bedroom where everything was red and black; bedspread, throw rugs, drapes, sheets. Elegguá's colors: deep, rich, excessive. The mirrored ceiling only heightened the suffocating feel to the room.

"What'd you find?"

Kincaid turned, a giant whose sandy hair and beard were going gray, a man whose sharp blue eyes and roguish good looks still made her breath hitch in her chest. He held up a black silk negligee with the nipples cut out. An "RK" was embroidered in red thread between the cutouts. "Bit small for you, Ryan," she said with a laugh.

"But not for you." He stepped around behind her, turning her slightly so she faced the mirror, and held the negligee up to her. "Not bad, but I don't think black's your color. How about red?" He reached into the drawer and with a snap of his wrist brought out a nearly identical negligee, except it was red, and exchanged it for the black. "Well?" He rested his chin on top of her head, watching her in the mirror.

"I'm not crazy about either one," she said.

"Picky, picky, Aline." He moved and turned it inside out so she could see the tag inside. "It's from Betsy's Lingerie, that ritzy shop in the Cove. If they do their own monograms, those would be special orders, right? And presumably they keep records."

"RK," Aline said, running her thumb over the embroidering. "It could be short for Rikki. Or maybe the *R*'s for Rikki and the *K* is for Kincaid, huh?"

"Yeah, that must be it. I wasn't in the Orient at all. I was living a secret life here."

"It wouldn't surprise me," she said.

"Thanks."

"Just joking, Ryan." *Sort of.*

"What's the *botánica* owner's name again?"

"Ortega. Manuel Ortega."

"Then the *K* doesn't stand for him." Kincaid's hand vanished in the drawer again, and he pulled out several items this time. A black garter belt. A low-cut black silk bra. A red silk teddy. Red panties with the crotch missing. The monogram adorned everything. "Maybe she was hooking."

"Her blond pal in the pink leotards said no. I asked. And Gene ran a check on her: no record."

"She might be lying, and not all hookers get busted."

"Maybe. But it's just as likely these were gifts from some guy whose tastes are a bit kinky."

"She might've been the kink and bought them for herself." He pointed at the mirrored ceiling. "My ex-wife had a ceiling like that when I met her, and she was definitely a kink."

"Ex-wife one or two?"

"One."

"You never told me she was a kink."

"You never asked."

Intrigued that she'd stumbled on something new about Kincaid, she asked what kind of kink ex-wife number one was. "Are we talking videos? Orgies? Whips and chains? What?"

He exploded with laughter, and Aline whacked his arm with the back of her hand. "Very funny, Ryan."

"But I really had you believing it for a minute, didn't I?"

"Ha. C'mon, let's finish searching this place."

Between them, they came up with: a gram of coke, about two ounces of Colombian, a tube of something prescribed by the same gynecologist Aline went to, an empty address book, a file of publicity photos. They also ran across a photo album from which most of the pictures had been removed. The few that remained were of Rikki as a girl of nine or ten: posing at the beach, hand on a hip, grinning for the camera; on a sled, in a tree, blowing out candles on a cake. In one, she stood between a man and woman, presumably her parents. The woman's image was blurred, but the man's face was quite clear, and he reminded Aline of someone.

"Does he look familiar?" she asked Kincaid.

He shrugged. "A young Ricardo Montalban." He turned the picture over. On the back was: *Me with Mom & Dad, D.C. 1962.* "Are her folks still alive?"

"Her buddy says no. But she also admitted that Rikki was pretty tight-lipped about her life."

"Into our *take* pile."

Aline set it on the couch with some other items and went into the utility room off the front hall, the last room to search. The only thing of interest they discovered was a small table covered with a white cloth. On top of it were glasses of water, containers filled with wilted flowers, a half-smoked cigar, a bottle of Florida water, half a fifth of rum, candles of various colors and sizes, and religious statues. There was also a coconut on a shallow clay plate which had been smeared with honey.

It was a homemade altar, common in homes where *santería* was practiced. Here, offerings were made to the saints, requests were voiced, prayers were uttered. The whole thing smacked of paganism, idols, earth religions, the very stuff that had triggered the Salem witchcraft trials and turned Catholics into butchers in the Middle Ages.

Aline knew that each item on the altar had a specific function, and probably represented particular saints as well. But the three-day seminar the department offered each year on ethnic customs had been too condensed to provide such details.

"What's the coconut mean?" she asked.

Kincaid rubbed his fingers through his beard. "The way I understand it, nothing in *santería* means just one thing or has just one purpose. Coconuts are used in divination, in the treatment of physical ailments, in spells. Elegguá likes them, so they're sometimes offered to him on Mondays—his day of the week. That's probably why this one's here."

"And the honey is used to sweeten his disposition?"

"Good, Al, you're catching on. Some of the *orishas* supposedly have sweet tooths, so the honey could've been used to draw a particular one. But since Rikki was wearing beads that are Elegguá's colors, the honey was probably part of an offering to him so he'd help her get what she wanted."

"The part in the movie."

"And whatever else she was asking for."

"And the glasses of water?"

The *orishas* gravitated toward water, he said. They also liked flowers, which were sometimes used in cleansing rituals, as were cigar smoke, rum, and Florida water. That word, *cleansing*, suggested communions and confessions, holy water and baptisms. She said as much, and Kincaid smiled.

"Same idea. Cleansings are generally for a person's spirit, to get rid of any negative influences he may have absorbed. In a typical cleansing, a *santero* sweeps a bouquet of white flowers up and down the sides of your body, over your head, across your feet, down your spine, and along your arms. If the *santero* feels that your spirit is *really* tainted, then he uses a pair of white doves, holding them by the feet as he sweeps them over your body. The doves are then killed and buried, which supposedly keeps the negativity from spreading to someone else." His eyes flicked over the table again. "Everything here is pretty standard."

But what they found in the freezer was not.

A plastic glass with ice in it and a piece of black cloth tied over it had been hidden in the back corner of the freezer, behind a bag of flour. They popped the block of ice from the glass, then broke it to get out the two scraps of paper inside. Both had traces of ink on them, but whatever had been written had long since vanished.

"Got any ideas about this one?" she asked.

"Just a guess. It's probably some sort of spell." Kincaid fingered the black cloth. "If you look at this in symbolic terms, black could represent death—either literally or figuratively. The pieces of paper might represent two of something—two ideas or two people—probably people. And the freezer . . ." He shrugged. "To preserve something or to kill it. This is where an expert would come in handy, Aline."

"I'm open to suggestions."

"I was thinking of Meg Mallory."

A reference librarian and the island historian: good choice. She'd lived on the island for fifty years, long enough for her to qualify as a Tango Fritter, even though she hadn't been born here. If she didn't know the answer herself, she would know someone who did. "If you talk to her, I'll handle the lingerie shop. Oh, Gene said okay on the consulting fee."

"But only after he gave you fifty reasons why it would be an unnecessary expense, right?"

"Please, Ryan, don't exaggerate."

"Twenty reasons?"

"Three."

"Let's hear them."

"You're not dependable, you're not—"

"Never mind."

She chuckled and poked him in the ribs. "Truth hurts, huh, Kincaid?"

He lit the cigar and blew smoke over the altar. "Got any requests for Elegguá, Al?"

Only a couple of dozen, she thought. "How many am I allowed?"

"One at a time." He passed her the cigar. "Puff a little on that while I light a couple of candles."

She blew smoke at Kincaid's head. "Now you're cleansed, Ryan."

"Tell it to the IRS."

She knew about his tax woes, of course, because Bernie had told her. "How much do you owe?"

His eyes skewed against the smoke. "Bernie must've told you."

"She said it was over ten grand."

"That's about right."

"What're you going to do?"

"Nothing. Hell, they've impounded the plane. That's worth at least twenty." He dripped wax from a red candle onto a plate and fixed the candle in it. "They'll probably sell it and keep the whole twenty, too, the bastards. What's your request?"

Clarity, a new job, a different career . . . The list was long and complex, a litany that reflected everything she wanted to change in her life. How could she choose just one thing? All of it was important.

"No requests?" he asked when she didn't say anything.

"I can't decide what should be first."

"It's just a game, Al."

"Then you go first."

He thought a moment, and blew out the candle's flame, like a kid making a birthday wish. "Your turn." He lit the candle again.

"What'd you ask for?"

"That's between Elegguá and me."

"I thought you said it was a game."

He sighed. "It is. I'll be in the living room. This smoke in here is getting to me."

She stood there after he'd walked out, irritated because he'd started this stupid thing, gotten her to play along, and then left. Typical. This was exactly what he'd done six months ago when

he'd departed for the Orient, and the year before that when . . .
and then . . .

"Aw, forget it." She crushed the cigar against the coconut,
blew out the candle, and marched into the hall, wondering what
Kincaid had wished for.

Aline's house rose from the hump of a man-made hill at the
dead end of Hurricane Drive. Like many of the homes at the
southern tip of the island, it was built on stilts that lifted it ten
or fifteen feet off the ground. Built of knotty Florida pine, which
had once blanketed Tango Key, it had vaulted ceilings, a sleeping loft, and large windows that shot from the tile floors to the
ceiling.

It had been her parents' weekend getaway when they'd lived
in Key West, where they'd owned and operated Whitman's
Bookstore. After they had died, Aline had given up her apartment in Key West and moved in here. In 1980 she'd opened a
smaller Whitman's on Tango's boardwalk, which she now owned
with her former manager, Mark Finley. Since the bookstore was
Finley's sole job, he ran it and kept it profitable. Aline took care
of the paperwork and filled in when she could for the three part-
timers. The arrangement worked well.

The bookstore, of course, remained a career option, but not
one that interested her very much. She'd already done it. She'd
started this Whitman's from scratch and had made a success of
it. There was no challenge to it now. Her job still provided that,
but she was fed up with police work—homicides, B&Es, drug
busts, drunken brawls, all of it.

It pays the bills, practical Bernie would say whenever Aline
complained.

Take a leave of absence, Prentiss would advise.

Don't give me that mid-life crisis shit, the chief would grumble.

But the point was that she felt as if her life had stalled. It was
like an old song whose familiarity comforted her and conferred
a sense of roots, but whose words and music no longer made
her feel good.

She stepped into the house, flicking on lights as she went,
listening for the click of Wolfe's claws against the tile. She didn't
hear them. She whistled for him. He didn't appear. Mating season, she thought. Wolfe had wandered off in search of a lady
skunk, leaving through the hinged panel at the foot of the front

door. He'd done it before, but he'd always checked in when it got dark, just to let her know he was okay.

In the kitchen, his bowls were overturned. Water had puddled on the floor. The newspaper and stack of mail she'd left on the kitchen counter had slipped into the sink. The potted plants on the sill had been knocked over, and one had broken, spewing clumps of black dirt and bits of clay pot across the counter and into the sink. It was possible he'd tangled with a cat that had found the hinged panel and made himself at home, that was what she wanted to believe, but a deeper instinct said no.

Someone had been in here and frightened Wolfe.

Aline set her briefcase on the counter, dropped her purse on the stool, and dug out her .38. The house *felt* empty, but just in case it wasn't, the gun gave her an edge. She removed her sandals and tiptoed into the hall, her thumb flicking off the safety on the gun.

She listened, but heard only familiar sounds—the pound of the surf a block away, the hum of the fridge, the ticking of the clock over the sink. She checked the downstairs closets, the back bedroom and bath, the utility room. She climbed the bamboo ladder to the loft, heart beating a little faster now, and peered over the top.

Nothing.

Up a little higher and she turned on the lights. There. Better. Much better. But nothing here looked out of place. The rainbow-colored hammock was strung near the window, her bed was covered with stacks of clean laundry, her bureau and nightstand were still a mess.

"Wolfe?"

She walked behind the hammock to open the window, but it was already cracked—not the way she'd left it this morning before she'd gone to work. She called for Wolfe again and this time, heard scratching.

"You up here, boy?"

Frantic scratching now, coming from the bathroom. Aline threw open the door, didn't see the skunk, said his name again. The scratching was coming from the linen closet, and when she opened the door, towels and bathroom supplies tumbled out. She heard him clearly now, growling the way skunks did when they were frightened or angry, and realized he was inside the wall.

She hurried back down the ladder and around the corner of

the alcove that jutted out over the carport. Years ago, before the extra bedroom at the back of the house had been built, the utility room had been here, with a laundry chute that had run from it to the loft. Later, the room had been turned into a closet, with a storage area and the old chute behind it. She didn't know how Wolfe had found it, but it was the only way he could've possibly gotten inside the wall.

Sure enough, the closet door was ajar. Bags of books leaned into boxes of Christmas decorations, which had toppled into a carton of board games. Shiny bulbs and Monopoly money and paperbacks and Trivial Pursuit cards were scattered across the floor and the top of the trunk everything had been resting on.

Aline leaned over the trunk, sneezed as dust flew up, and opened the pint-sized door to the storage room. She called for Wolfe and a moment later heard the click of his claws against the chute as he slid to the bottom. He shot past her, a black and white blur moving faster than she would've thought possible. It took her ten minutes to find him huddled inside the tub, behind the shower curtain.

He was a two-foot black and white striped skunk with an eight-inch tail that flicked back and forth as he growled and stamped his little feet, sure signs he intended to blast her. He couldn't, of course, he'd been de-scented, which he'd apparently forgotten. But he could still claw and bite and since skunks had terrible eyesight, she extended her hand slowly so he could smell her.

"It's me, boy. How about some Stinko Delight? You hungry? C'mon, I'm not going to hurt you."

Aline clicked the nails of her other hand against the edge of the tub, their code, the way she usually called him. His black raisin eyes squinted at her. His little rosebud mouth moved, as if to form words. His nose sniffed frantically at the air. And then his tongue darted out and licked the back of her hand.

She picked him up, and checked him over as he squirmed in her lap, struggling to escape. He didn't appear to be injured. She couldn't find any cuts or nicks or scrapes. But from the way he gobbled down the chicken and raw eggs she gave him, it was obvious he'd been in the chute most of the day, and that something had terrified him enough to keep him there. As she watched him, she realized the most stable relationship in her life at the moment was with this four-year-old skunk. The moral to *that* was too depressing to contemplate. But on a cheerier note, if it hadn't been for him, she wouldn't have noticed that the window in her loft wasn't the way she'd left it.

She climbed back up the bamboo ladder and searched the loft. Contrary to what Kincaid believed, there was an inherent order in the room's chaos, and it didn't take her long to notice that several things were missing. Her hairbrush. A bottle of Opium perfume, which she favored. The long T-shirt from Chile which she usually slept in. A tube of lipstick. Except for the perfume, nothing was worth more than ten bucks. Even the two twenty-dollar bills on the dresser hadn't been taken.

Aline turned slowly in place, eyes sliding through the room, pausing here, there, searching. Her gaze stopped on the framed photograph on the nightstand next to the bed.

It was facing the wall.

When she picked it up, her heart shuffled across the bottom of her chest, her eyes stung, a tongue of cold licked at the back of her neck. Part of the photo had been cut away, and only the half with Kincaid in it remained, his arm curving toward where she should have been.

4

Ortega licked his dry lips and stepped carefully through the brush, keeping his flashlight aimed at the ground so he could see where he was going. He couldn't hear anything but wind. It swept in from the Gulf, whistled over the cliff just beyond him, and whipped leaves and pine needles around his ankles. Every now and then his flashlight dimmed or blinked out and he shook it fiercely, swearing softly in Spanish, wishing he were anywhere but here. But this was another test.

The test of darkness in the old seamen's graveyard.

Padrino would be waiting for him, waiting for the shovel he carried, for the empty duffel bag that flopped against his thigh as he made his way through the dense thicket. He wished for moonlight, starlight, any kind of light that would strip away the dark. But the sky had clouded over, and he smelled rain in the air, just as he had the night Rikki had died.

The night he helped kill her.

No, I didn't kill her.

Padrino did. He, Manuel Ortega, only held her, doing what had to be done for the greater good, for the vision, for the knowledge. He was an apprentice, the only pupil of a sorcerer whose power would one day blind with its brilliance. One day soon.

When the moon turned black.

As he neared the graveyard, his throat went dry. A wave of sweat moved across his back and sprang through the pores of his hands, his face. Spirits walked here: he could feel them. They brushed up against him disguised as the wind. They breathed on his cheeks. Their spittle dampened the back of his

42

neck. They whispered to him in a language he didn't yet understand, and their voices seemed sharp, menacing.

"*Padrino*," he whispered. "Are you here?"

The wind swallowed his voice. Ortega moved forward slowly, shining the flashlight over the headstones. They stuck up from the dark like huge packs of chewing gum standing on end, and branches hung over them, skeletal arms that swayed, rustled, that chattered in the wind.

"Padrino," he said again, louder this time.

But it was only the wind who answered him, groaning like a woman at the moment of her greatest pleasure.

As he moved closer to the graves, the spirit voices got louder. The skin on his arms ruptured with goosebumps. Fear swelled against the back of his throat, a boil, a tumor, a fat heart that throbbed.

Forty Hispanic seamen had been buried here between 1910 and 1948, but it was the presence of one man Ortega felt most strongly, and he knew where that man's grave was. He had known since he was a child, when the stories about Armando Bacalao had been whispered with both reverence and revulsion. He was the greatest *mayombero* to ever come out of Cuba, and some said that if he had lived, his power could have defeated Castro. Others believed that Bacalao had faked his death and assumed a new identity when he'd denounced Ikú. The bones in his grave, they said, belonged to a man Bacalao had sacrificed as an offering to Ikú, to appease the god for his own defection. The only thing Ortega knew for sure was that *Padrino* possessed Bacalao's power. He had seen the power, tasted it, watched it. And one day that power would pass to him, because he had been chosen.

A man does what he must, he thought, and shone the beam over the headstones again.

"No lights."

Ortega whipped around at the sound of the voice; *Padrino* laughed silently and took the shovel. "You act like a child who's scared of his own shadow, Manuel. Come on, we have work to do."

Without the flashlight, the dark was thick, impenetrable, an inky abyss where the ground might shift at any second, where the trees might topple, where the dead might suddenly rise up and swell in the breeze like phosphorescent sails. But *Padrino* moved forward with the quick certainty of a man who knew these woods, a man who saw with the soles of his feet, the pores in his skin, a man of power. Ortega was honored that he had been chosen.

They stopped at the grave. The headstone leaned to one side, and the lettering on it was faded but still visible:

CAPITÁN ARMANDO BACALAO
17 de julio, 1901, La Habana, Cuba
4 de diciembre, 1948, Tango Key
MÍ VIDA PARA IKÚ

Padrino jammed the shovel into the soil and started to dig. Ortega set the duffel bag down, crouched, and cleared the dirt to the side with his hands. The wind moved against his back, the graveyard ghosts danced around him, the dark licked at the air he breathed. His hands were getting dirty. The black soil pushed up under his fingernails. Its wet smell swirled in his nostrils and stank of death. He hated this. But an apprentice was supposed to take orders, to learn, to remember. An apprentice did what he had to do.

The shovel struck something, and Ortega felt the dull, hollow sound inside his own skull. Now *Padrino* worked his way quickly around the grave with the shovel. It sank, hit, sank again. *Padrino* tossed the shovel aside and fell to his knees, and they both dug with their fingers until the edges of the coffin appeared.

"This is it, Manuel. Help me lift it."

It took them a few minutes to pull the coffin out, and when they did, Ortega felt a stab of disappointment. It was so *small*. How could such power be contained in a body that was so diminished? Perhaps the stories were true, after all. Perhaps another man was buried here, an ordinary man, a *campesino* Bacalao had sacrificed. But then the lid slid away from the coffin and *Padrino* sucked in his breath and Ortega knew Bacalao was buried here. He sensed the evil, the power, felt it like a weight in his bones, his blood, in the deepest recesses of his being. He felt the unseen something that hissed from the coffin, that changed the texture of the air, the temperature of the wind.

Ortega's heart lurched like a drunk in his chest, lurched with fear and awe and a need to flee. But *Padrino* switched on the flashlight and shone it into the coffin. The bones were small, no larger than a key deer's, and when *Padrino* picked one up and brushed it off, it was utterly white, like a pearl.

Padrino picked up more of the bones, and some of them broke and fell back into the coffin. They pulverized instantly. Tiny plumes of dust rose up, and *Padrino* leaned into them, inhaling them. Ants and bugs scurried out of the coffin; *Padrino* didn't seem to notice them. He stuck his finger through the skeleton's eye socket and reached up into the skull.

"Here, Manuel. Here was the true source of Bacalao's power. Here." *Padrino* spoke in Spanish and looked up at Ortega then, his eyes feverish, glazed, almost wild, and tapped his own temple. "And soon it will be here." His laughter was soft, wild, a little crazy. Then the skull broke off from the rest of the skeleton and his *padrino* lifted it in his cupped hands and told Ortega to shine the flashlight into the mouth.

The eyes lit up.

The holes of the nose glowed.

The skull turned bright and luminous, as though it were burning from the inside out, a white pumpkin, a macabre star, a new moon. *Padrino* then removed the flashlight and brought the skull close to his own face and slowly, very slowly, drew the tip of his tongue around the rim of the eye sockets. The tongue darted into the sockets, out, in again, then slipped down over a cheekbone to the mouth.

Germs, thought Ortega. *Diseases.*

"Beautiful," whispered his *padrino*.

"We should hurry," Ortega said, looking around nervously, more afraid now of the living than the dead. "It will be light soon."

Padrino told him to gather up the rest of the bones, wrap them in burlap, and put them in the bag. The skull was bound in black satin cloth and placed next to the other bones. *Padrino* also added dirt from the deepest part of the grave and a nail and a splinter of wood from the coffin. An earthworm was crawling from the dirt inside the hole, and *Padrino* picked it up, squeezed it between his fingers until it was dead, and dropped it in the bag. "Any time a worm appears in a grave, Manuel, one must kill it and use it in the *nganga*. It's a sign."

Ortega nodded. *An apprentice must remember.*

He forced himself to think about later, about what was to come. First, the bones would be pulverized and mixed with drops of their own blood. Then the worm would be chopped up with a pinch of dirt from the grave and the heart of the panther they had killed three weeks ago. The panther was important because it had been Bacalao's creature, his spiritual counterpart in the animal world. It was fleet and shrewd, a hunter who would now do *Padrino*'s bidding, because he possessed its heart.

The personal belongings of their next victims would be added to the mixture, so the panther would know their smell, their habits, their haunts. All of this, including Rikki's fingers, would be combined with the *nganga*, the source of the *mayombero*'s power.

It was the equivalent of a voodoo root bag, but more vast, more complex, like a small world that contained all the creatures and plants a *mayombero* would need for spells and magic. This little world was ruled by a *kiyumba*, the spirit of a corpse the sorcerer chose during his initiation and removed from a grave. Various parts of the corpse were used in the creation of the *nganga*, and if its spirit consented to work with the *mayombero*, then the pact was sealed for life.

Padrino already possessed the *nganga* that had served Bacalao so well throughout his short life. He had inherited it. Eventually, it would be passed on to Ortega and to it would be added *Padrino*'s bones and dirt from his grave and blood from Ortega and whoever *he* chose as an apprentice. The process was infinite, immortal, an ever deepening spiral whose borders were closed to all but the chosen.

And he, Manuel Ortega, had been selected to inherit the darkest magic, the darkest power. It made everything worthwhile, even Rikki. She wasn't really dead, after all. She too had been picked—and was now immortalized, living on in the *nganga*, endowing it with her considerable sensual talents. In her new life, she would be with him forever. They would hunt together, learn together, bound by magic. Surely she understood this and, in the greater wisdom she'd found in death, had forgiven him for tricking her that night.

As he tied the burlap around the bones, the damp wind brushed across his ear like lips, a ghost kiss. For just an instant he thought he heard Rikki's voice curling through the dark, a finger of smoke, a tendril of fog, *Help me, Manuel, help me.* He saw her slumping in his arms, felt the warmth of her blood on his hands, tasted that night's rain in his mouth.

Then there was just the moan of the wind and *Padrino* hissing, "Hurry up, Manuel."

His heart ached as he stood, as he hurried from the graveyard, away from the voices of the dead, away, dear God, away.

5

Kincaid sped through the rain, following Old Post Road out of town and into the hills.

This two-lane route, twisting around the periphery of the island as if embracing it, dated back to the turn of the century. Then it was little more than a horse and buggy path which wound through the wilderness between Tango to the south and the Cove to the north. The postmen who'd delivered mail once a month had traveled it on horseback after arriving on the ferry from Key West.

The ferry still operated, but like everything else on the island it bore little resemblance to its predecessor. Progress, Kincaid thought, had taken its toll on Tango. Whereas land here had once sold for a hundred an acre, the price of an average home now was about $250,000, the highest in the state. Gasoline was almost fifty cents higher a gallon than on the mainland, clothes and food were fifteen percent more expensive, and property taxes were absurd. No wonder people had to have two jobs to live here.

But despite the problems, and the way developers gobbled up bits and pieces of the island, there were tangible benefits: pollution-free air, limits on building that prevented the construction of high-rises, a wilderness preserve that covered the northeast tip of the island, and an unusual topography of hills and beaches, glades and wilderness. Tango remained the only place in Florida that Kincaid wanted to live, even in the bad times.

But maybe bad times had cycles like the moon, and his were almost over. Besides the consulting fees he would earn from the police department, the call he'd gotten late last night from Hannah Porter spelled income. He'd worked for her and her husband in the past, digging up background information for Porter's books. The jobs were usually uncomplicated, and always paid well.

Once he was high in the hills, the rain let up and the sweet scent of ocean and earth wafted through the windows. The pale light varnished the damp cushions of green, and everything sparkled—the brilliant red blooms on the acacia trees, the lavender periwinkles, the pines, the banyans. And then he rounded a curve and there was the lighthouse, rising from the lip of a cliff on the western slope of the island, a great bleached bone standing on end. It was over a hundred years old, a monolithic relic of the days when Tango was a dark green pearl floating in the Gulf Stream. Numerous stories had circulated about the place over the years—mysterious deaths among the lighthouse keepers, supposed hauntings by the Hispanic fishermen buried in the nearby seamen's graveyard, boats smashed to smithereens on the rocks seventy feet below it. But none of the superstitions that had grown up around it had prevented the Porters from buying it three years ago.

Kincaid pulled up to the imposing iron gate and got out. Three German shepherds raced from the trees on the other side, oblivious to the drizzle as they snarled and barked and leaped up against the slats. He rang the intercom and kept his distance from the gate; the pooches looked damn hungry.

"Yes?" asked a male voice with a slight Hispanic accent.

"It's Ryan Kincaid. Hannah's expecting me."

"*Ah, sí, señor.* If you will please follow the driveway to the front of the lighthouse and do not get out until I have leashed the dogs."

"Right." Like he needed to be told.

He heard a click and the gates began to creak open. He hopped back into the Saab, shut the windows, and drove through. The shepherds bounded along, keeping pace with the car, making enough racket to raise the dead.

The driveway twisted through beautifully landscaped grounds: hibiscus hedges that were trimmed into neat geometric shapes, citrus and mango trees weighted with fruit, sprays of ferns interspersed with clusters of bright flowers. This was Karl Porter's Walden, the place where he created his sci-fi space fantasies, his thrillers, his weird, dark tales of possession and madness.

Kincaid had met him and Hannah shortly after they'd moved here, when Porter did a signing at Whitman's for his latest book. The affair had been enormously successful; his name drew buyers in droves. But the aggravation Aline had gone through to accommodate Porter's numerous eccentricities had soured her on Porter the man, and to this day she still disliked him. She wasn't a woman who forgave and forgot, he thought, and no one knew it better than he did.

As Kincaid neared the lighthouse, a man in a yellow rain slicker emerged from the trees and whistled shrilly for the dogs. When they raced over to him, he snapped leashes on their collars and led them away. A moment later, Kincaid stopped behind Hannah's sleek white Porsche. In front of it was its twin, the bright red number that Porter drove, and in front of that, the family van.

Kincaid darted through the drizzle to the front door. It opened before he rang the bell, and Hannah ushered him into the hallway, her voice soft and breathy as she greeted him, and suggested they talk in the kitchen.

"I know I called you awfully late last night, Ryan, and I do apologize, but I wanted to get started on this right away. . . ."

He smiled to himself as she chattered nonstop, her wide pastel blue eyes blinking and rolling and laughing as she skipped from one topic to another. The weather. The new dogs. Her various illustrating projects with firms in Miami. The sales figures on Porter's newest book. Her garden.

She was just a wisp of a thing, five two or three, with short, fluffy blond hair, and a face pretty enough to stop traffic. She wore gold hoop earrings, her feet were bare, and her slender body was pressed into designer jeans. Her bright yellow T-shirt with WOODSTOCK across the front completed his impression of her as a sixties flower child.

Her incessant chatter characterized her as much as anything else, and Kincaid enjoyed listening to her. She possessed a childlike exuberance for anything that interested her. It led some people to dismiss her as a flake, and blinded them to a mind that was bright and mercurial and which complemented Porter's. Despite her youth—she was fifteen years younger than Porter—she was shrewd where he was trusting, detailed where he was not, left brain to his right. Ying and yang, the perfect balance.

They settled at the shiny black table in the kitchen, where the picture window overlooked the Gulf. The blue-green waters stretched through the mist like a mirage, stripping him momentarily of his sense of time. It was easy to imagine old fishing vessels churning through fog on these painted waters a century ago, following the glow of the lighthouse beacon. No wonder Porter had moved here. From his study in the old beacon tower, he had only to gaze out at this incomparable loveliness to lose himself.

"I meant to call you a couple of weeks ago when I heard you were back, Ryan, but then I had to go to Miami for a couple of days and it slipped my mind," Hannah was saying. "In fact, I sometimes feel like I spend most of my life in Miami, even though I've only got to be there once a week, when one company has its editorial meetings. Karl's tried calling you a couple times too. *Anyway*, he's started this new project and I'm *desperately* in need of some help. It may involve a trip to Miami, but other than that, it's stuff you can probably find here on Tango. The library doesn't have much, but we've got this *huge* Latin population on Tango, and since you speak Spanish and all, I thought . . ."

"What's the project involve?"

"Oh." Her laughter broke up the concentration on her pretty face. "Yeah. I got ahead of myself." Her small, white hands curled around her coffee mug. "He's doing a novel that involves *santería*. A real dark thing, really. I know I, for one, will *not* be able to read it if I'm alone here at night."

Funny, Kincaid thought, how you didn't hear or think about something for months at a time, and then suddenly it cropped up twice in twenty-four hours. "What do you need exactly, Hannah?"

"Stories. There're a few books on *santería* in English, and I can get background material from those. But Karl needs *real* experiences people have had with *santería*. Spells that have worked, secret rituals, the way a *santero* is possessed by a spirit when he goes into a trance, like that."

"I'll see what I can do. But it may take a while. *Santeros* are tight-lipped."

"Oh, don't worry about time. He's got a long deadline on this one. The zombie business in voodoo interests him, Ryan, so if there's anything in *santería* like that, it'd be good too."

"That wouldn't really be *santería*."

Her thin brows arched. "No?"

"I don't think so. Anything to do with the dead and rituals of the dead—the so-called dark side of *santería*—falls into *palo mayombe*."

She looked interested. "Karl mentioned that. What is it?"

He admitted he didn't know much about it, except that *palo* was the Hispanic equivalent of black magic. It dealt with death, destruction, and revenge, and its practitioners were called *mayomberos*. "They don't worship *orishas*, who're considered spirits of light, but work through a god called Ikú, who—"

"Ikú?" She sat up straighter. "Is that what you said?"

Kincaid nodded.

"C'mon, I want to show you something in the seamen's graveyard." She pushed away from the table. "The dogs found it this morning."

Outside in the drizzle, they followed a path through the mist that paralleled the edge of the cliff for a few hundred yards. The wind whipped up over the sides, a tempest that tasted of salt and wilderness. He was soaked to the skin before they reached the six-foot wall that separated the lighthouse property from the woods beyond it. The gate squeaked as they passed through it.

"The caretaker said he must've left the gate open yesterday or something. That's the only way the dogs could've gotten out." Hannah glanced up at him, her thin fingers sliding through her damp hair. "When he tracked them down, they were in the graveyard."

They cut away from the cliff now, through knee-high weeds, and into woods where the trees grew close and tight, as if they were protecting something. The canopy of branches was thick enough to keep the drizzle from touching them and took the brunt of the wind; but it whistled through this tunnel of wet green, a high-pitched noise that seemed at times almost human, as though some neighborhood kids were hidden in the brush, signaling each other with what were supposed to be bird calls.

When they reached the graveyard, the air seemed to change, growing cooler, silkier, softer, although he might've been imagining it. But this was a place where a man could imagine any number of dark and terrible things and believe absolutely that all of them were real or were about to be real.

The gravestones, perhaps forty in all, were as weather-beaten as the men buried here had probably been when they died. Weeds sprouted everywhere, flourishing on the graves, sticking out of the cracks in the headstones.

"Here," said Hannah, stepping carefully between the headstones now. In the middle of the second row she stopped. There were fewer weeds on this grave, and little growth around it. The earth, in fact, looked freshly dug. "When the caretaker found the dogs this morning, they were trying to get at a corner of the coffin that was sticking up through the dirt." She crossed her arms at the waist, and her hands vanished inside the sleeves of her rain slicker. "Like it had been dug up. But not by dogs."

"Grave robbers?" Kincaid chuckled. "I doubt that any of these guys had anything buried with them worth stealing, Hannah."

"Probably not. But it still gives me the creeps. This is what I wanted to show you, Ryan." She moved around to the right of the grave, crouched, and brushed her hand over the headstone. She pointed. "Ikú."

Kincaid moved closer. Captain Armando Bacalao, whoever he was, had been born on July 17, 1901, in Havana, and had died on December 4, 1948, on Tango Key.

"What's the epitaph say?" she asked. "I don't know Spanish."

" 'My life for Ikú.' "

Hannah gazed at him from the other side of the grave, drops of rain sparkling in her hair. "Should we dig it up, Ryan? And see if it's been broken into?" Her voice was softer, almost a whisper, as if she were afraid someone might overhear them.

Kincaid started to say no; what was the point? But he felt a weird little nudge just under his ribs and decided it wouldn't hurt. "Got a shovel?"

"In the shed. Be right back."

While she was gone, Kincaid strolled through the rows, spot-checking other graves to see if any looked freshly dug. None did.

It didn't take him long to uncover the coffin once Hannah came back with the shovel. The splintered wood around its edges told a grim little tale, and once he got the lid off, the coffin told the rest. The thing was empty.

"Did the dogs act up last night?" he asked.

Hannah shook her head. "No more than usual." She tore her eyes away from the coffin, her face sallow and gray in the light. "They're supposed to be watchdogs. That's why we got the damn things. We're pretty isolated out here, and Karl spends so much time up in the tower, where you can't hear a damn thing except the wind. He thought the dogs would be a good idea since I'm usually puttering around on the ground floor, and if something happened . . ." She shrugged. "I used to think he was just being overly cautious. Now I'm not so sure, what with that murder and all."

"It was probably just some kids from the high school, Hannah."

"But what would they need bones for?"

"These days, no telling. Does Karl know?"

"He knows the dogs got out and that the grave looked like it had been dug up. He figured the dogs had done it." She laughed a little, but there was something sad about it, almost wistful. "He's cautious, but he's not paranoid."

"Maybe you should call Aline and at least report it," he suggested.

"I hate to bother her. It's not that big a deal. Besides, you're probably right, that it was just some kids."

Kincaid eased the coffin back into the hole and covered it with dirt again. They walked back toward the lighthouse, Hannah quiet and pensive, hands lost in the pockets of her slicker. Once they were through the gate, she said, "Could you do me a favor, Ryan?"

"Sure."

"Stop by the tower and see Karl before you leave."

"I was going to."

"Good. I think he spends too much time cooped up in the tower. He needs to get out, get away from the book, from work. He needs to be with people other than me."

"He's been compulsive as long as I've known him, Hannah."

"This is different. Something's bugging him, and he needs someone to talk to, and it sure as hell isn't going to be me."

The way she said it hinted at problems and differences that were none of his business, and he preferred not getting involved at all. He liked the Porters, both of them, and didn't want to find himself in the uncomfortable position of having to choose sides. But just the same, he climbed the six flights of stairs that twisted like an intestine to the old beacon tower. The door was open, Porter's computer was on, but he wasn't at his desk.

"Karl?"

Kincaid stepped inside, into Karl Porter's private world, where the light was magical and strange and the only sound was the moan and whistle of the wind. Books were everywhere—stacked on the floor beside his desk, piled next to his computer, clumped in no apparent order on shelves. On a shelf under the window that faced the lighthouse grounds were a VCR, a TV, and a CD player. To Kincaid's left were a pint-sized fridge and a couch with folded sheets and a pillow at one end. From the looks of it, Porter wasn't just spending a lot of time up here; it was almost like he was hiding.

Kincaid walked over to the sliding glass doors that opened out onto the Gulf and saw Porter leaning against the railing in the corner, his thinning, dark hair blown about by the wind. He was as muscular, dark, and tall as his wife was petite, blond, and short, and from the back looked like an ex-jock.

When Kincaid slid open the doors, the wind assaulted him, burning his eyes and stinging his cheeks. The smell of the sea and rain filled him. "Hey, Karl," he shouted.

Porter glanced around. The wind seized his hair from the back and made it stand on end. He looked wild, uncivilized, as though he'd sprung fully grown from the sea, the wind, the elements. Then he grinned and hurried toward Kincaid, a hand smoothing his hair back over his head.

"Ryan, my God, it's good to see you," he said loudly, pumping Kincaid's hand, slapping him on the shoulder. His dark eyes squinted against the wind, creasing deeply at the corners. "I heard you'd gotten back. How was it? Isn't Shanghai the most incredible city you've ever been in? Did you get to Taiwan, Ryan?"

Kincaid laughed and suggested they go back inside. Once the doors were shut behind them, the wind kept prowling across the glass, hungry, restless, rattling it now and then like a beast that wanted in.

"Jesus, you look great, Ryan. This trip must've agreed with you. Make yourself comfortable." He gestured toward the couch and opened the fridge. Out came two Coors Lights, which Porter popped. He passed one to Kincaid and settled in the stuffed chair to the left of the couch. The last thing Kincaid wanted at 9:30 in the morning was a beer, and it must've shown, because Porter said, "Oh. I guess it's sort of early, isn't it. What the hell. I lose track of time up here. That's probably part of the problem. *Salud*." He lifted his can and drank.

He did it, Kincaid noticed, like he needed the beer. Needed

it badly. His hand trembled slightly as he set it on the coffee table. He patted his windbreaker, pulled out a pack of Winstons, lit one. "So tell me about the trip."

Porter was one of the few men whose passion for travel equaled Kincaid's. Where one of them hadn't been, the other had. What one didn't know about a particular city or country, the other usually did. Although he hadn't done much traveling since he'd married Hannah, Kincaid knew, Porter and his first wife had lived in half a dozen countries during their twelve-year marriage. And that relentless itch for foreign places had never left him. It was an itch Kincaid understood well.

"I keep hearing this tone in your voice, Ryan, that says it was a great trip, *but*. . . ."

"No problems with the trip, only since I got back. Uncle Sam's after my ass."

"Yeah, I heard about the plane." He took another swig of beer and sat back, the heel of his right foot resting against his left thigh. "About ten years ago they billed me for back taxes and I didn't have the money, so they impounded my copyrights. I eventually had to buy them back. They're mean fuckers, Ryan." He paused, a meaningful pause that meant he was working up to something. "How's Aline?"

"Busy. I guess you know about the body that was found on the boardwalk?"

"Yeah, I heard." Something changed in his expression, something small but significant that altered the shape of his mouth, of his eyes. "Sometimes I think the maniacs moved from Miami down here."

"It looks like *santería* might be involved."

"Really?" He flicked at an ash on his jeans and stabbed out his cigarette. "Why?"

Kincaid started to tell him, but changed his mind. It might be one of those details the cops weren't releasing to the press so they could weed out cranks. "Cops aren't saying much."

"If you pick up anything specific from Aline on *santería*, Ryan, let me know. I'm sure Hannah told you I'm desperate for some authentic stuff."

"I'll do what I can."

"This book was Hannah's idea, you know, and I think her instincts were right on target again. I feel good about this one, Ryan. Better than I've felt in a long time."

"Hell, they've all been good."

Porter rubbed a hand along the side of his face, sipped at the beer, shook his head. "Then you haven't read *The Percy Parallel*. That one was shit, Ryan. The whole time I was writing it I kept wanting to be somewhere else. Moving. Traveling. When this one's finished I think I'm going to do exactly that." He flung out his arms, a gesture that encompassed not only the room but the lighthouse, grounds, the view, his life. "Why not? I can afford it. I can afford to go anywhere, Ryan. The only reason I haven't is because of Hannah." He got up, pacing around the room now, as restless as the wind. "Hannah doesn't enjoy it. She likes being where she feels she's in control. If we went anywhere, we'd be staying in Hiltons, Ryan, and what's the point in that? I might as well not even leave the country if I'm going to stay in a fucking Hilton." He stopped, his face etched with a peculiar longing. "Is it worth it?"

"I don't know." Kincaid's situation with Aline wasn't quite the same as Porter's with Hannah. But it was close enough because the bottom line was travel, extended travel, nomadic travel, non-Hilton travel. "If I come up with any answers, Karl, you'll be the first to know."

"Women," Porter grumbled, plopping into the chair again, a leg hoisted over the arm, a hand digging for another cigarette. "I ran into Aline one night at the Pink Moose, did she mention it?"

"No." Kincaid sensed what he was working up to, so he saved Porter the trouble. "Was she with Martell?"

Porter's dark eyes flicked toward Kincaid and seemed surprised or disappointed, Kincaid wasn't sure which. "Yeah, she was with him. What do you think of him?"

"I'm afraid my opinion is biased." Kincaid wanted to laugh, to show Porter that he didn't take Martell too seriously in the overall scheme of things, but the most he could muster was a sick chuckle. "You know him?"

"Sort of. A year or so ago I needed some legal background for a book and contacted him. I told him I'd pay him a hundred and fifty an hour, which was twice what he was getting at the time. And you know what the little shit told me? That he'd do it for five hundred an hour. 'You can afford it,' he says. 'Your books are always on the *Times* best-seller list.' Now, I don't mind paying people for a job, Ryan, but c'mon. Anyway, I had Hannah contact him, but without his knowing she was my wife. He gave her the information for seventy-five an hour."

Martell: the Tango Casanova, Kincaid thought. It was enough to make him gag.

"I was loaded the night I ran into him and Aline, Ryan. I said some things about her current taste in men which she probably hasn't forgiven me for."

Kincaid laughed. "Good. I'm glad somebody said it." He pressed his palms against his thighs and got to his feet. "I'd better shove off and let you get back to work. Let's get together for drinks or dinner sometime soon."

"Great. I'll call you in a couple of days." Porter walked him to the door. "Good to have you back, Ryan."

Kincaid was halfway down the first flight when he remembered he hadn't told Porter about the pillaged grave. He started to turn around but realized that if he didn't leave now he would never make it back into town on time to meet Aline. Being late was a sure way to get off on the wrong foot with her, so he kept going.

If he had returned to the tower, he would have seen Karl Porter standing at his desk, staring at the revolver in his hand. He would have seen Porter lifting the weapon to his temple, pulling back the hammer, then weeping as he jerked his arm away and fired at the window.

As a pane of glass in the tower shattered, the only thing Kincaid heard was the howl of the wind as it swept furiously through Porter's private world.

6

Rainwater rushed off the awning in front of the Tango Cafe, creating a shimmering veil that made everything beyond it look luminous and strange. Aline felt as if she were peering into a probable world which hadn't fully solidified, which might dissolve at any second. In fact, maybe Kincaid had stumbled into this probable world and couldn't find his way back, and that was why he was late.

Yeah, sure, Al.

If she added up all the minutes and half hours she'd spent waiting for Kincaid in the nearly four years since she'd met him, the sum would surely be equal to a full day. Maybe several days. Maybe even as much as a week. And if she threw in the two six-month trips and the one three-month jaunt, then the figure soared. And good ole dependable Aline had welcomed him back after every trip except this one, now hadn't she? And this time she'd screwed up by requesting his help on a case. So she had only herself to blame.

Fortunately, Ferret's presence mitigated her annoyance somewhat. He'd strolled in out of the rain fifteen minutes ago and scooted into the other side of the booth like he'd been expected. She didn't know how he'd tracked her here—through Kincaid, maybe. But she didn't ask. She never asked Ferret how he knew what he did, where his information came from, who his sources were. It didn't really matter, because most of the tips he passed on checked out.

As she was sure this one would: that Rikki Baker had been

involved with two other men besides Ortega, and one of them was the owner of Platinum's.

"His name's Nick Uvanti." Ferret's skeletal fingers curled around his mug of coffee. "Koko to his close friends. He and Rikki were a pretty hot item for a while, then she dumped him. He didn't like it. He fired her. Then he hired her back a couple of days later and they saw each other from time to time, but not like before. He's got a house up near the Cove, but he can usually be found on his Chris-Craft at the marina."

"You know him?"

"He's placed some bets with me. He's sharp, rich, and thinks money solves everything, Sweet Pea. He also carries a piece and has a bodyguard who looks like Quasimodo. I heard he used to slap Rikki around when he drank. It's probably true. He's the type."

"What about the other guy she was supposedly involved with?"

"Don't know. The only thing I found out is that he exists."

Three men, then. Mr. X, "Koko" Uvanti, and Ortega. It was more than she'd had last night. "Is he Cuban?"

"Half Puerto Rican, I think."

"Are Puerto Ricans into *santería*, Ferret?"

"Beats me. Ask Ryan. He's the gringo expert on this stuff."

"Can I ask you a question, Ferret?"

His lips pulled away from his teeth, and for a second she felt that elemental fear that always struck her when Ferret smiled. "Since when do you ask permission?"

"When it's personal."

"Ah." He folded his hands and sat forward a little, his face serious now. "What's the question?"

"Why're you interested in this?"

"Sweet Pea." He flung out his arms. "I'm an information broker. This is my business. I need to *know* these things. Then I sell them. Or give them away. Depends on who's asking."

"C'mon, this is different for you. Why?"

Ferret's eyes softened, and he cocked his head, looking at her strangely, as if he'd just understood something new about her. "You're getting better, Al."

I am? At what?

"A year or so ago, when she and Uvanti were a regular thing, he brought her to my office a couple times when he placed bets.

I liked her. She made me laugh. But I always had the feeling that there was something not quite right about her.''

"Like what?''

"Oh, one night the three of us had dinner at this fancy place in Miami. Uvanti commented on the china; she knew what kind it was. Uvanti commented on the crystal; she knew what that was, too. She was a big reader, heavy stuff. Descartes. Spinoza. Dostoyevski. Tolstoy. It was like I was talking to this cultured, educated woman who just happened to dance in the buff for a living. It didn't add up.''

He glanced at something over her left shoulder, then back at her. "You're about to get company, so I'd better split. I'll be in touch.''

And just that fast he was gone and Martell strolled up to the booth. He was decked out in jeans, sandals, a T-shirt, and a windbreaker—strictly laid back.

"Ferret left in a hurry.''

"He has a habit of doing that. What brings you out on a Saturday morning, Si?''

"Breakfast.'' He sat next to her, forcing her to slide over so he'd have more room. "And you.''

"Sure,'' she laughed.

Martell clicked his tongue against his teeth and patted her knee. "Your cynicism's showing, Aline. I called your place a little while ago to see if I could interest you in breakfast and a ferry ride over to Key West. I heard about a new antique store.''

"If I didn't have to work, I'd love to go.''

"The stripper?''

She nodded.

"Any leads yet?''

"A few. There may be a *santería* link.'' Aline gave him a quick rundown, aware that his hand remained against her thigh, resting there, as if he'd forgotten about it. "We still haven't found her car—she drove a VW Rabbit—and we still don't know where she was killed.''

"Has Bill done the autopsy?''

"He promised he'd have something today.''

"Maybe I'll swing by the hospital later.''

As they went through their checklist of procedures—what the D.A.'s office would eventually need, what he would need, all the usual things—his hand slipped lightly over her thigh, a slow, distracted motion. When it stopped, his fingers were curled over the inside of her thigh, a little high to be merely friendly, and now his thumb made slow, tight circles in one spot. It raised goosebumps on her arms, but she didn't stop him, didn't push his hand away. She caught the scent of soap on his skin and rain in his hair, and something hitched in her chest. *Hormones. Six months of celibacy. That's all it is.*

But she suddenly imagined herself and Martell someplace private and secluded. A beach. A lagoon. It was night and a moon burned against a star-strewn sky and she was pressing up against him and his hands were slipping over her bare skin and his mouth was—

"Al?"

She blinked. Everything swam back into focus. Tango Cafe. Rain. Martell. The heat inside her lingered, bright, intense, almost painful. She knew he'd asked her a question but didn't know what it was and looked at him blankly.

"What?"

"As soon as you've got your notes typed up, could I see them?"

"Sure." The pressure of his hand was intrusive now, it irritated her, and she reached down to push it away. But his hand was already gone. His fingers were laced together on the surface of the table. But she was sure that . . . no, she wasn't sure.

"How about dinner tonight?"

She started to say no, she would be too tired. But she saw Kincaid's Saab pull up to the curb, a white shape as illusory as everything else on the other side of the water pouring off the awning, and yes, he was twenty minutes late, and yes, she thought dinner with Martell sounded like a fine idea. "Around eight?"

"Eight it is."

"Now I've got to run. Scoot over, Si."

He did and she stood quickly and was on her way out the door as Kincaid stepped down from the Saab. Aline felt Martell's eyes on her, on her and Kincaid as they stood under her umbrella, deciding who would drive. She caught Kincaid's quick glance toward the cafe window as she hurried around to the other side of the Saab. Before she ducked into the car, she looked toward the window and smiled at Martell, who was still watching them, and then Kincaid looked around and his eyes met hers over the roof of the Saab and she smiled at him, too.

Aline closed her umbrella and was still smiling as she swung her legs inside the car. She had an almost overwhelming urge to press her face into her hands and giggle. This was fun. She was enjoying herself. She liked the frown on Martell's pleasant face as he'd watched through the window and Kincaid's moody silence as he popped the Saab into gear and pulled away from the curb. But most of all, she liked how she felt, as though she had discovered some elementary secret other women had always known but which had somehow eluded her until now. A secret about men, about men and women, a secret about herself.

The island's equivalent of Little Havana was known as El Pueblito. The Little Town. It had modest concrete-block homes with tricycles in the small yards, blazing acacia trees, oleander bushes, and old cars parked at curbs. It had been settled in the 1820s by Bahamian and Cuban seamen. They had fished the warm Atlantic waters for turtle, crawfish, stone crabs, and clams, and managed to eke a living from the sea despite the heat, malaria, and yellow fever.

The community burgeoned in 1831 with the inception of the cigar industry in Key West. In 1868 many cigar makers in Havana migrated to Tango and Key West because of the numerous nationalist uprisings in Cuba against the Spanish. Some found employment in the Key West factories and others turned to the sea for their livelihoods.

Aline wondered out loud if *santería* had arrived with the first wave of Latins or later, in 1959, when so many Cubans had fled.

"Probably with the first wave," Kincaid replied. "I imagine it was practiced just as frequently back then as it is now. Did you know Karl Porter's working on a novel that involves *santería*?"

"It doesn't surprise me. That's right up his alley. When did you see him?"

"This morning. That's why I was late."

A reasonable excuse, as usual. She listened as Kincaid told her about his visit. "Why would anyone steal a skeleton?"

"Beats the hell outa me. But this Bacalao character might be worth checking into. The library keeps historical records on the lighthouse."

"Why bother? I'm not going to waste time looking for a grave robber, Kincaid." She looked over at him. "Unless there's something else you haven't mentioned."

"Just a hunch, really."

"What kind of hunch?"

"I don't know yet."

Which was exactly the problem with hunches, she thought.

A few minutes later they turned into a small shopping strip with nothing but Hispanic stores in it. The *botánica* was flanked by a used bookstore on one side and a Cuban coffee shop on the other. The front window was jammed with religious statues of all shapes and sizes, crucifixes, medallions, candles. Large glass jars, which bore colorful labels, contained herbs, dried flowers, and things like crushed eggshells, dried lizards' tongues, lodestones, snake oil.

Inside there was simply more of everything that was in the window. Some of the statues were five feet tall and stood in mute grandeur along the aisles, hands outstretched, beatific expressions on their faces. Some wore crowns. Some were black. Some had rosary beads laced through their fingers. African face masks rested on shelves next to mason jars; bars of soap were placed alongside dried flowers and spices; snake skins hung next to jars of honey and boxes of cigars. There seemed to be no particular order to anything. It was as if she'd stepped into an enchanted place suspended between worlds or dimensions. If she blinked, it might vanish.

The air smelled sweet—of incense, scented candles, of fresh flowers from the fridge against the wall. Cigar smoke permeated everything. "I'll cruise," Kincaid said. "You ask if Ortega's in."

She nodded; she knew the routine.

She wandered over to the counter. A short, plump man asked if she needed help. He was nearly bald, his green-tinted aviator glasses rode low on the bridge of his nose, and his yellow guayabera shirt barely covered the roll of fat at his waist. "Is Manuel Ortega in?"

"He's busy, señora." His small, serious eyes flitted restlessly about, insects on the prowl. "I am his partner, Jaime Seroz. Is there something I may help you with?"

"I need to speak to him."

"I'm sorry, he—"

Aline flashed her I.D., and Seroz immediately changed his tune.

"I will get him, señora. Excuse—"

"Hold on."

"Yes?" Hopeful: as if he thought she'd changed her mind about Ortega.

"Tell me about Rikki Baker, Mr. Seroz."

"Rikki."

Like he couldn't quite connect the name with a face. His eyes blinked rapidly twice, paused, blinked again, like a code.

"Mr. Ortega's girlfriend. Rikki Baker."

"Rikki. *Sí*. Rikki." Tears swelled in his eyes and he looked away, down at his plump, dimpled hands. "Forgive me, please," he said softly. "It is still a shock." He slipped two fingers up under his glasses and rubbed at his eyes. When he looked at her again, the tip of his nose was bright red, as if all the blood in his face had rushed into it when his head had been bowed. "She was a good person, a daughter of Elegguá. She understood that it was a great honor to be chosen by an *orisha* of Elegguá's stature."

"Why?"

Two lines jutted sharply down between his eyes, a crooked frown that said no one had ever asked him why before, because of course the answer was obvious. "He guards the doors of opportunity. Without him, nothing can be accomplished, señora."

"What doors? I don't understand."

"*De la oportunidad*," said Kincaid, coming up behind her, his Spanish smooth, flawless. "*De todo.*"

"*Exacto*," agreed Seroz, nodding, then rattled off something in Spanish she didn't understand.

Kincaid asked Seroz to speak English, and he switched. "She was not Hispanic. She had no teacher, no *madrina*, but the first time Manuel—*el señor Ortega*—threw the coconuts for her, asking which *orisha* she belonged to, the answer was Elegguá, and so it remained."

"He didn't take very good care of her," Aline remarked.

"The ways of the *orishas* are sometimes not clear to us, señora, because we do not see the whole picture. They do."

The words echoed with the simplicity of Catholic catechisms. "It doesn't change the fact that she's dead, Mr. Seroz. Or that her fingers were chopped off. Or that the killer dumped her body. Or that she and Mr. Ortega were having an affair."

"An affair?" He raised his eyebrows, which threw his broad forehead into a chaos of tiny wrinkles. "No, no, I believe you are wrong. Manuel was her teacher, señora. He was guiding her through the studies so she could become a *santera*. She had already received Elegguá's *collares*—the necklaces—the first step."

"My understanding is that they were lovers, Mr. Seroz."

His pudgy little cheeks puffed out with annoyance. "I think not . . . he . . ."

"But you can't say for sure, can you?"

The bamboo curtain that hung over the door behind the counter moved, and a man who looked like a young Ricky Ricardo stepped through. Black hair that was slicked back with something, eyes as dark and hard as walnuts, well-dressed, a lot of jewelry: early forties, she guessed. But it was hard to tell for sure. Latin men aged well. His English was flawless. "Is there a problem, Jaime?"

Seroz shot off something in rapid Spanish. The man nodded, strode forward, smiling widely, extending his hand toward Aline. "I am Manuel Ortega, Detective. We would be more comfortable talking upstairs."

Aline introduced Kincaid as her partner. Ortega, a paragon of courtesy, shook Kincaid's hand and ushered them through the bamboo curtain and up a flight of stairs. His office wasn't large, but had a sense of spaciousness about it, due in part to a mirrored wall and the long windows. The combination of colors disoriented her and it must have shown, because Ortega waved a hand through the air and commented on it.

"The most powerful colors."

"Oshún's colors," said Kincaid as they settled in a pair of wicker chairs with red and yellow cushions.

Ortega, now seated behind his desk, looked pleased. "My *orisha*. The goddess of love. Marriage. Our version of Venus." He stroked a topaz on his little finger. "Rikki was my student." Dark eyes sliding from Aline to Kincaid, speaking to them both. "For a year or so. In the beginning, it is true that we were lovers. But not later. I do not know what else to tell you."

"She remained your student once you were no longer lovers?" Aline asked.

"But of course." The question seemed to surprise him. "Our physical relationship made her learning easier."

Spare me. This was sounding less like Catholicism now and more like a sixties rap. Brotherhood, peace, free love, amen. She started firing questions at him. He'd known her about a year, right? More or less, Ortega replied. Which? More? Less? Could he please be more specific? Ten months, he said. Yes, it was about ten months. How did they meet? At Platinum's. How did the *santería* business begin? She wanted protection. From who?

From what? He didn't know. From a person? Was it a person she needed protection from? Was it maybe Nick Uvanti?

Ortega seemed uncomfortable now. "Perhaps. She did not love him, she did not even like him, but she found it difficult to break away from him."

"Why?" asked Kincaid.

"I did not ask, señor."

"Because he was abusive?" Aline asked.

"I don't know."

He was covering something, Aline thought, but didn't press it. Not now. Not just yet.

"Who else was she involved with, Mr. Ortega?" she asked.

"I do not know."

"But there *was* someone else besides you and Uvanti?"

"Yes, I think so. But that is only from what she did not say, señora. You understand what I mean?"

"When did you last see her?"

"Just before she was going to leave for Miami, where she was to try out for a small part on a TV show. Or a movie. I forget. I gave her new *collares*, red and black beads, so Elegguá would be with her."

"When was this, do you remember?"

He thought a moment. "Ten days ago, I think."

"Did she have her car at the time?"

Blink, went Ortega's eyes. "Her car? Why would she need her car? I came to her apartment."

"And you're sure it was ten days ago?"

Blink, blink. "Yes."

Aline realized she couldn't ask Ortega where he was the night of the murder, because she didn't know yet when Rikki was murdered. Wouldn't know until she had the results of the autopsy. And until then, she didn't have anything else to ask him. But Kincaid did.

"Do you know anything about *palo mayombe*, Mr. Ortega?"

They were standing in his office doorway then, and Aline noticed the way Ortega leaned into the jamb, as if his knees had gone suddenly weak. "*Palo?* No. Not much. I know that some people refer to it as the dark sister of *santería*. But I disagree. *Palo* came from the Congo, not Nigeria, and its practitioners do not work through the *orishas*, señor."

"They worship Ikú, don't they?"

"Yes. And others."

"Aren't *santeros* sometimes cut into *palo* for the herbal knowledge?"

Ortega's arms folded at his waist, a protective stance. "I have heard it happens, yes."

"And don't some of their rituals involve mutilations?"

Ortega smiled, regaining his self-confidence. "You seem to know more than I do about it, Señor Kincaid. Perhaps you can tell me the answer."

Kincaid's smile could have frozen the balls off a horse.

"No need, amigo. I think you already know the answer. *Hasta luego*."

Inside the Saab. Windows sealed, doors locked, tires hugging the wet streets. She felt safe in here, and wondered why she would think of the Saab in that particular way. *Safe from what?*

Aline pulled her legs up against her and rested her chin on her knees. "I need an opinion, Ryan."

"The answer's yes. I think he's hiding something."

"That wasn't the question."

Kincaid looked over at her, his blue eyes pale, puzzled, perhaps a bit wary. She knew he thought she was about to ask something that would disturb the delicate balance that had existed between them since they'd left the cafe. "What's the question?"

"Can you think of a reason why someone would steal a bottle of Opium perfume, a nightshirt, a tube of lipstick, a hairbrush, and part of a photograph?"

His mouth slid into a smile. "I'll have to give that one some thought. But offhand, it sounds like a pledge night at the frat house, Al."

"How would you know, Ryan? You were never in a fraternity."

"For your information, I was president of a fraternity."

"At the University of Miami?"

"Where else? That's where I went to school."

"You never told me this."

He laughed, and she realized she'd been taken again. "The kid who cried wolf. You're going to do that once too often, and I won't believe anything you say from then on."

"You're too gullible."

"Only with you."

"How come that doesn't sound like a compliment?"

"Because it isn't."

The wipers slipped back and forth across the windshield, filling the silence with their monotonous drone. A minute passed. Two. He finally spoke. "So who got ripped off for all this stuff?"

"Me."

"When?"

She told him what had happened.

"The two twenties were still on the bureau?"

"Yes. What do you think?"

"That it'd probably be a good idea if you had some sort of security system installed, Al."

"It costs too much." Besides, that wasn't what she meant and he knew it. She said as much.

"What do you want me to say? That a picture is a kind of effigy? Okay, it is. And he's got an article of your clothing, strands of your hair from the brush, and two items that you use frequently—perfume and lipstick. It's enough to use in a spell. More than enough. The only thing better would be some of your blood. Or a piece of your skin, Al. Or a spot of your saliva. Is that what you want me to say?"

"I don't know." *Yes. No. Yes. Convince me I'm not imagining things.* "Yes, I guess so."

"But on the other hand, it might not have anything to do with *santería.*" He braked for a light at the intersection. "It might just be a fluke, Al, someone who broke in to take a look around and that was all he picked up before he ran into Wolfe. He spooked and hotfooted it out of there, not realizing he'd frightened Wolfe worse than Wolfe had frightened him. There may not be anything to it at all."

"But you don't really believe that, do you?"

"No." He paused. "And neither do you."

7

I

The Tango Key library was a converted conch house with a gable roof, several porches, and the typical decorative wood known as "gingerbread." It was one of the oldest buildings on the island, and there was something about it that made it look like a house in a fairy tale, Kincaid thought. A magical place where nothing inside was what it seemed.

When the island's first postmaster had constructed it in the early 1800s there was only a single floor and a barn on the five acres of land where the family had grown some of their food. In 1905 it was purchased by Henry Flagler, who'd intended to use it periodically while he was building the railroad that eventually connected Key West to the mainland. He'd torn down the barn, erected the additional floor, refurbished the place, and then never lived in it. Five years later he sold it to Tango County and it became a library.

Inside, Kincaid climbed the creaky stairs to the second floor, where the air smelled of coffee and cedar from the paneled walls. The door to Meg Mallory's office at the end of the hall was open. She was sitting at her cluttered desk, a seventy-five-year-old librarian and historian who looked sixty. Her feet were propped in a windowsill, and she was paging through a thick tome in her lap. Pale light bled into her salt-and-pepper hair and struck the lenses of her bifocals when she looked up. She peered at him over the rims as if she didn't know him.

"I wasn't gone *that* long," Kincaid said.

"Ryan." She laughed and swung her feet to the floor. "I thought I was hallucinating. I heard you were in Nepal."

69

"Wrong trip." He caught the faint scent of lilacs as he bussed her on the cheek. "The gossip machine here should provide better updates than that."

"Aw, hell, it's not very reliable anymore. It breaks down periodically, you know, and there's no one to fix it. Just like my memory. Move that stuff, Ryan, and make yourself comfortable." She gestured toward the books stacked on the chair in front of her desk. "Now let's see, was it Australia?"

"The Orient." He cleared the books and settled down. "You still running marathons?"

"Ten-k runs mostly, although I may try New York's run next spring."

"Ambitious."

"Or masochistic. You do much running on your trip?"

"Not as much as I would've liked." He talked about pollution counts in places like Tokyo and the throngs of people that made running nearly impossible in Hong Kong, and in the back of his mind kept puzzling over the things that had been stolen from Aline's. There was something about it he wasn't seeing, something related to *santería*, something intrinsic to rituals that preceded certain types of spells. But he couldn't pinpoint it.

He explained to Meg that he needed to find an expert on *santería*, preferably a *santero*. She thought a moment, sitting forward, fingers forming a steeple under her chin. "There's a woman I know who lives out in the hills, Ryan, just north of the cat's nose. Her name's Anna Riviera. She's a *santera*, and I've known her for years. She doesn't have much use for most of the *santeros* on the island, but she knows everyone."

"Is she any good?"

A dimple appeared in the corner of her mouth. "I guess that depends on what you're looking for. Protection, a love potion, herbs, a reading, a healing, information . . . maybe protection from the IRS?" The dimple vanished. "I heard about your plane."

"What'd they do, publish it in the paper or something?"

"A friend of mine works out at the airport and was there the day the Feds came out to impound it."

Terrific. He wondered what else had been circulating on the grapevine about him in his absence. "All I need is some information. It involves the murder of the stripper. Did you hear about it?"

"On the news this morning. But they didn't mention that it involved *santería*."

"That's a maybe, and it's just between us, Meg."

"I think this woman can probably help, Ryan. She isn't crazy about gringos, though, so it might be a good idea if I go out there with you."

"How do you know her?"

Meg sat back, her chair squeaking. "Oh, about fifteen years ago, when my husband was so ill, she was recommended to me by a Cuban woman I knew who thought she might be able to help him. She threw some shells, then some coconut rinds, and told me a few things, all of which happened. She also gave me a list of herbs and explained how to prepare them for my husband. I figured we had nothing to lose. The doctors had already written him off; they said he had three months to live. So I followed her specifications on everything, and within a week he was out of the hospital. Two months later there was no sign of cancer in his pancreas. He lived another seven years and died of a heart attack." She shrugged. "I know it sounds outrageous, Ryan."

The scar on his stomach burned. "I'm not a complete skeptic."

"I'll get in touch with her today, and we could go out there tomorrow if you'd like."

"What time?"

"How about if we meet at the Tango Cafe around noon? If something changes, I'll call you."

"Make it eleven and we'll have lunch."

"Great."

"One other thing. I need information on the old seamen's graveyard up at the lighthouse. Who's buried there, something about them. Got any suggestions?"

"Sure. The lighthouse has been one of my island projects for years." She swiveled in her chair, scanned the shelf behind her, and plucked out two slender books and a three-ring notebook. "Take these with you. The little things were published by the Tango Women's Society. The notebook is stuff I've compiled over the years, and if you lose it, Ryan, I'll have your head."

"I'll return everything tomorrow morning. I really appreciate this, Meg."

He started to stand, but she reached across the desk and touched his arm. Her fingers were cool, dry, but communicated a sense of urgency. "This is probably going to sound silly or superstitious or something, Ryan, but if you're going to be delving into *santería* at all, you need to watch your step."

His scar burned and twitched, as if commanding him to pay attention. But he patted her hand and whistled a few bars from *The Twilight Zone*. "Don't worry about it. *Santería* may not even be involved in the homicide."

"You don't understand. You're going to be asking questions, poking around, digging for answers. Word gets out in the Latin community, and if a *santero*'s mixed up in this, you could find yourself in big trouble."

"Hexed, huh?"

She drew her hand away and tilted her bifocals back into her hair. Her dark eyes pinched with annoyance. "Don't make a joke out of it, Ryan. As absurd as this stuff sounds to the Western mind, a lot of it works."

Kincaid apologized for his glibness, gave her hand a quick squeeze, and left. All the way downstairs the scar itched and burned. He knew he was imagining it; the scar was too old to produce any sort of sensation. But it didn't change the fact that he felt it. A doctor had once compared it to the discomfort an amputee often experienced in a phantom limb, real but not real.

The difference, though, was that nothing had been amputated during the exploratory surgery that had produced the scar. Instead, a viscous mass the size of an orange had been removed from his large intestine. The baffled surgeon had described it as a ball of matter that contained gnarls of black hair, chips of bone, fingernails, teeth, clumps of dirt, and a swatch of burlap the size of his thumbnail. He didn't have any explanation for how it had gotten inside Kincaid.

But the Cuban lab tech who'd shown it to him several days after his surgery had known exactly what it was. *A trabajo*, she said. *A spell*. It was not the worst she'd seen, but if it had gone untreated it eventually would have killed him. When he asked how it had gotten inside him, she shrugged. *A santero's magic, señor. An act of revenge.* Then she had given him the glass jar with the thing floating in alcohol inside it. A reminder, she said.

For several years, until Aline had tossed it out, it had sat on the mantel in his den like a child's excised appendix.

* * *

The bowels of the Tango Key Hospital were a cool, eerie twilight ruled by the dead.

Kincaid's shoes whispered in the hall. Now and then he heard the clatter of the freight elevator trundling between the floors above him, delivering patients from surgery, taking them to intensive care, bringing them to the lobby to be discharged. The hospital morgue and autopsy room were down here, and so was the cubbyhole where Bill Prentiss hid out when he didn't want to be found.

The morgue was unlocked, and as usual the cloying sharpness of hospital cleansers masked the smell of death. A body bag rested on a gurney next to the autopsy table, awaiting Prentiss's scalpel. The wall of metal drawers gleamed brightly in the wash of fluorescent lights; Kincaid wondered which one held Rikki Baker. He stopped in front of the door to the darkroom. A red light glowed overhead.

"Bill?"

"Hey, Ryan. Be with you in a second."

Several moments later the red light blinked off and the door opened. Prentiss, dressed in jeans, a T-shirt, Reeboks, and a chef's apron, looked like a male model down on his luck. He needed a shave, his eyes were bloodshot, his dark curly hair was mussed. He blinked against the glare of the lights. "Is it Sunday yet?" he asked.

Kincaid laughed. "So this is what happens to you when Bernelli goes away for a weekend."

"Yeah, shit. She's the timekeeper in the family. C'mon in. Some curious things in this case, Ryan. The Baker woman has had some pretty extensive plastic surgery, for one. New nose, tucks under the eyes, at the jaws, something done to the shape of her mouth. Excellent surgery, too, I might add.

"Her stomach contents didn't tell me too much. She'd had some apple pie right before she was killed; the stuff wasn't even digested. I've also got some X rays you'll find mighty interesting."

The darkroom was large, well-equipped, and smelled like chemicals. Prints floated in a tray of water, a strip of negatives was sandwiched between glass in the enlarger, and a dozen X rays were clipped to a wire suspended over the sinks. Prentiss removed two of them and fixed them to a lit panel against the wall.

"That's her sternum you're looking at. You can see the path the knife made. It tore straight up into her heart. Slender blade, with a jagged edge on it. I was hoping part of the knife had broken off in her, but no such luck. It would've given us a lot more to work with. But I was able to get a negative cast of the wound, which I'm going to pass on to Harry Topper in the lab. He'll be able to glean more information about the weapon from it.'' He tapped the second X ray. ''What you're looking at here are her hands. What was left of them. Her fingers were amputated with something sharp but not necessarily heavy. The cuts are clean, Ryan, straight through the bones.'' He shut off the light inside the panel. ''The serotonin levels in her blood say she was dead when the fingers were chopped. I'm placing her death at somewhere between late Sunday evening and early Monday morning.''

''What're the other X rays of?''

''Her head, arms, legs. I was looking for fractures, breaks, anything that would indicate a struggle. The only thing I found was a fracture in her upper left arm. Bones can break in a lot of different ways, and sometimes it doesn't even take much to do it if the bone's weak to begin with. But the way this bone is fractured makes me think it may have happened by her arms being jerked back. Maybe when her fingers were chopped off, for example. Or maybe because she was restrained by someone behind her while someone else in front stabbed her. The angle of entry and path of the knife could only be done from directly in front of her.''

''Couldn't the fracture have happened if she struck something in the struggle? Or by someone hitting her? Or maybe when she fell?''

''Possible. I'm not ruling out any of those things. I'm just saying to keep in mind that you may be looking for two people. I also found traces of gunpowder on her thighs, around the abdomen, in the pubic area. I don't know what it means, since she wasn't shot. I took samples of the stuff and sent it to the lab.''

''Anything else?''

''Yeah.'' He paused, rubbed his chin, and pulled down another X ray, which he fixed to the panel. ''I don't normally take X rays of the internal organs before I start the autopsy, but for some reason, I did this time. Take a look, Ryan.'' And he flicked on the light.

Kincaid didn't have to be a doctor to recognize the shape of a fetus, curled in its silent, watery world.

"Christ," he whispered. "How far along was she?"

"Nine or ten weeks. I sent the fetus to the crime lab in Miami. Hopefully it'll give us a DNA fix on Daddy, and once we've got that, there's only a one-in-two-billion chance of being wrong."

DNA was a genetic signature, and its testing had been used for several years to help determine paternity in civil suits, Kincaid knew. Its use in criminal matters was much more recent. But the statistics so far were encouraging. Out of thirteen cases in South Florida in which DNA comparisons were used, twelve ended in convictions.

"How long will it take to get a fix?"

"It depends on how jammed up they are in Miami. I asked for priority, so maybe that'll hurry things along. In the meantime we'll have blood types to work with. I couldn't find any signs that she'd been raped—no indication of forced entry, no bite marks. This guy was no Ted Bundy. But there had definitely been recent sexual activity. I think I got a good enough sperm sample so we can get the guy's blood type from it." He flicked off the light on the panel and stared at the dark X ray. "Sometimes I hate this fucking job," he said softly.

2

Two hundred years ago, the northern shore of the island, with its cliffs and hills and rocky juts, had been the ideal hiding place for pirates' ships. They plundered the Spanish vessels which they lured inland, hid their treasures in the deep pine forests that covered the island then, and left their indelible mark as surely as the Hispanics had.

Pirate's Cove was now a rich man's village with a two-million-dollar marina, neat little streets filled with exclusive shops, and homes that would make the hearts of Palm Beachers palpitate, Aline thought. Its infamous heritage was commemorated in the names of things—Treasure Shops, Doubloon Drive, Pieces of Eight Theater—and in the motifs that local businessmen used. Full-masted ships as logos, for instance, and awnings shaped like pirates' hats.

The main road through downtown was Tango's equivalent of

Rodeo Drive or Worth Avenue in Palm Beach. Small, exclusive shops lined the main boulevard. Porsches and Lamborghinis stood at the curbs, raindrops balled on their shiny hoods. Colorful umbrellas sprouted from sidewalks like exotic mushrooms. And under them were the Cove ladies, decked out in full regalia—gold and diamonds, alligator bags and shoes, designer shorts and skirts.

It took Aline ten minutes to find a parking spot, and when she did, the meter didn't work. So she slapped her official police sticker on the inside of the windshield and darted across the street.

Betsy's Lingerie Shop, where Rikki Baker's negligees had been purchased, was the sort of place where underwear started at $25. It was busy busy busy. Sales clerks floated through the perfume-scented air, their voices soft and obsequious. *Yes, ma'am. Certainly, ma'am. Here's your size, ma'am. Of course, ma'am.* Aline, dressed in jeans, a cotton blouse, and sandals, felt like a thorn among roses, a leper among beauty queens. Several clerks instantly assessed her as a waste of time and cast disparaging looks her way. It came as no surprise when she stood at the counter and was blithely ignored by the three sales clerks who were suddenly busy with tasks: counting money at the register, wrapping gifts, sorting merchandise. Aline finally spoke to the pert little thing closest to her, the one sorting silk robes.

"Are you the manager?"

Head bowed, hands fussing with a bow: "Yes, ma'am, I am. If you'll wait just a minute . . ."

"I've already waited five minutes."

"I'll get someone to help you, ma'am."

"You're the one I need to speak to."

A sigh now, a little show of temper as she tossed a hanger into a box of hangers behind her. "If it's about a return, you'll . . ."

Aline dropped her badge on the counter. "It's official."

"Oh." A nice, wide smile now. "Of course, Detective, uh . . ."

"Scott."

"We can talk in my office. Won't you come back this way, please?"

Her office was a nook at the back of the store and was barely large enough for the two of them. Aline brought out her bag of goodies and emptied it on the desk. Two black negligees with the RK initials embroidered on them. "These were bought here, and I need to know if your shop also did the embroidering."

The woman checked the label and the stitching on the initials and nodded. "Yes. This is definitely our work. These two little knots here are our embroiderer's trademark."

"Is embroidery a special order?"

Suspicious now, eyes narrowing ever so slightly: "Well, yes, but . . ."

"I'd like to know who placed this order."

"I'm afraid that's not possible." She shook her pretty little head. "I just don't see how we could trace something like that. Not everyone special-orders at the time of purchase."

"What difference would that make?"

"Look, Detective. All we'd have to go on would be receipts, and it would take *days* to go back through all of the receipts."

"You're not computerized?"

"Only with sales figures. Not who buys what and when."

"But the customer's name would be on a special order, wouldn't it?"

Frowning, squirming in her chair: "Well, yes, but . . ."

"Her name's Rikki Baker. I'd like you to look through the receipts and see if she placed an order for these initials. If so, when."

She jerked a small metal box toward her and flipped open the lid. It was jammed with pink and yellow slips. "That's just special orders for the last six months, Detective. How the hell am I—"

"What's your name?" Aline snapped.

"Linda. Linda Drewson. Why?"

"All right, Linda. Watch closely." Aline dug her fingers behind the card that said B and pulled out a stack of slips. She dropped them in front of Linda. "This is how you do it. One by one, for every single box until you find Rikki Baker's name. R for Rikki. B for Baker. Got it? However it's listed. Red initials on black negligee. Very simple. If you don't think you can do it, then I'll be glad to get a court order to do it myself. Any questions?"

Her mouth plunged at the corners. "No."

"Fine. I'd like an answer by Monday." Aline pulled out a business card and dropped it on her desk. "Call me at home or at work."

Tersely: "I'll call you as soon as I have something, Detective."

How sweet it is.

8

When the last customer left that afternoon, Ortega locked the *botánica*, drew the shades, and walked up and down the aisles, collecting the items they would need for tonight.

Three yards of black silk, a bottle of crushed eggshells, garlic, pepper, a burlap bag. He carried these things into the storage room under the stairs and locked the door behind him. He set everything on a shelf, then pulled a bookcase away from the paneled wall. From his pocket he pulled out a remote control device similar to those used for TVs. He pressed the middle button, heard a familiar whir, and a moment later a panel about half as tall as he was slid slowly upward.

Ortega hunkered down, ducked his head inside, and turned on the lights. The air smelled a little musty, despite the air-conditioning vent he'd added in here several months ago. But some fresh roses or a stick of incense would take care of the worst of it. He retrieved his little treasures from the shelf, and a moment later he was inside the secret room.

He could tell from the construction that it was the oldest part of the building, and guessed it had been used for contraband of one kind or another through the years. He'd stumbled across it a long time ago, shortly after he'd bought the shop, when he was spraying for bugs.

There had been nothing in the room then except some empty boxes and a panel in the floor, which was a second exit. He'd cleaned it up, added the remote-controlled door, and hired a Cuban he knew in Miami to knock out the wall between the room and the storage closet in the *botánica* to give him a little more space. Now it was fully equipped. A cot. A small fridge. A pantry stocked with food. A gas stove. A sink and running water. He even had a tiny bathroom and a small kitchen: the comforts of home on a smaller scale.

Back then, he didn't understand why the room mattered so much, why he was spending so much time and effort fixing it up. He thought it might be some childhood thing, the result of growing up in a house with brothers and sisters and cousins and second cousins and aunts and uncles, a house where privacy was something only the rich gringos had. But now he understood. Now he knew he'd been digging into the darkness within himself, preparing for his destiny.

Against the far wall was a trunk of his *abuelita*'s things. His grandmother had died ten years ago and left him her house, where he and Seroz now lived, this trunk of useless clothes, and the money he had used to open his *botánica*. Next to the trunk was the altar.

He arranged his treasures here, lit two tall black candles, and removed the lid from the black iron cauldron in the center. It wasn't really an *nganga*—he wouldn't be entitled to one until his initiation was completed—but in Ortega's mind, it served the same purpose.

The ashes and dust on the bottom were the remains of human bones, lizards, bats, creatures that crawled, that flew, that dug, that hopped. There were herbs and spices, bark and graveyard dirt. He had even added a lock of Rikki's hair because he wanted her to be with him. The problem, though, was that his *nganga* didn't have a spirit to rule it. He had not yet dug up a corpse from the graveyard and gone through the ritual that would seal a pact between him and such a spirit. That would come when he had completed his initiation with his *padrino*. In the meantime, he was fortifying himself, preparing himself just as he had when he'd fixed up the room. But now he knew why.

He laid out his instruments. A long needle. A sharp kitchen knife. Black thread. He reached for a glass jar covered with tinfoil. Holes were poked in the foil so the centipedes inside could breathe. Three centipedes. Once there had been a dozen. He made a mental note to replenish his supply.

He rolled off the rubber band that kept the foil secure against the top of the jar, picked up the needle, and impaled one of the centipedes. It squirmed and wiggled, struggling frantically, but it didn't die. Not yet. These creatures were surprisingly hardy.

He flicked it off the needle with his finger. It writhed on the black cloth that covered the altar, its tiny legs pumping frantically.

Ortega watched it a moment with detached interest, as though he were a scientist observing a creature he was about to dissect. Then he passed the needle through the tip of the candle flame. Back and forth, again and again, until the tip of the candle glowed orange. Now he swirled it in the ashes and dust in the cauldron. It was important to request Iku's blessing.

He set the needle aside, lit a cigar, blew smoke over the centipede. He anointed it with rum. *One who is sensual*, he thought. *A second who is fleet of foot. A third who has the power. A fourth who hunts and protects.*

"This is for the fleet of foot."

Ortega picked up the knife, held the blade in the flame for a moment, then pressed it against his palm and whipped it across. The pain was sharp but brief. He squeezed blood from the cut and watched the drops roll into the caldron. Food for Ikú.

"Protect me," he whispered. "Guide me." He went into the bathroom and opened a bottle of alcohol, which he poured over the cut. He put a Band-Aid on it and returned to the altar.

The centipede had somehow managed to crawl almost to the edge of the table. He rolled it back, tore off a long piece of the black thread, and threaded the needle. Then he picked up the centipede and eased the needle through the center of its body until only the thread ran through it.

He tied the loose end of the thread around the tip of the needle and hung it like a necklace from the base of the candle. The centipede was still alive. That was good. It was a sign that Ikú was pleased, that he would help Ortega and *Padrino* tonight. It meant that when the centipede died, so would the one who was fleet of foot.

Ortega imagined what she would look like, what she would be wearing, what she would say, what he would say, what *Padrino* would do to her before she died, and how he would watch— learning, absorbing, remembering, just as a loyal apprentice should.

This one would be easier for him than Rikki had been.

This one he would enjoy.

9

I

Think it through. Perfume and a nightshirt, lipstick, a hairbrush, a photograph. Aline could see the stolen objects in her head as she drove, lined up like sale items on a department store counter.

She tried to connect them with something else, with *santería*, with rituals and incantations and spells. She imagined the intruder emptying her bottle of Opium perfume into an iron pot, then adding strips of her nightshirt, flecks of her lipstick, hairs from her brush, and setting fire to her photograph. But it all smacked of bad horror movies, of silly superstitions about things that went bump in the night, and she started to laugh.

Then she thought of the grotesque thing that had been removed from Kincaid's stomach, the glob that had floated in a jar of alcohol on his mantel, the medical anomaly. And the superstitions suddenly didn't seem quite so easy to dismiss.

She swung into the parking lot in front of Stile, Penn & Associates, the only gynecological and obstetrics office in the Cove and probably the only one in South Florida open on a Saturday. The building looked like it had been slapped together from old driftwood and was tucked back into a holt of pines across the street from a park.

During the season, the parking lot was jammed with expensive cars. But now, in late May, the dead season, the lot was half empty. The cars were more modest because they belonged to the people who lived at the south end of the island. *Peons like me who work two jobs,* she mused, and poked her Honda into a spot under the sagging branches of a banyan.

Wayne Stile had been Aline's gynecologist for at least twenty

81

years. He was a kind Southern gentleman to the core, and one of the few physicians she knew who seemed to take his Hippocratic oath to heart. But this was the first time she'd ever visited him in an official capacity, and she hoped there wouldn't be any problems. Even Southern gentlemen could be stubborn when it came to ethics.

She waited in his office, a spacious wood-paneled room with half a dozen degrees on the walls, photos of his wife, his kids, his grandchildren, and the South Carolina beaches where he'd spent his childhood. He strolled in about ten minutes later, looking tan and fit. "If it isn't my favorite darlin'." He hugged her hello and in that soft, lolling drawl asked how she was doing and if she was getting enough sleep and working too many hours and did Whitman's have any new books on colonial times he should know about.

"Actually, Wayne, I need to ask you some questions about a woman who was one of your patients."

"Ah." He settled behind his desk and reached for one of the four pipes in a stand to the left. "Well. *Was* one of my patients, hmm? That past tense, coming from you, worries me, darlin'."

"Rikki Baker. We found her body last night. It was in this morning's paper."

"Only paper ah read is on Sundays, and offhand, ah don't recall her name. But that's not surprising. Tell me what you need."

Aline explained.

He patted tobacco into his pipe, lit it. "Let me ring for her file."

It took him a few minutes to go through it when it arrived, and he sat there nodding to himself and puffing on the pipe. The scent was sweet and pleasant and reminded her of Kincaid, of the pipe he'd smoked on their trip to New Zealand. The sheets on their bed and the inside of the car they'd rented had smelled like this, of Cherry Blend. Even her memories of the lakes, hills, and meadows were imbued with this fragrance, and filled her with nostalgia for what had been. But with it came the bitter taste of her frustrations during Kincaid's long absences, when her personal life was suspended in a kind of limbo.

"The dancer, I remember her. Sure. A lovely woman. Single. Effervescent. What a bloody shame." He looked up. "Has Bill done the autopsy?"

"I'm sure he has, but I haven't spoken to him yet today."

Stile fiddled with his pipe, tapping at the tobacco with a match, puffing, tapping again. He was mulling something over. How much to say or not say. "Well, you'll know sooner or later, Aline. Rikki Baker was pregnant."

Double homicide: that was her first thought.

"Who was the father?"

"Ah don't know. And in light of how she died, Aline, ah don't feel ah'm breaching confidentiality by telling you that she and ah had quite a lengthy discussion." He held up a sheet of paper. "Ah always try to jot notes to refresh mah memory, and ah see here we talked about her options: carrying the child to term and keeping it, giving it up for adoption, or terminating the pregnancy."

She had already had one miscarriage, he said, and was concerned she might have another if she carried this child to term. Stile had told her not to worry about it, she was in excellent health. But the conflict went deeper than that. She was single, she wanted to pursue a modeling or acting career, but the idea of being a mother also appealed to her. She told Stile she needed to think about it, and he said if she was going to terminate, it would have to be within the next few weeks. "She was just three weeks pregnant then. We had to verify it with a blood test."

"I thought you had to be at least six weeks before you could tell."

He smiled. "Not anymore, darlin'. And we don't use rabbits, either."

"When did this conversation take place, Wayne?"

He consulted the file. "March twenty-eighth."

Ortega as a daddy? A DNA fix on the fetus and a sample of his blood would answer that, *if* she could get a sample of Ortega's blood. "Did she tell you anything at all about the father?"

"He didn't know she was pregnant, and she had no intention of telling him, since they were no longer seeing each other. Ah got the impression their relationship was erratic. On again, off again. Ah do remember telling her that if she was going to go through with the pregnancy, she wouldn't be able to continue with the kind of, uh, dancing she was doing. That would mean a loss of income. Ah suggested she ask the father for financial help. Ah don't know whether she did or not; she didn't seem too worried about finances. Or if she was, she didn't say so."

"Did she tell you what he did for a living?"

"He did 'okay.' Ah believe that's the way she put it."

"Do you know if he was Hispanic?"

"Ah think she mentioned that she 'dated around' and one of the men was Cuban. But ah don't know if he was the father of the child, Aline. Maybe she didn't know either." He tapped the pipe against the side of an ashtray and set it down.

"There's one other thing, too, Aline. Sometimes when a patient is in a moral quandary about the abortion issue, she asks if ah know of someone in the clergy she can talk to. Ah usually recommend a Catholic priest I know. He isn't exactly an advocate of abortion, but he isn't opposed to it either. Ah think of him as one of these new breed of priests the church badly needs. Anyway, ah know Rikki saw him because he called the following day just to touch base."

"What's his name?"

"Lukas Carver. He's at St. Joseph's in El Pueblito. You may have to get a court order to get him to tell you anything, but he's worth a try."

She added church to her Sunday agenda, and ten minutes later headed toward the marina and Nick Uvanti's yacht.

2

Lester's Bar: island landmark, neighborhood hangout, local color. If the place was still standing in a hundred years, Kincaid mused, it would probably be a prized artifact for sociologists and historians who sought to uncover the quirks of late-twentieth-century man.

Kincaid was seated at his usual booth in the back, away from the jukebox. From here he could see the front door, the corner of the pool table in the room to his left, and the bar to his right. Twirling stools, which dated back to the bar's days as a soda fountain, still lined the counter. The ornate spigots that had once flowed with Dr. Pepper and root beer now bubbled clear and cold with the cheapest draft beer in town. The movie posters on the walls attested to Lester Senior's love of Hitchcock. Huge glass jars were clustered at one end of the bar and were filled with beef jerky and hard-boiled eggs in vinegar. There were no

records on the jukebox recorded beyond 1960. The bar existed
in a permanent time warp, and was the perfect place to look
through the books Meg had lent him.

He started with the slender volumes on the history of the
lighthouse. Some of it he already knew, but much of it was new.
It had been built over a two-year period, beginning in 1870, by
a group of fishermen who lived on Tango. The hazy old photograph of the finished product showed a much smaller and stunted
version of the present lighthouse. At the turn of century it had
been bought by the Feds and reconstructed: the walls were reinforced and the tower—minus glass—was added. It was manned
by three men, who were killed in 1909 during a fierce storm that
slammed into the keys. To this day, no one could explain why
the men had left the sanctuary of the lighthouse during the storm.
They were the only fatalities on the island, and although the
lighthouse had escaped damage, a superstition grew up around
the place, and it remained empty for two years.

In 1911 the island hired two men from Miami to work the
lighthouse full-time. For the next twenty-three years the place
was always staffed and functioned efficiently. But by 1934 the
keys had been hard hit by the Depression. Eighty percent of the
people in Key West were destitute or on relief. On Tango, that
figure stood slightly higher. There was no money for things like
lighthouses, and it was shut down again.

After that it fell into disrepair, until the lighthouse was "purchased from the county." In other words, thought Kincaid, when
the Porters bought it.

The rest of the little books were filled with ghost stories and
local lore about the lighthouse that had been passed down over
the years. Kincaid set them aside and opened Meg's notebook.
It was jammed with newspaper and magazine clippings, hastily
scribbled notes, typed pages, none of it in any particular order.

Meg apparently subscribed to the same *I'll get to it later*
attitude that Aline did. But after nearly four years of digging through the mess in *her* drawers and closets, the notebook was a cinch by comparison. He started in the middle and
worked his way in one direction, then the other. It only took
him ten minutes to find the first reference to the old seamen's
graveyard, a brief biographical sketch of the first man to be
buried there, in 1910.

Kincaid skimmed it and moved on until he found something

on Bacalao, the last man to be buried in the graveyard. He was the only child of a Cuban cigar maker and his wife, who had left Cuba in 1902, a year after Bacalao was born. They settled on a small farm in the hills, which Bacalao worked until he was eighteen, when both his parents drowned during a storm at sea. He inherited a great deal of money and within two years owned a fleet of fishing vessels and a larger farm.

At the age of twenty-five he married a wealthy Tango woman whose father was a banker. They had one child, a son born in 1944, four years before Bacalao was killed when his ship smashed into a reef. His body was recovered, and his wife had him buried in the graveyard.

On the surface, his life appeared quite ordinary. But in one of Meg's scribbled notations was a reference to the stories that Bacalao advanced himself through black magic, which he had supposedly learned from the Nigerian nanny who had accompanied his family from Cuba. These rumors were fed by the men who worked his ships and tilled his land, by the people who knew him and kept their distance from him.

During the late thirties there was a spate of brutal murders on the island which hearsay attributed to Bacalao, even though the evidence was never enough to formally charge him. Kincaid couldn't find any specifics on who was killed or when or if an investigation had even taken place. Nor was there anything on what had happened to Bacalao's wife and son after his death at sea. It seemed important, although he couldn't have said why, since this had only a marginal connection, at best, with his job for Hannah.

"Aren't we the studious one."

"Hi, Ferret." Kincaid didn't glance up.

The little man sat down on the other side of the booth, set down his beer, and dropped his racing form and notes on the table. His hand slid into Kincaid's line of vision, headed for the slender books, turning them so he could read the titles. Kincaid raised his head. Ferret in shades, damp hair combed back, pale blue guayabera shirt limp on his thin shoulders. Racing attire.

"The lighthouse, huh?"

Kincaid explained. Ferret tipped his sunglasses back onto the top of his head and jerked his thumb toward the poolroom. "Porter's in there losing his shirt."

"He can afford it."

"He's not a sloppy drunk, I'll say that much for him, but booze doesn't do much for his pool game."

"When're you heading out for the races?"

"A few minutes. Want to come along?"

"Thanks, but I'll pass."

Lips drawing back: "Hot date, Ryan?"

"Business."

Ferret pressed the tips of his skeletal fingers together, still smiling. His dark, weasel eyes said he was playing. "I hear a certain stripper at Platinum's is meeting Ryan Kincaid, private eye, for drinks after her act and that he's got some questions to ask about her buddy Rikki Baker. That's Starr with a double R, Ryan."

The skin across the back of Kincaid's neck tightened, and something cool rushed over his arms. There were any number of ways Ferret could've found out about his visit to Platinum's this afternoon. From the bartender, for instance, who had directed him to Starr. And of course Kincaid had asked Ferret her name last night, at Platinum's. A lucky connection, that was all. But somehow Kincaid didn't think it had happened like that, and the little man's game annoyed him.

"If you're that clever, Ferret, how come you don't know who killed the Baker woman?"

Now those skeletal fingers slipped up the front of his guayabera shirt, fiddling with the buttons. His lips drew away from his teeth. White, sharp teeth. "Hey, I'm not a psychic, Ryan." He rapped his knuckles on the table and scooted out of the booth. "She knows more than she's telling, amigo. Catch you later."

Kincaid watched him weave through the crowd until he disappeared through the front door, into a shaft of late afternoon light. Then he got up for a refill on his beer.

Porter was at the end of the bar, salting a hard-boiled egg in time to a Buddy Holly tune. He didn't look drunk, and he didn't slur his words when he greeted Kincaid; but now and then his dark eyes glazed over or blinked too quickly, and his voice was a shade too loud.

". . . rain was driving me nuts up there in the tower. You know what the wind begins to sound like if you listen to it for eight hours straight, Kincaid?" His teeth sank into the upper third of the egg with an almost savage pleasure. "Like a woman. It begins to sound like a woman. A woman in pain, a woman complaining, a woman bitching, a woman when she comes.

There's a noise a woman makes then, Ryan. Sometimes it's a whistle. Sometimes it's a groan. Sometimes it's both, like she can't quite decide what the occasion calls for." He lopped off the next third of the egg, shook more salt onto what remained, washed down the bite with a slug of beer. His dark eyes flicked from the egg to Kincaid's face. "That's what the wind sings to me all day, even when it's not blowing."

He brushed his hands together. The gesture had an air of finality about it. And for a moment, there in the dim wash of light from the bar, he looked like a man in terrible pain. His mouth opened, then snapped shut, as if he were about to confide something and had changed his mind.

"Game of pool, Ryan?" The words came out a tad too crisp, as if it were an effort now to keep from slurring them. "Twenty bucks a game?"

Kincaid shook his head. "Can't. I've got to split. I'll call you tomorrow about dinner."

"Great. Fine. That'd be good." His head bobbed. He knocked back the rest of his beer and rubbed his hands over his face. "Do I look as bad as I feel, Kincaid?"

"Can you drive?"

"Drive." The word rolled off his tongue. He squinted his eyes and tried to focus on the jar of hard-boiled eggs. The harder he tried, the more inebriated he looked. "Yeah, sure," he said after a few moments. "I can drive. No problem. Cars are never a problem. It's driving my life that's a problem, Ryan." Then he laughed. It was laced with such bitterness, it seemed to cut through the very air he breathed. "Jesus, listen to me. I sound like a soap opera. Talk to you tomorrow." And he wandered off toward the poolroom again, swaying slightly to the music.

3

Nick "Koko" Uvanti's Chris-Craft was easy to find, even in a marina where half the boats whispered of big money, family money, fortunes earned and lost in a single day. It was a sleek, lovely vessel, at least eighty or ninety feet long, Aline guessed, with shiny redwood railings and redwood panels on its side. It

gleamed in the late afternoon sun, white against the blue waters,
an empress of the high seas. Music floated from its deck, and
people teemed at its stern. A party was in progress.

How convenient. She would not only get to see how the other
half lived but would have a slight edge over Uvanti, because
God forbid that his friends should know a cop was questioning
him about a homicide.

She made it up the walkway before she was stopped by a man
with a body that rivaled Schwarzenegger's and a face that looked
like a smashed grapefruit. He was wearing an expensive Italian
suit, and when he grinned, his gold tooth flashed. Quasimodo,
for sure.

"Invitation, ma'am?"

She pulled out her badge. "I'd like to speak to Mr. Uvanti."

The gold tooth disappeared. His small blue eyes seemed to
sink into his cheeks like globs of fat. "Right this way, Detective
Scott."

She caught a whiff of cologne as he turned, a musky fragrance
that mixed with the smell of salt in the air. She followed him
away from the party and music and up a flight of stairs. The
room they entered was lavishly decorated—brass light fixtures,
French Provincial furniture, heavy blue velvet curtains at the
windows which were tied back with gold cords, a solid oak bar,
a Persian carpet on the floor. In one corner was electronic equipment—oversized TV screen, VCR, CD player.

"If you'll wait here, ma'am, I'll get him." The floor seemed
to shake as Quasimodo left.

Aline wandered around the room, touching everything, glancing through Uvanti's collection of tapes and music, pausing in
front of the paintings and prints on the wall. She didn't have to
know much about art to recognize some of the artists' names.
Wyeth, Dalí, Botticelli. No wonder there was a security camera
scanning the room.

"I picked up the Botticelli at an auction in Rome. One of his
better pieces, I think."

Uvanti's voice startled her; she hadn't heard him come into
the room. He was casually but expensively dressed and wore a
lot of jewelry—chains, rings, a diamond stud in his left ear. His
thick black hair was meticulously styled and brushed his collar
in the back. He stood a couple of inches taller than she did, five
ten or so, and was well-built. A weight lifter, but not like his
pal Quasimodo. Her immediate impression was that Uvanti had

come from a humble background he would just as soon cover up and forget.

"I love the Dalí etching," she said.

He smiled pleasantly, hands clasped behind his back. "I did a lot of work with the Dalí Museum over on the Florida West Coast, and the etching was Salvador's way of saying thanks."

Salvador: the message was loud and clear. Uvanti, the millionaire, was playing gracious host to a pedestrian cop. *Fuck you, pal.* She got right to the point.

"Where were you between Sunday evening and Monday morning, Mr. Uvanti?" When she'd called Prentiss on her way over here, he'd been unable to give her a more specific time range for Rikki Baker's death, so this would have to do. "This past Sunday and Monday."

Uvanti was no longer smiling, but his gaze remained steady, direct, a little unnerving in its intensity. "You should be more up front, Detective Scott. Ask what you really want to know. Did I kill Rikki? No."

"I asked where you were, Mr. Uvanti. And that's precisely what I want to know."

"I was here on the boat, entertaining some people from out of town." He turned and strolled over to the bar. "Would you like something to drink?"

"No. I'll need to talk to your staff to verify your alibi, Mr. Uvanti."

"Fine. I'll have Max take you around before you leave."

"Max?"

"The man who met you on deck."

Quasimodo.

She went over to the bar and sat in one of the high-backed stools. "I'd also like the names of your guests so I can speak to them as well."

Uvanti's dark, disturbing eyes impaled her. "They're business clients, Detective. I'd prefer to keep them out of it."

She didn't give a damn what his preferences were but let it pass for the moment. "How long were you involved with Rikki?"

"Off and on for about a year and a half. Almost from the day I hired her." He poured a double shot of Stolichnaya vodka into his glass and added a dash of Perrier and a slice of lime. "I don't suppose you ever saw her dance."

"No."

"She was good. Real good. Innovative."

She wondered what could possibly be innovative about taking off your clothes in public. "I understand you also fired her at one point."

He sipped at his drink, his unflinching gaze inscrutable. "Then I hired her back three days later."

"Why did you fire her?"

"Business reasons."

"Oh? I thought you just finished telling me what a terrific dancer she was."

He lowered his glass to the bar and smiled. "You're beating around the bush again, Detective."

"So are you. My understanding is that you fired her because she was seeing someone else. Several other men, in fact. I also hear you beat up on her when you were drunk. Is that direct enough for you?"

His dark eyes smoldered. He pinched the top of the skewer in his glass and stirred with a vengeance. "Rikki was free to see whoever she wanted, Detective. I just didn't like the idea of her hanging out with that scum *santero*. You know about him? About Manuel Ortega?"

"Why don't you tell me what *you* know about him, Mr. Uvanti. And about the others."

"Only one other that I know of, but that might be wrong; and no, I got no idea who he is. Don't much care. She liked taunting me with her other lovers. She got off on it. Anything she got off on, she was good at. That's why she was great on stage, Detective. She got off on having that kind of power over the men in her audience."

"Did she hook?"

"No."

"How can you be so sure?"

"My girls make enough money so they don't have to. And they know the rules. If you hook and I find out, if you do drugs and I find out, you're gone *that* fast." He snapped his fingers. "I don't need trouble with cops and drugs and lowlifes, Detective. It's just good business sense."

"Did she have any family?"

"Somewhere, but she never talked about them, and I didn't ask."

"So her parents are still alive?"

"That was my impression." He walked over to the electronic corner, plucked a tape from the collection, and popped it in. "I also had the feeling she didn't get on with her family and hadn't seen them in years.''

"Any close friends?"

He shrugged, aimed the remote control device at the VCR, and the tape whirred to life. "Starr. She works at the club. And a couple other women she talked about from time to time, but I never met them. Look at this, Detective."

He nodded toward the huge TV screen, where a brunette in a sleek silk number and spiked heels undulated to an African beat. Blue and red lights flashed around her. She stopped at the front of the stage, head thrown back, hair a cascade against her shoulders, hips moving, grinding. With a flick of her wrist, the silk slipped off her white shoulders and thunderous applause drowned out the music. Uvanti froze the frame and Aline saw a very pretty woman with a pouty, sensuous mouth, breasts like marble, a tummy as flat as an ironing board.

"That was only one of Rikki's faces."

Aline thought of the K on Rikki's negligee: *Koko?*

"Here's another one of Rikki's faces."

He fast-forwarded the tape, hit PLAY. No music now. No silk outfit or flashing lights. Rikki was performing for an audience of one: stretched out on a chaise lounge in the sun, naked body oiled, a hand sliding up the inside of her parted thighs, wide eyes as coy as her mouth, smiling, beckoning. A bright red nail now circled her navel, then dipped lower, moving, moving. Her head dropped back, and her other hand slid up through the oil to her breasts.

"She liked the camera." Uvanti glanced at Aline. "Would you like to see another Rikki Baker face?"

"Not particularly."

"I would." Martell strolled over to them. He was dressed in a three-piece suit and had a drink in one hand. "Hello, Detective Scott."

Formal: Martell was hunting his own leads. "Hi."

He glanced back at the screen. "So let's see some more."

Uvanti's chuckle was soft, almost lewd. "Sure." He hit the PLAY button again. Moonlight on water. A slow pan of a beach, then a leisurely zoom on a solitary figure in a string bikini strolling across wet, glistening sand. "A pensive, restless Rikki," Uvanti commented.

The woman waded into the water, reached around behind her, and unfastened the top of her bathing suit. She flung it away from her, and the camera followed its arch into the moonlight and its rapid descent. A moment later, the skimpy bottom followed. The camera slid back to Rikki, who was stretched out in the shoals, waves washing over her, legs spread wide, arms extended. A crucifixion. Or bondage.

Two figures materialized in the moonlight, dark ghosts who moved toward her, one closing in at her feet and visible only from the chest down, the other approaching her head, his naked back to the camera. The man at her feet reached Rikki first. He knelt between her open thighs, a worshiper paying homage, and touched his mouth to her belly. His hands slid over her breasts.

Rikki's head thrashed from side to side, as though she were trying to break free of her bonds. There was no sound except the soft breaking of the waves and breathing, his, hers, and now the other man's, who leaned over her, pressing his mouth on hers.

"Fantasy games," said Uvanti.

"Who're the men?" asked Martell.

"Actors who needed the work." Uvanti stopped the video. "There're quite a few of these, Detective. I have copies if you'd like to take them with you." He smiled. "As research."

"The only thing I need, Mr. Uvanti, are the names of your guests."

"I thought we straightened that out."

"I won't mention the homicide unless I have to. Now let me have the names."

He didn't look too happy about it but said he would have Max put a list together and she could pick it up on her way out, after she'd talked to the staff. Fine, she replied, and the three of them walked out onto the deck, where sun blazed orange against the horizon, spilling color across a bank of clouds and into the Gulf.

Uvanti excused himself to go find Quasimodo, leaving Aline and Martell alone at the railing. But the wind was too strong, and they moved back around the corner, to the left of the stairwell, where the wind couldn't touch them.

'What're you doing here anyway, Si?" Aline leaned against the metal railing.

"Same thing you are, only my way. I knew Nick was always hitting on his girls, and it made sense that he'd hit on Rikki. So I decided to take advantage of my invitation to this little get-together." He knocked back the rest of his drink. "Good ole Koko courts people on Tango, Aline." He jerked his thumb toward the stern, where the party was. "Back there you'll find an aide from the mayor's office, and most of the major hot shots in the Cove crowd."

"Poor boy makes good?"

"Something like that." His elbow pressed against her arm. "We still on for dinner?"

She looked over at him, prepared to make a crack about how easily he tired of the way the other half lived. But he touched her chin with his index finger, drawing her face closer to his. His tongue slid slowly across her lower lip, as if tasting it. His hand slipped under her hair, cool against the back of her neck. She turned and he turned, and now his hands were at the sides of her face, tilting her head slightly so their mouths fit perfectly.

She had never been kissed in quite this way. Her awareness seemed focused entirely on the shape of his mouth, his teeth, the slow insinuation of his tongue and its glide across her own teeth. The smell of the salt air mingled with the odor of the metal staircase and the scent of Martell's skin and the Scotch he'd been drinking and the faint aroma of her own perfume. The light in her head blinked on, off. Time slowed. Time pulsed. Time became a skein of delicious sensations.

His hand at her shoulder, the small of her back, burning across her ribs. A thumb idled on the curve of her breast, moving in lazy circles against her blouse. Desire licked at her skin. She ached. She burned. Her clothes were too hot. His mouth at her throat, her ear, whispering. Her skirt slid up in back. A breeze kissed her knees. His hardness against her thigh. His hand against the back of her thigh, her buttocks, fingers cool against the silk of her panties. Her hips moved against him as though they were separate from her, unconnected to her, seeking a forbidden something here in the salty shadows, the heat. And then something snapped in her head.

She could hear it, a noise like dried leaves crackling underfoot, the noise ice made when it broke up, when it shattered. She pulled away from him, cheeks flaming with embarrassment. Her hands moved in quick, jerky motions over her clothes, smoothing them into place. She walked out of the stairwell, over to the railing. The wind cooled her cheeks, dried the sweat on her face, cleared her head. Her fingers curled tightly over the wood. She blinked several times and breathed deeply, filling her nostrils with the smell of water and salt and sunset, and gradually the throb inside her subsided.

A crescent of sun still glowed above the horizon, and neither Uvanti nor Quasimodo were anywhere in sight, so only a few minutes had passed. She didn't know why the time should matter, but it did.

Martell came over to the railing, raking his fingers through his dark hair, the scent of his skin thick in the air. "I, uh, didn't mean to . . ."

"Forget it." She felt like a tongue-tied adolescent caught necking in the backseat of her father's car. Aline smiled quickly, trying to dispel the tension, and over Martell's shoulder saw Quasimodo lumbering around the corner. "Company."

"Eight?" he asked quietly.

"Make it nine." She moved rapidly away from him, wondering if the heat of those few moments showed on her face.

Yes, yes, said the members of the staff and crew. Mr. Uvanti was on board last Sunday night. No, he never left. Yes, they were quite sure. The party went on until four or five in the morning, and Mr. Uvanti slept on board that night and had breakfast here the next morning.

Yes, they were absolutely certain.

The crew's memories were unanimously perfect.

10

The Saturday-night cover charge at Platinum's was fifteen bucks, which bought you nothing more than a seat at the bar. But when Kincaid handed over his money to the well-dressed bouncer at the door and gave his name, the man nodded and escorted him to a booth on the upper level.

The booth was private, sequestered on two sides by tall plants and on the other two by Japanese silk screens. A bottle of Chilean wine was on ice, and the closed-circuit TV was on.

"When you need something, sir, just press this button," said the bouncer, pointing a thick finger at a red button on the TV console, "and someone will be over to take your order. Ms. Starr will join you after her act." The bouncer then proceeded to pop open the wine, and Kincaid sampled it. The sapid taste stirred memories of Chile, of Aline, of the Christmas they'd spent together there shortly after they'd first met.

"Is that to your liking, sir?"

"It's fine."

The bouncer filled his glass. "We like to know how our customers feel about the various acts, so we encourage everyone to express opinions." He punched a blue button on the TV and a small panel slid to one side, exposing eight square buttons. He pressed the one that said KEYBOARD, and a rectangular piece of the table popped up, revealing a computer keyboard. "This button clears the screen." He tapped it and the screen went blank. "This one brings up the name of the woman currently onstage. And this one here provides a list of comments. If you want to make additional remarks, sir, you just use the keyboard. You can also bring up our wine list, the menu, and your tab. Any questions?''

"Impressive," Kincaid said.

"It's all the newest technology, sir."

At a minimum of fifteen bucks a head, Kincaid thought, Uvanti could afford it. He tipped the bouncer and settled back with his wine, glancing from the stage to the TV as one of the acts got under way.

Costumes were lavish, the dancing in most cases had been choreographed, and all of the women were lovely and young, in their twenties and early thirties. Uvanti's private harem.

The music for Starr's act was a strange meld of Latin rhythms—samba and reggae, salsa and drums. The dancing was sometimes wild, sometimes erotic, but always controlled. It conjured images of prehistoric tribes living in fear of gods whom they worshipped and placated with rituals and blood and offerings. The act was smooth, surprisingly tasteful.

Like the other dancers, Starr was never completely nude. There were always tendrils of silk, of color, that covered some part of her milky skin. But she tantalized, she teased, she seduced with movements that held the promise of a little more. He was impressed. If she was as good at talking about Rikki Baker as she was at dancing, the evening wouldn't be a total waste.

She swept into his booth fifteen minutes after her act had ended, a woman with baby blues and a 1930s face who was dressed like a twenty-first-century space dweller. Metallic jumpsuit, bits of glitter in her electric blond hair, bright red lips that matched her nail polish. She wore enough quartz crystal jewelry to power a dozen radios, and so much perfume it settled around Kincaid like a mist.

She slid into the booth, jumpsuit rustling, and immediately held out her wineglass, which he filled. "I'm just *dying* of thirst, babe. Thanks. Cheers." She clicked her glass against the edge of his, tipped it to her mouth, and drained it like water. "Much better. Would you . . . ?" She held the glass out for more, and he obliged her. This time she took small, dainty sips. "Isn't this just the *best*? Well, it's not as good as some of the Californian stuff, but South America just doesn't hold a candle to the good ole U. S. of A., now does it. Besides wine and bananas and the Copacabana, what else do they have? *Nada*, that's what." She laughed gaily and leaned toward Kincaid. "The best place to be in the U. S. of A., though, is right here on Tango. I don't like cities much. That's why Tango suits me. Small, but big enough, you know?'' Another pull on the wine and it was gone and Kincaid filled her glass again. ''So what'd you think of the show, babe?''

''You're good. Where'd you learn to dance?''

Baby blues dropping to her glass, a finger stroking the rose crystal at her throat. ''Oh, I picked it up, you know. Here, there. Koko's just the greatest to work for. That's Nick. Nick Uvanti.'' Blues on Kincaid again. ''You know him?''

''Not personally.''

''Well, he's tops. I mean, the pay's good and we don't have to take off all our clothes, and we can come up with our own routines and all. Not Broadway.'' She gave a quick little laugh. ''But we get some scouts in here from time to time. Nick's got connections. He helps his girls.'' Another small laugh, more wine. ''My astrologer did his chart, and she says he's like, you know, a highly evolved soul. But my channeler thinks he needs to redirect his energies into something a little more, uh, well, spiritual.'' Her fingers grazed Kincaid's arm and a wry smile reshaped her mouth. ''But that would put me out of a job, now wouldn't it.''

And so it went for the next twenty or thirty minutes, her astrologer, her channeler, her yoga instructor. Her sun and moon, her karma, her past lives. He was waiting for something he could seize on as an opening.

''. . . My channeler says that any time someone dies violently, like my friend Rikki did, it's because the soul has chosen to pay off a huge karmic debt. But I have some trouble with that. I mean, why choose to be murdered? It seems like there'd be better ways of paying off a debt.''

''What's your channeler say about who killed her?''

She shrugged, stroking the rose quartz again. ''Not much. My channeler's guides don't like to interfere like that. But I figure it had to have been some guy she was seeing, you know. Not Koko.'' She looked at him quickly. ''Koko would never hurt a soul.''

''I heard he beats up on women when he drinks too much.''

She gave an impatient wave of her hand. ''Oh, that's nothing. He doesn't mean anything by it. Rikki used to get pretty upset whenever it happened. And then she went to this *santero* for protection from Nick and ends up getting involved with *him*.

That's how she was, hopping from guy to guy, and every time she swore this was *the* man, her karmic link. Personally, I think her karmic link was with whoever killed her. That's who her debt was to. Now it's canceled." She shrugged and gazed pensively into her empty glass. "She was a good friend, but I wonder now just how well I really knew her."

"Why?"

She smiled coyly. "Mr. Detective. You don't waste any time, do you." Before Kincaid replied, she went on. "Rikki was like that saying. Oh, how's it go?" Baby blues fluttering to Kincaid's face once more. "Something about still waters . . . Well, anyway, it's like there were layers inside her, you know, and she only let you see this layer or that, but never all of them. Listen, babe, how about if we go someplace else? I hate sticking around here once I'm finished."

"Dinner?"

"I never eat dinner, babe. Can't afford the calories. How about if we drop in on the party at Koko's yacht? It'll be fun. Good food, booze, plenty of everything, and all of it free. It'll give you a chance to check him out for yourself." Another quick laugh, and now her hand dug into her small, shimmering purse and brought out a compact. She snapped it open, withdrew a tube of lipstick, and painted her mouth very carefully. "You like this color, babe? Rikki thought it might be a shade too dark for my skin, but I kind of favor it."

Sure, the color was just fine, Kincaid said, nodding, and knew he was going to be nuts in an hour.

She stopped at the desk to pick up a canvas bag. *I always carry extra clothes and makeup*, she said, and then chattered all the way outside to the Saab, her arm hooked in his, her silver heels clicking against the pavement. "Hey, babe, you never told me what sign you are."

I'm too old for this shit. "You never asked."

She heard the annoyance in his voice and glanced at him, frowning a little. "I'm asking now."

"November," he said. "Scorpio."

"Ah," she breathed, as though this told her everything. "No wonder."

And now he was supposed to ask, *No wonder what?* But he kept quiet, curious about how she would recoup.

"And your moon?" she asked.

It wasn't quite what he expected. "I don't know."

"You've never had your chart done?"

As though he had breached some unwritten ethic.

"No." They reached the Saab and he unlocked the passenger door and hurried around to the driver's side, hoping she would shut up or change the subject once they were on the road. But she didn't. The second they were both inside, she proceeded to dissect his personality.

"My guess is that you're a double water sign, see, Scorpio sun and a moon in Cancer or Pisces. Probably Cancer. So you're like real intuitive, artistic, and the home's important to you, roots are important to you. You're emotionally evasive, babe. In fact, emotionally you're like a crab, always scurrying sideways to avoid confrontations. Then we get to your rising sign, and I figure that's Gemini. Restless, always moving, traveling, with a mind like lightning. How am I doing so far, babe?"

"Okay." *Damn close.* He pulled away from the curb and headed for the quickest route north.

"Let's take the Old Post," she said. "I like that road. You mind?"

Yeah, he minded plenty. It would take twice as long to get to the marina, and he didn't think he could stand much more of her. But on the other hand, if he played along she might still prove to be a source of information.

He kept going west, toward the Old Post Road, and Starr continued with her analysis. Kincaid tuned her out and opened the sunroof. The moon hadn't risen yet, but the sky was clear and dusted with stars, and the air smelled of pine and salt and jasmine.

". . . I bet you haven't heard a word I've said, babe."

"Every word."

"Then you don't listen too closely. What I said was, pull off the side of the road."

The hard edge in her voice snapped his head toward her. Starlight touched the smile on her mouth and struck the snub-nosed .38 in her hand.

"Shit," he muttered.

"Now. Pull off into the trees." And she cocked the gun.

Kincaid's mind raced, eliminating his options at a depressing rate as he downshifted into third, second. He wasn't armed, and the gun he usually carried in his glove compartment was at home. He knew he could overpower her easily enough, but probably not fast enough, not before she fired. So that left one choice, the worst choice when you weren't in a position to bargain.

"I think I like you better as a flake."

"Very funny. Into the trees, and don't kill the headlights."

"So if you aren't Starr, what am I supposed to call you?"

"Stop right here."

He halted between two pines, about two hundred feet in from the road. She pressed the muzzle of the .38 against his temple and with the other hand pulled the car keys from the ignition. The gun slipped to his neck; his pulse throbbed against it. "Put your hands on the steering wheel, babe, where I can see them. Nice and easy now. Good. That's just fine. Now listen real closely, because I'm only going to say this once. We're going to get out of the car." She moved away from him, toward her door, the gun trained on his head. "I know how to use this, and if you make any sudden moves, I'll shoot first and be sorry later. Got it?"

"I speak English."

"Good for you, babe. Now put your hands on the steering wheel and keep them there until I tell you to get out."

Her door opened. She scooted out, never taking her eyes from him, the gun never wavering. *A pro. But on which side?*

"Put your hands on your head, babe, and get out."

He did.

She moved slowly around the back of the car, her eyes fixed on his face, the gun at his chest. Mosquitos buzzed around their heads; she ignored them. "Glad to see you can follow directions," she said. "Hands on the roof and spread your legs."

She frisked him with the same smooth control that showed in her dancing, and she did it like a cop. When she didn't find a weapon on him, she whipped his wallet out of his back pocket and kept the .38 hard against his spine.

"Okay, here we go. A driver's license. Lousy picture of you, Kincaid." She slapped the wallet down on the roof. "Turn and keep your hands on top of your head."

He moved around slowly until he faced her. She had kicked off her high heels and held her weapon with both hands now, a classic police stance. Definitely a pro. "Now who the hell do you work for, and what's your interest in Rikki Baker?"

"Since when do Feds work undercover as strippers?"

It caught her attention, but she didn't lower her weapon. "I'm asking the questions."

Kincaid's blood pressure inched steadily upward. "And I'll answer them when I see your I.D., *babe*. Or better yet, if I'm under arrest for something, I'd like to know what I'm charged with."

She hesitated, then she let go of the gun with one hand, unzipped the jumpsuit far enough to reach inside, her eyes never leaving his face. She set a badge and I.D. on the roof and slid it toward him, then zipped up the jumpsuit again.

"Take a look and start talking."

Detective Fuentes, FBI. The flash and glitz were absent from her mug shot and in the picture, she was a brunette, not a blonde. "I like you better with dark hair," he remarked.

"I got tired of it," she snapped, and scooped up her badge and I.D.

"What division?" Kincaid asked.

"Hey, I answered your question, now you answer mine."

"Consultant to the Tango P.D. on the homicide. Simple. Mind if I take my hands off my goddamn head?"

"Show me I.D.," she said, and Kincaid laughed.

"What kind of I.D. would you like? A business card with a magnifying glass on it? Or maybe a laminated thing from Private Eyes of America? Call Gene Frederick if you don't believe me. He hired me. You know who he is. You were talking to him outside of Platinum's. You were wearing pink leotards."

Another hesitation, lengthier this time. "Why's the police department need to hire a private eye?"

"Because they're understaffed, and I've done work for them before. What division are you with?"

Silence.

The dark beyond them rustled with noises. Frogs, crickets, things scurrying through the brush. A mosquito dive-bombed Kincaid's head. "The battery's wearing down. I'd appreciate it if you'd make up your mind so we don't both end up walking to Uvanti's yacht."

Silence.

"Okay, look. Let's drive to the police station. Better yet, let's drive over to Frederick's house and get this thing straightened out. The address is 330 Azalea Drive."

After another moment, she slowly let the hammer down and dropped her arm. She retrieved her I.D., unzipped her jumpsuit again to put it away, zipped it back up, and walked over to the car. "Let's talk inside. The mosquitos are eating me alive."

"So?" he asked once they were inside the Saab, the head-lights off, her weapon back in her purse.

"Missing persons, abductions, whatever you want to call it, it amounts to the same thing," she said.

"I don't get it."

"You're not supposed to. Drive."

He held out his hand, palm turned up. "You've got the keys."

"Oh." She shifted, slid her hand into a pocket, pulled them out, dropped them in his hand. "Let's get to Uvanti's."

Kincaid removed the car key from the case and held it. "Nope. You explain, then I'll drive."

He saw her hand flick toward her purse, but this time he was ready for her. He grabbed it and jammed it down between his seat and the door. "Okay, Fuentes. Let's hear it or you're going to be walking back to town or to Uvanti's yacht—either way the distance is about the same. And you won't have your gun."

She glared at him; those baby blues were as hard and cold as a winter sky at twenty thousand feet. Then she slipped her hand under her hair and flicked it off her collar. "I knew I didn't like you."

"I got all night, lady."

She turned her head toward the window, offering her profile, long, red-tipped fingers sliding up one cheek, through her hair, a lioness. "What the hell. You're going to know soon enough as it is. Baker wasn't Rikki's last name. It's Chamberlain. Regina 'Rikki' Chamberlain. She's been missing for nearly five years. Ring any bells?"

Vaguely. "Just get to the point, Fuentes."

She impaled him with those baby blues. "*Detective* Fuentes."

"Yeah, fine, whatever."

"Chamberlain: as in U.S. senator from Florida. Five years ago, when her old man was just a congressman, she walked out of a marriage to one of his aides, walked out of a cushy life in D.C.'s upper crust, walked out and wasn't heard from again, Kincaid. For a while it was on the books as an abduction. Then it was just another missing-persons case. Then Chamberlain was elected to the Senate and the FBI went through some changes and Chamberlain poured on pressure and I was assigned the case. So here I am."

"Nice of you to share what you knew with the local cops."

Calmly: "I wasn't entirely sure about her until this afternoon."

"Sure."

"Think what you want," she snapped.

"Here's what I think, Fuentes. Chamberlain was elected to the Senate a year ago. So give or take a few months for the workings of the bureaucracy, I figure you've been on this case six months, maybe nine at the outside, and you *know* this one's big. If you solve it, if you find the wayward daughter, it means kudos back at the home office. A promotion. But then the unsuspected happens. Rikki gets killed. So you weigh the odds and decide to find her killer because that's going to be *real* big. Headlines. Am I warm yet?"

"Yes and no." She'd been sitting back against the door, gazing at him, listening, arms crossed at the waist, her face a mask. But now she sat forward and reached into her breast pocket. She brought out a cigarette and a lighter. "Mind if I smoke?"

"Yes."

"Too bad."

"Why ask?"

Her smile could've chilled Jell-O. "Manners." She lit the cigarette and blew smoke up through the sunroof. "Fact. Rikki had plastic surgery. That made it real tough to identify her by photographs. Fact: I couldn't get prints from her apartment or her car or anywhere else because she had no prints. They'd been burned off medically, with acid, at the same Swiss clinic where she had her plastic surgery. And I've got the documents to prove it, Kincaid. This woman did *not* want to be found. And until I was sure, I wasn't about to tell Chamberlain squat."

"Go on."

A deep drag on her cigarette, head tilting back, mouth forming an "O" as she blew a smoke ring toward the sunroof. It lifted into the pine-scented air and seemed to hover for a second, circling a star, then dissolved. "Last week she and I had dinner and drinks together one night. She got blasted, and I drove her home and went through her purse. I found an old photo that looked promising, and even though it was pretty blurred, I sent it off to the lab. They worked their computer magic, and I got the word back this afternoon that it was definitely the missing Chamberlain.

"She's an only daughter, who would've inherited part of what already amounts to a small fortune. Chamberlain is a good ole boy who made a bundle in citrus before he took on politics." Her cigarette glowed in the dark, a beacon. "And he's very, hmm—how can I put this? Possessive. I guess that's as good a word as any. *His* citrus groves, *his* political office, *his* family, *his* daughter, who—"

"—ran off, and his pride couldn't handle it," Kincaid finished.

"Yeah. It was a personal affront." She paused. "He's an asshole."

"Does he know?"

"That he's an asshole?" She laughed. "Arrogance blinds, Kincaid. As for Rikki, I'm sure he knows by now. The I.D. was made. And my guess is that he'll be here tomorrow or the next day. No fanfare, no fuss, no advance warning to the cops involved in the case. Mr. Ordinary Joe enjoys having the element of surprise in his favor."

"Why'd she take off?"

Fuentes shrugged. "Chamberlain had mapped out her life— marriage to the right young man with a bright future, a certain lifestyle among D.C.'s movers and shakers, charity functions, and so on. It wasn't the life she wanted. So a year into the marriage, she walked out."

"Kind of drastic."

Fuentes shook her head. "Not really. She wasn't strong enough to stand up to him. He's formidable, Kincaid. You'll see what I mean."

"So who killed her?"

"No telling." She opened the door, leaned out, ground her cigarette into the dirt and pine needles. Then she shredded it. "Uvanti, Ortega, maybe Ortega's business partner, Seroz. You met him?"

"Briefly."

She shifted in her seat again. "He and Ortega are on-again, off-again lovers. Rikki told me that much. When she and Ortega stopped sleeping together, she contended it was because of Seroz."

"Rikki was nine to ten weeks pregnant."

"*What?*"

"And there may have been two killers, not one."

She mulled this over for a moment or two, her face in profile again, one hand clasped around her hair in back, fanning her neck with it. "How about if we drive around for a few minutes before going to Koko's party, babe?" She asked it in her Starr voice, and Kincaid laughed.

"You do that real well."

"I minored in theater."

"And the dance training?"

"Three hours a day, seven days a week, from the age of eight to eighteen. My parents had plans for me, too." She smiled and let go of her hair. It tumbled to her shoulders again. "I went to law school instead and then applied with the FBI." She glanced at him as he backed out of the trees. "What about you?"

"Scorpio sun, moon in Cancer, Gemini rising," he quipped, and she laughed.

11

I

The Flamingo was the oldest hotel on the island, the grande dame of Tango. Set back on three acres of land crisscrossed by horse trails and the Tango inlet, Aline thought it looked as though it belonged on the Mississippi River during Mark Twain's day. Wraparound porch with rockers, huge floor-to-ceiling windows, banyan trees with Spanish moss draped over the branches like lacy shawls.

Inside, the place was gracious and laid back. There were sitting areas decorated in wicker, throw rugs like colorful islands against the pine floors, piano music from the bar that floated through the lobby. It also had one of the best restaurants on the island, and Saturday nights were always busy.

She and Martell went into the bar to wait for their table and got a booth near the window. It looked out onto the back of the three acres, where pines and banyans loomed darkly in moonlight.

Martell glanced around for a waiter. "I think it'd be faster if I got our drinks at the bar. What's your pleasure, Al?"

"Bailey's over ice."

"Coming up."

He slid out of the booth, and Aline watched him move through the crowd, pausing now and again to greet someone. White slacks and a black shirt had replaced the three-piece suit he'd worn on Uvanti's yacht and made him look very unlawyerlike. He could've been anyone—a man she'd recently met, a business acquaintance, an old friend she hadn't seen in a while.

And who're you kidding, Al?

She rubbed her finger across her lower lip, where it seemed that the taste of Martell's mouth still lingered.

"Aline, hi."

Hannah Porter stood in front of the booth, her small white hands clutching a black beaded purse. She was leaning into the table because of the press of the crowd at her back, and her sapphire choker swung away from her white throat, a mesmerizing blaze of blue light.

"Hi, Hannah." Aline motioned her into the booth. "You're going to be crushed if you stand there. Scoot in."

"Thanks." Her fingers brushed her fluffy blond hair back; twin sapphires gleamed in her ears. "God, if I'd known it was going to be this crowded tonight, Karl and I would've eaten in. He wandered off ten minutes ago to get drinks, and I haven't seen him since. So how've you been anyway?"

"Not bad. You?"

"Just *swamped* with work." She lit a Marlboro with a delicate gold lighter and drew in the smoke as if she was addicted for life. "I picked up a couple of new magazine clients in Miami, and they're *real* picky about their illustrations. It's gotten so I didn't have all that much time to help Karl with research for his book, so I hired Ryan."

"He mentioned it. He also told me about the grave, Hannah."

She wrinkled her nose. "Pretty creepy, huh? Just the kind of weirdness I don't need when I'm out there alone, I can tell you."

"Look, if Karl's out of town and you don't want to stay at the lighthouse alone, you're always welcome at my place."

"Thanks, I appreciate it. But Karl's not out of town that often. He's just out, you know?"

"Out?"

"Out drinking. And then he doesn't bother coming home. When I remind him that even E.T. knew enough to call home, he acts like I'm trying to pen him in or something." She gave a small, defeated shrug and stabbed out her cigarette. "I don't know, Aline. He came home half in the bag this afternoon, slept it off, and here we are. I mean, this happens from time to time when he gets stuck on a book, but it's never been quite this bad. Last week he stayed out all night, and when he rolled in the next morning I was pissed. I jumped all over him. We had a terrible argument and I . . . I accused him of seeing someone else. He denied it. I asked him where he'd been, and he said he was too looped to drive so he checked into a motel. I called the motel and asked for his room, and the clerk told me no one by that name was registered. I . . .'' She stopped and shook her head. ''I'm sorry, I didn't mean to dump all over you.''

''Don't worry about it.''

''Maybe the four of us should get a table together for dinner.''

''I'm not with Ryan.''

''Oh. Sorry. I just assumed . . .''

''Everyone does. I'm here with Simon Martell.''

Her expression attested to Martell's reputation on the island as a ladies' man. ''You're *really* playing the field, Allie. What happened with you and Ryan?''

''I guess it's more of what *didn't* happen.''

Hannah rolled her pretty eyes. ''Sounds familiar. Karl's not too crazy about Simon, you know, so maybe we should just . . .''

But it was too late. Martell appeared just then and Porter was right behind him, and neither of them looked happy about the seating arrangement. But they were both too civilized to do anything about it. So the four of them spent the next half hour squeezed into the booth, making small talk that was punctuated by embarrassing pauses. More than once, Porter sat forward, his back to Martell and Hannah, excluding them as he talked to Aline. It irritated her. It reminded her of the night at the Pink Moose when she and Martell had run into Porter and he had drawn her aside and told her what he thought of her taste in men.

''Karl, do you mind?'' Aline touched his arm. ''I can't talk through you.''

''They aren't listening, anyway.'' But he sat back, pouting like a child, sipping at his drink. Aline, who was at one end of the booth, leaned forward to say something to Martell about checking on their table. But he and Hannah were yukking it up like old friends, his arm stretched along the booth behind her. It was obvious he found her immensely attractive—what man in his right mind wouldn't?—and it was equally obvious that she wasn't immune to his charm, which was not so surprising either, considering the state of her marriage to Porter. But it irked her. And worse, she didn't know who galled her more—Martell for being so flagrantly obvious about his passion for women, any woman, or Hannah for playing coy in an attempt to make Porter sit up and take notice. Who needed it?

Aline got up to check on their table. What was the name

again? asked the hostess, drawing her finger down the long list of names. "Martell." She spelled it for the woman.

"I'm sorry, ma'am, we don't have that name on our list. But I could add it if . . ."

"Check again. We had a reservation."

"A problem?" Martell asked, coming up behind her.

"They don't seem to have our reservation."

Martell's brows shot up. "Look, I called in for a reservation, I gave you my name when we arrived, and we've been sitting in there for forty minutes, waiting for our table."

Aw shit, she thought. A scene. She didn't need a scene. "Forget it, Si."

"No. I want a table. And if you can't provide one," he snapped at the hostess, "I intend to complain to the management."

The hostess, a sweet young thing who was probably a transplant from the mainland, looked flustered. "Sir, every table is filled. I can probably get you something outside, if you'd like."

"When?"

"Five minutes."

"Fine. We'll wait right here."

Three minutes later they were seated at a table on the back veranda. It was lined with flower boxes and huge clay pots that billowed with ivy and jacaranda and impatiens, hibiscus and jasmine. Ceiling fans turned slowly overhead. She could smell the sweetness of the Tango Inlet, grass, the distant pines. She hated to admit it, but the table was probably better than anything they would've gotten inside. She said as much, and Martell grinned.

"Sometimes it pays to make a scene. Especially when your date's about to make an exit."

"I was just going to check on the table."

"And then split, if it wasn't ready."

She met his gaze and knew she was as transparent to him as water. He laughed softly and leaned toward her, fingers resting against the back of her hand. A light touch, but it made her knuckles burn. "I'm a likable person, Al, really."

"Uh-huh." She slipped her hand out from under his and opened her menu. "Sometimes."

"You're hard as nails," he said, and gave an exaggerated sigh as he reached for his own menu.

She smiled a little, pleased that she'd redeemed some of the leverage she'd lost this afternoon on Uvanti's yacht. Martell saw it and chuckled. "Truce?" he asked.

"For now." And she smiled again.

2

Kincaid watched Fuentes in her Starr persona, working the crowd on Uvanti's yacht. *Listen up, babe. How ya doin', babe? Nice to see you, babe.* Her silver heels clicked against the deck, her red nails tapped her glass of wine, her hips swayed to the music pumping from the reggae band in the main salon.

Interesting paradox, this woman, he thought, but there were still certain things about her story that bothered him.

He picked at the hors d'oeuvres spread, got a Corona beer from the bar, and asked one of the waiters if there was a phone on board that he could use. Sure, the man said, and led him to a paneled library on the lower deck.

Impressive, Kincaid thought. Floor-to-ceiling books, a Tiffany stained-glass lamp, oriental vases, an authentic rolltop desk, and two pen-and-ink drawings signed "Picasso." If these were the originals, they were probably worth more than the yacht.

A bottle of Grand Marnier and several glasses stood on a wet bar against the wall. An unfilled pipe rested in a crystal ashtray next to it. The only things missing were slippers and a roaring fireplace.

The leather chair at the desk was softer than any chair had a right to be and sighed with Kincaid's weight. He got out his AT&T credit card, dialed the operator, and requested a number in Miami. It belonged to Slater, a guy in the Drug Enforcement Administration with a weakness for the horses whom he'd met through Ferret. He answered on the first ring, just as he always did, and there was no mistaking the deep baritone of his voice. "Yes?"

"It's Ryan."

"Hold on."

A buzz, a click, a netherworld, then: "Okay, the line's secure, Kincaid. I thought you vanished in Nepal."

"Not yet."

"Got a tip?"

"Sure. Last race at Calder tonight. Our boy says it's Catch-Me-If-You-Can."

"Got it. So what's the question, Kincaid?"

"Name's Miranda Fuentes. She says she's FBI, abductions and missing persons. I want it verified."

"You holding or should I call you back?"

"How long's it going to take? I'm not at home."

"Let me see if the computer's going to cooperate. Hold on."

Kincaid waited. He heard the music from upstairs, distant and pleasant, a horn offshore, the cool whisper of air from an overhead vent. His fingers wandered—into the rolltop's cubbyholes, into drawers, through papers. There was nothing of interest. This room, he thought, was mainly for show.

"Okay, Ryan. Give me her name again. Let's see what we've got."

Kincaid spelled her name. He heard the man on the other end tapping it into a computer.

"Here she is. Fuentes, Miranda. Born in the Big Apple thirty-six years ago, mixed parentage. Mother's American, father's Argentinian. B.A. in criminology from Georgetown, Phi Beta Kappa, law degree from Georgetown, *summa cum laude.* Divorced, no kids. She graduated third in her class from Quantico two years ago, spent a year in the D.C. office, was assigned to Miami under special investigations. Four months ago she took a leave of absence. Still on leave."

"What's special investigations?"

"It covers everything from drugs to abductions to you name it."

"Any reason given for the leave?"

"Nope, just that it's personal."

My ass. No wonder she hadn't told the cops anything. "Anything on how long her leave is going to last?"

"Max of six months."

"That means they're holding her job for her."

"Yeah. How much did you place on Catch-Me, Kincaid?"

"Two grand, split three ways."

"Good enough. Talk to you later."

He made two more calls, one to Aline, the second to Chief Frederick, to tell them about Senator Chamberlain's probable arrival tomorrow or the next day. When he reached answering machines, he left them both messages to call him as soon as possible. All the way back upstairs he stewed about Aline not being home; it meant she was out with that horse's ass Martell.

When he reached the deck, Fuentes found him and hooked an arm through his, steering him toward the railing. The breeze off the Gulf was warm and thick with salt. "Has Nick ever met you?"

"No."

"Ever seen you?"

"Not that I know of."

"Good. Let me introduce you. You're Ryan Kane, okay?"

They went through a metal gate with an EMPLOYEES ONLY sign on it, and up another deck. Here, Japanese lanterns around an S-shaped bar swung in the breeze and threw off soft twilight that barely illumined the Jacuzzi where two couples were laughing and drinking beneath the stars. "Hope you're not modest, Kincaid," she whispered, then waved her hand and called, "Koko babe, I got someone here I'm just *dying* for you to meet. C'mere."

"Help yourselves to drinks, Starr," Uvanti shouted back, "and come on over. Water's great. You know where the towels are."

"We're on our way, babe."

Uvanti's pinky ring bloomed red and huge against the bare shoulder of the woman he was with, a brunette whose tan said the sun was her religion and whose constant sniffle attested to cocaine as her god. When she wasn't talking, he was. Kincaid couldn't have repeated what they'd said if his life depended on it, but Uvanti was too buzzed to notice that he wasn't listening. Now and then the woman's hand dipped into the bubbling water; it didn't take a Sherlock Holmes to figure out what it was written all over Uvanti's face.

When Fuentes offered to get refills on the drinks, Kincaid's eyes followed her as she climbed out, water shimmering against her naked back, rolling off the flare of her hips, her buttocks like pale moons. She strode over to the bar, as uninhibited in her nudity as you'd expect a stripper to be.

"She's got the best ass in the club," Uvanti remarked, gazing after Fuentes as his hand slipped down his date's back. "She's hot. Good choice."

As if she was a horse he was betting on, Kincaid thought, and felt, inexplicably, like slugging him. He didn't know what the hell he was doing here in a Jacuzzi with an aging Casanova and his giggling bimbo, and decided he'd had enough of Nick

Uvanti for the night. He excused himself and walked over to the chaise lounge, where clean towels were stacked. He knotted one at his waist and joined Fuentes at the bar.

She had put on a terry-cloth robe and tied it loosely at the waist, but as she moved around mixing drinks the folds fell open, revealing a curve of thigh, the swell of a breast, a flash of white skin like satin.

"Here's your drink, babe." She said it loudly enough for Uvanti to hear, then leaned across the bar, brushing her mouth against his, a taste of fruit, chilled and sweet. "Don't go away."

Uvanti took the drinks, and Fuentes stood there for a few moments, chatting with him and the bimbo. Then they got out of the Jacuzzi and vanished down another set of stairs. Fuentes came back over, hands fussing with the tie on the robe. "What'll it be, babe?" She ducked behind the bar again.

"Whatever's cold."

She opened two Heinekens, set them on the bar, then claimed the stool next to Kincaid. It squeaked when she sat on it and squeaked again when she hooked her heels over the horizontal bar near the bottom and raised her bottle to her mouth. Sipping. Setting the beer down.

"Well?" Those baby blues shone in a face now scrubbed clean by the Jacuzzi, and her thick, wet hair coiled like braids over her shoulders. "What do you think?"

Kincaid thought of Aline, Aline with Martell. Then he leaned toward Fuentes, thumb sliding over her lower lip, and cupped her soft face in a hand and kissed her. She didn't touch him, but her mouth opened against his. She no longer tasted of fruit, but of beer and the dark and something else, something indescribably good. She didn't stop him as he untied the belt at her waist and slipped his hands inside, to that tiny waist, against that soft, damp skin.

She didn't move as he slid the robe off her shoulders and licked at a drop of water on her collarbone, and still didn't move as his hand slipped up under a breast, sculpting it with his fingers. The nipple rose against his palm and her heart beat fast and hard against his hand, and when the stool moved, Kincaid moved with it, standing in front of her now, her back against the edge of the bar, her thighs spreading slightly to accommodate him.

Her robe fell open all the way and his hands glided over her thighs and she sucked his tongue into her mouth, kissing him so hard their teeth clicked. But she still didn't touch him. Her hands were clenched into tight fists against her thighs, huddled there like tiny frightened birds. He worked one open, caressing the knuckles, memorizing them, and she pulled in a sharp breath as his thumb fit into the crease at her upper thigh. *You started this*, it whispered. *Let's finish it.* His tongue slid over her teeth and curled around her tongue, and she lifted her hips slightly, moving against the pressure of his hand, drawing it deeper between her thighs, into that warm, pale quick, the color of light.

She made a small, strange sound deep in her throat, a kind of purr, and then suddenly wrenched her head back. Her eyes snapped open. Those baby blues blazed with something that might've been panic or desperation, he didn't know which. Her arms jerked up and she yanked his towel loose and dug her nails into his shoulders, pulling him closer. She emitted a low, broken moan, of pain, pleasure, despair, hunger, all of them, none of them, he couldn't tell, it didn't matter. Her head dropped back and she slid forward on the stool, nails biting into his arms, pushing him away, pulling him closer, her breath coming in gasps, her mouth seeking his.

She started to shudder as her orgasm tore through her, his finger driving her. A sob exploded from her lips like some lost thing and she collapsed against him. Kincaid's arms closed around her waist and her legs locked behind him and he thrust himself inside her, the edge of the bar pressed against her spine. He impaled her and she crucified him and the stool toppled.

Her arm shot out, knocking over a bottle of rum, her hand seeking something to grab onto, anything. Kincaid hooked his hands in her hair and the world spun, stars tipping out of orbit, the reggae beat pounding at the air, the smell of her skin everywhere, her chest heaving against his, her skin slapping his, her mouth open against his shoulder. And then it was over and there was only a huge silence, as if the world had been vacuumed free of sound.

Gradually, he became aware of his breathing, and hers, filling the stillness, the dark, this small world of spilled rum and sea.

3

In the dream, the sun was darkening. Wind blew fiercely through the trees, fighting her, trying to hold her in one place. It whipped branches across her cheeks and hurled sand and leaves in her face, and she kept running. She couldn't hear the man behind her; the wind was too loud. But she sensed him, knew he was closing the gap between them, knew that the wind helped him. She shouted for Kincaid, but he didn't come. She raced on, stumbling like a drunk in the pines, the dark spreading. Half the sun was gone.

Aline stumbled again and slid through the twilight, rolling down a steep cliff. She landed on a rocky beach, waves crashing around her, water swirling at her ankles. The man shouted and her head jerked around and she saw him as he leaped, as he changed, two legs becoming four. He struck the sand as a panther and charged toward her. She scrambled up the face of the cliff, clawing at rocks, at dirt, and now hands were grabbing onto hers, helping her, and she sprawled over the lip of the cliff, her cry lost in gulps for air.

She lifted her head and saw Rikki Baker, face grotesquely swollen, stumps where her hands should've been. Aline screamed and leaped up and crashed into Ortega, who was laughing, and knocked him down. She ran, and suddenly she was standing over an open grave that swarmed with spiders and worms and ants, and the bones inside rattled as they sat up, and skeletal arms reached out for her as she toppled, screaming.

She lurched from the dream and came to sitting straight up in the dark, heart racing, hand twisted in the sheets, Martell's palm against her damp spine, his voice reaching her as if from a great distance. "What is it? What's wrong?"

Wind rattled the windows and snapped branches against the glass. She swung her legs over the side of the bed and felt her feet against the hard floor. Her fingers grappled for the lamp. Light, she needed light. She hit the switch again and again, but nothing happened and her panic crested and she yanked open the bureau drawer and grabbed for the flashlight. She turned it on; the beam struck the ceiling. She nearly wept with relief.

The hands of the clock stood at midnight.

"What're you doing, Al?"

"The lamp doesn't work."

"The wind must've knocked out a line somewhere."

She didn't care what had caused it; she just wanted light. She lay back, holding the end of the flashlight against her chest, staring up at the circles of illumination on the ceiling. She heard Wolfe somewhere in the house, coming home from wherever he'd been, his claws tapping against the floors, a comforting sound. Familiar. Most of all that.

The wind whined and moaned at the edges of the glass, and she sensed the nearness of the dream in the noises. It hovered just out of reach, the dream did, and she knew if she closed her eyes she would be standing over that grave again, peering inside.

Bacalao's grave.

A cliff somewhere, a rocky beach.

Ortega.

A dark sun.

Kincaid, who hadn't helped her.

He'd left a message on her machine, and she'd called back but had reached *his* machine and wondered why he hadn't returned *her* call. Maybe she should call him now. She would've liked to talk to him now.

But Martell was reaching for her, nuzzling her neck, his mustache tickling her skin. He gently pried the flashlight loose from her fingers and turned it off.

"Don't," she whispered, reaching for the flashlight.

"Come here," he said, reaching for her as she rolled onto her side, into the heat and safety of his skin, his hands.

Later, she slept and dreamed again.

12

Ortega saw her.

She appeared on her front porch in jogging shorts and a tank top, and glanced up and down the street, looking for traffic. But there was none. Not at this hour. She trotted down the steps and walked quickly toward the playground where she ran every morning before work, the place where he and *Padrino* waited.

He liked the bounce in her step and her long legs and the way the wind blew her dark hair. He liked the way she swung her arms at her sides and held her head high. A proud woman. Ikú would be pleased.

He pressed back into the hibiscus hedges that lined the jogging track and snapped the cord in his hand, pulling it taut. It lifted an inch from the dirt track and held on the other end, where it was tied around the trunk of a pine. If for some reason she eluded this trap, *Padrino* was a hundred feet ahead, waiting for her.

Now she limbered up near the swings, falling forward at the waist, fingers brushing her toes, shorts hiking up in back. There was enough light from the dim street lamps for Ortega to see the soft curve of her buttocks and a flash of her panties and the long lines of her legs. She had such beautiful legs, his little *gringa*, slender and tight from all the running. But most important, she was fast.

Fleet of foot.

Now she was moving. Now the wind slipped through her hair, sweeping it away from her face. Her arms were loosely curved at her sides, her fingers were not quite curled into fists.

At ease in her bones, her skin, she rounded the first curve, her shoes kicking up dirt, pine needles, leaves. Now the wind was at her side, blowing strands of her hair across her eyes. She brushed it back. She was another two hundred feet closer.

A cold sweat erupted on Ortega's face. In his mind, he could see the centipede on the black string; it was almost still.

She was a hundred feet away, passing under the light, sweat glistening against her throat and face. Now she was past the light. Seventy-five feet. Sixty.

His hand tightened on the cord. His heart climbed into his throat.

Less than fifty feet.

He could hear her breathing. He could almost smell her.

Twenty feet.

Ten.

Five.

Now she was at the rim of the darkest stretch on the track, coming, moving toward him. . . .

And then she stopped.

To tie her shoe. Jesus. To tie her stupid shoe.

She was breathing hard.

She wouldn't be going fast enough when she reached the cord; it might not trip her. They had no backup plans for something like this; he didn't know what he was supposed to do. *Padrino* hadn't told him, he—

She passed him. Passed the cord. Ortega swore softly under his breath and shot from the bushes just as *Padrino* lurched out onto the track and slammed into her. They both went down.

The woman screamed, but the wind swallowed it. She kicked loose of *Padrino*'s hold on her legs and scrambled to her feet, stumbled, screamed again, but by then Ortega had tackled her.

She sprawled in the grass to the side of the track. Ortega straddled her back, one hand clamped tightly over her mouth, the other bending her right arm back until he heard something snap. She screamed into his hand, bit at his palm, cried out, struggled as valiantly as he had known she would. He was proud of her, his little *gringa*, so proud of her will to live, to escape.

Padrino reached them, the knife glinting in the half-light as he grabbed her by the hair and slashed the blade across her throat.

Her head flopped against the grass. She made soft, gurgling noises, wheezing as she tried to suck in air, eyes bulging in her face. Ortega let go of her arms and stared at her neck, fascinated by the blood, mesmerized by it.

"*Apúrate*, Manuel," hissed *Padrino*. "Get the fuck off her."

Ortega leaped up, and *Padrino* rolled her over and dropped to his knees beside her. He turned her head to the side. Pressed a plastic cup against the corner of the slash, catching the blood as it pumped. She was still alive, her eyes wide, terrified, huge, screaming in pain, screaming for air, and Ortega stroked her cheek with the back of his hand, whispering to her, wanting her to understand that her death was an honor. He told her to close her eyes, to let herself move into the darkness. Someone would be waiting for her. She must not be afraid. Ikú would love her, take care of her. Ikú would be pleased.

Her blood stopped spurting.

Ortega felt for a pulse at her wrist.

He touched her eyes gently, shutting them.

Padrino held the cup at the slash a few moments longer, then capped it, set it aside. They dragged her into the bushes. While *Padrino* returned to get the cup, Ortega snapped open the tool case, removing the instruments that would be used. Then he unlaced her shoes, eased them off, stripped her socks.

Beautiful feet. White, damp, incredibly soft. He rubbed them, kneaded them, massaged them, and imagined that she purred, sighed, that she whispered to him.

"It is a great honor to be chosen by Ikú," he said, moving his hands up her lovely, long legs, across her muscular calves, pausing at her knees. Even her knees were nice. Not many women had lovely knees. Rikki's knees, for instance, had been knobby and ugly. But these . . .

"Turn her over," said *Padrino*, setting the cup of blood carefully in a pouch in the tool kit. "Quickly, Manuel. It'll be light soon."

Ortega rolled her onto her stomach. He got the pint of rum from the kit, uncapped it, tilted the bottle to his mouth. He swished the rum around inside for a moment, then sprayed it in a fine mist across her feet. *Padrino* lit a cigar and blew smoke around them. He spoke in an ancient tongue now, repeating words that had been passed down through generations of sorcerers, fathers to sons, masters to apprentices. Ortega didn't know what the words meant, but he felt their power and knew it would one day be his when he joined the hermetic circle.

Now *Padrino* set the cigar aside and picked up the cutting

tool. It was metal, with a razor blade inside, a tool which in ordinary hands would be used to cut wallpaper. *Padrino* adjusted the blade to its required length, three inches, and Ortega held the woman's foot firmly between his hands. Down came the blade, slicing vertically on either side of her Achilles tendon, then straight across on the top and bottom. A neat rectangle two inches long and an inch wide, as was required. Blood bubbled to the surface; Ortega wiped it away and *Padrino* peeled back the skin. He sliced deeper at the top and bottom, severing the tendon, then removed a piece of it.

It went into the pouch with her blood.

"Rum, Manuel."

He picked up the bottle of rum again, spun the cap, and poured it into *Padrino*'s cupped hands, washing them clean. Then he washed his own hands and poured rum over the woman's feet.

When they were finished, they carried her three hundred yards to a drainage ditch. *Padrino* hurried off to get the kit and bring the car around, and Ortega knelt beside her. He scooped leaves and pine needles around her and over her, making a kind of coffin, talking to her, telling her about himself, about his work, about *Padrino*. Just before he covered her face, he leaned over her, kissing her lightly on the mouth, and let his index finger slide through the blood at her neck.

He rocked back on his heels, pressing his thumb and finger together, watching the way the blood filled the tiny swirls and crevices in his own skin. Such a deep, fiery red, such a healthy red. His tongue darted out, licking at the blood. The taste pleased him. It was slightly metallic and almost sweet, and he felt a part of her entering him, flowing through him, running hot and thick in his own blood. He leaned over her again, licking the blood from her neck and throat and yes oh God yes, he heard her soft, urgent whispers, telling him she forgave, she understood, she was honored.

Then he scooped up a handful of leaves, raising them above her face, and let them fall. They fluttered down in the wind, the twilight, covering her, his little fleet-footed *gringa*.

BILONGOS
May 19–25

13

I

Aline woke up alone, which didn't surprise her, but she'd hoped for a little more from Martell. Hadn't he ever heard of bedroom etiquette? Didn't he know you at least stuck around long enough the next morning for breakfast? But maybe he hadn't wanted to feel obligated about spending the day with her. Hell, maybe all the rules had changed in the nearly four years she'd spent with Kincaid.

She decided to swim this morning instead of going for a run. She pulled shorts on over her suit, then fed Wolfe, who seemed uptight and fussy, nipping at her hand to tell her he wanted a larger serving of chicken, please, and would she mind getting up a little earlier from now on? Especially if she was going to have guests who were up before she was and didn't bother feeding him?

She hadn't even heard Martell leave, and the note from him on the fridge didn't tell her much: *Got a message on my machine from old man Griber, who's going to be in town this a.m. Call you later.*

So she'd been preempted by the old trapper in the swamp. Good. She felt better. She checked her answering machine in the den to see if Kincaid had called back, but the light glowed green. Usually he returned her calls quickly, but maybe he'd gone to the races in Miami with Ferret and had called her before he'd left and then gotten in late last night. If so, he'd be sleeping in. She decided to call after her swim.

It was warm and humid outside, and last night's wind had diminished to a strong breeze. But it had blown sand and leaves across the driveway and into the carport. Her Honda—a two-month-old silver Prelude for which she'd gone into debt—was covered with a thin skin of sand and salt. One of these days she was going to have the carport enclosed. It hadn't mattered so much when she was driving around in a ten-year-old vehicle with more rust on it than metal. But this was her first new car ever, and she wanted the paint job to last more than six months.

She retrieved an old beach towel from the back and walked around the car, rubbing off as much salt as she could without using the hose. But once she started, the salt and sand smeared. She opened the door to the storage room behind her, where she kept the hose, and switched on the light.

When Kincaid had lived here, this room was spotless, everything in its place. The tools had been on the upper shelves there near the air-conditioning unit, the hose had been wound neatly on the metal spike near the door, her bike had stood between the wall and a trunk. Although things were still roughly where they belonged, the absence of tidiness was almost painful. It was as if her presence alone could disrupt even the most orderly room.

She wondered if Martell had this penchant for neatness.

Probably.

The hose, of course, was only half on the metal spike and the rest of it was tangled on the floor. She started unraveling it, pulling it around the edge of the air conditioner, so she'd have more room. She bumped into a beach chair and spun around to kick it out of the way, and that was when she saw it, pinned close to the air conditioner on the clothesline that ran along the far wall.

A black chicken.

A dead black chicken.

Its wing had been clipped to the line with a clothespin. Its throat had been slit. Blood had pooled and dried beneath it. For several beats she didn't move, she simply stared at the thing, chills racing along her spine, hands sliding over her arms, air stalled in her throat. She took several quick steps back, and the air in her lungs hissed out.

"You sick fuck." The sound of her voice seemed out of place in here, in her own storage room,

which wasn't locked, it's never locked

and the ice on her back laced through the skin to her heart.

It was another moment before she moved again, and several

more before she jerked open the chest with her gardening tools in it. She pulled on her gloves, snapped out a plastic garbage bag, and approached the chicken slowly, as though she believed it would suddenly flutter to life and lift off the line and charge toward her, the panther in her dream.

Aline pinched the clothespin and the bird dropped into the bag. She carried it outside, where the light was better, where the air smelled of spring and life. Black thread was tied around its beak and each of its legs, and another piece bound the legs together. What did *that* mean in *santería*? What did the black chicken represent? Her? Was she "tongue-tied" in this case? Were her hands and feet "bound," preventing her from moving forward? Were her ankles "shackled"? Did the fact that the chicken was hanging mean something? What?

She nudged it back into the bag, put it in the car, and sprinted back to the house for her keys, her swim forgotten.

2

Kincaid liked the easy familiarity with which Fuentes bustled around his kitchen, grinding up coffee beans, measuring cream into the mugs for cappuccino, setting out the cinnamon. She was wearing one of his shirts, which cut her off at mid-thigh, and had rolled the sleeves up to her elbows. Only two buttons were fastened, so whenever she moved he caught a glimpse of skin so white it seemed luminous. Stripped of jewelry and makeup, naked of artifice, Fuentes looked younger, fresher, prettier. But not innocent.

"So what's it going to be, Fuentes? *Huevos rancheros?* Omelets? Oatmeal? Something fancier? Name your pleasure." Kincaid was standing in front of the fridge, perusing the contents. "Maybe something pedestrian like French toast?"

Her laugh was low, husky. "I suppose you even do windows, huh, Ryan."

"Everything except skunk litter," he replied.

She laughed. "*Skunk* litter?"

"Never mind. How about omelets *and* French toast?"

"With real maple syrup?"

"Let's see." He dug to the back of the fridge and found a bottle of maple syrup. "You're in luck. The real stuff, straight from Vermont."

"You didn't buy *that* on Tango. I've looked everywhere." The cappuccino machine sang as she frothed the milk in the mugs, and the aroma of Colombian coffee filled the kitchen. She filled his mug and passed it to him. "Unless you Fritters have a shop we transplants don't know about."

"My ex-wife sent it to me last Christmas."

"Where's she live?"

"Which one?" He cracked eggs in a bowl and whipped them.

"How many are there?"

"Two."

"Kids?"

"No. You?"

"No."

He waited for her to say there was an ex-husband, but she didn't. He wondered if her reticence was a professional hazard or just a personal tendency, and decided to press a little. "No ex?"

She shrugged and caught the tomato he rolled her way and began slicing it. "Yeah, there's an ex. But it didn't last long, a couple of years."

Bitterness laced her voice, made her mouth go tight and hard. Then she looked up, baby blues smiling at him, a slice of tomato held between her teeth, an offering. He nibbled and she nibbled and their mouths met. "Yum," she murmured, sliding her fingers through his beard as his hands vanished under the shirt, seeking her soft bottom, the flare of her hips, more of last night.

Her bare feet stepped up onto his, and, laughing, they moved back toward a chair at the table and fell into it, Fuentes straddling his lap. She locked her arms around his neck and pressed up against him, making that strange sound way in the back of her throat, that soft purring that got louder as he mouthed her breast through the shirt.

"I think breakfast has just been delayed," she said. "If the chef approves."

The chef, thought Kincaid, would forgo a week of breakfasts for this, for the light quickness of her hands freeing his erection, the sweet taste of her mouth, the scent of her hair. She eased herself down over him, gave a subtle grind of her hips, and moved, slowly, impaling him, eyes open, watching him, inscrutable.

"Do you think Uvanti killed her?"

"Maybe." He rolled the T-shirt up to her breasts, where light from the window behind him bleached them a bone white. He could see the tiny blue veins in the skin and the way the nipple's color deepened when he touched it. "But I think he's the type who'd play the mourning bit to the hilt, and he's definitely not doing that."

"Hmmm." A twitch, then a swift, controlled tightening of muscles as she lifted, sank, swiveled, and Kincaid gripped her hips. "Even when he and Rikki were an item, he lived just like he is now."

He held her still, slipping in deeper. Her eyes glazed; she took small, delicate nibbles along his lower lip and sucked in her breath when he moved again. .

"Why did you take a six-month leave of absence from the Miami office?"

Fuentes pulled back, made a futile attempt to mask her astonishment, but it was as vivid as the color of her eyes. "I'm impressed, Kincaid." Another grind, not as subtle this time, not as delicate, not playful. "What else do you think you know?"

He ticked off what his source had told him, and she suddenly lifted up, breaking the contact between them, and walked back over to the counter. She grabbed the brick of cheese and grated it with a vengeance, her hand moving so fast it blurred. Kincaid pulled himself together, watching her for a moment. "That's it? A tantrum?"

She slammed an onion against the counter and took a knife to it. "I don't appreciate your methods, Kincaid."

"I don't like being lied to."

Fuentes dropped the knife and spun, arms clutched at her waist. "As I said, it's none of your business, Ryan."

He sipped at his coffee and gazed out the window, where a scudding of dark clouds kissed the tips of the pines. "Then I guess it won't hurt if the local cops know about you."

"That's subterfuge, and you know it."

Kincaid turned his eyes back to her. "All I'm asking for is the truth, Fuentes. Why the obsession with Rikki Baker? Why the leave of absence if you were already working on the case?

Is there a rule that says Feds can't go undercover as strippers? Yes? No?''

She answered with a hard, cold stare.

"You know what I think?"

"I'm sure you'll tell me, whether I want to hear it or not."

He said he believed she'd been removed from the case for some reason, perhaps for the same reason that impelled her to pursue the case on her own, so she took a leave of absence. The stripping angle was a good way to get to know Rikki—and with her dance background, it came easily. But stripping also provided her with an outlet for her repressed sexuality—turning on without being touched, without getting involved.

Her expression didn't change as he spoke, but her eyes did. The blue deepened, and that same panic or desperation he'd glimpsed last night bled into them. He'd struck a nerve, a deep one.

For a second or two she didn't do anything, didn't speak. Her eyes misted, she looked down at the floor, at her painted toenails, then her arms dropped to her sides. When she spoke, her voice was neutral, detached, as if they'd just been discussing ordinary things. Would he mind if she used his shower? she asked. She needed to get cleaned up and then get going, she had errands to run. He said the towels were in the hallway closet and he would drive her back to the club to get her car. She shook her head. She could walk to the club from here, no problem, and she left the room.

He finished his coffee and looked at the stuff spread out on the counter and wasn't hungry anymore. The doorbell rang. *Go away*. But when it pealed a second time, he strode into the hall to answer it.

He heard the drum of the shower.

He opened the door and Aline held up a green garbage bag and said, "Could I come in a second, Ryan? I need some advice on what the hell this means."

Christ. "Now's not a good time, Al."

But she missed the cue—she thought he meant he was hung over or not quite awake—and she swept past him, assuring him it would only take a minute, all she wanted him to do was look at this thing, explain it to her or tell her where to find someone who could. In the living room, she stopped in the pale light that streamed through the picture windows and frowned ever so slightly at the noise of the shower.

She looked a question at him.

"Yes," he replied.

Her eyes slipped to the bedroom door, which was partially ajar, and he knew she was seeing the rumpled sheets, the comforter puddled on the floor, and the shimmering outfit Fuentes had worn last night, which was draped over the back of a chair. She turned her head toward the kitchen, which was separated from the living room only by a counter. She saw the makings for breakfast, smelled the coffee. In seconds, Kincaid thought, Aline had assessed the situation, weighed it against his mood and hers, his needs and hers, and accepted what was.

"This'll only take a second, Ryan."

She opened the bag and he peered inside, then took it from her and set it on the floor, folding the edges back until the chicken was exposed. She told him where she'd found it. "What do black chickens mean in *santería*?"

"I don't know. But I'm meeting Meg Mallory at eleven, and she's taking me to a *santera* she knows. I'll find out from her. Mind if I keep this?"

She gave a short, curt laugh. "You must be kidding." She bundled it up quickly and held it out. "It's all yours. What was the urgent message you left on my machine, anyway?"

He quickly told her about Senator Chamberlain. Her face drained of color, and she raked her fingers through her hair. "Great, this is just great." She made a crack about the family photo they'd seen in Rikki's apartment, about Daddy's resemblance to Fernando Lamas. "How did you . . ."

"I'll explain later."

Her eyes darted once to the bedroom door, then back, and he nodded, confirming her unasked question.

"Does the chief know?"

"I couldn't get hold of him."

"I'll call him when I leave here. He's going to want to know how reliable the information is, Ryan."

"Very."

As her hands busily worked at bundling the bag again, she gave him a quick rundown on what she'd found out yesterday— Dr. Stile, the lead on the priest, the lingerie shop, Uvanti's perfect alibi. They stood at the same time and Kincaid reached for the garbage bag with the dead chicken in it.

The shower went off, the clatter of pipes ringing out, abnormally loud in the silence, a kind of mockery. They just looked at each other, then she pointed at the bag. "Your friend's going to think you're weird, you know."

He smiled. "Yeah, probably."

"Guaranteed."

She smiled and so did he, and the weight of everything left unspoken rolled along between them as he walked her to the door.

When he came back inside the house, Fuentes was standing at the window, wearing his shirt and a pair of jeans. Behind her, the garbage bag was open and the chicken exposed.

"Where'd the chicken come from?"

He told her, speaking to her back.

Then: "The cop. Is she ex-wife one or two?"

"Neither."

3

St. Joseph's Church was in the heart of El Pueblito. It wasn't the largest church in the neighborhood, but judging from the number of cars jammed in the lot and squeezed in at the curbs, it looked as if it was the most popular.

Aline had to park three blocks away, in an alley next to a coffee shop. She started across the street, but the enticing aroma of coffee and freshly baked pastries reminded her she hadn't eaten breakfast and drew her back.

The place was crowded with couples and families—men in white suits and silk guayabera shirts, women in spring dresses, little girls in frills. At the back of the shop a clutch of elderly men played a noisy game of dominos. They laughed and shouted for more *cafecitos* and greeted friends in robust voices and tight *abrazos*.

Unlike Little Havana, this Latin neighborhood was small enough to be a community in the truest sense of the word. If you didn't know someone, then you probably knew his second cousin or a friend of his sister's. Tight families, common ideologies, strong religious beliefs, a support system. It meshed and functioned like a well-oiled machine and was going to make information hard to come by.

Aline bought a pastry and a *cafecito* served in a tiny plastic cup. It was loaded with sugar, but so what? She deserved a sugar lift after her visit to Kincaid's.

She strolled toward the church with her coffee and her pastry, trying not to think too closely about who had been taking a shower at Kincaid's. She passed cafes where the sidewalk tables were filled, and cut through a park where Cuban teenagers were decked out in acid-washed jeans, high-top sneakers with colorful socks that matched their tank tops, and lots of jewelry. A couple of guys were break-dancing to music that throbbed from a portable CD player, and kids had gathered around to watch.

She wondered where Kincaid had met his guest for the night, and who had been making breakfast. Probably Kincaid. Breakfast would be omelets or French toast or both, or maybe something a little more elaborate like *huevos rancheros*. They would linger over coffee and the Sunday paper, and before he left the house to meet with Meg Mallory there would be another romp in bed.

She felt a sharp jab of something shaped suspiciously like jealousy and decided there were distinct disadvantages to knowing someone as well as she knew Kincaid.

When she reached the church, the double doors were open and people were spilling out. A priest was shaking hands and talking with people as they left. He was a tall, pleasant-looking man, probably in his mid- or late forties. His dark hair was graying.

Aline stood off to one side at the bottom of the steps, finishing her coffee. When the crowd had cleared, she trotted up the steps and caught the priest as he was turning to go back inside.

"Father? May I talk to you for a minute?"

His smile eased the gauntness of his angular face and smoothed the pinch of fatigue at the corners of his chocolate eyes. "Sure."

"I'm looking for Father Carver."

"I'm Father Carver."

She introduced herself, and the smile disappeared by degrees, as though he'd been expecting this visit and dreading it. "I'd like to ask you a few questions about Rikki Baker."

The smile was completely gone now. His dark head bobbed once, twice, resigned. "Let's talk in the rectory. It's more private."

She followed him inside the church, past pews and confessionals and statues that gazed down in mute judgment. They exited through a side door, a gate, and into a courtyard that was lush with trees and bushes. Birds trilled sweetly in the shadows, as though they were blessed. A breeze carried the sounds of music from a radio and the scent of food from a cafeteria just beyond them.

"Would this be all right?" He stopped at one of the benches arranged around a small fountain.

"It's fine."

His hands moved across the thighs of his black slacks—large hands with thick fingers and carefully clipped nails. He waited for her to say something, a sure sign that he wasn't going to help her at all. So she got right to the point.

"I understand you counseled Rikki Baker about her pregnancy."

"Yes."

"Did she ever mention to you who the father was?"

Dark eyes serene, mouth as flat as a hyphen. "No."

"Can you tell me anything about her that might help us determine who killed her?"

"Detective Scott, my sessions with Rikki were confidential. I don't feel that in good conscience I can—"

"Her fingers were chopped off to the knuckles," she blurted. "Her heart had been pierced by a blade at least six inches long that tore straight up from her sternum. I found a *santería* altar in her apartment. I need your help, Father Carver. Please."

The breeze swirled leaves at their feet and blew spray from the fountain their way. Carver sighed, sat forward, back, and shook his head. "She was a very confused young woman. I know that she told the child's father about her pregnancy and he got angry and blamed her for not using birth control and wanted to know how she could be certain the child was even his. He broke off the relationship.

A few days later, I think it was, he got in touch with her again and said he'd been thinking things over. If she wanted to keep the child, he would give her enough money to pay for her hospital bills, doctors' visits, and to cover the months she wouldn't be able to work. In return for this, he wanted her to leave the island."

"What'd she decide, do you know?"

"She said she didn't need the money. She felt like he was trying to buy her off. But about two weeks ago I got a call from her and she said she was going to be moving to Miami, where she could get work on TV. She was going to keep the baby.''

"Do you know if the man was Latin?''

"She never said. I know he was older than she, though, and he did well financially.''

"Did she talk about her interest in *santería*?''

Carver fingered his clerical collar and shifted around on the bench, turning sideways so that he faced her. "What do you know about *santería*, Detective Scott?''

"Not enough.''

His smile was patient and a little sad. "A wise answer. Let me ask you something else. Was there anything in Rikki's apartment, besides the altar, that was connected to *santería*?''

Aline told him about the plastic cup covered with a swatch of black cloth and the two scraps of paper frozen in the ice. "I figured it was some sort of spell.''

That last word seemed oddly powerful now, imbued with all the arcane strangeness of any ritual in Catholicism. The priest nodded. "It's a specific spell to create enmity between two people. It's used primarily by *santeros*, but there are variations of it used by *mayomberos*. Have you heard of *palo mayombe*?''

"*Santería's* equivalent of black magic.''

"It's quite a bit more than that, but the analogy will do. As a priest in this parish, I see the side effects of both *santería* and *palo*.'' He explained *palo*'s origins and how it differed from *santería*. Much of it was what Kincaid had told her, but vastly expanded. "Let's say you found out your husband was having an affair with someone, Detective, and you wanted to put a stop to it. You'd go to your local *santero* and explain the problem and he would tell you how much it would cost to do a *trabajo*. A spell. One of the *trabajos* he might recommend would be the one you found in Rikki's freezer. It might or might not work. If it didn't, you might take a more drastic measure and consult a *mayombero*. His *trabajo* would be much darker.''

"In what way?''

Carver rubbed his jaw. "Typically, in cases like this, the *mayombero* goes to the cemetery and digs a hole in a dark corner. He buries a silver coin—a quarter, fifty cents, the amount is unimportant. This little grave symbolizes the grave of the man he's going to kill. The wayward husband.

"The *mayombero* takes some of the earth from this symbolic grave and wraps it in a black cloth. At home, he lights a candle which has been stolen from a church. He heats a straight pin in its flame and runs it through the body of a live centipede that's been tied up with black thread. He says the man's name three times and puts some of the dirt in a piece of clothing that belongs to the man. These then go into his *nganga*, which I'll explain in a minute. The centipede is pinned to a tree, and the *mayombero* commands his *kiyumba*—a spirit—to kill the man and make him suffer just as the centipede is. The victim usually dies violently a few days later. Centipedes are popular among *mayomberos*."

"Good against evil, and evil wins," she remarked, thinking of the black chicken, the black thread.

"What I'm saying, Detective, is that these things are real. They happen. Spells work. They work for the same reason that prayers do. If you put enough energy into something, negative or positive, you're going to get results."

The source of a *mayombero*'s power, he said, came from his *nganga*. Part of his initiation involved digging up the corpse of a person who had recently died. The more evil the individual had been, the better suited his *kiyumba* or spirit would be to the *mayombero*. The head, toes, fingers, ribs, and tibias of the corpse were removed. The death had to have been recent enough so the brain was still present, even if it was decayed. The bodies of white men were preferred, because it was believed their *kiyumbas* were easier to influence than a black man's. Some *mayomberos* preferred to have the brain of both a black and a white man, so attacks could be carried out on anyone, regardless of skin color.

"Once the bones are removed, a ritual is enacted in which a pact is sealed between the *kiyumba* and the *mayombero*. Then the making of the *nganga* begins. It includes anything a *mayombero* thinks he might need to carry out his work—worms, spiders, bats, frogs, cats and dogs, herbs, spices, the list is practically endless. All of these things become part of the world within the *nganga*. The *kiyumba* rules this little world, and the *mayombero* commands the *kiyumba*, who has agreed to obey him."

This "power pack," he said, could be kept in an iron cauldron or in a burlap bag which was hidden in the darkest corner of the *mayombero*'s house. "There have been some *mayomberos* who've added things to their *nganga* which they believed would increase their power."

"What kind of things?"

He thought a moment. "Let's go to my office. I have something to show you."

They walked through the courtyard and across a basketball court, where the breeze swirled into dust devils that bit at her ankles and cheeks. The sun had popped through the clouds, and heat radiated from the black court in waves. She slipped on her sunglasses, thought of the black chicken again, and asked Carver if he knew what it meant.

"Chickens and doves are used in spiritual cleansing rituals in *santería*, but I don't know if they have any particular meaning."

"Suppose the chicken's dead and its legs and beak are bound with black thread?"

"My guess is that the desired outcome is silence and immobility about something. In *santería*—and in *palo*—everything is a symbol for something else. Was it a chicken or a rooster?"

"A chicken."

"Then the intended victim is female. Was the throat wrung or slit?"

"Slit."

"I imagine some of its blood was taken. That would symbolize the blood of the victim. Was there anything inside the mouth?"

"I didn't look."

"Where was it found?"

She had a difficult time getting the words past her throat. "That's significant too?"

"Absolutely. If it were found on a front porch, at the entrance of the house, it would mean the victim's opportunities concerning this situation would be blocked. Symbolism."

"It was on a clothesline. What would that mean?"

He shook his head. "That's a good one. I don't know." He opened the door to his office. It was large, paneled, and simply furnished, with an oak desk and bookshelves and a sitting area under a window that overlooked the back of the church property. From a shelf he pulled out a photo album and set it on the coffee table, turning it so they could both see it.

"Since I was assigned to this parish five years ago, I've been collecting information on *santería* and *palo* so I could deal with some of the problems I come up against with parishioners. You see, there isn't any clear-cut policy on *santería* within the church. They just pretend it doesn't exist. So we do the best we can, stressing the positive aspects and chastising the negative."

He opened the album and paged through it slowly. There were articles cut from newspapers and magazines, photographs of altars and animal sacrifices and common spells, lists of ingredients used in certain spells. A treasure trove of information. "This is what I wanted to show you." He stopped at a grainy black-and-white photograph of a handsome young man with thick, dark hair and Rasputin eyes. "He was one of the most infamous *mayomberos* to ever come out of Cuba. His name's Armando Bacalao. He's—"

"—buried in the old seamen's graveyard," she said softly.

"You've heard of him?"

"Indirectly." Her bones seemed to shift and slide around her, as though her body were being rearranged at a cellular level. "His grave was robbed yesterday."

Carver's head raised slowly, as though the movement hurt him, and he crossed himself. *"Dios mío,"* he whispered. "Then it's true."

"What?" The room was suddenly too warm, the air too still, and she squirmed on the couch. "What's true?"

He paged quickly through the photo album, talking as he did so. "During the thirties, there were a number of unsolved murders that happened here on Tango. Some people said Bacalao was behind them. You see, part of what made him so powerful was his deviations from the established rituals in *palo*. One of those deviations involved adding to his *nganga*, as we were talking about before. It's believed that he used certain body parts from these victims."

He stopped at an article from the *Tribune* dated in early May 1934: BRUTAL MURDER OF DANCE-HALL GIRL BAFFLES POLICE. "Her fingers were chopped off," said Carver, his voice so quiet it was nearly inaudible. "She was killed at home on the night of May twelfth, the same date Rikki was killed."

He flipped to the next page. EX-OLYMPIC RUNNER FOUND DEAD AND BRUTALIZED ON BOARDWALK. "This young man was killed on May 18, 1935, fifty-four years ago last night. One of his Achilles tendons was removed."

A third page. BODY OF LOCAL PALMIST WASHED UP ON EAST BEACH. "Her eyes were removed. May 25, 1936."

Aline couldn't lift her head, blink her eyes, couldn't speak. She saw Carver's hand turning the next page and already knew what it was going to be. HOMICIDE DETECTIVE BRUTALLY MURDERED. "September 22, 1937." Carver said. "Detective Abel

Whitkins had been working on the murders for three years when he got a telephone tip from an anonymous caller. He was supposed to meet the man on the Tango ferry. He never made it to Key West. He was stabbed and his skull was crushed and his brain was removed."

"But none of these other murders have happened."

The priest rubbed a hand over his face. "If I'm right about what's going on, I suspect you'll have another homicide to deal with. Maybe not an ex-Olympic runner, but a close enough approximation. I don't know the details on the wound that killed Rikki. I couldn't bear to read the newspaper article. But I think if you look back through the old files on the dance-hall case, you'll find that the stab wound that killed the dance-hall girl in 1934 will duplicate the one that killed Rikki."

"But what makes you think there'll be another murder so soon?" *Last night, it would've been last night.* "The ones Bacalao committed were a year and a week apart. And why would anyone be duplicating those murders to begin with? I don't understand."

"Power." Carver shut the photo album; it made a soft sound, a kind of sigh. "All of it has to do with power. Maybe by compressing the time element, the killer feels he'll increase his power; I don't know. But I *do* know that by using Bacalao's bones, the killer draws on the power he had." He paused. "Find your grave robber, Detective, and you'll have your killer. My guess is that Bacalao's bones have been pulverized and are now part of another *mayombero's nganga.* And the *mayombero* wants all of the power Bacalao had, so in a sense he's paying homage by duplicating the murders."

"Why did the pattern of murders change with Whitkins? I mean, up until then, Bacalao had been committing the murders a year and a week apart."

Carver shrugged; his smile was thin, mystified. "I don't know. But presumably Bacalao had a reason. But I'm sure of this much. If there *was* a homicide last night, you can be sure there'll be another one on May 25, unless you find him before then."

"And a final murder on September 22," she said.

"Yes."

"Of a cop."

"If the killer is following in Bacalao's footsteps, then it would be the cop who's investigating Rikki Baker's murder."

It couldn't get any clearer than that.

14

I

The old *santera*'s house was in the hills near the cat's left ear, set back in trees that shaded it from the worst of the summer heat. It was a two-story building with white pillars at the front and a wide driveway steep enough to give you shin splints. Kincaid thought it looked cumbersome among the other houses on the block, all of which were newer, brighter, sleeker.

Meg Mallory explained that the place had been built at the turn of the century by Anna's grandparents, who were the wealthiest black family on the island at the time. Nothing else had existed up here then.

He parked the Saab alongside a diesel Mercedes which was at least twenty years old, box-shaped, shiny, the color of chocolate. A girl with pigtails was crouched near a bicycle on the shaded lawn, playing with a Siamese kitten. She waved as they got out and called, "Hi, Mrs. Meg. Come see my new kitten."

The child's name was Josie, and she had to tilt her head back to look up at Kincaid. "Wow, you're tall."

He laughed and stroked the kitten, which was now snuggled in Josie's arms. "What's his name?"

"Bandit."

"Is your Nana home?" Meg asked her.

"Sure, she's out back in the garden. C'mon. I'll show you."

She led them around the side of the house, where an old woman in denim coveralls and a floppy straw hat was digging furiously at weeds flourishing at the base of a rose bush. She was short, thin, and spry, and Kincaid wouldn't even venture a guess at her age. She hugged Meg hello and greeted Kincaid with a wry, knowing smile that left him with the impression that she knew something about him she couldn't possibly have known, since they had never met.

They settled at a white aluminum table covered by a multi-colored umbrella in the outside patio. A maid in a white uniform served cold drinks while Meg and the old woman caught up on news. Her dark eyes kept slipping toward Kincaid, almost as if his face seemed familiar to her but she couldn't place it.

"You have a question," she said suddenly, gazing at him, sitting forward. "Please ask so it will stop poking at me." She sounded annoyed, and Kincaid, remembering Meg's warning that the old woman wasn't nuts about gringos, addressed her in Spanish.

"Is there any ritual in *santería* or *palo* where amputated fingers are used?"

In Spanish, she said, "Well. You are an interesting combination of contradictions, señor." Then she looked over at Meg and switched to English, speaking as if Kincaid weren't present. "His Spanish is excellent, Meggie. But who is he and why should I tell him anything?"

Meg smiled and explained that Kincaid's interest concerned a homicide. The old woman's thin, spidery fingers laced together on the tabletop. "Are you familiar with the *nganga*?" she asked.

"Yes."

"That is the only time I can think of when fingers would be used in established rituals. But since I am not cut into *palo*, I cannot speak with authority on these things." She smiled again, playing with him now. "But that is not your only question."

"Do you know anything about Armando Bacalao?"

"I assume that since you know that name, Señor Kincaid, you are also aware of what Bacalao was."

"More or less. A kind of master black magician."

"In your terms, yes, I suppose we could refer to him that way."

Kincaid questioned her about the murders he'd supposedly committed, but she didn't know anything more than what he'd read in the books Meg had lent him. She had been away from the island during the thirties. Had he, toward the end of his life, denounced *palo*? Kincaid asked.

Yes, that was her understanding. "His son was supposedly abducted in the forties—1947, I think—and since Bacalao was a rich man and had his share of enemies, it was not implausible. But there were rumors that his wife had actually sent the boy to live with relatives elsewhere because she feared he would turn out like his father.''

''She was an American, right?'' Kincaid asked.

''Yes. After his son vanished, Bacalao felt that the gods he had worshipped for so long had betrayed him and he denounced Ikú. A year later he drowned at sea.''

''What happened to his wife?'' Meg asked.

''I think she left the island. I do not know if she's still alive.''

''And the son?''

She shrugged, palms turned up. ''*Quién sabe?*''

''In one of the books Meg lent me, there was speculation that Bacalao hadn't died, that he'd faked his death, and that someone else was buried in his grave.''

''There are many stories. Personally, I believe that he died. I met him once. Years ago. I was only a young girl, twelve, thirteen, I cannot even remember. He was renting a house from my grandparents then and came by to pay the rent. He was still in his twenties then, quite handsome, quite polite, a gentleman.

''I was practicing my piano lessons. He asked me to play *Für Elise*. I did, and he gave me this.'' She reached into her upper pocket and pulled out a shiny gold charm—either a full moon or a sun with a crescent moon impaled against it. It was attached to her key case. ''I keep it for good luck.'' She stroked it with her thumb. ''Much later, when these stories were circulating about Bacalao, I was going to throw it out. But my grandmother, I remembered, pointed out that it was given in a generous spirit, with no malevolent intent, so I kept it.''

''What do you know about Manuel Ortega?'' Kincaid asked.

She cupped her hands around her glass of iced tea. ''So many, many questions, señor. I knew his grandmother quite well, but I haven't maintained a close contact with him. Why don't you tell me what you would like to know?''

''Is he cut into *palo*?''

''Possible. His herbal knowledge is quite good, and there are *santeros* who are cut into *palo* for that knowledge.''

''He was involved with the woman who was murdered. She was his student. She'd already received the *collares*.''

''He has taken on students over the years. Exactly what are you saying, señor? That you think he killed this woman? Amputated her fingers?''

"He's a suspect."

She gazed off to her left, where her granddaughter was playing with the Siamese kitten. Sunlight slipped down her long,
slender nose, and for a second she looked almost regal, an aging, dethroned queen. "I have not seen Manuel for a while."
She drew her eyes back to Kincaid and fanned herself with the
straw hat. Her hair was utterly white, and strands had curled
against her damp, wrinkled forehead. "We had a disagreement
over advice he had given to a friend of mine. I felt he had misled
her about his abilities and charged her too much for a *trabajo*.
He is a capable *santero*, but often overestimates his abilities. He
is, how should I say this . . ." She paused.

"Unscrupulous?" Kincaid prodded.

"In some respects, yes, but it's because he's blinded by ambition. It's not uncommon among *santeros*. Many of them are
young when they become involved with *santería*, and they do a
few *trabajos* that work and have some success, and suddenly
they believe they are tremendously powerful and they seek
shortcuts. But there are no shortcuts."

"Is he unscrupulous enough to kill someone if he believes
the person's death will benefit him in some way?"

Annoyance shadowed her features again, and she sat back.
"Señor, you are asking me to draw a conclusion I'm not qualified to make."

So he changed the subject and asked about animal sacrifices,
specifically black chickens. "Chickens and doves," she said,
"were common sacrifices in *santería* and had numerous uses.
The blood was offered to whatever *orisha* was being invoked,
the bones were pulverized, and the feathers were plucked and
used in other rituals. Unless the bird had been used for a spiritual
cleansing, it was always eaten afterward by the *santero* and his
family, because it had been consecrated by the *orisha* to whom
it was offered."

"That's not exactly what I'm talking about." Kincaid excused
himself and returned to the Saab for the garbage bag. When he
came back, he set it on the ground near the *santera*'s chair and
folded back the edges of the bag, exposing the chicken.

"Good Lord," Meg said quietly.

The old woman didn't say anything. She picked up her gardening gloves, slipped them on, knelt on the grass, and grasped
the chicken by the legs. She turned it over, examining it in much
the same way a vet would a sick animal, poking, prodding,

parting the feathers with her fingers. She withdrew a Swiss Army knife from the pocket of her coveralls, sliced through the thread around the chicken's beak, then pried it open. She used a twig to scrape something out of its mouth and set it on the table.

A wrinkled bit of paper no larger than a fortune in a cookie: she smoothed it out with a gloved finger and looked at him.

"Is Aline the person who found this?"

"Yes."

She pushed the paper toward him. Aline's name was typed on it. Just her name, nothing more.

"Was the chicken dead when she found it?"

"Yes."

"In *santería*, we call spells *trabajos*. In *palo*, they are known as *bilongos*. And this one is normally used with salt and the animal is alive when its mouth is bound. The idea is that when the animal dies, the person whose name is on the paper will also die. But since the chicken was already dead, señor, I believe this is mainly a warning of what she can expect. Throat slashed, feet bound, lips sewn together. Is this Aline a friend of yours?"

"Yes."

"Has there been anything else like this that has happened?"

He started to say no, then remembered the thefts. Perfume. A nightshirt. Lipstick. A hairbrush. Her photo. When he told the *santera*, she nodded.

"The perfume would attract the *kiyumba*. Tell her to wear no perfume or a different brand. The same with the lipstick. What is her attitude toward *santería*? Toward *palo*?"

"Skepticism, but maybe not as much as before."

"Will she do as you ask?"

Not usually. "I guess it would depend on what I ask."

"This is not an idle threat." She gestured toward the chicken. "It means that certain forces have already been activated. I can't negate the spell, but perhaps I can lessen it somewhat."

"How?"

"By disposing of the chicken in a certain way and then preparing something that your friend should carry with her."

Talismans, Kincaid thought, wishing he could summon some skepticism of his own and laugh it off. But the scar on his stomach, silent for a day, now began to itch and burn again. "Whatever you recommend."

She left for a few minutes and returned with three things—an egg inside a glass, a white candle, and a small, homemade white bag. "If we knew the name of whoever had worked the spell against her, it would be much easier to annul *his* spell with another. Since we do not know who he is, this is the next best thing." She tapped the edge of the glass with the egg in it. "Aline should fill it halfway with water and during the next nine days keep the glass prominently displayed in her home. Every morning she should light the white candle and invoke Santa Clara to bring peace and harmony into her life. At the end of the nine days, the water from the glass should be thrown into the street and the egg was to be taken to a park and smashed on the ground. Santa Clara should be invoked again and asked that the evil disappear from Aline's life in the same way the egg was broken."

"And the white bag?"

"Inside is garlic, parsley, a bit of camphor. Evil spirits can never resist camphor. This bag has been taken to seven churches and dipped in holy water. She should carry it on her at all times."

Aline, he mused, was going to laugh, argue, debate; she was going to think he'd lost his mind. But at this point, why discard any possibility?

"These things, combined with my disposing of the chicken, will only alleviate the effects of the spell. Until you know the person's name, there is not much more we can do. If anything else like this is done against her, please let me know, señor. It will then be necessary to counteract the effects."

As though all battles took place on two levels, he thought, the physical and the spiritual.

"There is something else about Bacalao you should know," the woman said as she walked them around to the front of the house. "Or rather, about the legend of Bacalao. The date of his death, December fourth, is believed to be significant. It's the feast day of Changó, who was the *orisha* he denounced when he was cut into *palo*. Lightning, which is ruled by Changó, is what sank his ship. Some *santeros* feel this is an example of the very real power of the *orishas*—that Changó killed Bacalao as an act of revenge."

"What do you think?" Meg asked.

The woman's smile made the deep creases in her face move and shift. "Such coincidences aren't uncommon in *santería*. But what you really need, Señor Kincaid, is someone who would give you the *mayomberos'* opinion on this."

"I don't suppose they're listed in the Yellow Pages."

She laughed, the first time she'd done so, and it was a low, dry sound, almost a wheeze, the sound of a desert wind rubbing up against cactus. "There's a man I know who's something of a scholar about *palo*, even though he isn't a *mayombero*. He's away right now but should be back in a few days. I'll talk to him and then get in touch with you."

As Kincaid dug into his wallet for a business card, Josie and her kitten came running around the side of the house. The girl scooped up the kitten before it reached the driveway and came over to stand next to her grandmother, the kitten snuggling into her arms.

"Can I have one too?" Josie asked when he passed the business card to her grandmother.

"Sure. I think I've got another one in here." It was tattered around the edges, but Josie didn't seem to mind.

"Neat," she said. "The magnifying glass reminds me of Sherlock Holmes."

Kincaid chuckled. "That's the idea." He glanced back at Anna. "Call me when you know something."

She gestured toward the glass and the small white bag. "Make sure your friend gets those."

"I'll do my best." But he suspected his best wasn't going to be good enough.

2

Some people looked normal and weren't, Aline thought. Others didn't look normal and were. And still others didn't look normal and weren't and never would be. Harry Topper, who was in charge of the Tango crime lab, fell into that category.

He was thin, pale, and his clothes never fit him right. His slacks were too short or too long, his shirts were too large or too small, and the colors were all wrong. Khaki and jungle greens that exaggerated his pallor: he would've looked better in soft blues and cheerful pastels. His face was pleasant, perhaps even cute in an old-fashioned way. But Aline rarely saw his face because it was usually bent over a slide or turned toward his computer.

Topper loved his computer. Topper loved his job. Topper, whose father was a Miami mortician and whose mother was a pathologist, had been born to forensics the way other people were born to money. His only professional problem, really, was that he spoke a language few people understood. So his articulation was slow, precise. He pronounced each syllable like a drama student who'd been coached to sharpen those Ts and close those Os, and all the while, his brain whirred, translating the technical to the mundane. As a result, his response to her *Hey, Top, got anything for me?* was as dilatory and measured as it would've been if she'd asked for the chemical composition of the human body.

"What I've got, Aline, is going to make your life easier, believe me." He slid his chair from the microscope to the computer without looking at her. His hands played the computer keyboard. "One. Rikki Baker had intercourse with a man who's got A negative blood. Two. The fetus she was carrying had O blood. Three, she had A positive blood. That means whoever she had sex with didn't impregnate her, because if you cross an A pos with an A neg, you do *not* get Mr. Universal Donor, O. In fact, since she was A pos and the fetus was O, the daddy's got to be an O."

"How's that going to make my life easier? That means one out of every two men out there could be the daddy, Top."

"I'm not so sure the percentage is quite that high." He looked at her now, his eyes almost as pale as his skin. "The gunpowder Bill found on her during the autopsy?"

"What about it?"

"It had traces of a thermoplastic adhesive on it. Vegetable glue, quite clear, and it kept the gunpowder stuck to her stomach and the inside of her thighs."

"For five days?"

"Sure. Pretty ingenious, really, and I think that's what bothers me the most, Aline. A lot of *premeditation* went into this. They kill her, amputate her fingers, ditch her car, and then stop to spread gunpowder on her. Real ritualistic."

"They? You're sure it was two people?"

"Absolutely. The knife's angle of entry, the broken arm . . . Oh. I almost forgot. We have her car. A couple of campers in the preserve ran across an abandoned car last night and called it in. One of the patrolmen answered the call, and it was towed into town. It's in the garage, and I found a few things that are pretty interesting. Got time to take a look?''

"You bet."

They rode over to the garage on a golf cart that Topper drove like a madman, whipping left then right to avoid potholes. "If we knew where she was killed, Aline, it might help make sense of some things. Like how far they had to cart the body to the dumpster, whether they were using two cars or one, not to mention what the blood spatters could tell us."

Aline gripped the edges of her seat as he swung into a wide loop and screeched to a stop in front of the warehouse.

It was shared by the police department and the Coast Guard. Official vessels and vehicles that needed tune-ups, paint jobs, and repairs were brought here, and so were boats and planes seized in drug raids. There were several cigar boats, a twin-engine Cessna with tip tanks, cars, and a couple of vans.

Rikki Baker's VW Rabbit was parked in a separate area of the warehouse where the department kept large items related to ongoing investigations. Bright red. Hatchback. Two-door. Nothing unusual, except for the deep gouge in the paint between the tracks of the luggage rack on the roof.

"The gouge is recent; the metal hasn't even started to rust yet," Topper said. "I got to wondering what could've made a gash like this, and I decided it might've been the edge of a bike pedal. Like if you're in a hurry and you jerk the bike off." His arms came back, showing her what he meant. "And look at this mark on the other side. It could've been made by a bike seat. "So I tried out some different bikes, see, the ones we've got around here, and this is the one I came up with that's closest."

He wheeled a ten-speed over to the car that had been resting against the wall. "It's a twenty-three-inch frame. The seat's up as high as it can go. Try it and you'll understand my next point."

She mounted it but couldn't sit and pedal at the same time, even when she lowered the seat. "So the guy who rode it is taller than me?"

He grinned, pleased that his show-and-tell had gotten his point across. "And you're what? Five seven? Eight?"

"Eight."

"Okay, and I'm five eleven and I had no trouble pedaling it. So I think it's safe to assume he's at least as tall as me."

Ortega, she thought, was shorter than Topper, probably no more than five nine. Seroz was about the same height. It didn't eliminate either of them as suspects, since there were two men involved in the murder, but it gave her plenty to think about. Like why a bike was used. And where it was ridden.

September twenty-second.

Topper set the bike aside and opened the hatchback. "Back here, on the carpeting, I found traces of gunpowder." He pointed at several dark stains. "Blood. Hers. I ran it through already."

"Anything else?"

"That's not enough?" His mouth puckered, and he looked so disappointed, she laughed and slipped an arm around his shoulders, giving a squeeze.

"You've done great, Top. But if you come across anything else . . ."

"I know, I know. Call you anytime." He flashed a grin and jammed his hands in the pockets of his khaki slacks. "That's what they all say, Al."

Back in the lab, she called the station and Penny the dispatcher answered. "Any developments?" Aline asked.

Penny, whispering hoarsely: "His Highness the senator strolled through the door ten minutes ago, Al. The chief said give him an hour. And make sure you've got your ducks lined up."

What fucking ducks? The only thing she could tell Senator Chamberlain was that the man who'd killed his lost daughter was at least five foot eleven inches. Swell.

She said she'd be there in an hour, hung up, and dialed Lester's bar, looking for Ferret. He hadn't been in, she was told. She called his garage, and he picked up on the second ring.

"Yo."

"*Yo?* What kind of way is that to answer the phone?"

"Sweet Pea, this is a private line. Only people who got this number are friends. Friends forgive your quirks. And by the way, you should call your machine more often. I've been talking to it for the last two hours. I've got a lead you're going to like. A friend of Rikki Baker's asked her to look in on her place—water the plants and whatnot—while she was out of town. I'm trying to run down the address or the woman's name. I hope to have something soon."

"Does the friend work at the club?"

"Don't know, Sweet Pea. Like I said, I'm working on it. Is Ryan there by any chance?"

"No, I'm at the lab. Why?"

"Catch-Me won last night. Won big."

"How much?"

"Oh, I figure Ryan's share is somewhere in the vicinity of seventy-five."

"Grand?"

"Hundred. But don't say anything to him. I want to see his face when I tell him."

And he would take the money and run, she thought. And maybe he would even take his new lady along, just as he had once taken her. The notion depressed her more than it should have.

"Sweet Pea?"

"Yeah?"

"Did you run a check on that friend of Rikki's? The blonde in the pink leotards?"

"Only the usual, to see if she has a record. She doesn't. No reason to take prints."

"Keep an eye on her."

"Why?"

But Ferret had already hung up.

15

I

Kincaid spent an hour in the library after he and Meg left the *santera*'s, then drove over to Rikki Baker's apartment.

He wasn't sure why he'd come back. He and Aline had thoroughly searched the place, and so had forensics, but there was always a chance they'd missed something—something small but vital.

He sat in the silence of her living room, bare feet flat against the rug, grounding him, eyes closed, his breathing deep and even, his hands resting on his thighs. The trick was to turn down the noise in his own head and sink into a place where he could hear the air whisper to him, where the rooms would nudge him in this direction or that.

The softness of the cushion beneath him. The thickness of the rug between his toes. Sun's warmth against the back of his neck, spreading like melting butter across his shoulders, down his spine. As he approached a state much like sleep, images flickered behind his eyes. Rikki Baker's hands like crude clubs. Fuentes climbing from the hot tub on Uvanti's yacht, white skin gleaming. The black chicken. Ortega grinning like Ricky Ricardo. Aline at his front door. Fuentes grimacing, sobbing. The images came faster and faster until they blurred together, until they were a pale, luminous river of sensations, impressions. And then he felt it, a soft nudge just under his ribs.

Kincaid focused on it, trying to seize it, find it, draw it out. There. To his left. Toward the bedroom.

But we searched the bedroom.

The nudge instantly disappeared, and he waited, as patient as a yogi, certain it would return. It did, but with it came an intense burning across his stomach, where the scar quivered and twitched, reminding him.

As though he could possibly forget.

Minutes passed.

The air whispered.

The nudge got stronger.

Kincaid opened his eyes and got up, moving slowly toward the hall, feet sighing against the rug. Down the hall now, wood floor cold against his soles. He stopped in the bedroom doorway, eyes roaming through the red-and-black motif, across the wide bed, the mirrored ceiling, the bureau where he'd found the red-and-black negligees.

Close, but not close enough.

It was like playing Pin the Tail on the Donkey when you were a kid, stumbling around with a blindfold on your eyes as someone called out that you were warm or cold or hot. Except the cues this time came from some small voice inside. Instinct, intuition, a hunch, one bit of information connecting with another and another until a new picture emerged.

Inside the bedroom now. At the bureau. Opening a drawer. *Cold.* Not in here. He moved to the nightstand next to the bed. Empty: Aline had cleaned it out. He pulled back the spread: the sheets and bedding had been stripped by forensics. He upended the mattress, looking for tears, holes, but couldn't find any. He stood quietly a moment, eyes closed again, waiting.

Still cold.

He turned forty-five degrees.

A little warmer.

His eyes opened, and he was staring at the closet.

Her clothes still hung inside, arranged in no particular order. She had favored bright, flashy outfits for work, not unlike what Fuentes had been wearing last night. He recognized some of the labels. Designer stuff, expensive, the kind of clothes women in the Cove wore. And there were probably enough shoeboxes and sweaters to match every outfit.

In the shoe department, in fact, she would've qualified as the Imelda Marcos of Tango. Kincaid dropped to his knees and went through the shoeboxes stacked against the wall. Some were empty, most were not. A real collector, this Regina ''Rikki'' Chamberlain.

When he was satisfied the shoeboxes contained nothing of

interest, he crawled into the closet, under the hems of dresses, the cuffs of slacks. He felt along the wall, nails digging under the carpeting, seeking a loose edge or corner. He found one, but when he pried the rug back, there was nothing except concrete block and carpeting tacks.

If Rikki had owned this place, if it had been a house instead of an apartment, a floor safe would've been more likely. But still, it felt right, so he jerked the rug back a foot from the wall on either side.

He didn't find a safe, but he knocked loose a piece of the wide baseboard. He pulled it the rest of the way off the wall and rocked back on his heels, grinning.

The hole it had covered was large enough to fit his fist into. He stretched out on his stomach, pulled his penlight from his shirt pocket, and shone the tiny beam inside. The hole was at least six inches wide, six deep, and four high. Something was pressed up against the back; he dug it out with the penlight. It was a drawstring bag as soft and gray as a dove, and inside was $5,000 in hundreds, a key with a number on it that looked like it fit a safety deposit box, a passport, and an appointment book.

Kincaid fixed up everything, so the closet was the way he'd found it, and walked into the bedroom, where there was more light.

The appointment book covered two years. At first the entries seemed so ordinary, he couldn't figure out why she'd bothered hiding the goddamn thing. *M for lunch. Nassau. M stays over. Work: 9–2. Party with N. Shoot video. Work: 4–12. Days Inn. M for dinner & show. Work: 9–2. Caicos. Pick up bks. Seamstress. Dentist. Days Inn. Send pub photos to Miami.* But as he kept paging through the months, he detected several patterns.

The Days Inn entries were always underlined in red. From November through the end of March, they fell on every Wednesday without fail and also appeared at least one other day of the week. After that, they stopped.

M probably stood for Manuel Ortega or Miranda and *N* was Nicolas Uvanti. So who was she meeting at the Days Inn? And why was that entry always starred? And how come the entries stopped at the end of March?

Another thing he noticed was that every four to six weeks without fail there was a Nassau or Caicos Islands entry, with a flight number and time under it. Sometimes the trips were made on holidays—Easter, for instance, Thanksgiving, Christmas, days when she would not have been working at Platinum's. When he picked up the passport to see if the dates coincided, he suddenly realized he was looking at a diplomatic passport. The picture inside showed a pretty brunette who looked exactly like the photograph of Rikki that Fuentes had shown him last night. The new and improved Rikki, after plastic surgery in a Swiss clinic.

He pulled out his wallet and withdrew the clipping from the *Miami Herald* that Meg had given him when they'd been digging through library files for information earlier. A photo of the old Rikki, the woman who'd vanished five years ago. He set it alongside the passport picture. The old and new Rikki looked alike only in the color of the eyes, a vibrant blue, mischievous, almost coy.

No wonder she'd felt anonymous enough to pursue a career on the tube, he thought, and flipped to the back of the passport. The entry and exit stamps here matched the dates for the Nassau and Caicos trips. The last one she'd taken was two weeks before she was killed, with another scheduled in late June.

He didn't know what the hell any of it meant, but he had a good idea where to start looking for answers.

The five grand, the appointment book, and the passport went into a pocket of his windbreaker, and he slipped the key inside his running shoe. He left by the rear stairs, where he wouldn't be noticed. But he never made it past the second landing. One moment he was trotting down the steps and the next moment something slammed him from behind and he was flying.

His arms shot out to break the fall, but it was too late. He crashed into the clutch of metal trash cans at the bottom of the stairs. Lids hurled loose. Cans toppled. The clattering din was the last thing he heard before his head struck the wall, knocking him out.

"On your feet, Kincaid."

"Leave me alone," he tells the voice.

"You're in deep shit, Kincaid, and it's about to get deeper. Now move, move, there isn't much time."

But his legs won't work, his arms hang uselessly at his sides, his fingers are frozen. "Help me," he says. "Something's wrong."

And suddenly the voice starts to cackle and the dark splits open, spitting out twin glowing red orbs. They dive straight for him like tiny fighter planes. They burn through his skin and

*burrow into his muscles, his bones and blood. He screams. The
scar on his belly ruptures, spewing chips of bone, of teeth, ragged strips of flesh. One of his eyes pops from his head and rolls
down his cheek like a tear. Part of his large intestine springs
from his gut, a jack-in-the-box. It slides down the inside of his
leg, and slithers off into the dark..*

*He lunges forward, grabbing for it, screaming for it, begging
it to come back, to return to where it belongs. The cackle shrills
from someplace deep inside him, a hideous keening, and then
teeth sink into his neck, tearing, sucking, drinking his blood,
and he screams again and tries to tear free, and his fingers snap
off, brittle as toothpicks and—*

He came to in the hallway where he'd fallen, arms thrashing,
head snapping right, left, spit and blood drooling from the corners of his mouth, his scar on fire. The fierce pounding in his
head slipped into his right temple as he pushed himself up to
his knees. He stayed like that for a moment, on all fours, the
stench of garbage rising in waves around him. When he lifted
his head, a silver tabby cat was sitting on the lowest step, gazing
at him with one amber eye; the other was the color of milk.
Kincaid rocked back on his heels and grabbed onto the edge of
the open door to steady himself.

It swung and he swung with it, stumbling out into the warm
alley, empty cans and bottles rolling down the steps in front of
him. He weaved about thirty feet and fell into the wall. He
leaned into it, clutching his stomach, the scar blazing and throbbing against his arm, and slowly sank to his knees in a patch of
grass.

After a while, he had no idea how long, he lifted his right
hand to his temple and felt the warm, sticky ooze of blood. A
lot of blood. Handkerchief, he thought. His fingers fumbled
with the zipper on the windbreaker's pocket. He found the hanky,
but realized the appointment book, passport, and five grand
were gone.

He sat down in the grass, hanky pressed to his temple, and
pulled off his right shoe. He felt almost giddy when the key fell
out. *Good, Ryan. A positive sign. Now all you have to do is get
your ass to the car.*

Shoe back on. Legs drawn up against him. Head resting
against his arms. The throbbing eased some and he slowly raised
his head. The silver tabby was directly in front of him now,
watching. An enchanted cat, he thought, and started to laugh,

but it hurt too much. The cat blinked; Kincaid blinked back. It evidently meant something to the cat because it strolled over and rubbed up against him, purring. It was a scrawny little thing with battle scars on its nose and head, the tip of one ear missing, ribs protruding, no collar.

"Gotta split, fella," he said softly, stroking the cat, then taking the hanky away from his temple.

Bright red blood. It had nearly soaked the handkerchief.

He struggled to his feet and inched forward, one hand against the wall as he made his way toward the end of the alley, the quickest route to where he'd parked the Saab. The tabby pranced along beside him like an escort, stopping when he stopped, moving when he moved, keeping pace with him, a shadow, a witch's familiar.

By the time he reached the Saab he felt better, but his head was still bleeding. The passenger door was unlocked, the keys were in the ignition, and the old *santera*'s egg talisman was gone. *Someone who knew enough to take it.*

But the little white pouch was still in the glove compartment, which had been locked, with the first-aid kit. Alcohol swab. Gauze. Tape.

Drops of blood warmed his eyelid. Christ oh Christ, the fucker had gotten him good.

He peered into the rearview mirror when he'd finished. Already, blood was seeping through the gauze. He knew what his next stop was going to be. He shut the passenger door and scooted behind the wheel. The cat purred at his ear.

Its cool, moist nose brushed his cheek.

"C'mon, fella, out. You can't come with me." He leaned over and opened the passenger door, pointing at the sidewalk. "Out."

The tabby climbed over the top of the passenger seat and settled down, that single amber eye watching him hopefully.

"Please?"

Blink, went the eye, and closed, knowing the issue was settled.

Kincaid shut the door, started the car and pulled away from the curb, his head bleeding, the stray cat purring with contentment beside him.

2

The door to Aline's office flew open five minutes after she'd arrived, and Bernelli charged in. Taffy eyes wide, blond hair mussed by the breeze, slender figure pressed into a denim skirt, cotton shirt, high-topped sneakers with pink socks. She plopped down in the chair in front of Aline's desk, lifted her feet onto the edge, and lit a cigarette, all before Aline had drawn a breath.

"*What* is going on?" The words rushed out in a cloud of smoke. "Penny gave me a rundown, but my God, I drive to Miami for the weekend so my parents can see my son, and the whole island unravels. Now quick. You got five minutes to fill me in before we meet with Mr. Clean and the rest of the tribunal." She jerked a thumb in the general direction of the conference room.

Aline passed her a sheet of paper that listed the pertinent facts on the case, such as they were. "I put this together, hoping you'd get back in time, Bernie. I feel like a witch about to face a trial where the verdict's already in."

But Bernie wasn't looking at the paper. She was gazing at Aline with eyes that possessed the knowledge of a friendship that went back twenty-five years. "You didn't, Al."

Aline knew exactly what she was referring to—Martell—and was instantly on the defensive. "So what if I did?"

"Knock it off, huh?" Bernie's feet slipped to the floor and she threw up her hands, cigarette burning between her fingers, ash growing by the nanoseconds. "How could I, Claudia Bernelli, possibly judge the wisdom or stupidity of your sleeping with Si Martell, especially in light of my own promiscuous past? As a matter of fact . . ." Her eyes darted around, seeking an ashtray. Aline sighed and pulled out the half shell she kept around for Bernie's butts and the chief's cigar.

"Thanks." Bernie tapped the ash into the shell. "As a matter of fact, Al"—she leaned forward, dropping her voice—"I was kind of curious if Si, you know, lives up to his reputation."

High school slumber party talk. "Yeah. He does."

A wry smile. "That's it? No details?"

"Bernie, you're a voyeur at heart."

"I know. Ain't it delicious?" She giggled, rubbed her hands together, and picked up the sheet. "Down to work." She scanned it, shook her head. "There's not much here."

"It's more than we usually have in less than forty-eight hours. What do you know about Chamberlain?"

Bernie stabbed out her cigarette. "Citrus. Bucks. Eight years in Congress. Fiscally conservative, liberal on social issues, hard-nosed on crime. A real mix. Besides Rikki, there's a son, and a fruitcake for a wife."

"A certified fruitcake?"

"Wouldn't surprise me. She's just one of these women who talks a lot and doesn't say much. Her big deal is fighting drugs. I caught her on Oprah a couple months back. She could use a facelift and a new hairdo. Too much Florida sun, you know. So what's the deal with this *santería* shit, Al? Is it for real?"

"I guess that depends on what you mean by real." Aline handed her another capsule of information and Bernie swallowed it, nodded, jotted some notes on the sheet of paper, looked up, a slight frown creasing her flawless skin. "September twenty-second is when the cop was killed back when?"

"Yeah." Something sour swelled in Aline's throat. She pushed a packet of papers across the desk. "There's everything I could dig out of the department's back files on the four murders. It follows pretty much what the priest told me." Detective Abel Whitkins, she said, was supposed to meet his anonymous caller around midnight on the last ferry off the island. He never showed up in Key West. His body was found in the hills two days after he disappeared. His brain had been surgically removed. The coroner said he had never been in the water and theorized that whoever killed him had probably gotten him off the ferry in the trunk of a car.

After his murder, no one would touch the case. It was still open.

"So you're saying you've been targeted just like Whitkins was?"

"I don't know. I don't even know for sure if there's going to be another murder. Maybe there won't be. Maybe there will be, but not until next year. In that case, my number won't be coming up for another four years."

"What'd the coroner's report on the dance-hall girl say? Are the knife wounds on the dance-hall girl and Rikki pretty close?"

"Yes. You think I'm being paranoid?"

"I think you're being too calm."

"But there's been no second murder."

"Not that we know about. Have you told Gene?"

"No, he's been with Chamberlain."

"If you're right, we might be able to use this to our advantage."

"Exactly."

"Doesn't Kincaid know a lot about *santería*?" Bernie asked.

"The chief hired him as a consultant."

"Uh-huh." She picked at her thumbnail. "At whose prodding?"

"Aw, hell. I felt sorry for him. Because or the IRS and all."

"Uh-huh." Bernie smirked, and Aline knew what *that* meant too.

"You're wrong."

"I'm right and you know it." She sat forward again, slender arms resting parallel to the edge of the desk. "It's like this, see. You love each other. Everything else is irrelevant."

Aline burst out laughing and got up, gathering the papers together. "Irrelevant to you, maybe. You're not the one who had to sleep with travel posters over her bed. You're not the one who had to know how long it takes to fly from New York to Auckland, New Zealand. You weren't the one who got deserted six months out of the year. And marriage wouldn't change any of that, Bernie."

Bernie rolled her eyes. "And on top of he's got no future, right?"

"Exactly. And by the way, he has amusements of his own, okay? Now c'mon, let's go meet Senator Clean."

Chamberlain was lean, handsome, well dressed, had thick white hair and expressive dark eyes. He really did resemble Fernando Lamas, until he opened his mouth. Instead of an accented, cultured voice that made you think of Spanish royalty, of high courts and women in satin, his echoed Jimmy Carter, but thicker, much thicker. It was backwoods Florida. It was moonshine and incest. It was straight out of *Deliverance*.

He sat to Chief Frederick's right, the afternoon light striking him from behind and spilling over the shoulders of his white suit. His clothes were impeccable. Tailored. Color-coordinated. As though he were dressed by his publicist. His hands were folded on top of a file. His unlit pipe lay on its side in an ashtray to his left. He stood and shook their hands when Frederick introduced them, and even flashed that famous smile TV cameras loved so dearly. But there was nothing behind it except white teeth; he was an utterly cold man.

"Gene has briefed me on what's transpired so far, and ah want you to know mah resources are at your disposal," he said in that long Southern drawl. "Before ah left Washington, ah contacted a friend of mine in the bureau who kindly provided a computer link and code which you can use to tap into their computer banks. If you require additional help, ah have two agents on call in the Miami office who can be here in an hour." He paused, his bushy brows rising, questioning.

"Right now, I think we prefer to handle it ourselves, Senator, although we'd like to use the computer link," Frederick replied.

His face remained inscrutable. "Of course. Whatever is easiest for you. Ah thought some background on mah daughter might help and—"

"Excuse me," said Aline. "But I'd like to know how you found out your daughter had been killed. I'm a little unclear on that."

"I still subscribe to the *Miami Herald*. The—"

"You couldn't possibly have recognized your daughter from that picture, Senator. She'd had plastic surgery since you'd last seen her."

Despite his polish, he looked a bit uncomfortable now. His fingers slipped up to the knot of his tie, loosening it. "Ah'd prefer not to get into it, because it's really not relevant to the case."

"*Anything* about this case is relevant." Frederick's voice was quiet, but terse.

Chamberlain thought a moment, then shrugged. "Ah still don't see that it has any bearing, but perhaps it'll help." Last Thursday, the D.C. office received a fax of an old picture of Rikki from the Miami office with an I.D. request, Chamberlain explained. A positive report was sent back to Miami early Friday morning, and he was notified by the Washington office. He was on a plane to Miami by Friday evening, trying to find out who had requested the I.D. All he was able to discover was that the request had originated on Tango Key. "Then when ah saw the picture in yesterday's *Herald*, ah knew it was mah daughter."

"How? She'd had plastic surgery."

Even the sadness in his smile was strained. "Ah might not have recognized her if it hadn't been for the tip from the bureau. But once ah saw the picture, it seemed obvious. Surgery didn't alter her eyes, Detective Scott."

"But she was still alive on Thursday."

"Uh, yes. Unfortunately, the Miami office doesn't have a

record of who sent the request, since it's done by department codes, or who received the positive I.D. But we believe it might be an agent who was removed from the case about five months ago and then took a leave of absence from the bureau."

Bernie asked why the agent was removed from the case. Chamberlain claimed he didn't know, which Aline rather doubted, but she let it slide. "So in other words the agent is still working on the case on his own?"

"Apparently."

"What's his name?"

"We're here to discuss the investigation of my mah daughter's homicide, Detective Bernelli, not an FBI agent who is no longer on the case."

Aline glanced at Frederick. His hair was just as white as the senator's, but that was where the resemblance between them ended. Frederick was thin, intense, often hot-tempered and demanding, but she couldn't imagine working under anyone else. When she'd started out in the department he'd been chief of homicide; now he was chief of police. And one of the things he did exceptionally well in that position was sway the opinions of people like Chamberlain. When he spoke, his voice was quiet and measured.

"Senator, the more information we have, the better equipped we'll be to find your daughter's killer. We need your cooperation."

This elicited a sigh from the senator; the shadow of quick assessments curled in his eyes. "Her name is Miranda Fuentes."

Kincaid's source. And his overnight guest. She didn't understand the connections, but she knew she was right. She didn't have much time to dwell on it, though, because Chamberlain launched into his prepared speech about his daughter.

Five years ago, he said, she was married to one of his aides, living in a lovely townhouse in Georgetown, and was active in community work, charities, fund-raising. He made it sound as if his daughter had been living the life of an American princess whose every desire, every whim, was fulfilled.

"And then one morning she just walked out of the house and didn't come back. Her car was abandoned at the railroad station. She took nothing with her, so of course we immediately thought she'd been abducted. But we didn't receive a ransom request. And when the bank notified us that the money in her trust had been gradually withdrawn until it was now depleted, we realized she had planned her disappearance."

"How much money?" Aline asked.

"About a hundred thousand. We suspect that at least half of that was used for her plastic surgery, in Switzerland." His pause, Aline thought, was for dramatic effect, so they'd have time to appreciate just how shrewd his daughter had been.

"Ah hired the best detectives money could buy, but nothing ever came of it. Then after ah was elected to the Senate, ah had some help from the bureau."

"No one ever heard from her?"

Chamberlain's eyes slipped toward Aline. They were hard and cold now, muddy stones that sat heavily in his cheeks. "Yes, ma'am, her husband received several letters from Europe in which she apologized and explained she needed to live her life her own way, that she wanted to pursue her dancing."

"And that's it?" asked Bernie. "There was never anything else?"

"No." His voice was dead calm. His fingers moved slowly along the edges of the file in front of him. "It practically destroyed our family. Mah wife had a breakdown. Mah son blamed me, and to this day we are not on good terms. Rikki's husband divorced her and remarried, but that marriage fell apart and so did his career. So you can see the toll of one young woman's selfishness and delusions is enormous."

Aline didn't particularly like the way the picture was shaping up. Chamberlain's search for his daughter didn't have much to do with concern or love or understanding. Rikki had offended and humiliated him, and he was unable to forget it, even now that she was dead. Aline was tired of listening to him.

She'd intended to expand on the *santería* angle for him, including what the priest had told her and what she'd dug from the old homicide files. But what was the point? Chamberlain's singular vision had afflicted him with a terrible myopia. The bottom line was that he simply wanted his daughter's killer found, and it didn't matter to him how it was done. If Frederick wanted to fill him in once she'd passed on the information, fine, let him. But she had nothing more to say.

The phone pealed, interrupting Chamberlain's monologue. Frederick answered it, and when his eyes flicked toward Aline, she knew what the call was about.

The second body had just been found.

16

I

"In my *head*? You have to shoot the Novocain in my head, Bill?"

Prentiss sighed. "Relax, okay? I numb the skin with something first and then I give you the shot. You won't even feel it. Your only other choice is no Novocain, and believe me, Ryan, without Novocain it's going to hurt like a son of a bitch when I stitch it up."

They were out on Prentiss's screened patio, next to the pool he'd put in when he and Bernelli had gotten married. A pleasant breeze flapped at the screen and carried the fragrance of roses and freshly mown grass from the yard. "You sure it needs stitches? Couldn't you just sort of press it back together with a bandage or something?"

"If you want me to do this, then you do it my way, Ryan, or drive yourself over to ER."

"Okay, okay."

Prentiss unsnapped his bag. "I think you've gotten more pigheaded over the years, Ryan."

"Only when it involves pain." He watched the silver tabby, who'd made herself right at home. One moment she was prowling the edges of the pool as though it were a lagoon in some marvelously wild place, and the next moment she was gobbling down more of the tuna fish and milk Prentiss had put out for her.

"What're you going to do with your little friend over there?" Prentiss asked as he worked.

"You could give her to Bernie for Christmas."

"We already have a dog and two rabbits, Ryan."

"I was afraid you were going to say that."

"Maybe Al would take her."

"I don't think Wolfe would be too thrilled about it. Ouch! Jesus, that burns."

"It's alcohol. I've got to clean this out. Sit still. Got any ideas who knocked you out?"

"None. It happened too fast."

"You going to inform the senator about the key and the rest of the stuff you found?"

"Not just yet. What're you putting on there now? It smells funny."

"This numbs it. You know how many times I've stitched you up in the last ten years, Ryan?"

"I don't keep count."

"Maybe you should."

They'd had this conversation innumerable times before: that Kincaid should get into a "less hazardous" profession and "settle down," as though marriage were synonymous with longevity. He wasn't even going to dignify Prentiss's remarks with a few of his own, because he knew what the response would be. Prentiss was as familiar with his and Aline's history as Kincaid was with Prentiss's and Bernie's. That sort of intimacy seemed to ride tandem with life on Tango.

Prentiss and Aline had always been close. They'd been born thirty seconds apart in the Tango hospital; he'd been her first lover. Kincaid and Bernie, on the other hand, had had a brief affair before he had met Aline.

Full circle.

And for him and Aline, perhaps it was a closed circle.

"Feel anything?" Prentiss asked.

"No."

"Good."

Kincaid watched as he threaded a rounded needle that looked like a medieval instrument of torture. He grimaced and glanced at the tabby again. She was chasing a leaf. "You sure the cat's a girl?"

"She's missing balls, Ryan."

"What do you think happened to her bad eye?"

"It looks like her retina is detached. She probably got a claw through it in a fight. Feel anything?"

"I'm numb from the nose up."

"So what're you going to call her?"

"I'm not keeping her."

"If you take her to the Humane Society, she'll be put to sleep in three days."

"I'll get Ferret to adopt her."

"Sure."

"She could be the mascot at Lester's Bar."

"Yeah."

"Maybe the Porters would take her. They've got plenty of space up at that lighthouse."

"They also have three dogs."

"Frederick likes cats."

"He's got four cats of his own."

"Shit."

Prentiss chuckled. "Okay, done. Six stitches. I'll need to see you in ten days to take them out."

The silver tabby was rolling over near his feet now, offering her tummy for a scratch. Prentiss looked at Kincaid, who sighed.

"Okay. I'll call her Unojo. One-Eye."

"The noble decision, Ryan."

An hour later, after dropping Unojo at home, feeding her, and changing his clothes, Kincaid strolled into the Tidy Laundromat in downtown Tango. It was hot and noisy inside, and the air smelled of soap and burned fabric. There were kids and moms and baskets of clothes everywhere. But he found Geneva Syncow where she usually was on Sundays, seated in one of the benches against the window, her nose buried in a book.

"Any good sex scenes?" he asked, stopping in front of her.

Her dark eyes flicked up, spitting fire, ready to do battle. Then she saw him and her grin dimpled her plump cheeks. "As a matter of fact, there *are* some sex scenes, Ryan, and I was going to make a crack about how you're going to get yourself belted one of these days. But it looks like someone already did it. What's under that bandage, anyway?"

"Six stitches. I fell into some garbage cans."

"Right," she laughed. "So what's today's fine question?" She patted the bench beside her and shut her book. He noticed it was Porter's newest one, *The Percy Parallel*, which he hadn't read yet.

"Any good?"

"His best."

"He thinks it's one of his worst."

"Well, he's wrong." Her hand vanished into her purse and came out with a bag of M&Ms. She tapped some into her palm and offered him the bag. He shook his head. "There's this man, see, John Percy, who creates a clone of himself who takes his place in his marriage, which has gotten awfully rotten and . . . well, anyway, I don't want to spoil it for you. So what's your question, sweetie? I know you don't make a habit of hanging out in laundromats."

Kincaid pulled out the small key from Rikki's apartment. "What's this look like to you?"

Geneva, who'd worked at Island Bank for fifteen of her thirty-seven years, rolled her eyes. "You're going to have to come up with tougher questions than that, Ryan. It's a key to a safety deposit box." She took it from him and turned it over in her palm. "One of ours, too."

"How do you know?"

"Ours are blue and red."

"Can you find out which box it fits? And look inside? I need to know what's in there."

She popped several M&Ms in her mouth and flicked her long, straight hair off her shoulders. "No can do, sweetie. We're talking major-league infraction, Ryan. I'd not only lose my job for a stunt like that, but I'd probably go to jail, too."

"It's important."

"It always is."

"Real important."

Her soft gray eyes crinkled at the corners. More M&Ms vanished into her mouth. "How well do you know Karl Porter, Ryan?"

"Well enough."

"Okay, I'll tell you what. If you get him to autograph this book, I'll see what I can do about this key. But I'm not promising anything. Like I said, I could get myself in deep trouble. Give me some details."

He did.

As she listened, she devoured the M&Ms, nodded her dark head, tapped her nails against *The Percy Parallel*. "Senator?" she interrupted. "Oh, dear. I don't know about this, Ryan."

"Please."

"Can't the cops do something? I mean, a safety deposit box is the same as a house. You get a search warrant."

"And then her old man would know about it. I want him kept out of this."

"Oh God," she groaned. "What I do for my friends. I hope you appreciate this, Ryan." She thought a moment. "Okay, let's see. I'll have to go in early Tuesday or stay late or something. But I'm not removing anything from the box."

"Why wait until Tuesday?"

"Because I have tomorrow off, and if I suddenly went in, it'd look weird."

"Just list the contents and if there's any written material, make copies."

"Copies," she repeated. "Shit. It'll *have* to be before or after hours then."

"Whatever's easiest for you."

"What would be easiest for me, Ryan, is not doing this at all."

He lured her away from that train of thought by suggesting that she meet him and Porter for drinks at the Moose some night.

"You're kidding."

"Do I look like I'm kidding?"

"Oh, God, what the hell would I *say* to him? I'd have to lose fifteen pounds first and get my hair cut and—"

"You're married, kid, remember?"

She gave an indignant sniff. "Really, Ryan, what's *that* got to do with anything? You're so provincial sometimes."

"Do we have a deal?"

She dropped the bag of M&Ms into her purse. "Oh, I suppose so. As long as you uphold your end of the bargain."

"That's what a deal is, Geneva."

She held out *The Percy Parallel*. "To Geneva, with love, okay?"

"You don't want to finish it?"

"I've got another copy at home. I always get two copies of his books, Ryan. One to read and a second just in case something happens to the first. For the collection, you know."

Of course.

"I'll phone Tuesday," she called after him. "And don't forget what the inscription's supposed to read." She giggled. "And if he wants to make it a little racy, that's okay too."

Kincaid laughed.

2

The park was in an ordinary neighborhood west of town where there had never been much crime. It was a place where young families and single people with ambitious dreams bought their first homes, investing in a future that seemed to promise everything. White, educated, middle-class. Teachers, secretaries, social workers, and nurses like Greta Manaccio, who had been found by another runner, a young man. He was leaning against a tree, and looked like he might have fallen over if it hadn't been there. And because he was nervous, he overexplained everything.

He'd known Greta casually, he said, because he saw her every morning on the track. They were usually the only ones out here before six, with Greta arriving ten or fifteen minutes before he did. On Sundays, though, he rarely ran and had come out here this morning since he knew he wasn't going to get to run tomorrow and he liked to get in a certain number of miles a week. He'd found her when a couple of squirrels were chattering up a storm over near the ditch.

"That's when I saw . . . her toes sticking up out of the leaves . . . and her hand . . ."

"And you called the police station right after that?" Bernie asked.

His right foot swung back, running shoe against the trunk, and he looked down for a second. "I brushed the leaves away first. I guess I just couldn't believe it was a body." He raised his eyes again. "Then when I realized it was Greta and that her throat had been . . . slit, I, like, lost it. I raced home to call the cops."

"What time does she usually run on days when she works?" Aline asked.

"She's out here by five fifteen at the latest."

"And you didn't hear any screams?"

"No. My air-conditioning was on. Everyone's been running the air. I bet no one heard anything."

Aline glanced over toward the ditch, where two of Prentiss's Skeleton Crew were lifting Manaccio's body onto a stretcher. She didn't want to take a look, didn't want to know for sure if the woman's Achilles tendon was gone. But she surrendered to her compulsion to do so as they were sliding the stretcher into the back of the ambulance.

She lifted the bottom of the sheet that covered Manaccio, raised the woman's leg, and stared at her feet. Everything blurred. The blanket of still, oppressive air clamped down over her, and her chest felt like it was filled with flaming rags, crushed glass, tiny daggers. Her eyes watered and burned, as if she'd stuck her face too close to a bottle of ammonia. She thought she might puke. Then her vision cleared and seemed preternaturally sharp. She could detect the tiny highways of lines that ran through the dry blood on the right sole and the clean, precise incisions that sliced vertically on either side of the heel, and its horizontal counterparts. Bloody tissue filled the hole where part of the woman's Achilles tendon had been removed.

Fingers, a tendon, eyes, a brain.

She let the leg drop. Jerked the sheet over the woman's feet again. Slammed the door to the van. Stepped back. She distanced herself, waiting for her breath to return to normal, for her heartbeat to settle.

People of particular professions or with particular talents chosen apparently at random, following a pattern of murders that had taken place more than fifty years ago, she thought. Dancehall girl: stripper. Ex-Olympic runner: jogger. Palmist: psychic? *santero*? another palmist? What? What was the eighties equivalent of a palmist? *And what's the eighties equivalent of a homicide detective?*

Easy. A homicide detective. A weird laugh bubbled in her throat and she pressed the back of her hand to her mouth and stared at the blank white rear doors of the ambulance.

May 25.

September 22.

Follow Ortega and you'll have it.

Maybe.

"Al?"

Bernie stopped alongside her. "I talked to Manaccio's next-door neighbor." She gestured toward a woman standing next to the young man who'd found Greta. "She saw her last night around eleven thirty. Manaccio was just getting home from the three-to-eleven shift at the hospital, and the neighbor was out walking her dog. They talked a few minutes. Manaccio was complaining about having to work seven to three today because she was filling in for someone else. She said she was still going to run at the usual time. Five fifteen.''

"So what I need to ask Ortega is where he was between five and . . . what time does it get light?''

"Six thirty or so.''

"Okay. Six thirty. And you know what he's going to tell me? That he was at home, sleeping, and how am I going to disprove that?''

"You're not.'' Bernie lit a cigarette and blew the smoke up, up toward the trees, the patches of sunlight. "But if we tail his ass from now through the twenty-fifth, maybe we can prevent the third murder from happening.''

And the fourth? Can we prevent that one, too? Huh? Can we, Bernie?

17

Ortega dreamed of the Cuba he had never seen. He dreamed of soft green hills and fields of sugarcane, of women in white summer dresses and outdoor cafes, and it was in one of those cafes that he saw Rikki floating toward him in a plaza, her hair a dark cascade behind her, arms outstretched, mouth forming his name. He leaped up from his table, his chair toppled, and he raced across the busy Havana street, shouting for her. But when she neared, he could hear her sobbing, *Why, Manuel? Why did you kill me?* The knife was sticking out of her, she was covered in blood, and she lurched forward, toppling into him—and melted right through him.

He spun and she was sprawled there against the cobblestones, blood pooling around her. He slipped his arms under her, whispering to her, explaining that she and his other pretty *gringa* were special, they were chosen. Her head snapped up and her eyes rolled back in her head until only the whites showed, glowing like damp full moons. *He'll betray you, he'll betray you, betraybetray*, and then she threw her head back and laughed and laughed and began snapping her fingers off at the knuckles and hurling them at him.

Eat them, Manuel. Eat my fingers.

One struck him in the cheek and penetrated the skin, and he pulled on it and couldn't get it out. He felt its nail digging into his gums, loosening his teeth, growing longer and longer as it burrowed up through the roof of his mouth, toward his brain. He felt it split in two like a piece of wood, and one sharp splinter inched toward his eyes while the other continued a slow, painful spiral through his sinuses.

Eyes, Manuel? Are you going to take the woman's eyes? And

the other woman's brain? Are you? Hmm? Do you like how that feels, Manuel? Are you going to watch your padrino kill those women like he killed me? Hmm?

He cried and pleaded and clawed at his cheek, trying to grab the finger. *Don't worry, Manuel,* said *Padrino. I will take care of everything. Haven't I always taken care of everything? Believe in me, Manuel. Believe in the power of Ikú.*

Believebelieve, he chanted.

Betraybetray, whispered Rikki.

And he came to in his bedroom, the voices swirling around him, calling to him, each voice demanding that he listen, pay attention, that he do this, do that, and the phone was ringing and he didn't know what day it was and his head was burning up with fever.

He fell back against the pillow, tasting blood in his mouth and sinuses and a deep throbbing pain in his cheek. The phone kept pealing. He snatched it up.

"*Dígame,*" he rasped.

"It's me."

Betrayer, whispered Rikki.

"*Dígame.*" He pressed the heel of his hand against his eyes and tried to block out the soft chant of her voice in his head. But he couldn't. She was part of him. And even now he felt the other woman, the runner, stirring inside him, weeping because she couldn't run.

"Hey, Manuel, wake up," *Padrino* said sharply.

"I'm awake."

Betrayer.

Why can't I run?

Betray—

Why—

"Are you still sick?"

Have I been sick? Yes. Of course. He was sick now. He vaguely recalled Seroz giving him aspirin, taking his temperature, Seroz fussing over him like a mother.

"I still have a fever."

And inside the bright haze of the fever, he saw himself and *Padrino* in Rikki's VW that night, in the woods, fixing the gunpowder to her thighs, part of the symbolic offering to Ikú. He heard *Padrino* chanting softly in the ancient tongue as he blew cigar smoke over Rikki's body, sprayed her with rum and Florida water. Ortega smelled the stink of her blood thickening in the car as *Pa-*

drino's chanting grew more frenzied, as he began to tremble, to shake, as his eyes rolled back in his head and Ikú possessed him.

And that was when the unspeakable thing happened, when *Padrino* fell on top of Rikki and pumped inside her and . . .

"*Manuel, wake up,*" *Padrino* snapped.

Ortega rubbed his eyes, almost hating the man on the other end of the phone. "I'm awake," he said flatly.

"Are you alone?"

"Yes."

"Wrong, Manuel. Get the portable phone and walk out into the yard and look through that hole in the fence. Go on, get the goddamn portable."

He did, and threw off the sheet and reached for the shorts on the old rocker under the window. His *abuelita* had given him the rocker before she died—and the house after she died. Funny, that he should think of her now, that old blind woman rocking, rocking, her knitting needles clicking together like false teeth.

He looked around for his thongs but couldn't find them. He hated going outside barefoot. You never knew what sort of things were in the grass. Parasites no larger than an atom. Germs. Microbes that ate flesh.

"Why don't you just tell me what's outside," he said into the portable phone.

"Go look."

Firm. Commanding.

Betraybetray
Why can't I run?

"Shut up," he hissed to the voices inside him. "Shut up."

He opened the sliding glass doors in his bedroom and stepped out onto the concrete stoop. A bright, sunny day. *Which day?* Already hot. *Is it summer yet?* The light lanced through his eyes.

"I don't want to step onto the grass without my shoes," he told *Padrino*.

"What?" He exploded with laughter, and Ortega's humiliation was quick and intense, a wild heat.

"*Chíngate,*" Ortega spat, and slammed his thumb against the OFF button, disconnecting them.

He set the phone down and stared at the fence.

He couldn't see the hole, but he knew where it was. He had carved it when he was five years old, during a hot summer afternoon when he'd been visiting his *abuelita*. He'd been using a pair of old scissors and a butcher knife he'd stolen from the kitchen, and he'd carved it so he could watch what went on in the street.

Nothing had changed in all those years, not really.

Betray—

Why can't I—

No. Some things had changed.

He looked down at the grass, grimaced, stepped down onto it, and hurried across it to the fence. He crouched and pressed his eye to the hole.

The phone rang; he ignored it.

His eyes slipped left, right, left again. Ah. There. Parked under the folds of the ceiba tree at the corner. A white car. Maybe a Ford. He saw two shapes in the windshield, but couldn't make out who they were, whether they were male or female, but it didn't matter because he knew they were police.

Following me.

For how long?

What's the date?

Monday.

No, Jesus, not Monday. He had gotten sick Monday. The lack of sleep the day before had done it. The anticipating, the planning, the worry. These things had made him ill. He had stayed home on Monday. Seroz had opened the shop.

Then today is Tuesday.

No, that wasn't right either. On Tuesday, he and Seroz had argued about the shop. He recalled this clearly. They had argued because Seroz wanted out of the business and Ortega didn't have the money to buy him out. They were stuck together, he and Seroz, like an old married couple whose affection for each other had soured over the years. He knew this had happened on Tuesday because during the argument Seroz had reminded him the shop closed at nine that night and they were always open until nine on Tuesday and Saturdays, and today could not be Saturday because then . . .

He squeezed his head between his hands and shut his eyes tightly and felt the rough wood against his forehead.

The police are following me.

Ikú would protect him.

The police are suspicious.

Of course they were. He knew this would happen. They had known from the beginning that it would happen. But he had an alibi.

That gringa cop.

He stood slowly and made his way back across the grass, through the hot sun, toward his bedroom. The phone was ringing again. He picked up the portable and held it to his ear, listening.

"Manuel?"

"I saw the car."

"We're going to have to change our plans."

"We need protection. First we need protection."

Betrayer, hissed Rikki.

I can't run, wailed the runner.

"I have a plan, Manuel."

"What kind of plan?"

"Ikú needs to be fed."

Ortega felt lightheaded with relief, because of course *Padrino* was right. Ikú was hungry. If they fed him, he would make things better. This was the way.

"When?"

"I'm not sure. It depends on how long they watch you. What they suspect."

Betray betray—

"No. It will only make the police more suspicious of me."

"You don't have to do anything. I'll do it. You watch. You help. You drive. But you don't have to do anything. This is *my* test."

He hurt. He burned. He wanted to lie down and go to sleep and dream of the Cuba he had never seen and let *Padrino* take care of everything. "Yes, okay. Your test. Call me later. Good-bye."

Good-bye, good-bye, laughed Rikki.

But when he blinked, he was still holding the phone and he heard *Padrino* saying, "Manuel? It will be someone we don't know. We've never met. And not on the island."

"Yes. Fine. I must go now." He switched off the portable and rushed into the bathroom and washed his hands again and again, first with soap, then with Clorox, then with hot water again. He fell back onto the bed, shivering, his teeth chattering, hands grappling for the covers.

Manuel, mí amor, said his *abuelita*.

Ortega turned his head toward the rocker and saw his *abuelita* sitting there, rocking, knitting, her white head bowed. "You're dead," he said softly.

And she lifted her head and her lips drew back and her skin smoked as it burned away from her face, and she laughed in Rikki's voice and said, "And so are you, Manuel. So are you."

He hurled the portable phone at her and it smacked the wall, bounced off, hit the floor, and the empty chair rocked.

Rocked slowly.

"Manuel?"

Go away. Ortega drew the sheet over his head. *Go away.*

"Manuel?"

"Estoy aquí." He threw the cover off his head. *"Que quieres, Jaime?"*

Seroz stopped in the bedroom doorway. Against the light in the hallway behind him, he looked like a squat, plump seal who was about to clap his hands in front of him and waddle wetly into the room. But he stayed where he was, as though he didn't want to get too close to the bed for fear of catching whatever Ortega had.

"Do you need anything?"

Peace, thought Ortega.

"No."

"Should I fix you something to eat?"

"No. No, thank you. I will get something later."

"Call me at the store if you want anything."

"Yes." *Go away now, Jaime.*

"Do you think you'll be able to work tomorrow?" He moved a little farther into the room now, smoothing a hand over his balding head. "I have things I need to attend to."

Ortega pushed up on his elbows. "If I feel better, I will be there. Otherwise close the store."

The foot of the bed dipped as Seroz sat down. His hand slipped over the white spread, straightening it, and his glasses slid down on his nose. "We need to talk, Manuel."

"Now? We have to talk now?" Ortega's voice rose a decibel, and he saw Seroz wince. "About what? What is so important that it can't wait?"

"About the *store*."

The store the store: the words echoed in Ortega's head, made his temple pound. "What about the store?"

Seroz's face turned bright pink. "What is *wrong* with you? I've told you four times that I want out of the business, Manuel. I want you to buy me out."

It seemed they had had this conversation before, but maybe he'd dreamed it. Yes, of course. A dream. Otherwise he would've remembered it. "I don't understand. Why—"

"I *told* you why." He was pacing around the room now, and

Ortega got dizzy watching him. "But you don't listen, Manuel. You hear only what you want to hear. You're involved in dangerous things, and I will not be a part of such evil. I . . . I look at you and I no longer know who you are or what you are becoming." He stopped next to the bed and gazed down at Ortega with his small, dark eyes. "Do you understand what I am saying? Are you listening to me? Are you *hearing* me?" He leaned over, his pink face so close to Ortega's that he could smell Seroz's breath, a faintly sour smell, of old coffee, smoke. *"I know,"* he whispered.

What was he talking about? What did he know? Was he talking about Rikki? How could he possibly know about her? "I don't feel good. Go away. Leave me alone."

He rolled away from Seroz and slipped down under his covers, into his cool white sheets, his pure sheets, seeking the dream of Cuba. But Seroz yanked the covers off him. "You think I'm *stupid*, Manuel? You think I don't know what you're doing? You think I know nothing about Bacalao? About Ikú? About the darkness in you? I can *smell* it on you, Manuel. I can *smell* it. And if *I* can, then the police can also. Do you hear me? That detective has been into the store, asking where you were early Sunday morning, Manuel. I told her you were here, because that's what I thought. I thought you were here sleeping. But now I am no longer sure, Manuel."

Ortega shivered in the cold air and drew his knees up against him and shut his eyes. "Go away," he whispered.

Some time later, he didn't know how long, a chilly finger slid down his spine and he rolled over and glanced at the rocking chair. There was his *abuelita* again, cackling, laughing. *Blood on your hands, Manuel. Blood on your hands, look at your hands, do you see the blood? Do you, mi amor?*

He leaped out of bed and ran into the bathroom and turned the water on as hot as he could stand it and thrust his hands into it. Blood swirled pink down the drain, but as soon as he washed it off, there was more of it, always more, and now the voices returned, Rikki's and his pretty little *gringa's*, *Betray betray, I can't run*, and his *abuelita* cackling, *Blood, blood.*

He poured Clorox into his hands, spreading it up to his wrists, and then used soap again. But the bleeding didn't stop until he scrubbed with Comet. Then he stumbled back into the bedroom, his face burning, burning, the skin on his hands as wrinkled as prunes but clean.

Pure. Uncontaminated.

18

I

At nine A.M. sharp, Kincaid saw Geneva Syncow's bright yellow Buick pull up to the curb across the street from the Tango Cafe. She was two days late because she had "run into problems," as she'd told him over the phone. But what the hell. Few things in his life ever worked according to any schedule he set up, so why should this be any different?

She breezed through the door in a white cotton suit, white sandals clicking against the tile floor, and spotted him at a booth near the rear of the cafe. As she joined him, she tipped her sunglasses back into her hair, brought her fingertips together just under her chin, and without preface said, "I believe in omens, Ryan. Did I ever tell you that?"

Oh oh. "I don't even get a good-morning?"

"I'm not so sure how good it is."

"How about breakfast?"

"I'm fasting."

"What for?"

She sighed. "To lose thirty pounds, Ryan. Not because I enjoy it."

"Coffee?"

"Unless you have something stronger. A lot stronger."

"The suspense is going to kill me, Geneva. What the hell happened?"

"Happened today? Yesterday? Where would you like me to start, Ryan?"

"With coffee. We'll start with coffee." He signaled the wait-

178

ress, who brought over a pot and mugs and left. "There was nothing in the box? Is that what you're trying to tell me?"

She let out a short, clipped laugh. "Ha. Tuesday, see, I got to the bank a little early, so I could scoot upstairs where the safety deposit boxes are kept, right? But the old biddy who takes care of that department had also come in early, so I couldn't do anything. 'This means something, Gen,' I told myself. 'This is significant.' I wasn't about to do anything with her up there, so I went back downstairs and called you. Right after that, my boss walks over and drops the morning *Herald* on my desk. The story on Rikki Baker being Senator Chamberlain's long-lost daughter is circled in red. He says he needs everything we've got on her because the senator has requested it."

"How'd he know where she banked?"

"Way I heard it is that he made official requests of every bank on Tango. And that's eight banks, Ryan. We got more banks on this island than we do churches. So yesterday I spent the entire day calling up everything on the computer having to do with Rikki Baker's accounts, and didn't get into the safety deposit box until last night."

"And?"

"Hold on. I'm getting to that. Bear with me. I went through her checking and savings and money market accounts. I didn't mention the safety deposit box because there was no record that she'd rented one. Which means it was *very* difficult finding out which box this goddamn key belonged to." She slapped the little key on the table. "Difficult, Ryan, not impossible. But I'll get to that in a second." Her plump hand dropped into her purse and returned to the table with a computer printout. "Rikki Baker's banking history, Ryan, has some *very* interesting things about it."

The woman's pay from Platinum's, after taxes, amounted to about thirty grand a year. Once a month there were additional cash deposits of between five and eight hundred, which Geneva figured were tips. "Even if she'd been making a grand a month in tips, Ryan, her total income would be around forty thousand, give or take."

"You're the numbers whiz."

"I don't mind telling you, Ryan, this one challenged me. I tallied up every check she'd written in the last year, went through her savings and money market statements, and what I found was that everything tallied to the penny. She was living precisely

within her means, saving X percentage of her income, spending
Y percentage. It was as neat and comprehensible an accounting
as the IRS would like from all of us. It was too damn perfect.
No car payments, credit cards promptly paid off every month,
and *no* checks made out to department stores, Ryan. That's what
really got me; it was just too unlikely for any woman who's got
a wardrobe like she did—''

"Wait a minute. You *knew* her?''

"I'd seen her waltz into the bank enough times to know who
the hell she was, yeah. And her clothes, Ryan, were straight out
of shops in the Cove. *Real* expensive numbers. You expect *large*
balances on credit cards for those kinds of clothes. Either that
or you know the woman's hubby is pulling in five million a year.
So I stayed late last night, and after the biddy had left I went
upstairs and spent an hour trying to figure out which box the
key fit.''

"And?''

"I found it. Box three fifty-two. It was rented two years ago
by Regina Chambers. Chamberlain, Chambers, get it? Very
close. There was another name listed on the box when she rented
it, but it had since been removed. Nicolas Uvanti, of R.D. number three, in the boonies outside the Cove. Inside the box was,
hmm, let me get this figure exactly right.'' She slipped on a pair
of glasses and flipped through the printout. "Ah. Okay. Here it
is. Eighty-two thousand, six hundred and fifty dollars. Nice
round figure, don't you think, Ryan?''

"Does Uvanti bank at—''

"No. I checked.'' She unclipped a scrap of paper from the
top of the printout. "This is a copy of a ledger sheet that was in
the box.'' She turned it toward him, red nail sliding down the
list of figures and dates. "She was keeping tabs on just how
much money was in here. The deposits started a little over a
year ago, with six thousand, and were made once a month there-
after.''

Kincaid glanced at the dates. Although he couldn't recall the
exact trip dates that had been in Rikki's appointment book and
stamped in her passport, he remembered some of the trips had
taken place on holidays. Thanksgiving and Christmas of last
year, for instance. The corresponding ledger entries fell within
five days of both those trips. Close enough. In fact, if he had to
take a wild guess at what all this meant, it looked like Rikki had
been using her doctored diplomatic passport to import or export

something for Uvanti in or around Nassau and the Caicos, and had been paid handsomely for it.

And maybe, just maybe, she had wanted out, but was afraid of what Uvanti might do to her. So she'd gone to Ortega for protection. But what was she bringing into or taking out of the country? Drugs? Dirty money? The Caicos were the Swiss banks of the Caribbean; the Bahamas were a favorite spot with the Medellín Cartel. He and Aline had found coke and grass in Rikki's apartment, but hardly enough to qualify for anything more than recreational use. That didn't rule out drugs as a possibility, but the more Kincaid thought about it, the likelier it seemed that Uvanti would be involved in money laundering rather than drugs, and had killed Rikki because she knew too much.

And the *K* on her negligees could stand for Koko, Uvanti's nickname.

But if he'd killed Rikki, then he had also killed the runner; both women's injuries were too specific to be coincidental. *If* his theory was correct, then Rikki's death had accomplished two things for Uvanti: silenced her and marked the beginning of some ritualistic reach for power that Uvanti believed would culminate on September 22, with the death of the detective in charge of the case.

Aline.

Perhaps Uvanti had had another goal in mind when he'd killed Rikki: to frame Ortega for the murder, thus evening the score between them for Rikki, for Ortega stealing Rikki's affections.

It seemed plausible, even though he sensed some pieces were missing.

But hey, no problem, he'd figure it out. His luck, after all, had changed. The bad cycle had ended Sunday evening, when Ferret turned over his track winnings, $7,500 and change, enough to get him through until the IRS released his accounts.

"What're you going to do with all this?" asked Geneva.

"Talk to Aline and see what she wants to do. She's the cop."

Geneva looked dubious and sat forward, a corner of her mouth dimpling. "I *know* you better than that, Ryan." She slid the printout across the table to him. "I know you so well, in fact, that I'm going to entrust this to you. But if you *ever* show it to anyone in a position to figure out it came from me, I'll mess your credit up so bad, Ryan, you won't be able to buy dog food on Visa."

He laughed. "My lips are sealed."

"Fine. Now where's my autographed book?"

"In the car. I'll go get it." A white lie, he thought, glancing at his watch, but Geneva would love him for it in about five minutes.

Although it was still early, the air outside was hot and sultry, heat quivering inches above the pavement. He retrieved *The Percy Parallel* from the front seat, and as he locked the Saab again, Porter's red Porsche pulled up behind him. He hopped out, looking tan and fit and a far sight better than when Kincaid had last seen him at Lester's Bar on Saturday.

"This is the first time I've ever done a one-book signing, Ryan, I want you to know that."

"That's why breakfast is on me. I appreciate it. Really. She's helping me out on something, and the condition was your autograph. She buys two of everything you write, Karl."

"*Two?* Christ, for that I'll buy *her* breakfast *and* yours. So what're these stories you've got for the book?"

"I've lined up a local *santera* who'll talk to you, and there're some twists on the Baker case that you can include."

"From what I've been reading, it sounds like the twists are all political." They rounded the corner, out of the shade and into the sunlight. "I always felt there was something about her that didn't figure."

"I didn't realize you knew her." Kincaid glanced at Porter as he said it and caught the quick something that shadowed his eyes—fear, sadness, perhaps surprise. He wasn't sure what it meant. Maybe nothing.

"I saw her dance a couple of times." Porter's slow smile hinted at the weirdness of sitting in a smoky room, in a private booth, watching a woman undress onstage as though she were doing it for you, just for you. "So in that sense I guess you could say I knew her. You got the feeling when you watched her dance that she knew exactly what she was doing not only with her body but with her life." He stopped at the newspaper vending machine, fed a quarter into the slot, and plucked out today's edition of the *Tribune*. "You ever catch her act?"

"No. But I hear Uvanti has some interesting videos of some of her private acts."

"That's about his speed."

And then they were inside the cafe and Porter was asking where she was, where this wonderful fan of his was who bought two copies of everything he wrote. Kincaid nodded toward her and handed Porter the book he was to autograph. The air around him changed instantly, bristling with an ineffable something that was Porter onstage, smiling, charming, as handsome as a movie star.

Kincaid hung back, watching, admiring Porter's smoothness, his apparent sincerity as he introduced himself to Geneva, shook her hand, and slid into the booth across from her. The public Porter looked like a man on top of the world, at the pinnacle of his success, a man whose life worked.

His act was so convincing, Kincaid almost believed it.

2

Aline's office was shaped like and old-fashioned keyhole, round at the front, where it curved to a rectangular window that jutted out over the street two stories below. The window ran from floor to ceiling and offered a magnificent view of the city park.

On days like this one, when the tinted glass fractured bright sunlight, the window seemed almost enchanted, a window in a fairy tale, a place where Rapunzel might've sat, her hair falling to the street below, where her lover waited. Never mind that Rapunzel was the worst kind of fool, pining away in her tower, waiting for her lover to rescue her, doing nothing to change her own circumstances. The lure of the story lay in the separation of the lovers, in the ladder of hair he climbed to her tower, in the shearing of that hair by her bad-assed father. So what if Rapunzel was as insipid as most of the heroines in fairy tales? There were some curious parallels between her story and Rikki Baker's, and one important difference: Rikki had escaped.

Everything she'd done from that point on had been motivated by her singular goal to remain free. Perhaps, in the end, that was really what had killed her. The question was who had carried it out. Ortega? Uvanti? Both of them? Uvanti and someone other than Ortega? Mr. X and someone else they knew nothing about?

Two cops from another department had been tailing Ortega since Sunday night, while she and Bernie had concentrated on

Uvanti. But so far the trails were dead. Ortega hadn't left his house, and Uvanti had bounced back and forth between his club, his yacht, and his home in the Cove, Quasimodo always tight at his side.

Other leads had also turned out to be dead ends. Ferret had been unable to discover the name or the address of the woman whose house Rikki was supposed to keep an eye on while she was gone for the summer. All right, so it probably wasn't even important. But suppose it was? Suppose it was as vital as the embroidered initials on Rikki's negligees?

Another dead end. According to Linda Drewson, the snob at the lingerie shop, Rikki Baker had placed the order for the embroidery on her negligees. No mystery at all.

Then there was the manager at the Days Inn, who'd informed Aline she would have to get a court order before he'd turn over the computer printouts on who stayed at the hotel and when. He did, after all, believe in the right to privacy, and why should he make an exception for her just because she was a cop? Martell was going to take care of the court order, but no telling when that would come through. So here she was, with only two days between now and May 25, and no closer to answers. Even Kincaid's call a few minutes ago hadn't provided answers, only more questions. A spiral of questions, she thought, each level more impenetrable than the one before it.

She reached into her shirt pocket and pulled out the small white bag Kincaid had given her. *It's like a rabbit's foot, Al. Think of it that way. For luck.* Parsley, garlic, and camphor: the stuff of vampire stories. She felt silly carrying the damn thing—until she thought of the hideous jar that had been on Kincaid's mantel that had contained a mass of hair and chips of bone and teeth. Tangible proof of a *santero*'s revenge. The inexplicable medical oddity. The dreadful proof that a world so many people relegated to ignorance and superstition possessed a frightening reality. So she carried the white bag even thought it stank up her clothes and her purse and the inside of her car.

"What you need is a night off." Martell strolled into her office, looking dapper and very attorneylike in a three-piece suit.

"Tempt me with something, Si."

"Can you get off by four?" He shut the door behind him, and she watched him stride across the room as her fingers played with the tie on the white bag.

"Unless something comes up."

"We could sail over to Palm Key and have a sunset cookout. Fresh fish on the beach."

"Yeah?" She smiled as his face came a little closer. "And make it an early night? I've got surveillance at eight tomorrow."

"Perfect. I've got to see Judge Lawrence about the court order at eight thirty. He promised he'd have it." Martell took the white bag out of her hands, set it on her desk, and touched her chin as he kissed her. His mouth was cool, light, barely brushing hers. But it stirred a slow heat inside her, that same strange, almost languid desire she'd come to anticipate with him. "White Linen, right?" he asked when he moved away.

"No more Opium for me." Not since the old *santera* had told Kincaid how her stolen Opium might be used in a *santería* ritual.

"I like it. I like it a lot better than this." He picked up the white bag and made a face. "This reminds me of a pizza parlor or a kid who's got the flu, Al."

"Thanks a lot."

He untied the bag, opened it, tapped some of the contents into his hand. Flakes of garlic, leaves of parsley, and flecks of camphor fluttered into his palm. "I don't know, Allie." He shook his head as if to say it was all beyond him. "Just because some daffy woman gives it to Kincaid, you start carrying it around. Personally, I think it has more to do with him than with her."

"What it has to do with, Si, is two homicides. Now will you please put the stuff back in the bag?"

He did, and chuckled as he stood. "Sometimes you're real predictable." He ruffled her hair as if she were a child who'd just said or done something mildly amusing.

She jerked her head back. "Cut it out."

"See you at the marina at four."

If you're lucky, she thought, staring holes through his back as he opened the door and left.

3

During the tourist season, business along the Tango boardwalk bristled. You could rarely find a seat at one of the outdoor cafes, prices were hiked up, bikes were prohibited. But this was mid-week in May and it was a different world altogether, Kincaid thought, more like the boardwalk of his youth.

Kids whizzed past on their bikes, the hard-core sunbathers had the beach nearly to themselves, and most of the people seated at the outdoor tables were shop employees on their afternoon breaks. He recognized a handful of tourists who'd probably arrived for the eclipse on the third. The sky was clear, the sea a plateau of blue glass. With little effort he could imagine how it would look from three thousand feet up. He could almost see the smallness of everything, the way colors blended, the merging of shapes, the creation of new patterns.

And it was new patterns he sought now, as some part of himself processed and refined what he had learned this morning and gradually integrated it with what he had already known about Uvanti, Ortega, Rikki Baker. Eventually, probably when he wasn't thinking about any of this, a fresh idea would surface. It would be so clean, so unsullied, so simple, he would wonder why he hadn't seen it before. And from that point on, his path in the investigation would diverge.

Or at least that was how it worked in theory.

All too often, though, nothing happened. The old assumptions just wouldn't let go, and he got mired in them. That was what had gotten him into trouble in the *santería* case in Miami six years ago. His neat theories about *santería* as so much mumbo jumbo had made him myopic, and that myopia had nearly killed him.

In this case, what he refused to see might kill Aline.

He spotted Bernelli about three hundred yards before he reached Platinum's. She was seated at one of the outdoor tables, dressed like a tourist in white shorts, a haltar top, sandals, sunglasses, a magazine open in front of her. From where she was, she had a clear view of the club's two doors—front and alley.

He came up behind her, leaned over, and whispered, "Just who're you fooling, Bernie?"

Her head jerked back, and she peered up at him. "Very funny, Ryan. You just scared me into next week, you know."

"I guess Uvanti's inside."

"Uvanti," she said, poking her sunglasses higher on the bridge of her nose, "hasn't done a bloody interesting thing for the last four days. The only change in his routine is who he takes home for the night. You going to sit down or what, Ryan?"

"Don't want to blow your cover."

"You'll be good for my cover."

Kincaid laughed and pulled out one of the aluminum chairs. "That might be the nicest thing you've said to me in five years, Bernelli."

She tipped her sunglasses down low on her nose and gazed at him over the rims, those taffy eyes watching him like a cat's. "Contrary to what you believe, Ryan, I happen to like you, despite your drawbacks as husband material for Al."

"Truce." He held up his hands. "I've already heard all this."

"I was just going to say I never understood what the hell the big deal was. I mean, it's not beyond arriving at an equitable arrangement, Ryan. While you traveled and romanced honeys in Nepal and wherever, Aline would be free to pursue her own life here. A calculated risk, granted, but maybe neither of you is really cut out for monogamy."

"Monogamy was never the issue."

Oh? said her raised brows. "Well, it is now."

The remark had its intended effect, and its meaning was abundantly clear: Aline had told her about his company last Sunday. He started to change the subject when he saw Miranda Fuentes sail out the front door of Platinum's as if she couldn't get away quickly enough. No glitz for Fuentes today. She was strictly pedestrian in tight jeans and high-topped sneakers, lustrous hair pulled back in a loose ponytail.

She paused on the boardwalk, slipped on her sunglasses, and walked off quickly in the other direction, hips swaying. She moved with purpose, like a woman who was supposed to be someplace other than where she was.

"Catch you later, Bernie." He left before Bernelli could ask any questions.

Kincaid followed Fuentes at a distance of two or three hundred yards. When she ducked into a phone booth near the end of the boardwalk, he stepped into a shop's doorway, keeping an eye on her through the display window. She remained inside for nearly four minutes, and as she stepped out she dropped something into her purse. She continued to the end of the boardwalk and turned left, headed toward the alley that ran parallel to it. She was probably on her way to the public parking lot where many of the boardwalk employees left their cars.

He hurried after her but turned several buildings sooner, down a narrow, shadowed breezeway, so he would come out behind her. But before he reached the end of it, he heard her footsteps coming toward him. He hunkered down behind a garbage can until she passed, then crept to the corner of the building, keeping her in sight.

She went past Platinum's, her blond head as luminous as a moon in the alley's shadows, and Kincaid followed again, maintaining a safe distance. About a mile down the boardwalk, directly across the alley from Aline's bookstore, she stopped at a navy blue Jetta, unlocked it, slid behind the wheel. Kincaid waited until the Jetta had vanished down one of the side streets toward Route 2, then sprinted toward the Whitman's lot, where he'd left the Saab.

It didn't take him more than sixty seconds to reach the end of the side street that fed into Route 2, but he didn't see the Jetta to his right, in the traffic idling at the light. There was no sign of it off to his left, either, where Route 2 forked as part of it merged with Old Post Road.

So what's it going to be, ole buddy? Right or left?

Left: she'd said she liked the scenic view on Old Post. It was as good a reason as any.

A half mile later he glimpsed the Jetta hopping into the far lane and shooting off onto Old Post. He didn't know what pleased him more—that he was about to find out where she was going in such a hurry or that he'd been right about which direction she'd headed.

Kincaid switched lanes and kept three or four cars back as she sped into the hills. The afternoon sun slipped behind the trees, and long shadows fell across the road. Pine perfumed the air. Birds flitted past the Saab's sunroof.

Three miles from the airport, Fuentes turned onto a shady dirt road. It led, Kincaid knew, to the western tip of the lagoon that served as a landing strip for seaplanes. During the winter, the area was inhabited mostly by tourists, who rented cabins and bungalows along the lagoon at seasonal rates. He kept going for another couple hundred yards, then slowed, pulled off onto the shoulder, and swung around.

Her Jetta was parked in a carport of a cabin at the end of the road. The place was set back in pines, isolated from its neighbors by dense trees on either side. She must've been meeting someone here. No name on the mailbox, either, which fit. People like Fuentes made contacts away from home.

He parked in front, strolled up to the wooden front porch, and rang the bell. When no one answered, he knocked. When she still didn't come to the door, he turned the knob, encountered no resistance, and walked in.

He heard the shower.

A cozy room. Fireplace. Books. Throw rugs. A jungle of plants. More books. Wicker furniture. Floor lamps with old-fashioned lace shades. On the mantel were several photos of Fuentes with a nice-looking man. Here, the two of them on a cruise ship, standing against a railing, arms around each other, the backdrop of the sea behind them; there, the happy couple clowning for the camera; and here, okay, this explained it, a close-up of Fuentes and the man waving from a convertible with tin cans and streamers trailing from under a sign that said JUST MARRIED. So she *did* live here.

The shower went off.

Kincaid smiled to himself and sat down to wait.

4

"Hello, Detective." Quasimodo smiled, and his gold tooth flashed. "Mr. Uvanti's on the upper deck, at the pool." He pointed a thick finger upward, then let it fall until his arm was horizontal, the ubiquitous finger aimed at the stairs. "I think you can find your own way."

"Yeah, thanks."

Another grin, another flash of that gold tooth, then a small salute. "Sure thing."

Uvanti wasn't alone upstairs. He and a young woman with short, bright red hair were sunbathing. An old tune by the Doors boomed from a portable CD player next to Uvanti's chaise lounge. He tapped his feet to the rhythm and paged through a magazine as the redhead applied suntan lotion to his back, and he didn't look up until Aline's shadow fell over him.

He turned the music down. "Well, Ms. Scott. Pull up a chair and join us. This is Ginny." He sat back and patted Ginny on the thigh. "Get the lady a drink, will you, hon?"

Crack, crack, went her gum. "Sure. What're you drinking?"

"Water."

"One water coming up." She shuffled off, narrow hips swaying, finger snapping in time to the music.

"So what's on your mind, Ms. Scott?"

"Rikki Baker."

He tipped his glasses back onto his head, smiling. "I've told you everything there is to tell. My alibi checks out. What else is there to say?"

"Did you know Rikki was pregnant?"

He looked uncomfortable, and she expected him to deny any knowledge about the pregnancy. Instead, he nodded. "Sure, I knew."

"So the baby was yours?"

Uvanti shrugged, his eyes flicking away from her, to something behind Aline, probably the redhead. "She claimed it wasn't."

"Then whose was it?"

His gaze fixed on Aline again, eyes as small and hard as nuggets. "She didn't tell me, Ms. Scott. We weren't exactly on good terms then."

"Meaning you were no longer sleeping together."

A twitch at his mouth, sunglasses twirling in his hand. "Yeah, you got it."

"Here's your water," said the redhead, shuffling over, the glass extended.

"Thanks."

She stood there, green eyes telegraphing something to Uvanti, who tilted his head toward the bar, indicating that she should split. She did.

"Well trained," Aline remarked.

Uvanti bristled. "You got anything else on your mind?"

"Just a piece of information I'd like you to mull over, in case you haven't read the papers. It turns out that Rikki Baker wasn't really a Baker, see. She was Regina 'Rikki' Chamberlain, daughter of Senator Chamberlain. And what that means in prac-

tical terms, Mr. Uvanti, is that the Feds are now involved and
they're keeping a close eye on you. So watch your step. And
contact me before you sail off to any pretty ports on your pretty
boat here. Do I make myself clear?''

"I've got nothing to hide.''

"Good. Then you shouldn't have any problems.''

She stood, and Uvanti remained where he was, twirling his
sunglasses, the Doors album still playing, his eyes watching her,
assessing, measuring her against something in his own head.
"Oh, one other thing, Mr. Uvanti. What's your blood type?''

"How should I know?''

"You don't have any idea?''

"Look, Detective, you want to charge me with something?
Fine, charge me. You want to arrest me? Hey, great, go right
ahead. But I was on my boat the night Rikki was killed. And if
I remember correctly, you've already verified my alibi for this
past Sunday morning. You came by here on Monday, I think it
was, and Max verified that I spent the entire night on board
here.''

"I know when I was here, Mr. Uvanti.''

"Good for you. Then you're also bright enough to know that
if you arrest me without evidence, I'll be out on bond in an
hour.''

He was right, of course, and he also knew she couldn't force
him to have a blood test. Men like Uvanti always seemed to
know just how far you could push the system before it shoved
back.

"Don't forget to check with me before leaving Tango. And
that means any trips on the boat, too, Mr. Uvanti. See you
around.''

"I doubt it.''

As she walked away, she felt the weight of his gaze against
her back, pressing, digging, hateful.

19

I

Rooms always told a story, and the rooms in which Fuentes lived were no exception. The portrait of her that emerged as Kincaid poked around mystified and intrigued him.

She lived alone, and she liked things tidy. Each item had its place, its niche, its category. Books and music were arranged by type and alphabetized by author or musician. Her extensive self-help tapes on visualization and positive thinking and the numerous books on psychology indicated an intense inner search.

In fact, everything he discovered said that Fuentes was a controlled, disciplined woman, singular in her purposes, whatever they were. He sensed too that she had struggled for these traits the way other people did for wealth or fame, as though their attainment and continued reality were intrinsic to her emotional well-being. It explained a few things about that night on Uvanti's yacht and the morning after.

The look of panic in her eyes.

Her defensiveness.

Her sexual intensity.

He was betting that before the night on the boat, Fuentes hadn't been with a man since her marriage had hit the rocks.

She didn't see him immediately when she walked out into the living room; he was sitting where there wasn't any light and she was fiddling with the watch at her wrist. She was dressed completely in black—jeans, shirt, sneakers, even the scarf that bound her hair was black.

"Nice place," Kincaid said.

His voice startled her. But her recovery was quick, flawless, *controlled*. "I do have a doorbell."

"You were in the shower and didn't hear it." He pulled on the cord that hung from the floor lamp. Light spilled into his corner of the room. "I used to know a cat burglar who dressed in black."

He saw her eyes flick to the Band-Aid that now covered his stitches. Then she jerked a thumb toward the door. "Hit it, Ryan. I'm not in the mood for company." She continued toward the kitchen. "And don't slam the door on your way out."

He followed her into the kitchen and leaned against the sink, watching as she pulled a snub-nosed .38 and a shoulder holster from the drawer. Instead of putting it on, she set it on the counter, as if to make a point. "I figured you as the type who slept with her gun under her pillow."

This remark elicited a sharp, curt laugh. "Just goes to show what you don't know." She opened the fridge, brought out the makings of a salad, then went over to the pantry and returned to the counter with a can of tuna fish. "For a long time I didn't carry one," she said as if there'd been no pause in the conversation. "I thought that people who did attracted the circumstances in which they would have to use a weapon. Then I got shot at my first month out of Quantico and realized it wasn't the gun that attracted the circumstances but the job."

She whipped the tuna with mayonnaise and diced in celery and a hard-boiled egg. Kincaid thought of Aline, who never bothered mixing her tuna with anything because it was too much trouble.

"Don't just stand there, Ryan." Fuentes slid a pack of carrots across the counter toward him. "Make yourself useful."

"Where's the carrot peeler?"

"The drawer to your left. And while you're peeling carrots, Ryan, you can tell me how the hell you found me and what you're doing here."

"I followed you from the boardwalk."

"Why?"

"I wanted to know where you lived."

She looked at him incredulously and laughed. "Yeah, sure you did."

As if she couldn't quite believe that any man—even one who'd spent the night with her—would want to know such a thing.

"And I have some information you may find interesting," Kincaid said.

"In exchange for what? Truth?" She spat the final word, a reminder about Sunday, just in case he'd forgotten. "A roll in the sack?"

The last crack made him angry. "Look, Fuentes. I don't give a damn what kind of hang-ups you've got about men. You know things about these homicides that I don't, and I'm willing to pay for that information with some of my own. If the proposition doesn't interest you, fine. Then you can peel your own carrots."

He dropped the peeler and leaned against the sink again, arms folded at his waist. She looked at him, at the carrots, at him again, and exploded with laughter. "I can peel my *own carrots*? Jesus, Kincaid, who's the weirdo here?" Some of the tension dissolved. "All right, let's start over. Okay? Would that be okay with you?"

"Great. I'll leave and come back in."

"Yeah, you would."

"You're right."

And he did.

This time he rang the doorbell and she answered the door and he said, "Hi, Miranda."

"Hi, Ryan."

"You have a few minutes?"

"Just a few." She stepped aside and he came into the living room and shut the door softly behind him.

"So?" she asked, not moving, those baby blues fastened on his face.

"There was eighty-two thousand, six hundred and fifty dollars in a safe deposit box which Rikki had the key to. Uvanti's name used to be on the box as well. She was making monthly trips to Nassau and the Caicos and was traveling on a diplomatic passport. Smuggling. I figure drugs or dirty money. Right or wrong?"

She shifted her weight from one foot to the other, jammed her fingers into the pockets of her jeans, gazed at the floor for a moment. "Right and wrong." She looked up again, smiling now. "You like tuna fish salad, Ryan?"

Supper: idle chatter. The weather. Her bungalow here. Movies. Books. She cleared the table, and he rinsed the dishes and put them in the washer. Then she sat back down, legs folded under her, and lit a cigarette, ready for business.

"You first, Ryan." Those baby blues skewed against the smoke.

"Ladies first."

Her laughter this time rang sincere. "I figured you'd say that. Okay." A knee came up and she rested her hands against it, cigarette burning between her fingers. "You're right that Rikki was a courier. But not for dirty money or drugs. Uvanti's thing is art."

Sure. The art on the boat. "So he's smuggling art out of the country?"

"A little more complex. He's selling forgeries of the paintings *he* owns to dealers in the Caribbean, who sell to clients all over Central and South America. Very *good* forgeries which, based on their own merits, would be worth a great deal of money. I suspect he also has some other lucrative offshoots, like forgeries of paintings he *doesn't* own, but that's probably on a much smaller scale. Too easy to trace when you're talking about well-documented artists and their work."

"But why? He's already got a ton of money."

She stabbed out her cigarette and leaned forward, arms resting parallel to the table, those baby blues amused, smiling. "Money has never been the point with him, Ryan. It's the thrill of the game, the same thing that motivates some people to climb Everest or, hell, go to war. High stakes. The art thing started because he associates art with class. That's why he throws parties for all the society folks in the Cove. It makes him feel like he belongs. Personally, I don't think he gives a damn about the aesthetic value of what he collects. It's the idea that *he* owns something which other people covet."

"So go on about Rikki."

"She delivered the paintings, and the dealers paid her directly. Since the dealers didn't know these were bogus paintings, they thought it was a great deal because they avoided import taxes.

"Anyway, she brought the money back to Uvanti and he funneled it into various businesses—including Platinum's—and used some of the money to buy additional art. He paid Rikki more money than she'd seen since she'd cleaned out her trust fund and split for Switzerland. I'm sure the money you found is just part of what she had. The rest of it is probably in the Caicos."

"Who're his forgers?"

She shrugged. "There's one in New York, another in L.A., and probably a couple others we don't know about. They're Europeans whom Uvanti 'discovered' and then set up in business over here. I'm pretty sure Rikki was his only courier, but I think she was hoping to train me to take over because she wanted out. And this part is just supposition, Ryan."

She turned the pack of butts around in her hand, tapping one corner and then another against the table. "See, I think something happened on one of these trips, something got screwed up, and it frightened Rikki. It might've been something as small as some overzealous customs official checking her suitcases. But that's all it would take for her, because she was still a woman on the lam from a life she detested. Whatever it was, she ended her affair with Uvanti as a first step in terminating their business arrangement. About that time, she went to Ortega, thinking that a *santero* could protect her."

"Why a *santero*? Rikki Baker wasn't Hispanic. She was a WASP. How many would think of *santería* in those terms? Most of them haven't even heard of it."

Fuentes smiled and lit another cigarette. "The way Rikki told it, Uvanti comes from a family where *santería* was practiced. He practices it. She says he was always talking about how these spells worked. So I guess she figured that what worked for him would work for her. Granted, it's weird thinking, Ryan. But these people aren't what you could call normal."

Kincaid wasn't even sure what the word meant anymore. "Does Uvanti know Ortega?"

"Sure. Ortega was Uvanti's *santero* until Rikki came between them. Or so she said, anyway. I was never quite sure just how much to believe of what she said when it came to her relationship with men."

"It sounds like she confided in you quite a bit."

"Only on certain things, and it took me a *long* time to gain her trust."

"Did you know she was pregnant?"

She nodded. "And no, Ryan, she never told me who the father was. It could've been Uvanti or Ortega or someone else, maybe someone she met in the islands. She wasn't too picky when it came to sex. But I'm pretty sure she intended to go through with the pregnancy."

She blew smoke into the air between them, caught Kincaid's

flinch, and quickly waved the smoke away with her hand. She was gone, she said, the week before Rikki was killed. She didn't know anything about Rikki's supposed audition until she got back and one of the women in the club told her. "I figured that story was for Uvanti. I think she was going to split for the islands and get out of the courier business altogether."

"Do you know where she was killed?"

The baby blues darted away from his face, following a tendril of smoke. "Yes." She crushed the cigarette in the ashtray and pressed her hands against the table, fingers splayed, still not looking at him. "Here. She was killed in this cabin."

"Here," repeated Kincaid. "Hey, that's terrific, Fuentes."

Speaking softly: "She was going to water my plants while I was gone. I didn't even know about it until Saturday, because I have an apartment in town where I stay when I'm working."

Kincaid recalled Ferret's lead about a friend of Rikki's whose plants she was supposed to be watering while she was out of town. A lead that had gone nowhere. A lead that had been right in front of him all the time. "Great," he muttered.

"I couldn't go to the cops, Ryan," she rushed on, her hands sliding off the table and into her lap. "It would've put me in a terrible position."

"Ever heard of a crime scene, Fuentes?"

"I can do without the sarcasm," she snapped. "And for your information, I've had forensics training. I took pictures. I dusted the place for prints. I did everything you're supposed to do except call in a blood-spatter expert, all right?"

"Who'd you send the prints to?"

"To my contact in the bureau, a woman in the lab who knows what I'm doing here. And the only prints, Ryan, were mine."

"Is this the same woman you sent Rikki's old photo to?"

"Yes."

"And what makes you think that she's going to keep quiet if Chamberlain pours heat on her?"

"Maybe she won't. I decided the chance was worth it."

"Where was she killed?"

She pointed off to her left, at the wall near the fridge. "Whoever they were, she knew them. None of the doors or locks or windows had been jimmied. Only three of the cabins on the road are being used now, and they're at the other end, so I doubt if anyone heard anything." She stopped, rolling her lower lip between her teeth, her eyes fixed on him, waiting, seeking something in his face. "Her body was found on a Friday night, and I got out here that next morning. The place . . . reeked of blood. I cleaned it up and went back into town that afternoon to work, and that was when I met you."

"I know that part."

"Look, I realize the cop is a friend of yours. I know this has put you in a compromising position. But I couldn't risk Uvanti finding out that I'm not who he thinks I am. Not yet. Not until I find the forgeries for his next shipment. It's the only way to bust his operation at this point because I've got no other proof, and without proof, he'd beat the rap. He doesn't know about this place," she added quickly.

"If Uvanti killed her, don't you think he's wondering how come the cabin's owner didn't go to the cops?"

She shrugged. "Maybe. But more than likely, he's not thinking about it at all."

"How do you know there's going to be another shipment?"

"A hunch, mostly. But Uvanti's also made a couple of remarks recently about my being too bright just to dance and would I maybe be interested in making some extra money? I told him it would depend on what I'd have to do. That's as far as it's gone for now. But even if he hadn't said anything, Ryan, I know him. I know how he operates. He's not about to give up the thrill of this particular scam."

"Did you come here looking for Rikki or for Uvanti?"

"Both. We'd gotten a lead on him and a lead on her, and then the fine old senator found out some things about me and I was removed from his daughter's case. So I decided to do both on my own."

"It still comes back to why, Fuentes."

She sighed and raked her fingers back through her hair. "We went through this already. I'd rather not get into it now. I'm not even sure it's relevant anymore."

Kincaid let it pass. For now. "Just how're you going to find these forgeries?"

"I need either the forgeries for the next shipment or the originals of even one of the paintings he's already sold. And I've got a couple of ideas on where they might be."

"Officially, you're on leave. So one way or the other you're going to need help from the local cops, Miranda."

"I know. But first I'd like to check out my ideas, see if I'm right about where the paintings are." She hesitated. "I could use some help, Ryan."

"That depends on what's involved."

She sat back, arms crossed at the waist. "I'd like to hear what you have to say first. This *was* supposed to be an exchange. It's your turn to talk now."

So he did.

                                  2

Palm Key was an uninhabited island fifteen miles west of Tango, barely a mote in the vast blue of the Gulf. A good part of it always vanished during high tide, but it remained a favorite spot with weekend boaters and sunbathers. This evening, though, only one sloop was anchored in the cove. The couple who'd been on board were using another beach, so Aline and Martell had their strip of sand to themselves.

They swam and built a fire and feasted on clams steamed in seawater and wine Martell had chilled in the cooler. By dark a wind had risen, and it scooped up embers from the fire and flung them into the air, where they danced like lightning bugs. In the distance, lightning sutured the sky, but the storm was still so far away they couldn't even hear the thunder. Martell, scanning the heavens with a practiced eye, assured her they would be back on Tango before it started to rain. But even if they weren't, they could sleep on the sloop and head home at first light.

The idea appealed to Aline. She rather liked being on this tiny, lush island, away from her life, away from her job—away, that was all, just away. The shape of her existence here, now, seemed to have nothing to do with the life she lived on Tango. Murder did not exist here. Kincaid did not exist. Planes did not exist. It was as if Palm Key had slipped out of time or back in time, back a hundred years ago.

From here, in fact, the hills on Tango's western shore blocked the city lights, and all she saw was a dark form that lifted from the sea like a camel's hump. On top of it was a bright, pulsing glow that came, she knew, from the Porters' lighthouse, which she was seeing as it had existed a century ago.

"No wonder Porter writes such weird books," she said suddenly. "I mean, right now he's probably sitting up there at the top of the lighthouse, looking out on all this, conjuring things from the dark."

"Right now he's probably drunk." The firelight burned across one side of Martell's face and left the other side in shadow. For a few moments he didn't look like himself. It was as if she'd conjured him in much the same way Porter did his stories, molding Martell from the dark, the wind, the sand. It spooked her, and she hugged her knees against her and moved closer to the fire. "Besides," he went on, "whatever darkness Porter sees is in himself, Aline. He wrote weird books before he and Hannah moved into the lighthouse."

Hannah: the name curled into the air like blue smoke. Until Saturday night in the bar at the Flamingo, it had been *Mrs. Porter*. Now it was Hannah. "What do you think of her? Of Hannah?"

"That she married Porter for his money."

"Oh c'mon, Si," she laughed. "Stop being a lawyer for five minutes, okay? You two were pretty chummy Saturday night at the bar. You must've formed some opinion of her."

"By God," he said, smiling, "I think we've made progress, Aline. You actually notice what I do."

He was poking fun at her, and it irritated her. "It'd be hard to miss, since we were all sitting in the same booth."

"She was trying to get Porter to sit up and take notice. Besides, so what if I talk to someone else?"

The conversation had veered into something she hadn't intended, but the wine had loosened her tongue, and anyhow, he was missing the point. "You were hitting on her, Si, not just talking to her, which is fine, except do it on your own time, not mine."

Before he could say anything, she stood and walked toward the water, the wind blowing through her hair, sand biting at her ankles. She realized how buzzed she was from the wine and how much the sky had clouded over since they'd arrived. The moon and most of the stars were gone. The air had cooled. By dawn, Tango's rocky western shore would be blanketed in fog. The stuff would cling to the ground in the old seamen's cemetery and hover over the graves like ectoplasm. She could see it in her head, feel the chill of the place in her bones, and thought of her dream. She quickly immersed herself in the Gulf waters, a baptism of warmth, a purging.

After a while, Martell joined her and they sat on the shoals, sipping from the bottle of wine, talking, neither of them referring to their earlier disagreement, because there was nothing left to say. A clap of thunder and a brilliant shoot of lightning sent them scurrying for their things on the beach. The skies opened up, and they raced back to the sloop, laughing, drenched to the bone before they reached it. Only later did she realize that she couldn't remember what she'd done with her little white talisman. Had she left it on the boat? *Does it matter?*

The cabin was dry but cool and rocked in the swells. They stripped off their wet suits and wrapped up in thick blankets. Martell made hot toddies on the tiny two-burner stove. Just above it, on a shelf, was the skunk-shaped iron planter she'd given him, which billowed with ivy. The strands were so long, several of them had curled around slats in the unused burner. Aline started unraveling them, but Martell asked her not to. He liked them the way they were. They were the only greenery on board.

"And someday you'll forget and use this burner and they'll catch on fire," she said with a laugh.

"Not a chance. I'm not *that* careless."

They weren't going to be able to return to Tango in the storm, so Aline fixed up the aft cabin while he finished making the drinks. The bunk was barely big enough for the two of them but the cushions that served as a mattress were thick and soft and padded with a quilt.

They huddled under the covers, sipping their hot toddies as they exchanged stories. Her childhood in Key West and Tango, his in the Midwest, the odd connections that had led to their lives here and now. The alcohol, the storm, and their isolation had made them both talkative. She saw a softer, more circumspect side of Martell and felt comfortable with him in a way she hadn't before.

The lanterns hissed and flickered, spilling uneven light through the cabin. Shadows deepened in the corners, where the glow didn't reach. A slow heat spread through her bones as the bourbon in the toddy took root, as Martell's hands sculpted her from the rain and wind, from the lightning that blazed in the overhead hatch. In a moment of utter clarity the lightning illuminated his large hands, dark against her thighs, stroking with almost unbearable lightness, and in the next moment lightning burned the features from his face as he hovered above her, whispering to her, describing how her skin felt against his hands, his mouth. It wasn't so much what he said but the way he said it, the tone of his voice, its cadence, its rhythm, that excited her, that stirred a deep eroticism that had lain dormant in the months of Kincaid's absence. A huge ache filled her, and she reached for him, to guide him inside her, but something was wrong, he wasn't so hard, and he slipped away from her, murmuring that he wanted to make love to her, would she let him do that? Would she? Would she?

Aline felt the soft explosion of syllables against her breasts, her belly, between her thighs, and it seemed his mouth kept forming words even as his tongue made slow, moist circuits, speaking to her in a language that burned and consumed. Her body had never felt so sensitive, so tight and yet so boneless. She was fixed in the moment, she was free of it, she was drowning in it, burning in it. Now it was his hands, then a finger moving with a light but deliberate pressure against her, then his mouth again. His tongue was hot and sharp and a little cruel, and she hated him for it, wanted him to stop, to go on and on, she felt flayed and invaded and possessed and said, Please, please, and didn't know what she was asking for, a respite, an end, it didn't matter, it felt good, and seconds before she came he slipped inside her and the storm swept her up in its rage, its frenzy.

Through the night, she came to in fits and starts, like an old car that wanted to move but couldn't, and it seemed that no time had elapsed at all because it was still storming and Martell was still touching her, whispering to her, and the sloop was still rocking in the turbulent cove.

She dreamed that she was stumbling through the old seamen's graveyard, through fog that clung to her skin like silk. She could hear her stalker breathing. She could hear him calling her, first in Ortega's voice, then in Uvanti's, then his voice boomed like a foghorn from the lighthouse. Sobbing, she charged away from it, and suddenly she was on the Tango ferry.

Dark. No moon, no lights. She heard his footfalls on the deck. She ran past cars that were empty of people. She shouted for help, but no one was around to hear her. He got closer. He was laughing. The ferry churned through the black waters. She raced along the railing and nearly wept with relief when she saw a man standing there, a man in a trench coat and tie, a man she recognized as Abel Whitkins, the cop who'd worked on the Bacalao homicides.

"Help me!" she screamed, grabbing his arm.

But when he turned completely around, she saw that the top of his head was gone. "I can't," he said. "I'm dead." And then he laughed and she threw herself over the side of the boat and awakened with a gasp seconds before she struck the water.

The rain was a light tap dance against the deck, the windows. Martell was snoring. Her tongue felt thick and her mouth, sour. Her temple drummed the opening score to a hangover. She padded her way into the head, closed the door and turned on the light. Aspirin, she thought, and slid open the medicine cabinet. She found the bottle, tapped two into her palm. She reached for the small glass on the edge of the sink to fill it with water, and there was the little bag, her talisman, where she must've left it when she changed earlier.

She scooped it up, fingers tightening over it. She gulped down the aspirin and hurried back into the cabin, clutching the stupid talisman, pressing it against her once she was under the covers. She was afraid to close her eyes. The dream was waiting for her, and if she slept it would pick up where it had left off, and this time she would hit the water, feel it closing over her head, and Rikki Baker's killer would find her.

20

I

Ferret's jeep was parked in Kincaid's driveway when he got home the next morning. He was sitting on the porch steps, under a sky that sagged with clouds, watching the silver tabby wolf down a bowl of food.

"If you're going to own a cat, Ryan, the least you could do is be home to feed it. He was ravenous."

"She."

"Just what you need. Another woman in your life. She got a name?"

Kincaid stopped at the foot of the stairs, noticing the way Ferret was dressed—black fedora, white slacks, a black shirt, white shoes. Spiffy casual wear. "Unojo. One-Eye."

"God, even I could do better than that." He ran a long finger down the tabby's spine. She arched her back, purring loudly, and polished off what was left in the bowl.

"She likes you, Ferret."

"Don't get any ideas about pawning her off on me. I like cats just fine, Ryan, but I don't need one for a pet."

Kincaid chuckled. "C'mon in. I'll make a pot of coffee."

"I thought you'd never ask. I mean, it's one thing to let myself inside the house for a good deed, but quite another to just make myself at home." He whipped off his black fedora and followed Kincaid inside.

Once they were settled in the kitchen, Ferret remarked that Kincaid looked like hell. "Bad night?"

"No."

"Lack of sleep, huh. Let me make an educated guess. She's

blond, and when we first saw her she was wearing pink leotards.''

"Right." He brought the makings of breakfast out of the
fridge. "You eaten?''

Ferret spun on the stool like a kid. "Nope. And yes, I'd love
some of whatever you're going to fix.''

"I cook, you wash.''

The little man rolled his eyes. "You know, Ryan, you really
should stop imposing so many conditions on your friends. I'll
set the table.''

"And wash.''

Ferret sighed. "Yeah, yeah." He shuffled over to the cabinets. "So tell me about Ms. Starr, a.k.a. Miranda Fuentes.''

Kincaid's glance was sharp, annoyed. "You know, I've always wondered how you find out the things you do, Ferret. And
this seems like a good time to ask.''

"I spoke to Slater. He said you'd given him a tip on Catch-
Me and asked him to run a check on Fuentes. The connection
was just a lucky guess.''

There. A reasonable explanation. But it did little to allay Kincaid's suspicions that Ferret pulled information out of thin air.
"You want cheese in your omelet?''

"What kind of cheese?" Ferret asked, eyeing the brick.

"Jalapeño.''

"The hot shit, right?''

Kincaid laughed. "Yeah, the hot shit, Ferret.''

"Sure. And some Tabasco, if you don't mind. She's a Fed on
a leave of absence. What else?''

"That's about it.''

"Uh huh." Ferret popped a slice of jalapeño cheese into his
mouth, sucked air in through his teeth, and quickly filled a glass
with water and gulped it down.

"I told you it was hot.''

"Goddamn, Ryan," he wheezed. "Maybe you'd better hold
off on the Tabasco.''

"Right.''

Ferret carried dishes over to the breakfast table under the
window while Kincaid whipped the eggs and sliced in cheese,
mushrooms, green peppers. Neither of them spoke. The ticking
of the clock in the kitchen seemed abnormally loud. "You have
a case for this woman or what?" Ferret asked finally.

"I don't know.''

"I'm asking for a reason."

Kincaid wasn't so sure he wanted to hear the reason. "You always do, Ferret."

"No, I don't. Usually I just ask because I'm nosy."

"Sure." Kincaid flipped the omelets and popped bread into the toaster oven. Silverware clattered as Ferret finished setting the table. "Is there anyone in the county courthouse who owes you a favor, Ferret?"

He thought a moment. "It would depend on how big the favor is."

"A set of builder's plans or blueprints to Uvanti's house."

Ferret let out a soft whistle and smoothed his hand over his slick black hair. "That's big. What've you got in mind?"

"I need to know the layout of the house."

"I'll see what I can do, Ryan. But between the security system and Uvanti's thugs, the place is a virtual fortress. Even if you did manage to get in, you could have problems getting out. You ever seen the house?"

"Not yet."

"We can shoot up there in the van. I think you need to see the place before you decide to do this."

"I've already decided to do it."

"You still need to take a look."

"I've got to shower and make a couple of calls first. That should give you enough time to clean up."

Ferret made a face, and his eyes followed Kincaid as he got up. "The things I do for you, Ryan."

"Ain't it grand?"

2

"I'm beginning to think this is a waste of time," Bernie said, unwrapping the Egg McMuffin in her lap. "I mean, Ortega hasn't left the house since Monday, and no one except Seroz has been here. So what's the point?"

They were in the surveillance van across the street from Ortega's house, and the smell of the Egg McMuffin was making

Aline nauseous. "Do you *have* to eat that thing in here, Bernie?"

"Where do you want me to eat it? Outside?"

"What's wrong with eating breakfast at home?"

"Bill forgot to reset the alarm when he left this morning." She dropped the McMuffin in its cardboard container and set it on the dash. Then she popped the lids on the two coffees and passed Aline one. "And if you're going to be in such a rotten mood, Al, why don't you just go home and I'll pull this shift alone?"

"Sorry." Aline glanced back out the window and sipped at her coffee. It formed a sour pool in the bottom of her stomach, then seemed to slide off to one side as she shifted in her seat. "I'm just tired. Spending the night on a sloop off Palm Key isn't a real smart thing to do when you have to be at work by eight."

"Forget it. What time are you going to meet Si at the courthouse?"

"I don't know. He's going to call the station when he's got the court order and Penny will radio us."

"You *do* think he'll get it, don't you?"

"Sure. But the judge he's seeing is always late, so it won't happen at eight thirty." It probably wouldn't even happen by noon, she thought. But the court order for the Days Inn computer printout might be the best thing they had going for them today, late or not.

Aline dumped the remainder of her coffee out the window and quickly pulled her arm back in when she saw Ortega step out of his house. He was dressed in jeans, a blue guayabera shirt, and sunglasses. He hurried toward his old Buick.

"We're in luck," Bernie whispered.

"He looks like he's dressed for work."

They both slid low in the seat as Ortega glanced up and down the street. Aline watched him in the side mirror and caught the way his gaze lingered on the van. There was no reason for him to suspect that a vehicle with ACE PLUMBING written on the side would be anything other than what it appeared, but she sensed that he did.

Bernie waited until the Buick had rounded the corner before she cranked up the van. "No. Wait," Aline said, opening her door. "I'm getting out."

"Aw, c'mon, Al. Don't do this to me."

"Who's going to know?"

"I know, that's who. If you want to search his house so badly, we'll get a warrant and do it by the book."

"A warrant on what grounds, Bernie?"

"We'll think of something."

"We don't *have* anything. That's just the point. And *I'm* on the hit list, remember?"

"I'll wait."

"No, you follow Ortega. I'll catch up with you later. My car's just a block from here."

"What am I supposed to tell Penny when she radios?"

"Don't tell her anything. I'll go over to the courthouse from here."

Bernie sat there a moment, biting at her lower lip, fingers curled over the steering wheel. "Shit." She sighed, resigned now. "I'd do the same thing in your shoes. You have what you need to get in there?"

She grinned and patted her purse. "Always prepared."

3

Ferret drove like a little old lady. His hands clutched the steering wheel, his body was hoisted up on two pillows and tilted forward as he peered through the windshield. The speedometer needle barely brushed forty-five.

"Can you, uh, speed it up a little, Ferret?" Kincaid asked, glancing behind them at the string of cars. "It looks like we've got half the island's drivers on our tail."

The little man's eyes flicked to the mirror, then back to the road. "They can pass me just ahead, when the road straightens out. It's dangerous to drive over fifty on this road, Ryan."

"You're not even doing that."

Ferret gave him a dirty look. "I would appreciate it if you would stop being a backseat driver."

But he speeded up to just over fifty, and once they were on an open stretch, every car that had been behind them pulled out and whizzed past. Several honked. One man shot them the finger and shouted something Kincaid didn't catch.

"Jerk," Ferret murmured.

Ten minutes later the jeep climbed through a forest of ficus and melaleuca trees that blanketed a steep hill just outside of Pirate's Cove. The sun vanished and reappeared and vanished again. The air cooled. Ferret hung a left on one of the half-dozen roads that twisted off on either side of them. To their right, the trees gave way to a pasture where a dozen horses grazed.

"Uvanti's little pets," Ferret said. "A couple of them race at Calder."

"Any winners?"

"Yup." Ferret's lips drew away from his teeth, into that weird, hungry smile. "Catch-Me-If-You-Can."

Kincaid laughed and shook his head. "I'm beginning to get the picture."

"Hey, his tips have proven out in the past, Ryan. And I didn't ask if the race was fixed."

"Do I look like I'm complaining?"

"Just so we got it straight."

The pasture ended, and they passed several split-level homes set back away from the road. "Does Uvanti own the hill?"

"He'd like to, but a lot of the folks who live up here are old-timers, and when Uvanti offered to buy them all out a few years back they told him to take a hike. He's not too well liked."

"You ever heard anything about him being involved in an art scam?"

"So *that's* what this is about."

"Yeah."

"I know he's a big art collector, and I've heard rumors things might not be kosher, but I never paid too much attention to them. I stay away from men like him just on principle, Ryan, except for a few bets here and there."

"You know the Van Gogh that went for forty million at auction a couple years ago?"

"*That* was Uvanti?"

"Apparently. Fuentes says he bought it through a Japanese intermediary."

"Forty million. Jesus. I knew he was rich, but I didn't realize he was *that* rich." Ferret pulled off onto the shoulder, then cut into the trees until the van was hidden from the road. "We have to walk a bit. If you're going to go through with this, Ryan, I want you to take this route in. It's safest."

"You're the boss."

4

Aline had scaled the fence that enclosed Ortega's backyard and gotten into the house through the sliding glass doors in the bedroom, where the lock was old and rusted. A faint vanilla scent lingered in the room, which was as cool and still as a tomb and done mostly in yellows and reds of various shades, just like Ortega's office.

The bed wasn't made, and the nightstand was covered with bottles. Aspirin and cough syrup, decongestant, Vick's Vaporub. On the floor was a box of Kleenex and one white, furry slipper, turned on its side. It looked like poor little Ortega had a cold.

The only thing of interest in the bedroom was a .38, snug in a box, wrapped up in plastic, never used. Next to it was a container of bullets.

She went slowly and methodically through the house, not entirely sure what she was looking for, but confident she would know it when she saw it. She poked around in drawers, cabinets, always returning things just as she had found them. And in her mind she counted off the months until September 22, the anniversary of Abel Whitkins's death on the Tango ferry, the day that had her name on it just because she'd had the misfortune of being assigned this case. Plenty of time to solve the case and nab the killer, she thought, and wished she could really believe it.

Neither Rikki Baker nor the jogger had been killed in the same locations as the stripper and the ex-Olympic runner whom Bacalao had supposedly murdered. So location wasn't all that important. Neither was gender: the jogger was female, Bacalao's runner was male. The connecting elements between the murders were the dates and mutilations—fingers and an Achilles tendon. Since *santería* was a belief system in which symbolism was everything, then what did fingers and a tendon represent on a stripper and a runner?

Fingers were used to touch, express, pick up, put down, pull, eat, scratch . . . *Nonono. Touch, Al, the fingers represent sensuality and the tendon symbolizes speed.* Sensuality and speed: qualities Bacalao had sought and which his imitators perhaps coveted as well.

In the third murder that Bacalao had allegedly committed, the eyes of a palmist were taken. He had wanted her perceptions, her vision, her clairvoyance. *And Bacalao wanted Whitkins's brain because that was what he used to hunt and track him.* Just as she was doing.

Ortega's den. The vanilla scent that permeated the house came from here, from the dozen candles of various colors that adorned an altar. It was similar to the one she'd found at Rikki's, but with some interesting additions: squat, black candles into which little nightmare faces had been carved; a snakeskin curled like a shawl around the shoulders of one of the statues; an aquarium filled with black soil and ants, their intricate tunnels partially visible against the glass; a jar with a dead centipede in it that had been pierced by a needle and strung on black thread; and a dead frog whose mouth had been bound with black thread.

Black thread like the chicken. *And is there a piece of paper in its mouth with my name on it?*

Even if there was, she wouldn't be able to do anything about it legally. But at least then she would know for sure.

She spun the lid on the jar. Hesitated before reaching inside. The idea of touching the thing wasn't particularly appealing. *Just do it.* Her skin literally crawled when she picked up the frog. But it was no worse, really, than high school biology class, maybe not even that bad because she didn't have to dissect the thing, only open its mouth.

She broke the black thread with a nail file and used it to scrape the inside of the frog's mouth. A bit of paper rolled out, and she smoothed it open with the file.

It was blank.

Blank, for Christ's sakes.

She quickly tried to bind the mouth again, but the pieces of thread were too short, so she just dropped the frog back into the jar and tossed out the bit of paper. So what if Ortega noticed.

As she backed away, she suddenly felt as though she were peering inside Ortega's head, into the landscapes of his dark magic, into the sorcery of his dreams, his visions, his most private self. And she knew that somewhere on this altar was something that represented her. Not the frog, but what? The centipede? The ants? The black candles?

Four candles. She plucked them off the altar one by one, examining each under the light from the floor lamp. She was here. She knew she was. It didn't matter that none of the carved faces looked enough like anyone to tell which one might be her. She would take them all with her. Every single goddamn one. She dropped them in her purse and switched off the light and backed away from the altar.

Shadows eddied and shifted across the floor. She blinked, and now they seemed to be swelling, filling out, rising up, whispering to her. She shut the door behind her and stood for a moment in the hall, her back against the cool concrete. The pounding of her heart rushed into the silence. The phone rang, startling her. From another part of the house she heard Ortega's recorded voice.

The bedroom, she thought, and hurried back into it, into the odd shades of yellows, reds.

The beep sounded.

She waited for the person on the other end to say something, but the silence went on. Two seconds. Three. Four. Then breathing hissed into the silence like a toxic gas and goosebumps exploded on her arms. It was him, the other man, Ortega's silent partner. She felt him in the room, felt him as though he were standing behind her, grinning, whispering, *Ha-Ha, Ms. Detective. Ha-ha. I'll get you too, Ms. Detective. Take your brain, uh-huh, I will. . . .*

The sound of his breathing paralyzed her, curled through her, touching her all over inside, ghost hands that stroked and squeezed. She felt the dark twist of his derangement and his fearlessness, and now he seemed to be whispering, *Scared, Ms. Detective? Hmm? I know you're in there.*

Her arm jerked up, shot toward the receiver, fell on it. She wanted to lift it, the muscles in her fingers twitched and screamed and begged to do so. But she didn't. She couldn't. She squeezed her eyes shut and a sob slipped past her clenched lips and the heat of his madness seeped through her palm, into her blood. Then there was a click and a dial tone and the silence again.

Aline pulled her hand away from the phone so fast she knocked it to the floor. The receiver slipped out of the cradle, she grabbed it, slammed it back onto the cradle, rubbed it clean, and set it on the nightstand again.

The phone pealed.

The machine clicked on.

The breathing returned. She leaped for the sliding glass door, threw it open, slammed it shut. The sound pursued her into the heat, the smell of grass. She shoved the door closed and sprinted across the yard, purse slapping her hip, the breathing still behind her, pulsing, throbbing, fluttering, the noise like a hundred wings beating the hot, still air.

5

They had climbed a mile or more along a steep path lined with trees. The breeze, what little of it there was, didn't penetrate the dense foliage, and Kincaid's shirt was damp with sweat by the time they reached the top of the slope. About a quarter of a mile away and fifty feet below them, was Uvanti's home.

It was a perfect square built around a courtyard, large but not huge. A six-foot wall surrounded it, with an iron gate in front of it. It was set back from a paved road that, judging by the cars that whizzed past, was well traveled but not inundated. It looked ordinary enough, really, not impenetrable at all, and that worried him.

"Okay, what's the catch?"

"The security system, for one thing," Ferret replied, dabbing at his forehead with a handkerchief. "It starts just outside the wall. It's embedded in the ground and works on a combination of sound and light that are inaudible and invisible to human beings. It's like a force field, except you can walk through it, which of course disturbs it and lets everyone who's home know you're out there."

"Is there a generator?"

"No. But there's a cellar, Ryan, and I think that's where you'll find your paintings."

"It sounds like you've already seen the floor plans."

"I've been in there a couple of times, watching races and whatnot. I snooped around on my own." His teeth lined up in his mouth as he grinned. "And the information came in handy, huh?"

"Remind me to stay on your good side, Ferret. What else can you tell me about it?"

"Besides Max, the bodyguard, he's got three other guys who stay in the house. They live in the east wing there." He pointed. "Uvanti's living area is perpendicular to it. The other two wings are kitchen, living room, and so on. The cellar is directly under the courtyard. You get to it from the kitchen. I know there's another way down there, but I don't know where it is. The construction plans may tell you that.''

Kincaid settled on a rock, legs stretched in front of him, the sun warm against his face, eyes fixed on the house. "What else?"

Ferret smoothed his handkerchief on the ground and sat on it, pensive now, brow furrowing, sunglasses riding on top of his head. "Well, there's a storm pipe that leads from the road, along the side of the house and away from it and into the trees, draining water off the property, because it sits in a depression. Now, this part is rumor, so take it for what it's worth, but supposedly there's a tunnel from the cellar that feeds into it. Uvanti's escape route just in case, I guess.''

"Is there a way to get into the storm pipe?"

"Yeah. But it's in a ditch just to the right of the driveway, in full view of the house." ·

Kincaid nodded, thinking. A butterfly flitted past in front of them. Birds twittered and sang from the trees behind them. The scent of grass and earth and flowers seemed to congeal in the heat. "You think Uvanti killed Rikki Baker?"

"He had at least one motive that we know of separate from the *santería* stuff. He was also involved with her sexually. And on top of it, Ryan, he's a guy who does what he wants because he believes he won't get caught. So yeah, I think there's a good possibility he killed her and she just happened to fit into his *santería* plans. But in that case, he's also the man who killed the runner. And I'm still unsure about that part. But what I think doesn't really matter. You're the one who's going to do this job. What do you think?"

That he probably did it, Kincaid thought, and with Ortega's help. The two men's supposed rivalry over Rikki bothered him, but that might've been for show.

Ferret fanned himself with his black fedora. "You'll need some help getting to those paintings. Besides Fuentes, I mean."

"That an offer?" Kincaid glanced at him. The little man's hat whispered as it moved, stirring the heat. "Or just an opinion?"

Ferret supplicated the sky with his small, black eyes, his insect eyes. "Sometimes, Ryan, you ask the stupidest questions. Let's split. It's hot out here."

As they made their way down the path, there was a moment

in which Kincaid's affection for the little man in front of him shone with absolute clarity, and he felt absurdly grateful for the friendship.

6

Quick, now. Quick quick. Up the steps. Out of the light. Away from the crowds. Into the courthouse, where it's safe.

The small white bag in Aline's pocket burned against her hip, a reminder. *Garlic, parsley, a bit of camphor*: laughter gurgled in her throat, a deep, silly sound, almost a rumble, and died before it reached her lips.

Busy courthouse. Too many people pouring out. She didn't let them touch her. She slipped through them and past them like water, thin and almost invisible, a substance whose shape became the vessel into which it was poured.

Cool air against her face now. Martell nowhere around. Upstairs to his office. SIMON MARTELL, PROSECUTOR. His profession was burned in large letters into a wood plaque on the door; his name smaller, almost a postscript.

Sweat pimpled her upper lip, despite the cool air in the outer office. The secretary raised her eyes slowly. Pretty girl. *You one of Si's honeys?* Aline knew her name but couldn't remember her. "Is Si in?"

"Oh. Detective Scott. He was wondering what happened to you. Just a second, I'll buzz him."

Buzz, buzz. It hurt. She wanted to slap her hands over her ears. Her eyes burned. The talisman quivered in her pocket. The secretary spoke softly into the phone. Hung up. The door to Martell's office opened. He said something to her. She moved forward into his office. Nice view. Nice furniture. Nice. *I hate that word.*

She looked at him. He was angry. Why should he be angry? What did he have to be angry about? Had she done something? Not done something? Was he angry at her? Why? What had she done? Was Kincaid angry at her? No, Kincaid was—

Stop. Stop it now.

The door closed. Martell turned, sliding a finger under his

mustache as he smiled. "Got it." He wagged a computer print-out in the air. "When you didn't show up, I went over there myself."

Click, click went a wheel in her head as it cranked up. Turning. "To the Days Inn? You went over there? You can't do that, Si. There's not even a case yet."

His eyes grew dark, almost menacing. "I really wish you wouldn't pull that cop routine with me, Aline." And he slammed the printout on the desk. The noise startled her, jerked at her spine.

A light flashed behind her eyes, and she saw herself last night, on the sloop, inside the din of the storm as Martell devoured her.

Wrong. Something's wrong here.

She snapped to attention. "*Your* job was to get the court order for the printout, Si, and mine was to deliver it."

"Like I said, you weren't around." He slid it across the desk toward her, flipped it open. "Those dates your pal Kincaid got for Rikki's trysts at the Days Inn?" He stabbed a finger at the page. "I marked them. And there is *definitely* a case, Aline."

She glared at him, livid. "I don't give a shit if there *is* a case. You overstepped your job."

"Just look." Martell stabbed a finger at the printout; Aline imagined herself biting off the tip of it. "Go on. Look."

She did.

A red *X* next to a Tuesday last December. Another red *X* next to a Saturday in January. A third alongside a Tuesday in February. And on and on, back for at least a year, probably longer. And the name was the same. *John Percy. John Percy. John Percy.* She knew the name, but didn't know from where, her fatigue and anger like a wall she couldn't push beyond.

She glanced up at Martell, frowning. "Who is he?"

He sighed and rolled his eyes as though she were hopelessly obtuse, and jerked open his desk drawer. He dropped a book on the desk, spun it around so she could see the title.

The Percy Parallel by Karl Porter.

21

Ortega wandered restlessly around the shop, sniffling and sneezing as he dusted statues, moved them, rearranged objects on the shelves, then washed his hands and cleaned some more. Clean and wash, clean and wash.

He was here alone, and he hated it. Why weren't there any customers? What was taking Seroz so long with his errands? Why did he feel as if something terrible was about to happen to him? That Ikú had abandoned him?

The rear room, his secret room, tugged at him, beckoned. But he was afraid to go back there. It was haunted. Rikki lived inside it. So did the pretty little runner. Even now, he thought he heard them whispering and giggling, talking about him. If he went into the room, their spirits would seep through the pores in his skin. Their voices would rise and fall inside him. He knew. He knew they blamed him. He knew they didn't want to be Ikú's handmaidens.

Even though he had explained to them that it was an honor to be chosen, even though they had accepted their destinies, they had changed their minds. Women were fickle. Women could not be trusted. His *padrino* didn't understand that. *Padrino* believed women were like lumps of wet clay that could be molded and shaped according to his will. But Ortega heard these women's voices, and he knew what they really thought.

He slid open the door to the freezer at the back of the room and stuck his head inside. He breathed deeply of the cool, perfumed air. It soothed his hot cheeks and blocked out the sounds of the women's voices. Spirits couldn't track you as well when your scent was mixed up with other smells. Perhaps if he used a different shampoo and bath soap and alternated cologne in the morning, the women would lose his scent entirely. An excellent idea. Why hadn't he thought of it before?

He hurried to the front of the shop, locked the door, glanced into the street. The van that had been following him was gone. Good. But he still pulled the blinds, and then he plucked up one of the wire baskets his customers used and roamed through the aisles, collecting different soaps and oils, chuckling to himself. Perfect. Absolutely perfect. He would do a *limpieza* on himself, a cleansing with white lilies and powdered white eggshells. Then he would mix an *omiero*, the miracle elixir of *santería*, concocted from a hundred and one herbs, the favorite herbs of the seven major *orishas*. It would cure his flu, his spiritual malaise, it would silence the women's voices. It would protect him. The business with Seroz would clear up. The police would stop following him. He couldn't understand why he hadn't done it before.

Jaime doesn't understand what you are becoming, Manuel, Rikki whispered.

He pressed his hand over his ear, rubbing at it, rubbing away her voice.

He thinks you're evil.

Ridiculous. Seroz was limited by his beliefs of good and evil. He understood nothing of power.

He knows you killed me.

Impossible.

Run, Manuel, run, laughed his pretty little runner, his dead *gringa.*

"Leave me alone."

"Who, Manuel?"

His head snapped up at the sound of the woman's voice, and he saw Rikki coming through the doorway from the back hall, Rikki in shimmering silver, smiling, flicking her hair from her collar. He stepped back so quickly the wire basket bumped against the edge of the counter and he lost his grip on it and it crashed to the floor, spewing bottles and jars, bottles of soap, herbs. "What . . ." he whispered, and then he blinked and it wasn't Rikki at all. It was Anna Riviera, the old *santera* from the Cove, his *abuelita*'s closest friend when she was alive. He must have left the alley door unlocked.

"You look ill." She stepped around the counter and leaned

over, picking up things from the floor and setting them down. She knew what they were for. "Good idea to make an *omiero*, Manuel. It will cure your cold. But I doubt it will cure your other problems."

"I have no problems, señora." He scooped up the rest of the items on the floor and dropped them into the wire basket. "Except for the flu."

"Oh? I hear differently. And quite frankly, Manuel, the things I hear trouble me deeply, and if they are true, you are a disgrace to your grandmother's name."

Perspiration erupted on his brow. His vision blurred. He wanted to curl up at this woman's feet and beg for forgiveness. For understanding. For her compassion. "I . . . I don't know what you are referring to, señora."

His voice was soft, hoarse with his lie. She heard it, he knew she did, he saw the way the creases on her face deepened with amusement, disappointment. "Please." Gnarled hands up, as if warding off a blow. "Do not insult my intelligence with lies. I know about the slaughtered black chicken that was left in the detective's storeroom. I know about the things that were stolen from her home."

A vein throbbed at his temple. *Ha-ha, Manuel,* whispered Rikki. *Ha-ha, she's onto you.*

"I'm afraid I don't know what you're talking about, señora. Excuse me." He moved around her and reached for the broom and dust pan so he could sweep up the glass on the floor.

"Then let me put it more clearly, Manuel." She kept speaking in that same quiet voice, a voice that had never needed to shout to be heard. "The two women who were murdered were killed in exactly the same way as two of Armando Bacalao's victims more than fifty years ago. Bacalao's bones were removed from his grave. We both know what that means, don't we, Manuel? It means that a *mayombero* is duplicating the murders which Bacalao committed, as a kind of offering to him, asking him for *his* power and also for Ikú's help. It means this *mayombero* is using these women's body parts and Bacalao's bones to strengthen his *nganga*. And I believe, Manuel, that this *mayombero* has an apprentice."

Ortega's heart leaped into his throat. His hand tightened around the broom. Sweat oozed down the sides of his face. His voice, where was his voice? *Say something, fool. Say anything.* He managed to laugh, but it sounded false. He managed to smile, but his lips felt cold and thick. Cool air from the ceiling vent slid down the back of his neck and licked at his spine.

"Señora, with all due respect, you are wrong. Maybe you read this story in a book or it is something from a dream, I don't know. But you are no longer a young woman, and your memory . . ." He tapped his temple and shrugged, then finished sweeping up the glass. He dumped it in the trash can behind the counter. "I know how it is as one grows older. How the memory begins to fail. That's what happened to my *abuelita*, señora. I'm sure you remember that, no? Her sense of time got mixed up. She confused people. She thought I was her husband." He laughed and looked up at her, his fingers tightening on the broom. "Just as you think I am someone I am not."

She was still smiling, and he hated it. He hated how it made the lower half of her face crinkle like crepe paper. She was just a stupid old woman who

She knows, Manuel, cackled Rikki.

Ha-ha, Manuel.

She'll betray you, Manuel. Betraybetray

couldn't hurt him. Couldn't do anything to him.

"So who is the *mayombero*, Manuel? That scum Uvanti? I know about Uvanti. No? It isn't him? Perhaps it is . . . well, let that rest for the moment. Why don't you tell me about the black moon, Manuel? A friend of mine who is well versed in *palo* told me the significance for *mayomberos* of the eclipse on June third. The darkening of the sun. Would you like to hear what he told me, Manuel? Yes? No? You don't know? Ah, well, I will tell you anyway. The event called Black Moon is, hmm, how should we put this? Shall we call it a ritual? Hmm? Or a legend?"

She smiled as if challenging him to deny what she had said. For long seconds he simply stared at her, at her red cotton blouse and her white cotton skirt, an old woman with a wrinkled face and white hair and a body as thin and frail as an old cornstalk. His hatred was sudden, intense, and exploded from him like a hot, raging wind. Ortega jammed the handle of the broomstick into her stomach.

Her breath flew out of her, eclipsing a scream. Her eyes widened in her old, wrinkled cheeks. She stumbled back, clutching herself, and he cracked the handle over her head. It made a sharp, brutal sound that rang out in the silence, and her knees buckled and she doubled over, hands fluttering to her face.

He hit her again. And again. On the arm, the head, the side of the face, across the bridge of the nose. He heard the bone shatter. The handle snapped in two. She screamed, and he stabbed the broken end into her mouth with such force the jagged edges pierced the back of her throat and the handle shot out the other side, through her neck. The smell of her blood, the sight of it spilling over the floor, the handle, down the front of her clothes, incited him into a near frenzy. He kept pushing and grunting, impaling her, hating her, hissing, "Where's your power now, *vieja*? Where are your gods? Who's going to help you? Tell me! Tell me who's going to help you!"

He jerked the handle free. She slumped to the floor, her body twitching and shuddering like a puppet's. Her head flopped forward. Blood poured out of her mouth. Blood pooled on the floor at her sides. Blood. So much blood. Thick, red, still warm. Bits of bone and tissue floated in a pool near his shoe. Jesus God.

He jerked back. Rubbed his hands over his clothes. Clutched himself at the waist. Squeezed his eyes shut. Rocked back on his heels. *I killed her I didn't mean to kill her she shouldn't have said those things she had no right she didn't know anything she was guessing no one knows about Black Moon she shouldn't have taunted me she shouldn't sweet Jesus I killed her killedkilled*

A sob burst from his lips and he slapped a hand over his mouth and looked down at her, looked hard and long. Face smashed beyond recognition. Skull caved in on one side. Nose a bloody pulp. Blood oozing from the back of her neck. Arm twisted.

He had to do something. Get her out of here. Clean up the blood. Seroz would be back soon. Where was her car? Where had she parked it? Had she driven here alone? *The car, got to find the car and get rid of it.*

No.

First the body.

First he would take care of the body. And the blood.

He tried to move his legs and couldn't.

Oh-oh, Manuel, chanted Rikki. *What's happened here, sweetie? Manuel make a little boo-boo?*

Run, run, chanted his dead little *gringa. Run, run. Fleet of foot.* And her laughter echoed in the quiet, slapping the fetid air.

Look for the car first.

Yes. Of course. He would check first on the car. That made sense, didn't it?

He stumbled forward, past the counter, into the doorway that connected the shop with the hall, back to the staircase and the alley door. He opened it slowly, stuck his head out. He saw her old Mercedes parked at the fence on the other side of the alley. *Who knew she was coming here? Did she tell her granddaughter? Her maid? Did she tell anyone?*

He would worry about that later.

He bolted the alley door, raced back into the shop, pulled the bolt of black silk from the shelf. He dropped it beside her, unwound four or five yards of it. Scissors. He needed the scissors. Where were the goddamn scissors?

No time for scissors. He knelt, tore at the silk with his teeth, ripped it off the bolt with his hands. He grabbed her by the feet and pulled her away from the counter.

Her head lolled.

Her broken arm flopped like the body of a suffocating fish.

Blood splashed. Her blood on his hands. On his shoes. On his clothes. His face. The smell of it swirled in his nostrils. The strip of cloth fluttered down over her face. He rolled her over and wrapped the next length around the back of her head. Roll, wrap, roll, wrap, over and over again, down the length of her body until she was a mummy encased in black, a giant insect snuggled in her cocoon. *Good-bye, old woman, good-bye.* He laughed to himself, a soft, mad laugh he heard as music.

He secured the silk with masking tape, wrapping the tape around her just as he had done with the silk. Then he lifted her. Carried her over his shoulder into the back. To the staircase. He unlocked the door to the hall that led to his secret room. Down the damp, dimly lit hall. Into the storage room. He set her down. Pulled the shelves away from the wall. Pressed the button for the panel. Then he slipped her through the hole, Alice into the looking glass.

He turned on the light. Put the black cocoon at the foot of his altar. Hurried out again.

Cleaning liquids, rags, paper towels, a bucket of warm water and soap. *Clean quickly. Clean well.* Scrub spray wipe, scrub spray wipe. Every time he thought he had gotten all the blood, he would see another spot, another smear, another stain. The floor was bleeding. His hands were bleeding. He had to wash his hands half a dozen times and change the water over and over again, it was so pink, so dirty, the stink . . .

He ran out of rags. He used up four rolls of paper towels. Time ticked by. Traffic whizzed past outside. The stink of cleansers and blood made him dizzy. Once, as he was emptying the bloody water

into the toilet bowl in the back, his stomach heaved and he got
violently ill in the sink, and the bathroom echoed with Rikki's
laughter and the runner's chants of *Run, run, fleet of foot, oh yeah.*

In the shop again, he picked up the old woman's pocketbook
and carried it back into the secret room. He dumped the contents
on the floor, plucked out her keys, went through her wallet. He
took the money and left everything else.

He checked the floor once again to make sure he had gotten
all the blood, then wiped the area with Clorox. It killed the stink
of the blood. Now. Her car. He had to get rid of her car.

No. First he would call *Padrino* and tell him what had happened. His *padrino* would tell him what to do. *Padrino* would
take care of everything. That was his job. Ortega's job was to
learn, to remember.

His hand shook as he punched out the numbers of his *padrino's* private line. Two rings. Three. Four. Then: "Yes?"

"Es Manuel."

"Qué pasa, amigo?"

Ortega nearly laughed. He wiped his arm across his forehead
and smelled the blood and Clorox and cleansers on his skin. His
mouth tasted thick and sour. "I . . . I . . ."

"Speak up, Manuel. I can't hear you."

He vomited the story, his voice barely above a whisper, *Padrino* saying nothing, asking nothing, not even after he'd finished.

"Did you hear me?"

"Yes, Christ, I heard you. What did you do with the body?"

"I hid it."

"And her car?"

"In the alley. I have her keys."

"All right. Let me think. Jesus, I can't believe you've done this."

"She knew. She knew about Black Moon."

"Don't be ludicrous, Manuel. No one knows about Black
Moon."

"I'm telling you she *knew.*"

"All right, all right. Calm down. I want you to put the body
in the trunk of her car and . . . No, wait." Then, an excited
whisper: "Do you realize what you've *done?* This is wonderful,
Manuel. *She has the power.* She's the third. She's perfect. You're
brilliant, absolutely brilliant."

"But . . . but the date . . ."

"Forget the date. It doesn't matter. The *victim* matters, Manuel. Now here's what I want you to do . . ."

The knot in his gut loosened as he listened closely to what *Padrino* said about the body, the car, the old woman's eyes. He nodded and smiled, yes, yes, he understood, he understood what he had to do.

He washed up, changed into clean clothes, then opened his *abuelita*'s old trunk. A shawl, a wide-brim hat: he removed these things and put them on. From the old woman's purse he brought out lipstick, powder, rouge, mascara, and made up his face. Not very good, he thought, gazing at himself in the mirror, but good enough for this.

He stepped out into the back hall, listening for Seroz, wondering what he would do if Seroz suddenly entered the shop and saw him dressed like this. With makeup on. Ortega laughed aloud, laughed and laughed because of course he knew what he would do. He would kill Seroz. But he would do it quickly, cleanly.

In the secret room again, he hoisted the old woman onto his shoulder, paused at the alley door, looked both ways. Sunlight filled the emptiness. The air smelled clean and fragrant, of spring and hope and tomorrows.

He had backed the Mercedes up to the door, and now he popped the lid on the trunk, dropped the bundle inside, slammed it shut. He went back into the *botánica*, checking, double-checking. One last glimpse through the blind. No sign of cops. No sign of Seroz. Ikú was with him. Ikú protected. Ikú loved him.

He drove into the hills, toward the cat's right ear, where the wilderness preserve was. He was not stopped. He was not followed. He found the turnoff and hung a right. Every time the Mercedes hit a pothole, he heard the body rolling around, thumping up against the walls.

As if she were alive.

As if she were trying to get out.

Ridiculous.

She was dead. He had seen how dead she was. You could not be any more dead than she.

We are here, Manuel, whispered Rikki. *All of us. Your women. We are hereherehere*

Ortega switched on the radio and turned the volume high, drowning out the sound of Rikki's voice. He whipped off the hat, the shawl, rubbed at the makeup on his face with his hand, getting it off.

A mile or two in, the trees cleared and he could see the edge of the cliff, and there, off to his right, *Padrino* leaning against his car, a can of gasoline at his feet.

He waved Ortega over and patted him on the shoulder as he got out. "Well done, Manuel. But we still have a bit to do. Are you sure no one followed you?"

"Yes. Yes, I'm sure."

"Good. Are you all right?"

"Now. Yes. Now I'm fine." He inhaled deeply, pulling the fresh sea air into his lungs. The breeze cooled his cheeks. He tasted salt on his lips as he walked to the back of the car and opened the trunk. "Where should I put her?"

Padrino was gazing into the trunk. "Black silk. Good, Manuel. That's good. You did everything right. Just put her here on the ground and unwrap her head. I'm going to douse the inside of the car with gasoline."

Ortega didn't want to unwrap her head. He didn't want to see her face again. But an apprentice obeyed. An apprentice accepted his challenges by doing what had to be done. His hands trembled slightly as he started unwrapping the masking tape, then the silk. A soft breeze slipped through the trees and fluttered the edges of the silk, and for just a second he thought he heard the old *santera* whispering, *Helloooo, Manuel,* but of course it was only a trick of the breeze.

He didn't look at her face. He didn't look at her at all. He got up and walked over to the edge of the cliff while *Padrino* finished splashing gas inside the Mercedes.

Seventy-five feet below, waves pounded the huge, jagged rocks, and spray hung in the air like smoke. Over the years a handful of people had leaped to their deaths from here, so the place was now known as Suicide Cliff. An appropriate end for Anna Riviera.

Padrino called him over. His eyes seemed feverish, hot, as if he were on fire inside. "Do you realize how close we are, Manuel? How close we are to achieving a power held by no one else on Earth?"

Ortega didn't say anything; the look of madness in *Padrino*'s eyes frightened him.

Padrino held out the scalpel; it glistened in the light. "You want to do the honors?"

"Are you asking me or telling me?"

"Asking. It's your choice, Manuel."

"I would rather not."

Disappointment flickered in *Padrino*'s eyes, then he shrugged and crouched beside the old woman's body. Next to him on the ground was a glass jar filled with alcohol and a pint of rum. He took a swig of the rum, washed it around in his mouth, and shot it in a fine spray toward the woman's face. The drops of rum stood out against the dried blood, the crushed bones, sparkling and winking in the sunlight.

Next, *Padrino* lit a cigar and blew puffs of thick smoke toward the *santera*'s head. "When you get home this evening, Manuel, you'd better check your things. I think our detective was inside your place today."

"What? Why do you think that?"

Padrino looked up at him, smiling. "Trust me, Manuel. Just check your things."

He twisted open the lid on the jar, turned the old woman's head toward him, talking as he worked. "To preserve her power so that it passes into the *nganga*, the eyes have to be whole, Manuel, undamaged. So it's a good thing you didn't crush the bones around them. Otherwise a splinter might have punctured the eyeballs and we wouldn't be able to take advantage of this death."

The eye that now floated in the alcohol gazed up at Ortega; he looked away. But it didn't matter, he could still hear her whispering, *I watch you, Manuel. I watch and I wait.*

Then it was over, and his *padrino* tightened the lid on the jar and carried it over to his own car. He was grinning. He looked mad. Insane. He was a man possessed by something wild, something so dark, so hideous, Ortega wanted no part of it. But he didn't leave.

They put the old woman in the front seat of the Mercedes; the stench of gasoline floated out of the open door. Ortega slipped the gear shift into neutral and flicked a lit match into the Mercedes. The seat covers started to smolder, then burst into flame, tongues of fire zipping across them, crackling, leaping. *Padrino* pushed from the back and the car fell over the edge of the cliff, tumbling though the blinding blue like some huge and awkward beast, smoke spewing from its windows.

It struck the rocks and exploded. A fireball shot upward, quivering against the sky like a newborn sun, and then something lifted out of it. Ortega saw it, he did, a white, magnificent bird that soared up, up from the fireball, the smoke, up into the hot blue, its long wings beating the air, calling to him, *I watch, Manuel. I wait. For you. For you.*

DARKENING OF THE SUN
THE SUN
May 26–June 3

22

I

Kincaid strolled into the bedroom with two mugs of coffee and the construction plan to Uvanti's house, which Ferret had gotten for him, tucked under his arm. Unojo had claimed his side of the bed. Her silver head was resting against the sheet on Fuentes's thigh and turned slightly so she could see him. She blinked at him, two slow blinks and a fast one, a code he hadn't yet broken.

"I think she likes me, Ryan."

"I think she's jealous."

Fuentes laughed and lifted up on her elbows, her thick hair fanning across her shoulders as the sheet slipped off them. She stroked Unojo on the head, then gently moved her to the side, swung her legs over the edge of the bed, and reached for his shirt on the nearby chair. She shrugged it on and as usual fastened only one button.

"I wish you wouldn't do that," he said, passing her a mug.

Baby blues rising to his face. "Do what?"

"Button only one button."

She laughed again. "Okay, Ryan, what would you rather I do?"

"Button it all the way up." He sat at the foot of the bed. "Or don't button it at all." He spread the construction plan open between them. "Or take it off."

A roll of the eyes, a leg cocking up, elbow propped against it, hand supporting her chin. She smiled slightly, basking in the attention, and it dimpled a corner of her chin. Now that he had learned to read her face, he thought, it seemed as open to him as a child's.

"I thought we were going to talk business," she said.

"That was the idea."

"Maybe business can wait a few minutes, huh?" She leaned across the plans and locked her arms around his neck, nibbling at his lower lip. "We're shameless hedonists, Ryan, I hope you realize that."

"Worse than the Romans," he murmured, sliding his hands up under the shirt, against her cool, white skin. "Worse than the Greeks."

"Uh-huh." She tugged on him hard then, and they both pitched backward, laughing, tickling each other, rolling, startling the cat off the bed. The mattress dipped and swayed. The springs squeaked and complained. Fuentes squealed, wiggled free, tried to crawl away from him. But Kincaid grabbed her by the ankles, pulled her across the sheets, and flipped her onto her back. She squealed again and struggled, but he pinned her hands to the mattress and collapsed against her so she couldn't move and buried his face in her hair.

"You give, Fuentes?"

"Never." But her fingers curled over his hands and she moved her hips in that slow, sensuous way, as though she were dancing. "You could probably talk me into it, though, Ryan." She turned her head slightly, biting gently at his earlobe. "If you took off your clothes."

He sat up and stripped, and she laughed.

"You're *so* easy, Ryan."

"One of my better qualities."

She threw back the covers and he rolled in beside her, into the scent of her skin, her hair, into the blue softness of her eyes. They rolled and twisted and rearranged themselves, finding a peculiar symmetry of limbs that suited them, both on their sides, facing each other, her leg snaking between his. Their lovemaking was slow, languid, building like a morning heat that promised to peak at midday. He liked that. He liked the endless explorations of her hands and mouth, the way she controlled her movements, her muscles, a dancer's control. And he liked the way that control ebbed when he touched her in a certain way, when his hands whispered, *Like this?* and she responded by shifting her hips or biting her lip or pulling him closer.

"That night on Uvanti's yacht." She pulled back a little to look at him, her hand busy under the covers. "What did you think?"

"Of you?"

"Yes."

"I don't think I thought anything until you were at the bar making drinks."

"And what did you think then?"

"That you looked great in terry cloth."

"C'mon, Ryan," she laughed. "Be serious."

"That you were unapproachable but interested, just like I was. I guess that's what I thought." She moved her hips, asking. "What about you?"

"The same. Before that night on the yacht I hadn't been with anyone since before joining the bureau. And when it was happening, I kept thinking that if I didn't touch you, it wouldn't count, it wouldn't matter when it was . . ." She sucked the final word in with her breath and lifted her hips slightly and he slipped inside her. They rolled and she straddled him, lowering herself down against him just as the phone pealed.

"Great timing," she muttered.

"The machine will get it."

A moment later: "Mr. Kincaid, are you there?"

"Sounds like a kid," Fuentes said.

It took him a moment to place the voice: it was Josie, the old *santera*'s granddaughter. "I'd better get this."

Fuentes moved away from him, and Kincaid switched off the machine and picked up the receiver. "Hi, Josie. This is Mr. Kincaid. What can I do for you?"

"It's my Nana, Mr. Kincaid. I tried calling Ms. Meg at the library, but she's not there and they wouldn't give me her home phone and then I found that card you gave me with the magnifying glass on it and well, anyway, see, Nana wasn't here when I got home from school Friday and . . . and she still hasn't come home and I'm, uh, kinda worried about her."

"Didn't she tell the maid where she was going?"

"No. The maid wasn't worried, 'cause Nana sometimes goes away without telling us. But I think something's wrong and I was wondering if you knew what I should do."

"Is her car at home?"

"No."

"She didn't leave you a note?"

"No."

There was no reason to connect yesterday's explosion off Suicide Cliff with the *santera*, but once he considered it, he couldn't get it out of his mind. "Is her purse in the house, Josie?"

"No. Could you give me the number for the police, Mr. Kincaid?"

"Let me do this. I'll call the police and then I'll call Meg, and either she or I will come out to the house to get you, okay?"

"Okay. Thanks. Thanks a lot."

"You sit tight."

"I will. Wait, Mr. Kincaid. How long do you think it'll take you to get here?"

"Give us an hour."

"Right. Thanks."

He reached Aline's answering machine at home, hung up, and dialed her office.

"Bernelli, Homicide."

"Bernie, It's Ryan. Do you have anything yet on that explosion yesterday?"

"The lab's not *that* fast, Ryan. The car was blown into last week, and just about every piece of it went into the drink. The only thing we found was a dark brown panel from what the lab says is the wheel well. They're trying to I.D. the make of the car through the paint, and we've got drivers down there now. But I do have something else. . . ."

She told him about the arrest of Karl Porter at two this morning as he was leaving the Moose. Porter as Mr. K. Porter, the *K* on the negligees, the book on *santería*, Porter as John Percy in the computer printout from the Days Inn.

Kincaid heard Porter saying, *I saw her dance a couple of times . . . so I guess you could say I knew her.*

"Is he out on bond?"

"Hell no, and he won't talk to anyone either. He hasn't even hired an attorney. The senator's been pouring on the pressure since we brought Porter in, and unfortunately he went to the press. Porter hasn't denied or admitted anything."

"Could I get in to talk to him?"

"If he'll see you. So far he's refused to speak to everyone— his attorney, his wife, the chief, Aline. About the only thing we know at this point is that he's got O blood, which means he could be the father of Rikki's kid. But then, Uvanti's supposedly an O too."

"Hell, Bernie, I'm an O. And Rikki's last sex partner was an A negative. I'd like to try to get in to see Porter."

"Like I said, Ryan, be my guest."

He told her about the call from Josie Riviera. The girl's grand-mother drove an old-model dark-brown Mercedes, and although yesterday's date wasn't right, the fact that she was a *santera* fit the profile.

Bernie mulled this over, but not for long. "You want me to go out to the house and talk to her?"

"It'd be best if Meg was along, since she knows the family. I'll call her and call you right back."

In between calls, he briefed Fuentes, who was already getting dressed. She didn't comment one way or the other, but she didn't have to, her conclusion was written on her face: Porter wasn't guilty, couldn't be guilty, because Uvanti was their man. She said she would start breakfast and left the bedroom while he called the station again.

Aline answered and said she would meet Meg Mallory out at the *santera*'s house and would he please get over here and see if he could get anything out of Porter?

He said he'd be there in forty minutes or so.

Outside, heat clung thickly to the air, a portent of what sum-mer would bring. Sunlight bleached the gravel in the driveway, burned against the hood of Fuentes's Jetta, and threaded her hair with pale gold. He handed her the blueprints to Uvanti's house. "You'd better take this. I'll call you later. Unless you're work-ing."

"I've got three days off. Then boss man wants to talk about a promotion."

"To courier of his artwork?"

"Let's hope so." She leaned on the open car door, an eye winked shut against the glare of the light. "You think Porter killed her?"

"No."

A small frown creased her forehead, and those baby blues were soft, sympathetic. "Because he's your friend."

"Because I don't think he did it."

"Why not?"

"If he killed Rikki, then chances are good that he also killed the runner, which would mean he's deeply involved in *palo*, and it just doesn't fit."

"They're going to say he had a motive for killing Rikki. And that his *santería* project explains the rest."

"Ortega's a *santero*, Uvanti's involved in *santería*, and both of them had motives. They just haven't slipped up."

"Not yet. But you may have a hard time convincing the cops, Ryan, especially with the senator riding their asses. Porter is going to find himself in the unfortunate position of being Chamberlain's whipping boy."

"It's not his investigation, it's Aline's."

Fuentes gave a small nod, looked as though she was about to say something else, then apparently changed her mind. She slipped behind the wheel of her car. He shut the door and leaned down, elbows resting on the lower edge of her window, the sun hot against his back. "What is it?" he asked.

She smiled at his acuity and flexed her fingers against the steering wheel, not looking at him but gazing through the windshield. "I know this isn't the time to ask, but I'm sort of curious about something." She turned her head toward him. "Are you still in love with Aline?"

"I don't know."

Another small nod.

"What about you and your ex?" he asked.

"That was lifetimes ago."

"That's not what I asked."

Fuentes shrugged, tightened her long fingers over the steering wheel, looked away again. "I don't know."

Kincaid touched her chin, turning her face toward him. "You don't trust me, do you?"

"Trusting isn't something I do real well, Ryan."

"Then I guess we'll have to work on that."

She smiled ever so faintly, as though she didn't quite know what to make of the remark, then cranked up the Jetta and pulled out of the driveway with a honk and a wave.

Kincaid, puzzled by something he couldn't name, something without shape or definition, watched the Jetta until it vanished in the pines.

2

Children rarely made good witnesses, but Josie Riviera proved
to be the exception. She recalled, for instance, that her grandmother had received a call yesterday morning during breakfast
which had upset her. When Aline asked her to elaborate, Josie
said she thought it had something to do with Mr. Kincaid's visit
the week before, because she heard her grandmother say his
name.

Did Josie know who the caller was? Aline asked. Sure, she
replied with a nod, she'd answered the phone. The man who'd
called was Mr. Aponte, a friend of her grandmother's who taught
judo and karate in El Pueblito. When Aline asked what Mr.
Aponte's first name was, Josie shook her head; she couldn't
remember. But the name of the school where he taught was
Caribe.

"Did your grandmother say anything to you after she talked
to Mr. Aponte?" asked Meg.

Josie's fingers stroked and patted the Siamese kitten snuggled
in her lap. "Just that she had some important errands to run and
she might not be back when I got home from school."

"What kind of errands?" Aline prodded. "Did she say?"

"Grocery shopping, dry cleaning, like that. And I got the
feeling she was going to see someone, maybe Mr. Aponte."
Her wide dark eyes flitted from Aline to Meg. "Could I, uh,
stay with you, Ms. Meg, until Nana comes home?"

"You bet, honey. Why don't you go pack an overnight bag
and I'll talk to the maid. We can take Bandit, too, if you want."

Josie hurried off, the kitten racing along behind her.
"Where're her parents?" Aline asked.

"Her mother's dead. Her father's remarried and living somewhere around Daytona." She stared through the doorway to the
hall, where Josie had vanished. "I hope to God Ryan's wrong
about all this, Aline."

"I'm sure there's an explanation for her absence. Let's just
take this a step at a time, okay?" She gave the other woman's
arm a reassuring pat and wished she were half as confident as
she sounded.

3

Chief Frederick was on the phone when Kincaid entered his office, and he didn't look happy. Pink spots of agitation bloomed in his cheeks, his white hair was uncombed, as if he'd been running his fingers through it again and again, and he puffed urgently on a cigar as he paced back and forth in front of his desk.

He mouthed, *Stick around*, and Kincaid nodded and walked over to the window. He peered into the sun-washed street two stories below, watching Saturday traffic. Now and then the blast of a horn reached him, but mostly this office was cushioned from noise, sealing them in like astronauts in a space capsule.

". . . no, I don't think that would be a good idea, Senator." Frederick's voice strained with courtesy. "Threatening Porter isn't going to get us any answers, and right now I'd like to handle this *my* way, without any interference from you or the FBI. I'll call you at the hotel as soon as anything changes." He slammed the phone down, muttered something obscene about politicians, stabbed out his cigar.

"Your blood pressure's soaring, Gene."

He raked his fingers through his hair. "No fucking wonder I'm gray. That asshole wants to come down here and have a good ole heart-to-heart with Porter, who hasn't said squat since he was brought in. And no, Ryan, he doesn't want to see you. I asked."

"So I'll ask."

Frederick sighed, plucked his spent cigar from the ashtray, straightened it out, and lit it again. "Fine, go ask. But just so you know, Hannah Porter says Karl was gone all day yesterday, that he wasn't home the night of the twelfth, when Rikki Baker was killed, and that he didn't get home last Monday until around seven in the morning. And since he hasn't said anything one way or the other, he's got no alibi for any of the murders right now."

"Do you have the motel printout? I'd like to take a look at it."

Frederick riffled through the files on his desk, pulled out one, handed it over. "Those are copies of the pages with his name on it. The original's locked up. How's your head, anyway?"

He touched the Band-Aid that now covered his stitches. "No permanent damage." Kincaid opened the file and studied the list of names, pages of them with all the John Percy or J. Percy entries marked. "Did anyone talk to the desk clerks to see if they remembered Porter?"

"Yeah. I talked to three of them and showed them Porter's picture. They remembered him, all right. They remembered he arrived alone and left alone and always requested a room at the back, away from the main road. It would help if we had that appointment book you found at Baker's apartment, so we could compare the dates of her Days Inn entries with these dates. But Martell doesn't think that's going to be a problem in prosecuting him, especially once we've got that genetic signature back on the fetus."

"It sounds like he's awfully sure Porter's guilty."

"That's his job, Ryan."

And it would also be Martell's biggest case in two years, his ticket back into the limelight. "Then I suppose he's already got an explanation for Porter killing the runner."

"Obsession with his new project, the *santería* book."

"Sure." Kincaid dropped the file on the desk. "Does that mean Ortega and Uvanti are off the hook?"

"It means we're going to question Ortega again. As for Uvanti . . . ." Frederick shrugged. "We haven't got a damn thing on him."

"Oh? You're sure?"

Frederick twirled his cigar against the edge of the ashtray, knocking off the ash. "Unless you know something you've kept to yourself, Ryan."

"I might." Kincaid slipped his hands in the pockets of his trousers and turned back to the window, figuring the odds. He decided to risk it. "But it's got to be unofficial, Gene."

"Aw, Christ," he sighed. "Don't do this to me, Ryan. Not today, okay? I'm really not in the mood for it. I've got Chamberlain breathing down my neck, the press on hold, two women dead, and maybe a third, unless the old *santera* shows up. If Porter's not our man, then I need to know about it."

"My terms, Gene."

He grumbled, he argued, he threatened to lock Kincaid up and throw away the key. But in the end he came around because he couldn't afford not to, and listened without interrupting as

Kincaid told him about Uvanti's art scam and the Baker woman's involvement in it.

"I'd like to know who your source is, Ryan."

"Nope."

"Then it's just hearsay. I need evidence before I can arrest the man."

"I'm working on it. I only wanted you to be aware that Uvanti has a motive for killing Rikki that goes well beyond jealousy over losing her to Ortega or Porter."

"Fine. Now go see if Porter will tell you anything."

Porter looked like he was recovering from a mammoth drunk. He needed a shave, his clothes were wrinkled, his dark hair was uncombed. He was sitting back on the bunk in his cell, scribbling on a yellow legal pad open in his lap. Books were scattered at the foot of the bunk. He seemed oblivious to Kincaid's presence at the bars and the guard shuffling away from the cell to allow them privacy.

"I hear you're not taking visitors," Kincaid said.

Porter raised his head and gazed at Kincaid with eyes that were surprisingly clear. "It seems like the most prudent thing to do right now."

"You need anything?"

Porter chuckled. "Sure. But not anything you can get for me, Ryan." He looked back at the legal pad, scribbled some more, then slapped the pen down, set the pad aside, and came over to the bars. The two men regarded each other as if across an impassable chasm. Porter rubbed a hand over his face. "Go ahead and ask me, Ryan. Ask me if I killed her. Go on. Everyone else has asked. Why shouldn't you?"

"I already know you didn't."

Porter's laughter was loud and false, pierced with loneliness and despair. "Now, how the fuck can you be sure of that? Huh?"

"Cut the crap, Karl. If you don't want to talk to me, fine. But at least talk to an attorney. If you don't, they're going to appoint one anyway."

"You don't get it, Ryan. An attorney's not going to make a damn bit of difference one way or the other, not with Rikki's old man in the picture."

"Were you involved with her?"

Softly, as though it hurt him to speak: "Of course I was." His hands came up around the bars, gripping them so hard his

knuckles turned white. His dark eyes moistened, and he blinked
several times to clear them. "I was in *love* with her, for Christ's
sakes. The kid was mine. I begged her to keep it, to stay on
Tango until I could work out a divorce settlement with Hannah.
I offered to support her. I wanted to marry her. But oh no, she
wanted everything *now*, this instant. Well, it's just not that fucking easy to work out a settlement, and I wasn't about to just turn
everything over to Hannah."

"Where were you the night she was killed?"

"Hannah and I had had an argument, so I left and went into
town and had a few drinks and then I went by Rikki's. She wasn't
home so I went someplace else and had a few more drinks and
then drove over to her apartment again and she still wasn't home,
so I kept drinking and woke up the next morning on South
Beach."

"And when the runner was killed?"

Pain swept over his face, as palpable as the color of his eyes.
"I spent the night at Rikki's. I had a key. I . . . I just wanted to
be someplace where I could . . . could feel close to her or something."

"What about her relationship with Ortega? What do you know
about it?"

Porter paced back and forth in front of the bars now. "Not
much, really, except that she consulted him about things like he
was, I don't know, some sort of guru or psychic or something."

"Did you know she was sleeping with him?"

"Sure. And with Uvanti. They were her leverage, Ryan. She
figured I had Hannah so she needed a couple of men just to even
things up." He stopped moving, rubbed his hands over his face,
looked at Kincaid again. "She even did a spell on Hannah and
me. To separate us." His laugh was bitter. "Maybe I ought to
use that in the book." His voice broke, he sucked air in through
clenched teeth, whispered, "Jesus, Ryan. I didn't kill her. I
didn't kill anyone."

"One more question. Did you ever get in touch with that
santera whose number I gave you?"

"I spoke to her once on the phone, and we were going to get
together next week. Why?"

"She may be the third victim, that's why, and you're going
to get some questions. Pull up a chair and let's go back through
this from the beginning."

Porter sighed, shook his head, fixed his eyes on the floor.

When he glanced up again, his expression was resigned. "Maybe my attorney should be here too."

It was probably the wisest decision Porter had made since Kincaid had met him.

23

I

Caribe School of Judo and Karate was located in an old neighborhood on the edge of El Pueblito. Many of the buildings dated back to the late 1800s and were built by Cuban cigar factory workers and Bahamian fishermen. Simple pine structures with clapboard fences stood alongside two-storey conch houses and snug little bungalows. Huge banyans lined the streets, watchful sentries whose thick arms entwined over the center of the roads, creating a canopy of green.

The school itself occupied the bottom floor of a yellow conch house. Since the front door was open, she walked in. The room was stripped of furniture and a dozen or more students in white garbs sat on floor mats which were arranged in a circle around a small man who looked part Oriental and part Hispanic. He was sitting with his legs spread slightly, head touching his knees. As she watched, he grasped his left ankle and slowly brought it up behind his neck, hooking it there. Then he did the same with his right and rocked back onto his buttocks, arms extended at his sides.

He grinned in response to a groan from one of the students. "It's easier than it looks. Visualize yourself doing it, focus on the image, and then carry it out. Eventually you'll be able to hold the position for at least thirty seconds. Now, you try it."

His ankles came unhooked, his legs swung to the floor, and he stood. There was no separation to his movements, no apparent strain. It all seemed to happen in a smooth, singular motion as effortless as walking. He glanced around as the students started twisting themselves up like pretzels, grunting and groaning. Then he strolled over to Aline, gave a slight bow, and said, "Welcome. You wish to enroll in classes?"

"I'm looking for Mr. Aponte."

"I'm Carlos Aponte."

Aline introduced herself, and Aponte suggested they talk outside. He gave his class a few instructions, then they walked out onto the wraparound porch. Aponte straddled the railing as though it were a horse, and Aline settled in one of the wicker rockers. She explained what she needed to know and why. Aponte's pleasant face darkened.

"I warned Anna to be careful," he said softly. "I just had a bad feeling about it."

"Then you *did* talk to her yesterday?"

"Yes. I was out of town, and there were several messages from her on my machine when I got back. I called her first thing yesterday morning. She had some questions about *palo* and Armando Bacalao and wanted to know if I would talk to a private investigator named Kincaid who's working on the homicide of the stripper."

Aline nodded. "He's a consultant on the case. When you were talking to Anna, did she mention anything about going out later? Maybe to see someone?"

"No. She just said she would call Kincaid and give him my number and that I should expect a call from him."

"Did she mention anyone else besides Kincaid?"

"No."

"Why would she come to you with questions about Bacalao and *palo*?"

He ran his hands over his white trousers, a gesture as indicative of pensiveness as it was of reluctance. "You see, my grandfather was a *babalawo* here on Tango—a high priest of *santería*. That means he officiated at certain rituals, mediated disputes, and performed various other functions related to the religion, even though he wasn't a *santero*. He died in a fire several months after he mediated a dispute among a group of *santeros*, which included Bacalao, whom he ruled against. It was never proven, of course, that Bacalao was behind the fire, but in my heart I know that he was. As a result, the man and *palo* have become something of an obsession for me over the years."

"What did Anna want to know exactly?"

"Several things. If I thought there was a correlation between these murders and those that Bacalao committed; what had happened to his son; his *nganga*; his estate; his wife. She told me about the dead black chicken a detective found in her storage room." He paused. "I assume you're the detective she was talking about."

"Yes."

"Did you carry out her recommendations?"

Aline pulled the small white bag from her shirt pocket and held it in her hand. "Only this. The rest was stolen from Kincaid's car."

"So you believe in the power of *palo*? Of *santería*?"

"I'm superstitious enough to listen, Mr. Aponte."

He smiled and picked up the white bag. "You did more than listen."

"Considering that one of the people Bacalao killed was the detective who dogged him, I felt I had reason to."

"You don't have to justify your actions to me, Detective. I'm just trying to get a feel for what you think you believe, that's all. In *santería*, voodoo, witchcraft, in any occult practice, belief is paramount. In fact, in everything, belief is key."

She smiled at the simplicity. "If you don't believe, it won't work?"

"I'm speaking of root assumptions, Detective. Belief at the most profound levels. If these powers don't fit into your particular belief system, then they won't be part of your experience, therefore they can't possibly hurt you. But since you are involved in this case, there must be something in you, some belief—however buried—in such things. Therefore, it's wise that you carry the talisman, and it would be in your best interest if you weren't anywhere near Tango on June third."

"June third? Why? I thought Abel Whitkins was killed on September 22."

"He was. But the dates are secondary, Detective Scott, especially where this eclipse is concerned."

It took her a moment to realize he was referring to the impending solar eclipse. "What's the eclipse have to do with anything?"

"I'll try to explain. But there are several things I should tell you first." He opened the bag, sniffed at the contents, tied it again, and handed it back to her. "You see, this isn't just any *mayombero* who's committing the murders in homage to Bacalao. I believe your killer is Bacalao's son."

"Then he wasn't abducted?"

"I think his mother staged the abduction for Bacalao's ben-

efit. She knew he would never consent to the boy living elsewhere with relatives. She was afraid for him. I believe she sent
him to live with her sister in the Midwest.''

"Why do you think it's the son?''

"For many reasons. The precise duplication of the murders,
for one thing. Also, not too long ago there was a short piece in
the paper about a panther that was killed in the Tango swamp.
Its heart had been removed. That's a deliberate act, in line with
palo. Bacalao considered panthers his spiritual counterparts in
the animal kingdom. The heart would be used in the *nganga*.''

The panther in my dream.

"I feel that Bacalao's son somehow came into possession of
his father's *nganga*, then he decided to strengthen it by adding
his father's bones, so he pillaged Bacalao's grave in the seamen's
cemetery. Anna told me about the grave,'' he added, answering
her unspoken question. "And then he began duplicating the
murders his father committed, to pay him tribute. On top of
this, he knew the legends. About the Black Moon.''

She felt suddenly like a student at the feet of a sage, a woman
seeking enlightenment, and knew he was about to fill in a
vital piece of the puzzle. His voice when he spoke was soft,
measured, a cadence, a rhythm that drew her into it swiftly and
completely.

On the day Bacalao died, there was a lunar eclipse visible in
Africa, the continent on which both *santería* and *palo* were
born. Among *mayomberos*, this meant that Ikú was taking one
of his own back into himself. This spirit could only be reborn
during a solar eclipse, as the moon—known as the Black Moon—
passed between the sun and the Earth. According to legend, the
spirit's rebirth had to occur during the period when the sun was
completely blocked, and there had to be a sacrifice made to Ikú.
The ideal host for such a rebirth was an individual who had
consciously lured the spirit of the dead *mayombero* by honoring
him. This homage could be paid in a variety of ways—through
money given to his family or relatives; by acts committed in his
name; by the replication of his spells or *bilongos*.

The maximum possible duration of a total eclipse was seven
and a half minutes. If the spirit was to be reborn in an area
where only a partial eclipse was visible, then the blood of the
sacrificial victim would have to be drunk during that seven-and-
a-half-minute period to prevent the host from being consumed
by the light.

The Black Moon, Aponte said, was the most formidable symbol among *mayomberos*, a very specific archetype that personified the epitome of *palo*'s secret knowledge and power. Whoever inherited it was believed to be nearly invincible as long as he continued to honor Ikú.

"Which was where Bacalao failed. By denouncing Ikú after his son's supposed abduction, he turned all of that power against himself. Now, we civilized beings"—he smiled—"like to think of it all as superstition and coincidence. But *mayomberos* believe in it absolutely, Detective Scott, and if you want to find the killer, then you need to understand the depth of the belief, and the kind of fanaticism it instills. Especially if I'm right about the killer being Bacalao's son."

She wondered about Porter's background, where he'd been born, where he'd been raised, who had raised him, his return to Tango three years ago. "When was Bacalao's son born?"

"In 1945. He disappeared when he was just two, and Bacalao died a year later."

So he would be forty-four now, she thought. Porter was in his forties. So were Ortega and Uvanti. Terrific. "Assuming your theory is true about the killer being Bacalao's son, how would you go about tracking him down?"

"I wouldn't."

"How should I?"

"You shouldn't. As I said before, Detective Scott, the most prudent thing you can do is make sure you aren't within a hundred miles of Tango on June third. It doesn't matter that Whitkins was killed on September 22. Keep in mind the important element here is the eclipse, not dates. The power of the Black Moon is what the killer is seeking."

"You seem pretty certain this man's going to win."

"Not at all. I'm only saying that if you're on the island, he'll find you and try to carry out his plan. That's what a fanatic does, Detective. And most fanatics do it rather well."

It answered her question, and never mind if the answer wasn't particularly appealing. If the killer wasn't in jail, he would come to her.

And she'd be ready.

Aline spent two hours at the station. She listened to Porter's statement, which was issued in his attorney's presence, and listened to Kincaid, who believed in Porter's innocence, and listened to the chief, who said Porter's request for bond was denied, thanks to pressure from Senator Chamberlain, which was just fine with him because he wanted Porter to remain in jail until after the eclipse.

And then she listened to Martell arguing with Frederick about how to prosecute the case. When she reminded Martell that there were *two* killers, that Ortega and Uvanti were still suspects, and maybe he'd better not jump the gun, he got angry and told her *he* was the attorney and *she* was the detective, and since he didn't tell her how to do *her* job, he would appreciate the same consideration from her.

At the moment he was saying all this they were in the conference room, and Kincaid happened to poke his head through the door and hear it. "She's got a point, Martell, and it might be in your best interest to pay attention to what she's saying. More than one prosecutor has fucked up because ambition got in the way."

Aline saw the look on Martell's face and on Kincaid's and on the chief's and wanted to slide through the floor, to vanish, to go up like a puff of smoke. She expected Martell to explode, but he didn't. He spoke in a tight, controlled voice that reminded her of how he'd made love to her that night on the sloop, in the storm, in that precise, deliberate, almost cruel way, and she hated him a little now just as she had then.

"What you know about ambition, Ryan, could fit inside your thumbnail. Seems to me if you had a little more of it, you wouldn't have lost your plane to the IRS." Then he swept up his file and left the room.

"I need this shit." Frederick kicked the door shut. The slam echoed. "What I want *you* to do, Ryan, is to tell Aline what you told me earlier today. About Uvanti." He turned to Aline, poking the cigar at the air in front of her face. "And what I want *you* to do is listen, and then tell Ryan everything this judo fellow told you. And *then* the three of us are going to sit down and figure out a game plane. Everyone understand the rules?" His dark, angry eyes flicked from Aline to Kincaid and back.

"We speak English, Gene." Kincaid folded his bones into a nearby chair.

2

Aline bolted awake suddenly, blinking against the dark, senses straining for the noise that had jerked her out of a light sleep. *You imagined it. You dreamed it.* But she didn't move, didn't breathe too loudly, didn't get up. She struggled through the haze of her fatigue, trying to remember where she'd left her purse. Her gun was in the purse.

Think, think, c'mon. Where's the purse?

Then she heard it again, a small sound, a scratching, just outside her window. *He's here. On the porch outside the window. Jesus. Move. Do something.* Carefully, slowly, she slid off the bed to the floor and landed on her purse. She dug inside it for her gun. Found it. Flicked off the safety.

She crawled to the window. It was halfway open, and she hesitated under the sill, listening. There. She heard it again.

Aline moved to the side of the window and lifted up, peering through the glass.

Nothing there.

She crept to the other side and checked.

She didn't see anything, but he might be crouched under the sill, just as she was. Waiting, just as she was. If she went outside and circled around, she could surprise him.

No. Bad idea. She could surprise him right here.

She raised up and peered around the edge of the window, down at the floor of the porch, fear thick in her mouth. She couldn't see anything. It was too dark. Aline waited another moment, then slammed the window all the way up and threw herself back against the wall, the gun tight in her hands, ready.

When nothing happened, when there were no shots, no sudden movements, she leaned out. A raccoon scurried down the porch railing, then leaped onto a low-hanging pine branch and fled.

She burst out laughing and moved on unsteady legs toward the bed. She sank onto it, switched on the lamp, set the gun aside with hands that trembled, that were damp.

He wouldn't have come for her here.

He wouldn't dare.

Wolfe, sprawled at the foot of her bed, raised his head and blinked those dark raisin eyes at her. *Food?* he seemed to ask. *Is it time for a snack?*

"Yeah, why not," she said. "How about some Stinko Delight, guy?"

He leaped down from the bed and scurried over to the top of the bamboo ladder, glancing back at her as if to say, *C'mon, hurry up, please.*

They went downstairs. In the kitchen, she fed Wolfe some leftover chicken and fixed a Nightmare Chaser for herself, her mother's tea remedy for everything from insomnia to cramps. She sat at the counter and dug through the stack of papers and mail on the counter until she reached a legal pad. She turned a saucer over on the pad and used it to draw a circle.

Inside the circle, she printed *Rikki*. Using the edge of a 3 x 5 card, she drew two dozen lines out from the circle, so it now resembled a wheel and spokes. Then, as quickly as she could, without thinking about it, she jotted one or two words at the end of each spoke. Names. Events. Details about Rikki, Uvanti, Ortega, Porter. The art scam. *Santería. Palo.* From each of these words she drew a second spoke and jotted another word or two and so on until she had repeated the process four times and had to tape a sheet to either side of the original for additional space.

Within thirty minutes the entire case was diagrammed in a peculiar right-brain shorthand. Then she sat there, studying it, puzzling over it. She knew there were things she wasn't seeing, but that if she looked long enough she would begin to detect a pattern, a rhythm. It was like playing Boggle, a word game with lettered cubes. The object was to make as many words as you could in three minutes, using upended cubes that touched each other. They could touch in any way, and the words had to be at least three letters. It was always the simplest words she didn't see: *the, and, for, sex, love, cat, boy, girl.*

Aline spun the sheet around. Her head started to ache. Her eyes burned. She finished the tea and carried Wolfe and the papers upstairs. She fell asleep with the light on, the paper on her chest, Wolfe's head resting against her hip. When she awakened again, the hands of the clock stood at 4:00.

She got up and showered, then sat down on the bed again and studied the sheet for another few minutes. *I'm close. I can feel it.* The missing pieces were here.

"Porter." She tapped her nail against his name. "Porter, Porter. Something not right about Porter."

He was someone's fall guy. He was convenient. He was

framed. *Maybe. Be careful, Al. Be careful. Would he team up with Uvanti? With Ortega? Would he kill an old woman?*

No. It felt wrong.

All right. Uvanti, what about Uvanti? He *might* team up with Ortega, despite their competition over Rikki. Or because of it. *Eliminate the problem.* Rikki had been the problem. She, the runner, and the old woman had been steps to the goal. Power was the goal. The art scam was a postscript, then, to everything else, a moneymaking business, like the club.

How had Kincaid found out about the art scam? Who was his source? Someone within Uvanti's organization? Was it the same source who'd told him Rikki's father was Senator Chamberlain? On the sheet, leading off from Chamberlain's name, were: *FBI, Miranda Fuentes.*

Her gaze fell to Ferret's name. *Lead/Uvanti, watch Starr.*

And suddenly she knew. The babe in the pink leotards was Miranda Fuentes, his source, Rikki Baker's fellow stripper and friend, the woman who'd been in Kincaid's shower that morning. And for some reason he was protecting her identity.

Oblivious to the time, she called his house, and he answered on the third ring, his voice husky with sleep.

"Just a couple of quick questions, Kincaid."

"Al. Christ. I'm asleep. I'll call you later."

"This won't take long. Was Miranda Fuentes, otherwise known as Starr Abbott, the friend whose place Rikki was supposed to keep an eye on in her absence? And if so, Kincaid, was Rikki killed there? And if she was, why the fuck have you kept it to yourself? That's obstructing an investigation. Frederick could throw the goddamn book at you."

"It's not even light outside yet."

"Just answer my question."

Silence, then: "I had my reasons."

"Wonderful. And what about the crime scene, Ryan? And how do you know she didn't have something to do with Rikki's death? Just what kind of game are you playing, anyway? What's her involvement in this case? What's she know about Uvanti's art scam? Just who is she?"

"Calm down, will you?"

Right. Calm down. Lower your voice. Deep breaths. Good, very good. "I'm calm. Start talking."

"I think it'd be better if you heard it from Miranda."

Miranda: the name sounded like music when he said it. "I don't want it from her. You tell me, Kincaid."

"If you're free tonight, come over to the house around eight, okay?"

"So the three of us can sit around and discuss this? No thanks, Ryan. I—"

"Ferret will be here too."

"What's he got to do with this?"

"It concerns Uvanti, and we need your help. Look, I've really got to get some sleep. See you tonight."

The line went dead before she could say anything.

As the Honda climbed into the hills, she breathed a little more easily. It felt good to drive, to move, to be out of the house, away from town. She couldn't even see the town lights behind her because of the fog. So much fog.

It rolled across the road in front of the car, drifted from the thickets of pines, left a residue of moisture on the windshield. She felt like an explorer, sealed inside a small white capsule on wheels as it moved across the landscape of some alien world. And in this world, there had never been a Rikki Baker or any of the players in her life. *Santería* didn't exist here. Neither did Kincaid nor Martell or Miranda Fuentes. There was only the fog and the stillness and the whisper of the tires against the pavement of Old Post Road.

Now and then she caught a gleam of headlights behind her or someone passed her headed in the opposite direction. But for the most part, Old Post was deserted.

She turned right onto the dirt strip that led to Suicide Cliff. She'd been up here the day of the explosion, but there had been too many distractions and so many people mulling about that she hadn't really had a chance to look around. She didn't know what she expected to find, especially with the fog as thick as it was. But being here gave her a sense of purpose, made her feel as though she were moving forward, something she desperately needed right now.

The road ended in a small clearing. She swung off to the far right side, poked the Honda into the trees, and parked. The wind moaned along the edge of the cliff and whistled through the trees, strumming branches like strings on a musical instrument. When she stepped out of the car, her ankles vanished in fog. It swirled as though it were alive, tendrils coiling around the lower parts of her legs, licking at the backs of her knees. It spooked her, and for a moment or two she considered forgetting the whole thing and driving home. The conditions were hardly conducive for success. But what the hell, since she was here, she might as well poke around.

Aline turned on her flashlight and walked along the lip of the cliff, the beam bouncing against the fog lifting from the rocks below. The dampness chilled her. The wind blew her hair into her eyes. She zipped up her windbreaker and paused in a spot where the fog had thinned.

She could just make out the dark shapes of rocks seventy-five feet below, waves whipping against them, spray rising like smoke. According to one eyewitness, a young woman who'd been beachcombing about a quarter mile away, the Mercedes had exploded before it hit the rocks. Even a vehicle that had careened out of control wouldn't explode unless it hit something, and there was nothing to hit here where the car had gone over.

That made gasoline and a match the most likely culprits.

Was the old woman dead when the car was doused and set on fire?

The wind was so loud and she was so absorbed with her own thoughts that not until she moved away from the cliff did she hear a car. When she turned, it was too late.

Headlights blazed against the fog, burned through it like a pair of suns, momentarily blinding her. And then it charged her, bearing down on her, a tsunami, a bat out of hell.

24

I

Aline spun and tore toward the pines where her Honda was parked, but the car—*no, a van, it's a van*—cut her off. She swung away from it, but it didn't matter, it kept coming at her, bearing down on her, a fleet and deadly beast. She zigzagged. She weaved. Her arms pumped at her sides. She couldn't fathom how the driver had known she was here. Had he followed her from the house? *Does it matter?*

A shot rang out and she darted right, left, right again, the van turning as she turned, its engine screeching. She swung toward the cliff, and the van churned through the fog, gaining on her, faster and faster, and just before she reached the edge, she cut right again, toward her car, and hoped the van would keep on going. But the driver had anticipated her move and was already sweeping into a turn. Aline hurled the flashlight and heard it strike the van, but it didn't slow down. She sprinted parallel to the edge, breath trapped in her throat, the van racing alongside her. It was close enough for the driver to shoot her, but it was hidden by the fog so she couldn't see the driver or make out any details about the van.

Its nose suddenly lurched toward her, trying to force her over the edge. She switched back, hurling herself in the opposite direction, buying a few seconds—not enough, not nearly enough. The van's engine shrieked as though it were in pain, and she knew she wasn't going to make the trees before it swung back her way. So she did the only thing she could. She scrambled over the edge of the cliff, grappling for holds on clumps of grass, rocks, her feet digging, slipping, seeking purchase. It was easier than she'd thought it would be, and in seconds she was hidden by a layer of fog.

The wind deafened her. Spray dampened her face. She felt the vibration of the surf's relentless pounding against her palms. Her foot twisted, slipped, got stuck between a couple of rocks. When she tried to work it loose, she lost her hold on the clump of stone and brush she'd been clinging to and started to slide.

She gasped.

She grappled frantically to keep from tumbling backward off the cliff, grabbed at a bush, felt something wrench in her ankle. The white-hot pain lanced through muscles, tendons, bones, stealing her breath. For long moments she clung to the bush, tears stinging her eyes, the wind whipping her back, ankle shrieking, heart hammering.

I'm going to fall oh God I'm going to fall that's it

She tried to work her foot free of the place where it was jammed, but even the smallest movement pierced her to the bone. She shifted until the upper half of her body flopped over a slab of protruding rock. Slowly she moved her left foot, her free foot, to the trapped one. With the toe of that shoe, she worked the other shoe off her foot, leaving it jammed down inside the rocks, and hoisted herself onto the slab. She sprawled there, covered in sweat, face pressed into her arms, ankle throbbing, breath coming in small jerks.

After a while, she didn't know how long, she inched back onto the slab, the ledge, whatever she was on, and managed to sit up, spine pressed back against the cliff.

Above her, a light glowed in the fog. She dipped her head back, saw the beam dancing against the fog, skimming it, struggling to penetrate it. She realized that once the sun started to rise and burned off the fog, she would be as visible as a mole on a witch's chin.

Voices now, drones in the wind. She couldn't tell anything about them, not even how close they were. She pressed the heels of her hands against her eyes. *Think, do something, climb down, climb sideways, don't just stay here.*

Aline stretched out on her stomach and propelled herself forward with her hands and the tips of her shoes. Her ankle throbbed with every inch. When she reached the end, she peered over it, taking advantage of the flashlight's glare to look for a foothold. Nothing. More rocks and more fog. She crawled over to the other side of the ledge. Here the descent seemed gentler, with larger rocks and more clusters of weeds to grab onto. This side it would be.

She shifted around, lowered her legs over the edge. Her feet found a rock, maybe another ledge, she couldn't tell. But it was solid, sturdy, no surprises. Weight on the good foot. She checked for the glow of the flashlight, and even though it wasn't visible, she could still see. The sky, she thought. The sky was lightening. In another twenty or thirty minutes the sun would push up out of the sea.

Decide. Fast.

Aline pulled herself back onto the ledge. She crawled to the spot where she'd been, where the jut of rock above her protected her somewhat from being seen. She hunkered down, spine pressed to the rock, legs drawn up, the wind warm and damp against her face, and waited for the sun to rise.

She dozed off and snapped awake, certain she hadn't been asleep longer than a few minutes, it couldn't have been longer than that. And yet the sun flamed in a simmering blue sky and the fog was gone. The ache in her ankle had settled into a dull throb. It was swollen, as bruised as a piece of fruit.

Below her, the sharp protrusions of rocks and the tiny beach had vanished, submerged in high tide. The wind was stronger than before but offered no respite from the heat that even now radiated from the face of the cliff.

When she glanced up and saw what she had climbed over, she nearly swallowed her tongue. The overhang she'd mistaken for a ledge was actually a jut of limestone that looked like it might crumble at any second. It was wider than she'd thought but much shorter, barely protecting her from view on either side.

It was maybe four feet to the overhang, but she had no way of telling how far it was beyond that to the lip of the cliff. Worse, she didn't have the faintest notion how she was going to get out of here or if she even wanted to. The van might be waiting for her, the men might be . . .

Sit here long enough and you'll die of thirst or windburn. Scoot to the left now. Easy does it. Long way down. Longer down than up. Uh-huh. See anything? Nope, just clouds and blue sky and grass that grows sideways. Fine, fine, keep moving. One inch. Two. Stand up now. Turn. Grab those rocks. Left foot there. Right foot here. Pull. Nonono don't look down.

Hours passed. The sun beat against her back. Sweat soaked

her clothes. Her hands were slick with it. She tasted it on her lips. She smelled it on herself. All she wanted to do was get to the top, that wasn't too much to ask, really it wasn't, just this one small thing, top top top, and soon, oh God please, soon.

Her foot slipped once, knocking loose stones and dirt, and she sucked in her breath as she hugged the face of the cliff, certain that in the next instant the ground under her other foot would crumble and she would plummet like the stones, the dirt. But nothing happened, and she inched upward again, the top of the cliff less than four yards away.

The sun had moved in the sky. The muscles in her arms ached now. Her lack of sleep created white halos around everything she looked at. Shapes shifted and changed, rocks turned to sponge, weeds became razors that lacerated her palms. Nothing was what it seemed. Every time she checked to see how much closer she was, the top of the cliff was farther away. She didn't know how long she had been climbing, how many times she had stopped, how she had gotten so far down the face of the cliff without falling or breaking her neck. *But the sun has moved.*

She hallucinated. She dreamed with her eyes open. She quenched her thirst with an ice-cold bottle of beer. She conversed with Ferret about jai alai, with Kincaid about Fuentes, with Bernie about homicide, with dead Rikki Baker who sobbed, *You know the answer you know.*

And when she finally hauled herself over the lip of the cliff and sprawled in the dirt, she saw an old, wrinkled woman drifting toward her and knew it was the *santera*. Her mouth moved, but Aline couldn't hear what she was saying. *Louder*, Aline shouted. But the old woman started to fade, to dissolve like aspirin in water, and now the jogger sprinted past her, lifting her knees higher, moving faster and faster until she was just a blur of pastel against green trees, a violet sky.

The dead were keeping her company, she thought, and she exploded with laughter. She laughed until she cried, her cheek pressed against the warm dirt, the smell of sweat thick in her nostrils. Everything blurred. Ghosts danced. Death was a pastel painting and she was inside it. Then what was Kincaid doing here? He wasn't dead, was he? And if he wasn't dead, why was he here? He shouldn't have been here inside the painting with her, right?

Now she was rising. Now she was floating through the heat, the dim light, her body as weightless as a cloud, a matchstick.

Angels spoke to her, whispered to her, said her name again and again, touching her face, stroking it.

"Sip this, Al, sip it slowly," said the angel, speaking in Kincaid's voice.

"You're dead." she said.

"Drink this." Something cool and wet slipped past her lips, down her tongue, her parched throat. "That's enough. Take it easy."

She started to tremble, and the angel wrapped something around her shoulders. Her eyes closed, and she curled up inside the warm cocoon of the pastel painting, wondering why the angel had taken the wet, cool stuff away.

2

It was dark by the time Prentiss appeared in the coffee shop. Kincaid tried to read his expression as he walked over to the booth, but Prentiss had had too much professional practice at masking his thoughts. His face was as inscrutable as a chess player's.

"She's going to be okay, Ryan." He slid into the other side of the booth. "She's dehydrated, has some badly torn ligaments and tendons in her ankle, and a gash that required about six stitches. She's also got sun poisoning, thanks to her fair skin and who knows how many hours in the sun in ninety-degree heat."

"Can I see her?"

"I gave her a sedative. She'll be out until tomorrow morning. How'd you know where to find her, anyway?"

Because he'd figured it out. Because he'd had a hunch. Because he'd known, that was all, he'd known she would go to one of the crime sites.

He'd driven over to her place late this morning and left her a note, apologizing for his abruptness on the phone and asking her to call him. When he'd gotten back from Ferret's at two and discovered she hadn't called, he'd phoned the station. No one had seen or heard from her. Bernie speculated that she might have taken the day off and gone sailing with Martell. When that proved to be a dead end, he'd checked the usual spots—Lester's, the Pink Moose, the restaurant at the Flamingo—and Bernie had made the rounds of suspects. Ortega, Uvanti, and the light-house, even though Porter was still in jail and no one was there.

He'd found her at 5:30 this afternoon, prostrate in the dirt at the brim of Suicide Cliff, murmuring about ghosts and angels, and had brought her here, to the emergency room. "Did she say anything to you about what happened?" Kincaid asked.

"Shit, Ryan, she wasn't coherent. Did you find her car?"

"Yeah, it was parked up there. Purse and gun inside, money and credit cards still in her wallet, keys in the pocket of her jeans. There were a lot of car tracks, but hell, kids drag race up there. I think she just got careless and stumbled over the side and then had a hell of a time getting back up."

Prentiss ordered coffee. Kincaid took a refill on his and pushed away his half-eaten sandwich. "Got any ideas why her clothes stank of camphor?"

"Yeah. The talisman tore open. It was in her shirt pocket."

"The what?"

"The *santería* stuff."

Prentiss leaned forward, dark eyes scrutinizing Kincaid openly. "You *believe* this shit, don't you?" he said softly, as though it embarrassed him.

"Bill, I really don't feel like going into it now, okay?"

"Where is she? What's happened? Is she in a room? How serious is it? Will someone please tell me what's going on?" Bernelli had flown into the coffee shop so fast Kincaid hadn't seen her, and now she stood at the booth, hands fixed on her narrow hips, wide taffy eyes flitting from him to Prentiss.

"Have a seat." Prentiss patted the space beside him, and Bernie slipped into the booth. Kincaid sat through a recitation of Aline's injuries.

"That's it? That's all you know?" Bernie exclaimed when Prentiss had finished.

Prentiss rolled his eyes. "You see what I live with, Ryan? Do you understand now why I have the patience of a saint?"

"I want to see her," Bernie said.

"Me too," echoed Kincaid.

"She's six sheets to the wind, but c'mon."

She was alone in a double room on the fourth floor, curled up on her side, hair covering most of her face. Her left arm was attached to an IV. A catheter hose poked out from under the sheet and emptied into a plastic bag hooked on the side of the bed. She was so still, she looked dead. It wasn't until Kincaid leaned over the railing and heard her breathing that he believed otherwise.

"She's going to be in here until at least Saturday, off her feet. Otherwise those tendons and ligaments will never get a chance to heal," Prentiss said.

"Good luck keeping her here," Kincaid remarked.

"The chief's going to have someone parked outside the door starting around ten tonight. In fact, I think I'll stick around until he gets here," said Bernie.

Kincaid said he would stay, and Bernie glanced over at him, ready to argue, but she evidently changed her mind and decided to be snide instead. "I hear you have commitments elsewhere."

"Cut the crap," snapped Prentiss.

Bernie folded her arms at her waist. "Just stating a fact, Bill. I'm going to Al's to feed Wolfe." She turned on her heel and walked out.

Prentiss sighed, a deep cloying sigh that said, *Women, who can figure them out?* and informed Kincaid he'd be downstairs until midnight. He left, and Kincaid stood at the side of the bed for a while, then walked over to the window and gazed outside. City lights. Car lights. Starlight. Moonlight. Lights everywhere, except inside him. Fuck it.

He slumped in the chair by the window and closed his eyes, sinking, seeking that soft, cool place, satori, peace, a state of grace. But it eluded him as surely as the clarity of his own emotions.

Once, when Aline stirred, he returned to the bed. She hadn't moved. He crouched down, hands on the railing, peering at her through the slats as though he could divine some essential truth about her as she slept that had remained hidden from him. An answer about what had gone wrong. Some indication of what she felt toward him. If she felt anything at all.

Her face changed. She became Fuentes.

Kincaid shut his eyes and rested his forehead against the cool metal railing. *This is not a good space to be in, Ryan. Not good at all.* Two women. Two sides of himself.

"If you're praying, Ryan, I may puke."

Kincaid chuckled, stood, and turned around. Ferret's small, compact body was outlined in the doorway. He was wearing his black fedora hat and a trench coat. "You look like a flasher."

Ferret's lips drew away from his teeth in that strange, eerie smile, but his laughter was silent. He came over to the bed and leaned toward Aline. "I know you're faking, Sweet Pea," he whispered. "So listen up. I got a sure bet on next weekend's jai alai. You interested or what?"

"She's out."

"Drugs," Ferret sniffed with obvious disapproval, "never improve the situation. Prentiss oughta know better. But she can hear, Ryan. They can always hear. We still on for our meeting?"

"After I go back for Al's car. We're meeting at Miranda's place."

"Did she tell you about the invitations?"

"Which invitations?"

"Uvanti's going to have a little get-together on the night of the second. Look." Ferret held out a card that was pale blue, embossed in fancy silver script. *The pleasure of your company is requested on June 2, Ten P.M.—?* It was signed *Nicolas Uvanti.*

"This is going to make things a lot easier."

"You bet it is. Notice there's no name on it. You're going as Miranda's date, and I'm going to keep my date with the storm drain and his cellar."

Before Kincaid could reply, Martell sailed into the room, dressed to the hilt in a three-piece suit, as if he'd just come from court. The room filled instantly with the scent of his after-shave and the thickness of his overbearing presence. "How is she?"

"Out of it," replied Ferret.

"I can *see* that. Is she okay?"

"She will be," Kincaid replied.

He stopped on the other side of the bed. "Where'd you find her?"

"Suicide Cliff. How'd you know she was here, Martell?"

He heard the accusatory tone in Kincaid's voice, and his glance was sharp, angry. "Just what the hell is that supposed to mean?"

"You tell me."

"I don't have to tell you squat, Kincaid. But for your information, I got a call from Gene Frederick."

"Hey, hey," said Ferret, holding up his hands, patting the air. "This isn't the place to air your differences, guys."

Martell looked like he had plenty more to say, but he never got the chance because a nurse appeared and asked them to step outside. While they were waiting, a detective from robbery arrived to take up vigilance for the night, and the three of them left a few minutes later.

In the elevator, the silence was ugly, sticky, coagulating like blood. Martell stood to the left, staring at the numbers above the door; Ferret was on the right, staring at his shoes; and Kincaid was at the back, staring at Martell, his imagination plunged into overdrive. By the time they reached the lobby, Kincaid wanted nothing more than the satisfaction of sinking his fist into Martell's goddamn mouth.

"Got any ideas about who was after her up there on the cliff?" Martell asked as they crossed the lobby.

"Who says anyone was?" Kincaid snapped.

"I just assume that's what happened."

Funny, Kincaid mused, that Martell's conclusion about the events at Suicide Cliff were different from his own. "She wasn't coherent enough to tell anyone what happened. I think it was an accident. But one thing's for sure, Martell. *If* someone was after her up there, it sure as hell wasn't Porter, which doesn't do much for your case against him."

"Wrong. Porter was released on a three-million-dollar bond this morning. I guess Bernelli and the chief forgot to mention it to you, Ryan." He flashed his best *Fuck you* smile, pushed through the double doors ahead of Kincaid and Ferret, and hurried off through the parking lot toward his white Camaro.

25

The women never left him alone now.

They whispered to him in his dreams, danced around his bed, joined him at the table when he ate, accompanied him to the store. They taunted him, teased him, laughed at him. Right now, they were huddled in the backseat of his car, giggling. He saw Rikki in the rearview mirror, a hand cupped at her mouth as she murmured something to the old *santera*. Then she leaned forward, elbows resting against the edge of the seat, her mouth so close to Ortega's ear, he felt the warmth of her breath, smelled its stink.

You're asking for trouble, sweetie, by going to Nicky's yacht. He looks out only for himself, he's trouble, he betrays. And we know aaaallll about betrayal, don't we, Manuel.

The runner burst out laughing and chanted, *Run, run, Ortega,* and the old *santera* patted his cheek with a dried, gnarled hand and told him his *abuelita* was here, did he want to talk to her? Did he have anything to say to her? To explain to her? Did he want to tell her he was sorry? Hmm? Did he?

He switched on the radio and turned it up loud, drowning out their voices. He knocked the rearview mirror to the side so he couldn't see them anymore. But now he could feel blood seeping through the pores in his palms again, a warm, sticky ooze. He was afraid to take his hands from the steering wheel because he couldn't bear to look at it, to see the blood bubbling from the centers of his palms, his stigmata, his curse. But as it started to trickle down the insides of his wrists, his arms, Ortega jerked the wheel to the left and pulled off onto the shoulder of the road.

He grabbed the bottle of Clorox and the roll of paper towels from the floor, threw open his door, leaped out.

Don't panic. The women want you to panic, expect you to. Pay no attention to them. Concentrate on what you're doing. If you ignore them, they'll go away. They'll get bored and go away. Spin the cap. Pour. Right hand. Left. Oh God, the blood, so much blood . . . Stop it. More Clorox, pour on more. Now rub hard and fast, yes, good, hard and fast, again and again. It stings, Jesus, it stings bad. But it's supposed to, isn't it? Isn't it?

Gradually, the bleeding stopped. Half the Clorox was gone, running in rivulets around his shoes. He wiped his hands on towels. Bunches of towels. The stink of the Clorox made him sneeze, made his nose itch and run, but it was worth it to be pure again. He turned his hands over, examining them. They gleamed in their purity, glistened like white stones, winked in the warm morning light. And then, right in the heart of his left palm, a spot of blood appeared, just one tiny fleck blooming like a miniature rose. Ortega watched it, but it didn't grow, didn't spread. It was just there, burning bright red against his hand.

He frantically went through the glove compartment until he found a couple of tattered Band-Aids. He ripped one open, pressed it over his palm, then sat there watching it to see if the blood seeped through it. When nothing happened, he grinned to himself, giddy with relief, and drove on to the marina.

Uvanti's yacht was where it usually was, at the end of dock two, a giant vessel as sleek and lovely as any of his women. *Lovelier than me, sweetie?* Rikki whispered in his ear. *Did you know Nicky was going to name the boat after me? Hhmmm? Did you know that?*

Yeah, he knew.

Max the Monster, Uvanti's bodyguard, was standing on the deck, massive arms folded across his massive chest, watching Ortega as he came aboard. When he grinned, his gold tooth flashed in the light.

"Well, well, if it ain't the sorcerer. About time you got here. We've been waiting."

Ortega followed Max to the lower deck, where Uvanti's study was. The room was cool, with soft lighting and freshly cut roses that perfumed the air. Art covered the walls. Expensive art, a lot of it phony. *You know that because I told you*, Rikki whispered to him, Rikki, who was invisible now, tagging his heels like a friendly ghost.

Uvanti was on the phone, slowly turning the diamond stud in his left ear as he talked. One of his jewel-studded hands gestured for Ortega to have a seat. He didn't feel like sitting down, didn't even like being here, shouldn't have come. Suppose a cop showed up while he was here? He knew what conclusion would be drawn. He knew. But it was too late to leave now, so he sank into a royal blue chair. French Provincial, he thought, running a hand over the lovely wood. The real thing.

". . . *sí, bueno*," Uvanti was saying. "*Hasta luego.*" He hung up, swiveled in his chair, and rested his elbows on his desk, gazing at Ortega. He suddenly sniffed at the air. "*Amigo*, if that's cologne you're wearing, you need something new. It smells like a hospital. Whatever happened to Florida water?"

The Clorox, Ortega thought, but didn't say anything.

Behind him, Max the Monster cleared his throat, and when Ortega glanced back, he saw that Max had positioned himself in the doorway, blocking it with his muscular body. That was not a good sign.

"So. I will get to the point, Manuel."

Betray, betray, whispered Rikki.

Run, run, fleet of foot, laughed the *gringa*.

Shame on you, cackled the *santera*.

Ortega blinked and rubbed a hand over his ear, willing the voices to stop.

"What we have, Manuel, is some trouble with the cops, and I'd like to know just what the hell you've said to them about my relationship with Rikki."

"Nothing. They already knew about your relationship with her. I've told you that."

Uvanti's dark eyes darted to Max the Monster. "Did he tell us that, Max?"

"I believe he may have mentioned it, Nick."

"Uh-huh. But maybe he didn't tell us the whole truth." Those dark eyes slid back to Ortega. "Did you tell us the *whole* truth, Manuel?"

"I don't know what you're talking about."

"No? Well, let's see. There's the cops, like I said before. And then last Friday morning that spooky old Riviera woman comes nosing around here, asking a lot of questions about you and me and *santería*, Manuel. I didn't like that one goddamn bit, I don't

mind telling you.'' Uvanti shook his head and twisted the stud
in his left ear again. ''I don't like my name associated with
santería, you know that. We've talked about it. When our as-
sociation began . . . when was it? Two years ago?'' Eyes flicked
back to Max. ''Was it two years ago, Max?''

''Twenty-six months ago, Nick.''

''There. You see what an excellent memory Max has, Manuel? That's something you should try to develop. That and better
habits, like obeying instructions. Like following through on your
word. Twenty-six months ago, when I first came to you, you
gave me your word—*your word*, Manuel—that our relationship would remain confidential. That's essential in my kind of
work, Manuel. I explained all that to you. So how did the old
santera know about us? I guess that's what I'd like to know the
most, Manuel. I would really appreciate an answer to that.''

Betray, betray, chanted Rikki.

''I have nothing to say to you.'' He pushed himself to his feet
and stabbed a thumb over his shoulder, toward Max the Monster. ''And tell him to move.''

Uvanti's mouth twitched, as though it couldn't decide what
to do—smile, rage, fuss, hurl insults. His dark eyes impaled
Ortega, eyes filled with hatred, eyes whose madness Ortega had
seen many times before. He didn't know what sort of game
Uvanti was playing, but he didn't want to stick around to find
out.

''You don't frighten me.''

''That's good, Manuel. That's very good. Max, let him
through.''

Max the Monster moved to the side. But before Ortega was
through the door, Uvanti said, ''Hey, Manuel. Did you hear that
Porter got out on bond? And I hear from the local prosecutor
that the cops are going to be picking you up for questioning
now.'' He chuckled. ''And if you want to live to meet your
grandchildren, my advice is that you don't know me. Got it?''

Ortega ignored him and kept on walking, fear drumming a
frantic, wild beat against his ribs.

Betray, betray, laughed Rikki.

Run, whispered the pretty little *gringa*. *Run now.*

And once he was outside, he did. He ran through the salty
heat to his car, screeched out of the marina parking lot, and
raced home. He locked and bolted the front door, then rushed
into the backyard and peered through the hole in the fence,

checking for police. He didn't see any suspicious vehicles disguised as something they weren't, but it was just a matter of time. How much time? A few minutes? Hours? Maybe a day or two?

It didn't matter because the end result to him would be the same. Betrayal. That was the only truth.

He would go to the police and tell them everything.

But they wouldn't believe him. Why should they? He would tell them and they wouldn't believe and he would go to the chair.

Or worse, he would go to prison for life. No chance of parole.

Pack, he thought. He would pack a bag and—

And what, sweetie? asked Rikki, trotting along beside him as he hustled back inside. *How far do you think you'll get in your car?*

"Leave me alone!" he shouted at her.

A smile, a snap of her fingers, and she vanished, a genie in a bottle, a vision, a demon.

He locked the sliding glass door, drew the curtains, threw open his closet door, tossed a suitcase on the bed. She was right, Rikki was right. It was a four-hour drive to Miami. There was only one road from here to the mainland, and the police would catch him before he made it.

I'll rent a boat. Yes, of course, an excellent idea. It would require a deposit of several hundred dollars, but there was at least that much in the store register. It didn't matter that he didn't know anything about boats, that the only time he'd been on one he'd gotten violently ill. None of that mattered because he understood the truth now.

He understood everything. It had all been a lie. *Padrino* had set him up right from the beginning. The nature of power in the hands of a man without conscience was to corrupt absolutely. He had allowed himself to be corrupted. *Padrino* had molded him, sculpted him, created him for this role.

And no one will believe me.

So he would flee, he would—

Kill him, Manuel. Kill him and be done with it, said Rikki as she materialized at the foot of his bed. *Take the gun out of the drawer.* She pointed a long, red-tipped finger at the nightstand. *Go on, Manuel. Take it. Load it. And kill him. He deserves it. You know he does.*

"I've never shot it. It's never been out of the box." But even as he said it, he was moving toward the nightstand, opening the drawer, looking down at the box with the gun in it, reaching for it.

He would do it tonight.

No. On the third. During the Black Moon. Think of it, Manuel. Think of the rightness of such a death.

But the police would be coming for him, asking him questions, they would—.

You know where to hide, Manuel. Go on. Load the gun, pack it, and then leave. You know where to hide. He won't find you there. No one will. Not even Jaime.

Now he removed the gun from the box. Stripped away the plastic. Now his fingers closed around the container of bullets. Now.

The rightness.

26

I

June 1. One more day and she was out of this place, out of the wheelchair, out out out. *And the day after tomorrow is the eclipse*. No. She wouldn't think about that right now. She would think about what she was going to do today. A rerun of *Bonanza*? Of *Star Trek*? Another chapter in *The Haunting of Hill House*? A game of solitaire? Maybe a leisurely hobble down the hall to see what was going on at the nurse's station? Yeah, that sounded just fine. She needed the exercise. One more meal like breakfast and lunch and they'd have to roll her out of here tomorrow.

Aline swung her legs over the side of the bed and winced when she put pressure on her left foot. The stitches twitched. The torn tendons ached. Her sunburn itched. It was definitely the weirdest sunburn she'd ever had—right cheek and eyelids, right side of her neck, hands to the wrists, where the sleeves of her windbreaker had started.

She reached for the crutches and hoisted herself up, then let one of them drop back against the bed. There, that was better. Now she was only half an invalid. She hobbled to the door, and the rookie sitting just outside looked up.

"*Another* walk?"

"There's nothing on the tube."

He set his magazine aside and stood. "Okay, let's go."

"I'm only going as far as the nurse's station."

"I've got my orders, Detective Scott. The chief said if you left the room, I wasn't supposed to let you out of my sight."

This exuberant rookie, who couldn't be a day over twenty-five, had accompanied her on five walks today, sat in the sun room with her, checked her breakfast and lunch trays before they got to her, asked for I.D. from everyone who had walked through the door, even from hospital personnel, and yes, she appreciated it, really she did, and she understood he was only doing his job. But she'd had quite enough of it, thank you very much.

"Look, I'm only going as far as the nurse's station. You can see it from here. I won't be out of your sight. In fact, if you don't sit down, I'm going to scream. I'll throw a fit. I'll pull out my hair. Really."

He laughed and rubbed his chin, probably trying to figure out if she was serious. Then he nodded and picked up his magazine and sat down. "I guess it'd be okay."

She started down the hall, robe flapping around her knees, the end of the crutch squeaking against the shiny, polished floors. *Work, foot.* As she neared the nurse's station, the elevator doors opened and the blonde from Platinum's stepped out, a fake blonde, she thought, Starr Abbot of the pink leotards, Starr who was Miranda Fuentes, Fed, Kincaid's source, Kincaid's new love. Swell. *She* had never looked worse in her life, and Miranda, on the other hand, was the kind of woman people wrote songs about and composed love sonnets to.

She wore white slacks, a red print shirt, white sandals. A white leather bag was slung over her shoulder. Her voluminous hair was pulled away from a face so lovely, Aphrodite would've squirmed with envy.

When the chief had called earlier, he'd told her Fuentes would be stopping by and that Aline should cooperate with her. But for some reason, she'd thought it would be later, this evening, after dinner, during visiting hours.

"How're you feeling?" she asked.

"Bored."

Fuentes's mouth slipped into a smile. "I'm glad you're okay. Ryan told me what happened, that you never got a look at the van."

"It was too dark and too foggy."

"And there's still no word on Ortega, I understand."

"I imagine he's long gone from Tango."

"Is there someplace we can talk?"

"Out on the porch." Aline tilted her head toward the rookie

at the end of the hall. "But you'd better check in with my shadow first."

"Sure."

"Show him your Fed I.D. if you've got it." Then, just to make sure Fuentes understood that she knew what was what, she added, "He won't know you're on leave."

"I'm not anymore."

"Oh. The chief didn't tell me that part."

"Officially I was on leave and still am. But things changed when I spoke to Frederick yesterday afternoon and he called my boss at the bureau."

Miranda showed her I.D. to the rookie, then she and Aline continued down the hall and out onto the porch. There were a few other patients outside—in wheelchairs, playing cards and reading at the aluminum tables under the awning, standing at the railing. They claimed a table at the far end of the porch.

The view from here was magnificent: the deep blue of the sea to the south and the east, the town built right to the edge of it, the soft bruise of the hills to the north. The sky was clear, a deep, hot blue.

"I realize you pieced things together, Aline, and that I should have told you about Rikki being killed at my place. But I was afraid it would blow my cover at Platinum's."

"I don't suppose you told the chief about it."

"I told him the whole thing."

Surprise.

"Uvanti has approached me about 'acting as a business courier' for him. He didn't give me any specifics, other than to say Rikki used to do it for him and it pays well and would I be interested? I told him I might be interested, but I wanted to know a little more about it—what I'd be transporting, how much money we were talking about, who I'd be dealing with, and so on. He suggested we discuss the details tomorrow night at his party."

"And then you'll bust him?"

"Well, that depends on what's said. I'll be wired for sound, but just in case nothing comes of it, I'll still need evidence to bust him. Hopefully Ferret will be able to find that. If he does, a search warrant will do the rest."

She had it all figured out. *So what's she need me for?*

"Who's getting the search warrant?"

"Gene said he'd take care of it."

Gene: ah, well. That answered her question, now didn't it. Due to her injuries, she'd been shuffled to the sidelines on this case, and Fuentes had stepped in to take her place. The woman would have played a role regardless, but the situation had simply made it that much easier. The chief, who knew her well enough to understand how she would feel, had no doubt asked Fuentes to stop by the hospital for this little conversation so Aline wouldn't feel excluded. She appreciated the gesture, but who the hell needed it? She already felt like the disinherited relative.

"Does Chamberlain know you're back on the case?"

"Nope. And this part of the case doesn't concern him."

"Why're you afraid of him?"

"Who?"

"Of Chamberlain. That's who we're talking about, isn't it?"

She looked indignant. "I'm not afraid of him. He's just meddled once too often."

Aline could hear Chamberlain's good ole boy voice claiming he didn't know why the FBI agent had been removed from his daughter's missing person's case or why this agent would be pursuing the case now. Chamberlain hadn't been telling the whole truth, and neither was Miranda.

"Hey, look, if it weren't for Kincaid and the chief vouching for you, Miranda, I wouldn't be sitting here talking to you. So how about telling me just what it is between you and the senator? Why'd he have you taken off his daughter's case?"

The change in her demeanor was swift, and subtle—her spine stiffened, her mouth turned hard, and the blue in her eyes deepened, flashing with something that might've been anger or bitterness or both. "If you have any doubts about who I am, then call Gene. He's already checked me out through a friend of his in the bureau. He's agreed to this. He—"

"Does *he* know why Chamberlain had you removed from the case?"

Fidgeting now, eyes averted: "I don't know."

Liar.

As if she'd heard the thought, she suddenly said, "All right, he knows. But it's not relevant to any of this."

"Hey, I understand you think you're doing me a favor by coming here. But frankly, I don't need the aggravation. So good luck tomorrow night."

Miranda leaned toward her and tapped one of her long nails

against the surface of the table. "*You're* the one who stands to gain the most from this, Aline. With Uvanti out of the way, the only person to worry about then is Ortega, and if he's got any sense at all, he's long gone."

"I'm not totally convinced that Uvanti's behind this."

"It sure as hell isn't Porter. You said yourself that the thing with the van happened before it got light. And Porter wasn't out on bond until nine that morning, so he couldn't be the one who chased you."

"Hold it." Aline held up her hands. "Ortega's still loose, so please don't give me any bullshit about how much any of this is going to help *me*. All I did was ask a simple question, Miranda. And if you can't give me an answer, then we've got nothing else to talk about."

A moment passed. Two. Three. *Fuck it*, Aline thought, and reached for her crutch and pulled herself up. Before she reached the door, Miranda said, "I was married to Rikki's ex-husband."

2

Kincaid and Bernelli were exiting the Army-Navy store when someone called, "Hey, Bernelli."

They glanced around. A husky fellow with a gray, unkempt beard, white hair pulled into a ponytail, and a leathery face bounded up and pumped Bernelli's hand. "You're looking real good, Bernelli." His eyes slipped to Kincaid. "And I reckon you're the lucky doctor I've heard about."

Bernie laughed. "This is Ryan Kincaid. A friend of mine, Mr. Griber," and she introduced them.

Kincaid thought the old geezer looked relieved. "Nice to meetcha." The man's eyes flicked quickly from Kincaid to Bernie again. "Shore was sorry you didn't come out with Martell that night. He tell you about him and your partner comin' out to see me?"

"I heard all about it. So what brings you into town, Mr. Griber?"

He scratched at his beard and in his booming hillbilly voice said he always came in once a month and decided to tie it in with the eclipse this time. "Hell, there won't be another in my lifetime. I figure I'll find me a nice spot at the Moose and watch it from there. I called Mr. Martell's office to see if he needed any more statements or whatnot from me, but he'd already left."

"I imagine he'll be at his office tomorrow. I thought you saw him last week."

"Nope." He shook his head vigorously. "Haven't done seen him since he and your partner came out to my place."

"Well, stop by the station tomorrow and we'll have a cup of coffee."

"You bet, Bernelli. See you then."

"You just made an old lech *very* happy, Bernelli," Kincaid remarked as they walked on to the Saab.

"Ain't it the truth," she laughed. "My good deed for the day."

"What was that stuff about Martell?"

Bernie sighed. "I knew you weren't going to be able to resist that one, Ryan."

"I definitely have a problem with the man."

"And I suppose that doesn't have anything to do with Aline."

"You don't spend nearly four years with someone and stop caring when things end. Martell just isn't her type. He's no good for her."

"If he'd tone it down with his other *chiquitas*, he might not be half bad."

"That must mean he used Griber as an excuse with Aline."

"You really want the details?"

"Sure."

"Ha." She lit a cigarette and flicked the match into the street. "But okay. Since you asked. It's called bedroom etiquette, see. Leaving before morning. Got it? Does that satisfy your curiosity?"

"Yeah, fine. He used Griber as an excuse."

She hooked her arm through his. "Don't fret, Ryan. I'll still love you even if Aline ends up with Martell and you move to Miami to live with Fuentes."

"No way. I don't like Miami."

"But you like Fuentes."

"You're fishing," he said.

"You're right," she said.

They looked at each other and laughed.

* * *

Kincaid, Ferret, and Bernelli spent several hours at Fuentes's bungalow. They reviewed the construction plans of Uvanti's home, studied the city's schematic drawings of rain pipes and sewers in the area, and went over their plan until everyone was clear on who was responsible for what and when.

When the others had left, Kincaid and Fuentes walked down to the lagoon. The night was warm and humid, and the air was alive with the sound of crickets, frogs, the occasional hoot of a barn owl. The moon had risen, bright and nearly full, but in the distance, thunder warned of rain before dawn.

They settled on a strip of sand and dried leaves, under a live oak whose branches were strung with Spanish moss. The breeze off the water smelled of rain and fish, salt and summer. Less than three miles off to the left were the docks where seaplanes tied down. To their right, just beyond the beach, a dozen docks protruded into the water like dark, flat tongues. Most of them were empty now, but they wouldn't be in another week, once the summer renters started arriving.

For tonight, though, they had the beach to themselves, and their talk was mostly of small things, and only of the distant past or of the present. After all, it might be bad luck to talk about tomorrow night now that the others had left. And there was no point in discussing what might—or might not—happen once Fuentes returned to Miami. In short, the distant past was too remote to disturb the balance, and the present was simply easier to deal with. It demanded nothing of them. It didn't hinge on her feelings concerning her ex-husband or his toward Aline or even their feelings for each other. It was as clear and perfect as a gem and yet utterly unformed, in a continual state of becoming.

"When I was a kid, I used to sit in my uncle's backyard and watch the moon through this telescope he had." Fuentes leaned back on her hands, stretched her legs in front of her, and dipped her head back, eyes on the sky. "It wasn't a powerful telescope, really. I couldn't see Saturn's rings. But it was perfect for keeping an eye on the people who lived in the moon."

"The old Disney movie," Kincaid said. "About the woman in the hoop skirt who bounced and bounced until she bounced to the moon, right?"

"Yeah." Fuentes smiled, pleased that he'd guessed. "See her?" She pointed, and Kincaid followed with his eyes. "She's right there, off to the right a little."

"Who else lives in there?"

"Oh, the elves and the shoemaker, Cinderella, Snow White and the seven dwarfs, Mickey Mouse. All of Disney's characters were born in the moon. But so were the villains. See, over there?" Her finger slipped to the left. "They live in that shadow," she whispered. "And when the moon goes through its phases, it's because the good guys and the bad are battling it out." Her hand dropped to the sand again. "My grandmother's stories. She was American to the core, from the Midwest, and probably had a fit when my mother fell for an Argentinian. In college," she added. "That's where my parents met. Anyway, I think my grandmother used to spend a lot of time sitting on her porch in Iowa, watching the sky or something."

"She got tired of watching the corn grow."

"Probably." Fuentes chuckled. "I doubt if she'd ever heard of *santería*, but she had a story about an eclipse." She lit a cigarette and blew smoke rings toward the sky. "In her version, though, it's a lunar eclipse, when the moon passes through the umbra of the earth's shadow. She used to say that when it happened, it meant the bad guys had scored a victory. A biggie. Maybe a war or the conditions for a famine had started in some part of the world or someone who could've made a difference had just died. The world for her was black and white. Something was either good or it was bad."

"And for you?"

She shook her head and sat up, drawing her legs against her, elbows resting on her knees. "Nothing's ever been that simple for me."

Kincaid knew she was leading into something. He knew it not just by what she said and the way in which she said it, but because she reached for his hand, connecting them again.

"My ex called me."

The past: was he really surprised? "And?"

"I don't know." She stuck her cigarette into the sand and shrugged. "No, I *do* know. It complicates things."

"It shouldn't."

She shifted around, legs crossed Indian style now, moonlight spilling into her loose, wild hair, illuminating only one side of her face. "But it does." She told him then about the very thing that had puzzled him all along, the thing that explained her obsession with Rikki Baker. "For nearly three years, everything I've done has been because our marriage failed. And the marriage failed because he was so hung up on Rikki, he was incapable of loving anyone else. But now . . . I don't know, it's like Rikki's death released him.''

"And you."

"I guess." She shrugged and glanced out at the water. He felt her struggling to find the right words. "I don't know if it would work this time. We're both too . . . too much the same, too compulsive in the same ways, too solitary in the same ways. But I think I need to try."

"Then do it."

She smiled and looked down at the sand. "Just like that, huh?"

"It's only as difficult or easy as you believe it is."

Funny, he'd never thought it quite so simple before. But now that he'd said it, he realized it was as true for Fuentes as it was for him. She rocked toward him then, kissed him, locked her arms around his neck. She whispered that she wanted to make love here, now, on the beach, in the moonlight, and they did, and he knew it was probably for the last time.

27

I

Aline was released from the hospital at ten a.m. on the second day of June. Bernie picked her up and drove her home, the rookie tailing them, then parking himself on Aline's front porch.

The first thing Wolfe did when he saw her was nip her ankle, as if to make it clear he didn't appreciate being abandoned to the goodwill of others. But once he'd made his point, he wouldn't leave her alone. While Bernie smoothed open the plans to Uvanti's house and pointed out this and that, as though Aline were going to be there, Wolfe plopped down in the center of it. He sat between her and the chief when he stopped by, and later, blocked Martell's way up the front steps, growling and stamping his feet, swishing his tail. The only time the skunk didn't act schizophrenic was when Kincaid appeared late that afternoon. "He's been weird with everyone but you today."

"We're ole buddies. Tell her, Wolfe."

Wolfe backed away, then pounced on Kincaid's head when he lowered it to charge him. This, she thought, was what it would be like to watch your ex-husband play with his son on visiting day.

Even though she'd spoken to Kincaid on the phone, this was the first time she'd seen him since her mishap on Suicide Cliff. He was dressed for a scouting job—dark clothes, running shoes. He looked different somehow, changed, as if he'd been away on one of his trips and things had happened to him that he wasn't prepared to talk about. That he might not ever talk about. And maybe that was the point. Maybe the point all along was to realize that distance between even the closest of people was not such a bad thing, was perhaps even necessary.

"I just wanted you to know that if you don't feel safe here, Allie, you can always stay at my place. That rookie outside could drive you over."

"Thanks, but I'll be fine. You want something to drink? Eat?"

He shook his head. "I've got to meet Ferret."

"You're not going to Uvanti's party?"

"It doesn't start until ten. Ferret and I need to look the place over first. How's the foot?"

Aline shrugged. "Okay, but I feel married to the crutches."

He smiled, slipped his hands in the pockets of his trousers, glanced down at the floor, where Wolfe was gnawing at the tip of his running shoe. "I just want you to know it was never anyone's intention to push you to the sidelines on this case, Al."

As though he were personally responsible for how things had turned out, she thought. "I'm not blaming anyone. And let's face it, with this bum foot I'd just slow things down."

An awkward moment passed, then Kincaid glanced at his watch and said he'd better get going. She hobbled to the door with him, hating the blasted crutch.

"I'll call as soon as we know something."

"No matter how late it is."

"Right."

"And I'll leave the machine off."

"Okay." He slipped on his sunglasses as he stepped out onto the stoop. "Your sunburn looks weird."

"You're being too kind," she said with a laugh. "It looks ridiculous. By the way, thanks again. For the cliff."

"You already thanked me, Al."

"I did?"

"On the phone."

"Oh."

"You remember what I told you?"

"Nope."

"That now you owe me."

She laughed and didn't close the door until the Saab had swung out of the driveway.

2

It was light when he and Ferret left, driving a Buick from his garage that was as dark as the clothes they wore. Ferret didn't say much during the ride; he never did when he was doing a job. But he fiddled with the things in his flight bag, arranging and rearranging them. He tested his flashlight and the transmitter gizmo and then he switched on the radio and turned it loud and sat back, hands folded on his stomach, eyes closed.

"Don't fall asleep on me, man," said Kincaid.

"I'm programming for success, Ryan."

"With the radio blasting?"

Ferret glanced over at him. "Hey, you've got things that work for you and I've got things that work for me. You mind?"

Kincaid shut up.

He parked the Buick in the woods at the foot of the same hill they'd climbed the day Ferret had shown him Uvanti's house. Kincaid shrugged on his knapsack, loaded his .357, slipped it into his shoulder holster. Ferret, ever meticulous, fussed with the straps on his flight bag, adjusting them until he got them just right. Then he tied and retied the shoelaces on his running shoes, zipped and unzipped his dark windbreaker, and went through several other routines while Kincaid watched and waited.

"Ferret. How come you didn't do all this shit while we were in the car?"

"There're things you do in the car, Ryan, and things you do once you're out of the car. Synchronize watches."

"We already did it last night."

"That was then."

"Okay, okay," sighed Kincaid. "Five thirty-three."

"Got it." His lips drew away from his teeth in that strange, feral grin. "I'm ready now."

Ferret led the way up the twisted path, moving swiftly through pines, banyans, dappled sunlight. The eerie, tight quiet was broken only by the faint rustle of a breeze and squawks from a flock of green parrots that fluttered up from the trees. Once, when the breeze had stilled, Kincaid heard the bleat of a car horn somewhere beyond them. He and Ferret both stopped, listening. But there were no other sounds, and they continued up the hill.

When they reached the crest, the waning afternoon light

washed across Uvanti's estate, a bruised, deep light chopped up by long, sharp shadows. Through the binoculars, Kincaid counted half a dozen cars and a catering van parked to the left of the house, in the basketball court. In the front yard there were tables and a bar and a number of workmen bustling around, attending to details. Japanese lanterns hung from trees. A band was setting up on a wooden platform against the right wall.

They were up high enough to have a clear view of the courtyard in the center of the house. Here was a second bar and an L-shaped buffet table covered in white. "Looks like it's going to be more than just a small get-together," Ferret remarked.

"Better for you, especially with a band."

Ferret tipped his head back, scanning the sky like a soldier seeking enemy aircraft. "Even when it gets dark, it's going to be tricky getting from the bottom of the hill to that storm drain at the end of the driveway. I think I'll circle around and approach from those trees over there." He pointed off to the right. "The drainage ditch starts about three hundred feet out from the trees, and it's deep enough so that if I stay down I should be able to get to the storm drain without being seem."

"You're screwed if it rains, Ferret."

"The weather forecast calls for scattered showers late tonight, and clear skies after midnight. A little rain isn't going to affect me much."

But weather forecasts in South Florida were often wrong. Predicted showers became deluges, sunny days turned overcast and windy, mild temperatures shot for record highs. And if the thunderheads clustered over the Atlantic in the distance reached shore, it wouldn't take long for the storm drain to fill. The festivities would probably be moved into the courtyard, where—if the plans were right—an electronic roof panel would be activated, shutting out the rain.

"Don't worry about it, Ryan," said Ferret, digging into his knapsack. "You worry too much about things you can't control." Out came a red cloth napkin, which he smoothed open on the ground between them. This was followed by two ham and Swiss sandwiches on rye, two cans of apricot juice, and two more napkins. Ferret tucked his napkin under his chin, popped the tabs on the juice, passed Kincaid one. "Cheers, Ryan. Here's to success."

They clicked cans and sat back to wait for the action to start down below.

3

Ortega had spent nearly three days sealed up in his secret room in the *botánica*. It was oppressive. It was like being buried alive inside a coffin, the weight of the dirt as real and terrible as sounds from the life that was now closed to him—water gurgling in pipes, the cash register ringing, voices droning, Seroz on the phone with a customer.

He knew when it was dark outside because there were no more sounds from the *botánica* and he could hear the women, giggling and whispering here in the silence with him. He tried to ignore them, to concentrate instead on his escape and the preparation of a meager meal—hard-boiled eggs, toast, some fruit, a cup of instant coffee that was the worst coffee he'd ever had in his life. But his coffeepot had gone on the fritz this morning, and he had neglected to keep a backup in here. It seemed, in fact, that he had overlooked a number of small comforts which would have made his stay here much easier. But it was almost over.

After he'd rinsed off his dinner dishes and stacked them neatly on the counter, he stepped into the shower and pressed his ear to the wall. When he didn't hear anything in the shop, he went back into the room and sat at the edge of the cot. He slid the .38 and the box of ammunition out from under his pillow. He tested the gun before he loaded it, cocking it, firing it, the empty clicks echoing in the air. He held it straight out in front of him and aimed it at the far wall, imagining that *Padrino* stood there. "Bang, bang," he said softly, and laughed.

Bang, bang? Aw, c'mon, sweetie, you're going to have to do better than that.

His head snapped up. Rikki stood between him and the door, hands on her hips. How could she still have fingers? Hadn't he chopped them off? He raised the gun, aimed it at her chest, fired.

Oh really, Manuel, she laughed, striding toward him in her tight slacks, high heels clicking against the concrete floor. She lowered herself to the cot beside him. *Hon, you can't kill him from in here. You know that, don't you?*

Ortega loaded the gun and refused to look at her. He stood, shrugged on the shoulder holster, slipped the gun inside. Then he put on his windbreaker, zipped it halfway up, and sat again to put on his shoes.

In the shop, he heard the phone ring.

It's him.

Two rings, three, five, eight.

Then silence.

He's checking up on you, sweetie, Rikki said, following him into the bathroom. *He knows you're on the island.*

Ortega shut the door so he couldn't hear her. He turned on the faucet, picked up the bottle of Clorox, and disinfected his hands. That tiny spot of blood still bloomed in the center of his palm. He had even pressed a lit cigar against it in an attempt to burn it away, but the speck was impervious to everything.

Rikki knocked on the door. *Let me in. It's not nice to slam the door in my face.*

He didn't reply.

He raised his head and looked into the mirror. The face he saw was not his own. This face was gaunt, haunted, with dry, pale skin that creased deeply at the eyes, the mouth. And behind this man, stepping through the wood of the door, was Rikki, shaking her head.

Don't you know you can't keep me out, Manuel? We have a mission, you and I. Now you'd better hurry up and get going. And call him first.

Ortega spun and lunged past her. He threw open the door and stumbled out into the room, and when she followed him, he scooped up a glass jar from the altar and hurled it at her. It struck the wall and shattered, spewing clumps of dirt and two dead centipedes. Rikki laughed and laughed and called for the other two women, who appeared, surveyed the mess, and shook their heads.

So childish, remarked the old *santera,* staring at him with those gaping black holes where her eyes should've been.

So futile, chided the pretty little *gringa,* hobbling forward, blood running down the back of her foot.

"You're not real," he hissed. "Not real. Not real. Not real."

Then he turned his back on them, knelt on the floor, and pushed away the throw rug that covered the escape panel in the floor. He slid it open, shone a flashlight down inside, tested the rungs on the ladder. Everything seemed to be in good shape.

But first things first.

He let himself out through the panel, into the rear vestibule.

He unlocked the door to the *botánica* and slipped inside, into the cool, familiar scents of incense and candles and fresh flowers. There was no money in the register, but he unlocked the safe in the floor and took what there was, about $500.

Now his hand rested against the phone. Now his fingers were punching out *Padrino*'s number. Now his heart sped up. Sweat leaped across his back. He could barely breathe. He slammed the receiver down, eyes squeezed shut, hand gripping the edge of the counter.

I can't do it. I don't want to hear his voice, to . . .

You have to do it, Rikki said, stopping beside him, leaning into the counter. *You have to.*

Yes. She was right. He knew she was.

555-1697.

There.

It was ringing.

"Hello?"

That voice: so cool, polished, so smooth. A voice that mesmerized.

Betraybetray, chanted Rikki.

"Hello?"

Ortega's hatred poured out of him, seeping from his skin, his hands, radiating from him like an odor, and he knew *Padrino* felt it because he said, *"Eres tú? Manuel?"*

You won't live to see the Black Moon, he thought, then pressed his fingers down over the button, disconnecting them.

Behind him, the women applauded, even though he hadn't said anything.

4

Aline switched on the porch light and stepped outside. The cop Frederick had sent over, who looked like the twin brother of the rookie who'd stood outside her hospital room and accompanied her home this morning, was sitting on the bottom step and glanced around.

"Hi, Detective Scott. Everything okay?"

"Sure. I was about to fix dinner. If you're hungry, I'll fix an extra portion of everything."

"Thanks. But I ate before I came over."

"Okay. If you need anything, ring the bell. Sometimes when I'm up in the loft, I can't hear a knock at the door."

"Right. And lock up."

As if she needed to be told.

Bernie called while Aline was stirring a wine sauce she was trying to make from one of Kincaid's recipes.

"You okay?"

"This place is Fort Knox and I have my own knight outside the door, why wouldn't I be okay?" But even as she said it, fear spurted through her, a miniature geyser.

"You're wrong about this being Fuentes's case, Al. She wouldn't even *have* a case if we'd known from the start that Rikki was killed at her place."

"I wouldn't be much help, Bernie. If anything went haywire, I'd just slow you down."

"Nothing's going to go haywire. I . . . oh, I gotta run. The chief's here. I'll call you."

"Okay. Thanks. Be careful."

But she'd already hung up.

Her supper wasn't a complete success, but it wasn't a total failure either. Kincaid's wine sauce was better than what she'd made, but the chicken was cooked to perfection. She shared bits of it with Wolfe while she sat in front of the TV, watching a *Star Trek* rerun.

Around nine, Hannah Porter called and asked if her offer of a place to stay was still good. It looked as if Karl was going to be out drinking most of the night, she said, and she really didn't want to stay in the lighthouse alone. She sounded miserable and depressed, and who could blame her? Aline felt sorry for her and guilty about what had happened to Porter. She invited her to come on over, she could use the company too, and told Hannah to identify herself to the cop outside. What cop? Hannah wanted to know. Never mind, Aline replied. She'd explain when Hannah got there. She informed the rookie that a friend would be stopping by. No problem, he said, he would just have to take down her name.

Hannah breezed in a while later, blond hair windblown, cheeks flushed with color, an overnight bag in her hand, hoop earrings swinging. "*What* is a policeman doing outside and *why* are you on crutches and is that a *sunburn*?"

"You want all the answers at once?" Aline laughed.

"What I want, Allie, is to vegetate for an evening. Steer me to the bar and I'll make us some drinks."

They settled in the living room with a couple of Bailey's over ice. Hannah sat with her legs tucked under her, everything about her as soft and lovely as a photograph. Although she talked nonstop, her effervescence seemed forced, as though she were trying to convince herself that things were going to turn out just fine despite Porter's arrest, his drinking, their arguments.

". . . I just couldn't have stood another night up there, Allie. Since Karl's release, we seem to argue more than we ever did, and when we're not arguing, he's drinking, and when he's not drinking, he's gone. I don't want a divorce. I don't care about what's happened, about the business with Rikki. It's over. I just want to go forward."

"Does he know that?"

"I've told him, but it doesn't seem to make any difference. I know he didn't kill her, Aline. I know he didn't. He couldn't kill anyone."

"The charges won't stick, Hannah."

Her long, white fingers slipped through her hair, and she sighed. "God, just listen to me, going on about myself. I'm sorry. I always seem to be dumping on you, Allie. Now are you going to tell me what's going on?" She gestured toward the crutch resting against the side of the couch. Aline started telling her the story, picking her way back through what she remembered, censoring some of what she said. Hannah listened with absorption, refilling their drinks when they got low, interrupting now and then with a question. Aline experienced a peculiar catharsis in telling the story, a kind of relief, a lightness. But part of that might've been the Bailey's loosening her tongue. In fact, she seemed quite a bit higher than she should've been from just two Bailey's on a full stomach. Her vision kept blurring, and she finally excused herself and hobbled down the hall toward the bathroom, not entirely sure she was even going to make it.

The floor shifted like sand under her feet. The hallway tilted. She leaned against the wall, dizzy, nauseated, everything a blur, and opened her mouth to call for Hannah. But suddenly Hannah was there, taking her by the shoulders, saying, "Lean against me, Allie, that's right, I'll take care of the crutch, don't worry about a thing, you just had a little too much to drink."

"No," she whispered.

"What? What'd you say, hon? C'mon, lean on me. That's right. Sit here on the toilet seat and I'll get you a cold wash-cloth."

Water running. The floor swaying, buckling, the bathroom swirling. "My crutch," she said, gripping the edge of the sink, trying to stand. "Where's the crutch?"

"Sit down, Allie. You're going to fall if you don't sit down. Here, let me wipe your face."

Cool dampness on her cheeks. Hannah's voice a soft drone. She felt so dizzy, Jesus, and the inside of her mouth tasted thick and sour. "I need to lie down," she said, and tried to get up again.

"You need to stay put, and I'm not going to tell you again." She pushed Aline down roughly onto the toilet seat, holding her there with one hand, doing it even though Aline was taller and weighed more. "This drug is very potent, Allie, and it'd be better for you if you didn't fight it. I didn't want to give it to you, but it's the best way. Really it is. Just let it flow through you."

Her ears were ringing, and she wasn't sure she'd heard Hannah right, couldn't have heard it, must've imagined it, sure, she imagined it, Hannah was a friend, Hannah was

Karl's wife, it was Porter all along, they have a van, a dark van, and Hannah was on the cliff that morning while Karl was in jail, but why oh Christ why

Aline shouted, *"Nooooo!"* and her arms jerked up and she shoved Hannah in the chest, knocking her back, and pulled herself to her feet. But her body felt rubbery, boneless, nothing worked right, the room moved so much. Before she made it to the door, Hannah slammed into her from behind and Aline pitched forward with a scream.

She struck the opposite wall with her hands, breaking her fall, but it didn't matter, Hannah tackled her at the waist and they both went down. She had no strength to struggle, Hannah was riding her back, holding her hands behind her, telling her to stop, please stop, the drug was stronger, she should just let go let go let go. . . .

The front door opened. Aline screamed. Someone came running. The cop, it was the cop, oh please God let it be the cop.

"Well, Hannah, you've gotten yourself into a cute little mess."

"Don't just stand there, for Christ's sakes," barked Hannah. "Help me."

Aline screamed again and squirmed against Hannah's weight on her back, trying to throw her off, to claw at her, slap her, kick, bite, anything. The man, laughing, picked Aline up. She struggled, she fought, she screamed, and he clamped a hand over her mouth. She bit it, and he squeezed her nostrils shut.

"Beddy time, Aline."

I can't breath please no air give me air oh God oh

And she fell back into the soft darkness that waited for her, into the thick, powerful arms of the Black Moon.

5

They crouched at the edge of the trees, watching Uvanti's house.

The basketball court was lit up, and the glow from the lights inside the wall provided sufficient illumination for Kincaid and Ferret to see what was going on. A van had just pulled into the basketball court, and members of a band were getting out and carrying equipment up to the gates, which were open now. Several thugs in suits hung around outside. Two of them broke away from the group, strolled to the end of the driveway, then split up, walking off in opposite directions. The man closest to them spoke into a walkie-talkie as he cut away from the road and headed along the wall.

"This is the second time those two bozos have patrolled the grounds in the last forty minutes. Looks like a pattern to me," Kincaid said.

"Maybe they're expecting trouble."

"Yeah, that's just what I was thinking."

"Doesn't change anything."

"You sure?"

"We ferrets do just fine alone, Ryan." The little man grinned. "And we really don't mind being underground."

"In that case, I'm going to get going."

Ferret dug into his canvas bag and brought out a palm-size

electronic gizmo. "Contact me around eleven thirty. I should be in the cellar by then and know what's what, okay?"

"Right."

Kincaid pocketed the radio, shrugged on his knapsack, and took off through the trees, headed back toward the hill—and the black Buick.

6

Aline was moving and she heard buzzing.

An electric razor, she thought. Kincaid was shaving as he sat on the edge of the bed and as he shifted around, the mattress rolled like a ship in rough seas. Why was Kincaid shaving off his beard? She liked his beard. She couldn't imagine him without it. She wanted to get up and ask him why he was doing it and to ask him not to move around on the bed so much, she was tired, she was bushed. But it was such an effort to open her eyes. And what was wrong with her body? It felt abnormally heavy, as though someone were sitting on her, pressing her down into the mattress. She tried to break loose, but couldn't. She wanted to shout, but couldn't do that either. Her vocal cords didn't work. Nothing worked.

I'm dreaming.

I'm awake in a dream. I'm dreaming that I'm dreaming. I'm dreaming that I'm a prisoner in my own body.

Fear bubbled in her chest, her nostrils, at the corners of her mouth. *Wake up now. Quick. Quick.*

The buzzing was louder now, closer, and it wasn't an electric razor. It was voices. Two voices. A man's and a woman's. Aline tried to hold on to what they were saying, but the words faded in and out of the pounding at the back of her head and now the slow seepage of a memory filled her like air, like gas, like poison. She saw the man's face clearly in her mind and knew she was in a car, headed for her own death, and tried to scream.

"Jesus, Hannah, she's coming out of it. You were supposed to give her enough of that stuff to keep her out at least six hours."

"I did. I . . . what're you doing?"

A sudden, violent movement threw Aline against something.

She rolled. Hit the floor of the car. The car screeched to a stop. The door flew open and a warm rush of air blew over her. Someone lifted her and then she was staring into Ikú's face, into his dark, hungry eyes, eyes that smiled at her now.

"Hello, Aline. I hope that gag's not too tight. Or the ropes. Are they cutting into your wrists? Your ankles?"

She struggled in Martell's arms, but the drug had made her as floppy as a doll. He sat her up against the back of the seat and rolled the gag out of her mouth. "You can scream all you want, Aline. We're in the sticks, and no one will hear you. I want you to drink something for me, okay? And if you don't drink it, I'll have to pour it down your goddamn throat."

Her throat was parched, and it was difficult to form words. But she managed to whisper, "Why?"

Martell touched her cheek with the back of his hand, stroking, and she didn't even have the energy to jerk her head back. "Why you? It's nothing personal, Aline. It's just the way it has to be, that's all. The—"

"Hurry up!" hissed Hannah.

"Shut up!" Martell snapped without looking at her.

Hannah shrank back into her seat.

"The Black Moon is what I've been waiting for all my life," he went on, his voice soft and calm again. "Can you understand that, Aline? Can you understand what a mission is? What real power is?" He sat beside her, squirting something from a bottle into a Styrofoam cup. "When my mother died, I found a journal she'd kept for years. It had everything in it. All about him, about my father, the murders, why she'd never regretted staging the abduction, why she left him. He was dead by then, of course, but I went through all of his things and found the notebook he kept. Of *bilongos*. The ingredients of his *nganga*, everything I needed. He was a gifted, powerful man, Aline. Beyond good and evil, like any master magician."

"Si, please," said Hannah, fear coiling through her voice. "Hurry up. We haven't got all night."

Martell ignored her and kept stirring the stuff in the cup. Aline tried to keep her eyes focused on his face, his hands, but her vision shifted and slid around, as though her eyes were loose, rolling in their sockets like marbles. She could barely hold her body upright and as she started toppling to the side, toward the door, Martell grabbed her arm and pulled her back.

Keep him talking. "Porter," she said, her voice a rasp. "What about Porter?"

"He's a drunk, that's what," spat Hannah from the front seat.

"Well, that's not quite all," said Martell. "He's worth about forty million and once he gets the chair, that'll all go to Hannah." He smiled and in his eyes, she saw the dark hunger of his gods, his quiet madness. "And to me. I think Hannah and I planned things pretty well, don't you, Aline?"

Thinkthinkthink. Do something. "What about Ortega?"

Martell's mouth twitched with irritation. "He was weak." He held the cup up to Aline's mouth. "Now take a few sips of this."

She did, but she didn't swallow. She spat it out at him and, using her feet to push off, slammed her body into his. But she was so weak, he barely felt it, and it only made him angry. "Now that was really stupid, Aline." He clutched her chin, squeezing it hard, forcing her mouth open, and poured the stuff down her throat.

She coughed. She sputtered. She nearly choked. And almost immediately, she felt the drug streaming through her, infecting her, claiming her once again.

28

I

By the time Kincaid arrived at Uvanti's, the party was in full swing. The rooms and courtyard spilled over with people, the band outside was loud but not irritating, and the supply of drinks and food seemed endless.

Kincaid didn't see any familiar faces, not even Fuentes, who'd arrived an hour or so ago. He doubted there was anyone in the crowd who could identify him as anything but a man Starr Abbott dated.

He ordered a Perrier from the courtyard bar and wandered around, looking for Fuentes and a door to the cellar. The only one indicated on the blueprints was in the kitchen, which he found easily enough. But it was secured by two locks and there were too many people going in and out of the kitchen to even entertain the idea of picking them. Ferret had said he thought there was a second door, a staircase Uvanti had added after he'd built the house. It made sense; Uvanti was one of those men who always had another out. The most obvious location was someplace that was off-limits to employees.

That would put it in the north wing, Uvanti's private living quarters.

Kincaid made his way through the crowd, the smoke, the din, wondering where Fuentes was, keeping track of the time. At 11:25, before he reached the north wing, he decided to check in with Ferret. The only place where his privacy would be ensured was a bathroom, and the one he found was nearly as large as his living room: a sunken marble tub, a Jacuzzi, a window

290

filled with plants that jutted out over the outside deck, a skylight, sinks with gold faucets.

He sat on the edge of the toilet, kicked off his right shoe, pushed down the sock, and untaped Ferret's high-tech gizmo from the side of his foot. He hadn't been frisked when he'd arrived, but with so many goons around, why chance it? "Ferret, do you read me? Over."

There was no static when Ferret replied, but his voice sounded like he was speaking underwater. "I read you, Ryan. There must be five hundred bottles of wine down here, but so far I haven't found anything else. I'll keep looking. Contact me again in half an hour. Over."

"I've only found one door to the cellar. It's in the kitchen, and it's locked up tight. Have you seen any other staircase? Over."

"Not yet. Talk to you at midnight. Over and out."

As Kincaid taped the device to his foot, again, he wished he could hide his weapon as easily. He flushed the toilet, just in case anyone was out in the hall, then left.

One of Uvanti's thugs was in the hallway. His glance seemed sharp, deliberate, but Kincaid couldn't tell what it meant. Then the thug looked away and walked past him, into the bathroom, and shut the door.

Turn down the paranoia, Ryan.

He continued on to the north wing. The long marble hallway was lined with paintings from Uvanti's private art collection. Kincaid perused them, impressed in spite of himself, and followed the other guests into a room at the end of the hall. Here, under lock and key, under glass that was probably wired to an alarm system and impervious to everything but a nuclear bomb, was the $40 million Van Gogh.

A vase of blue flowers.

Forty million for a vase of goddamn blue flowers. I don't get it.

"Incredible," breathed one woman in a leather dress.

"Magnificent," exclaimed the man at her side.

"*Van Gogh*," whispered a woman in silk.

Fuckola, Kincaid thought, and moved on to the other paintings in the room.

"Well, Mr. Kane."

It took him a moment longer than it should have to respond to the name—the only name Uvanti knew him by—and he couldn't tell if the discrepancy had registered on the man. He smiled and gestured toward a painting to Kincaid's left. "You like it?"

His body stood between Kincaid and the identifying plate beneath the painting, so he couldn't see the artist's name. But the painting seemed familiar. It depicted two women, one standing inside half a seashell, another to her right, and off to the left, a man and woman with wings who were presumably angels. He knew he'd seen it before but couldn't recall where. "It's nice."

"Nice." Uvanti guffawed. "Yes, it's definitely nice. I'll give you a hint. The year was around 1460. The artist was a member of the so-called Medici circle, and did this painting for a member of the Medici family. It's probably his most famous."

Kincaid chuckled. "You'll have to give me more than that."

"A lack of concern with deep space. No great passion for anatomy, the bodies seem to float when they touch the ground, and yet, despite their etherealness, they're still voluptuous, don't you agree?"

Kincaid suddenly remembered. The Uffizi Gallery in Florence. He had gone there one morning because it had been raining and a museum was the best place to be when it rained in Florence. And he had seen this painting there. It had struck him, he remembered, because of the shell, of the woman who seemed to be rising out of it. Venus on the half shell, he'd thought, which was close. It was Botticelli's *The Birth of Venus*.

But what the hell was it doing here?

"Botticelli," he said, and gave the title.

Uvanti, who'd obviously pegged Ryan Kane as an artistic illiterate, slapped him on the back. "*Very* good, Mr. Kane. But it's not the original, of course," he added. "This is a reproduction done by an art student." He ran his finger along the lower edge of the painting. "See? No signature. But I guarantee you that if the painting had Botticelli's signature, this lovely reproduction could fool some of the art critics."

His hand remained on Kincaid's shoulder, urging him to the next painting and the next, away from the crowd and into a smaller room where there were more paintings. He pointed out why one work was better than another, how to identify the period and the artist, what to look for in good art. For the most part, as far as Kincaid's unpracticed eye could tell, these paintings were the real McCoy. So what was Uvanti's point about the

Botticelli? To flaunt his knowledge of art? To gloat? To let Kincaid know he was onto him?

And then it struck him.

Here. It's all in here. Ferret wasn't going to find anything in the cellar because there *was* no stash of paintings. Uvanti's private little joke, testimony to his belief in his own impunity, the way he got his secret thrills, was that the phony paintings were all hanging in these rooms, and perhaps even on the boat, among those that were authentic. That was the test. If the phonies passed the scrutiny of his guests, then they were shipped out.

With his courier.

Kincaid started to say something, but Uvanti spoke first. "I would advise you not to make any trouble, Mr. Kane. Max is right behind you, and he gets very annoyed when people don't follow my instructions."

Quasimodo poked a gun into the small of Kincaid's back and grinned when he glanced around, gold tooth flashing. "Walk, fucker."

"I believe you were looking for Starr, weren't you, Mr. Kane?" Uvanti's voice remained pleasant, he kept smiling, and his grip on Kincaid's arm tightened as he guided him through a door, into a study.

The door shut behind him.

Fuentes was seated in a high-back chair, mouth gagged, arms and legs tied. "This, Mr. Kane, is where we're having our private party."

He was no longer smiling, and he nodded to Quasimodo. "Frisk him, Max."

2

Ortega's exit from the secret room led to a manhole cover on a side street half a block away. He hurried down the road, bag over his shoulder, and stopped at a friend's garage. It was locked up for the night, but Ortega had a key and let himself in.

The old Pontiac he stored here was just where he'd left it. He opened the trunk, tossed his bag inside, and took out the phony license tag. He screwed it onto the back, then slid behind the wheel, praying the *orishas* had forgiven him for his blindness, his stupidity, and would make the car start.

It cranked up on the first try. The engine ran rough, and clouds of blue smoke spewed from the tailpipe. But the fact that it had started at all meant the saints were on his side. The car would get him where he was going.

He drove into the hills, up, up, away from the town, keeping well under the speed limit. The saints, after all, would only help a man who helped himself, and if he got pulled over for speeding, they would let him suffer the consequences.

The warm June air swept through the car. He relished the feel of it against his face, his arms. He drew it deeply into his lungs, purging the stale air from the secret room, and now and then he touched his hand to the bulge under his windbreaker.

The .38.

It glowed with a life of its own. It heated the skin against his ribs. He felt its reality just as he did Rikki's presence. Ortega knew she had followed him out of his secret exit and was with him here in the car. Every so often she touched his shoulder or his arm, as if to reassure him that he was doing the right thing, that she supported him, would help him. But for now she was quiet, watchful, waiting, expectant.

And so he drove, headed for Pirate's Cove Marina.

3

"I'm going to say this one more time." Uvanti tossed Kincaid's wallet onto the desk, where he'd been flipping through his I.D. "Our sensors picked up radio communication coming from the bathroom you used. Now who the fuck were you talking to?"

Kincaid, seated in a chair next to Fuentes, his hands and feet tied, shook his head. "I don't have any radio gear. Your pal there frisked me, Uvanti. You found my gun. That's all I had."

"Ms. Fuentes told us the same thing, Kincaid. And look what we found on her." He reached into his pocket and held up one of Ferret's gizmos. "A *very* sophisticated piece of equipment."

Kincaid glanced at Fuentes, trying to read her wide, terrified eyes, then looked back at Uvanti. "I don't know what you're talking about."

A nice, wide smile from Uvanti now as he glanced at Quasimodo. "Convince him we mean business, Max."

Quasimodo grabbed the front of Kincaid's shirt, yanked him to his feet like he weighed no more than five pounds, and sank his huge, powerful fist into Kincaid's gut. He crumpled to the floor, coughing, trying to catch his breath, black stars swimming behind his eyes. A foot slammed into his kidneys. He rolled to escape the next blow and heard Uvanti say, "Hold it, Max. Let's see if he has anything to say."

Uvanti's face was a blurred shape hovering above him. "How about a slightly different question, Kincaid? Are you also a Fed, like our little friend Miranda?"

It was a second before he could speak without gagging on his tongue. "You saw my I.D. I'm a private eye."

"Who hired you?"

Kincaid spit out blood. Uvanti helped him to a sitting position and wiped his mouth for him with a clean white handkerchief. "Mr. Kincaid's feeling a little sick, Max. Give him a glass of water."

Quasimodo came over with a glass in his hand, gold tooth flashing as he grinned. "You thirsty, man?" And he tossed the water in Kincaid's face.

"Oh, that wasn't very nice, Max." Uvanti crouched in front of Kincaid. "So who hired you?"

"The cops. And if they don't hear from me by midnight, your game's up."

"You're bluffing." But the smallest glimmer of doubt curled through Uvanti's eyes.

"Am I? You going to risk that?"

Uvanti glanced at his watch, at Fuentes, at Quasimodo. "Well, then, I guess we'll just have to put you two someplace safe until after the cops arrive, won't we? Take them downstairs, Max."

Quasimodo, ever obedient, removed the gag from Fuentes's mouth as Uvanti held a gun to her head, and cut through the ropes on her ankles. "And just how the hell are you going to explain the fact that we aren't here, Nick?" snapped Fuentes. "Don't you get it? The whole thing's a setup. They're *onto* you. They know about the art scam. They know you killed the Baker woman and the other two."

Uvanti patted her cheek. "Your concern is touching, honey. But I didn't kill Rikki or anyone else; Ortega's behind it. And I'm afraid the police aren't going to find any evidence to support your art scam theory. In fact, you two are the only ones who know about it. My story is that neither of you ever showed up at the party. Once you're dead, who's going to prove otherwise? It'll be their word against mine."

The man who thinks he can buy his way out of anything, Kincaid thought. And the hell of it was that he might just get away with it.

Uvanti glanced at Quasimodo. "Cut the ropes on his legs, Max. So he can walk to the cellar. And Mr. Kincaid, please don't try anything. I don't want to kill my pretty little Starr. Not yet." He smiled again and jammed the butt of his gun against Fuentes's cheek.

When Kincaid's legs were free, Uvanti told him to get up. He did, but with great difficulty. His kidneys throbbed, and he had to lean into a chair to keep from toppling over. Uvanti took the gun away from Fuentes's mouth, pulled her to her feet, shoved her over toward Kincaid. "Both of you get over to where Max is," he snapped.

Quasimodo was standing behind them, next to a bookshelf, his weapon aimed at Kincaid, his other hand resting on top of a book. He flipped it down and the entire shelf started to move. "Real original," Kincaid muttered.

Uvanti started to say something, but there was a sharp rap at the door. Quasimodo flicked the book back up, stopping the movement of the shelf, and said, "Who is it?"

"Simon Martell."

Uvanti immediately clamped a hand over Fuentes's mouth and pressed his weapon to her temple. "Don't even consider it," he hissed at Kincaid, then nodded at Quasimodo, who slipped his gun back into his jacket and cracked the door, blocking it with his immense body.

"Nick's busy," Quasimodo said above the music that drifted into the room.

Kincaid couldn't hear Martell's response.

He barely breathed.

A bead of sweat rolled into Kincaid's eye; he blinked it away. Behind Uvanti, in the dark hole of the partially open bookcase, something caught Kincaid's attention. Movement? *Or just wishful thinking?*

The conversation at the door continued.

The music seemed to get louder.

Time slowed, and everything in the room focused with utter clarity: Quasimodo at the door, Uvanti gripping Fuentes at the neck, the gun now at her back, and Ferret, easing himself out of the dark hole, coming up behind Uvanti, as silent and cunning as the creature he was named after. In one hand he gripped the .357 and in the other, a bottle of wine.

Easy Ferret. Easy does it.

And then he struck.

The bottle crashed down over Uvanti's head, showering him and Fuentes with glass and wine. Ferret, quick as lightning, leaped up and kicked the gun from Uvanti's hand before he'd even reacted. Now he stumbled back, groaning, gripping his bleeding head, and Fuentes hurled herself away from him. Kincaid slammed into Uvanti, knocking them both to the floor. Uvanti was still conscious and threw Kincaid off. He scrambled up and dived toward his weapon several yards away, but Fuentes—her hands still bound—threw herself over it.

Two explosions rocked the room. Screams erupted in the hall. Quasimodo, who'd taken one of the bullets, pitched forward and landed on top of Uvanti. The floor shook. *"Keep those people out of here!"* boomed Gene Frederick, and then the door slammed.

The sound echoed. It rose and fell in the sudden silence in the room. No one moved and then everyone moved at once. Ferret cut Kincaid's hands loose and helped him up. Martell was crouched next to Fuentes, picking bits of glass from her hair, her forehead. The chief and Bernelli were rolling Quasimodo off Uvanti.

"He's got more men around here," Kincaid said.

Frederick nodded. "We've taken care of them." He turned Uvanti over; the man's eyes fluttered open and he groaned.

"My head. Jesus, my head. I need help, I need a doctor, someone get me a doctor, my—"

"Shut up, dickhead." Frederick grabbed him by the front of the shirt and jerked him forward. "You have the right to remain silent . . ."

"You had a search warrant, so they aren't going to be able to say it was illegal entry," Martell was saying. "Ferret shot Max in self-defense, and I hardly think Uvanti's going to charge Ferret with assault when he was holding Miranda and Ryan hostage. Your case is going to stick, Gene.''

They were sitting in Uvanti's courtyard, waiting as Bernie and several other cops removed paintings from the walls, packed them up, and made a thorough search of the cellar and the rest of the house. They were surrounded by the remains of the banquet—crepes that were spoiling, bottles of open champagne that were going flat, pieces of honey-dipped chicken the flies had found, delectable deserts that had been knocked off the tables.

From where Kincaid sat, he could see the medic working on Fuentes in the kitchen, plucking slivers of glass from her face and arms. Birds twittered and swooped into the courtyard, announcing that dawn wasn't far off. Kincaid was so tired he couldn't even bear to think of moving, but Ferret was anxious to split.

Kincaid got up and went into the kitchen. Fuentes turned her head slightly. This elicited a grumble from the medic, who told her to sit still, please, he'd never seen so much glass in his life. ''You leaving?''

''Unless you want me to stick around.''

''How much more glass is there?'' she asked the medic.

''Enough to keep you here until daybreak.''

''You go on, Ryan. I'll call you later today.''

He kissed her on top of the head and felt strange, disembodied, as though he were outside his own bones, looking down on himself, Fuentes, and the medic. There was something wrong about the scene, about the distance he stood from Fuentes now. It was only a few feet, but it seemed immense, a gulf, an unbridgeable chasm. *It's over,* he thought. Just like that, it had ended, here, now, in the rubble of Uvanti's scam.

It depressed him.

When he and Ferret left a few minutes later, Martell walked out with them.

''How'd you know they were in there?'' Ferret asked.

''I didn't. It was just a lucky guess. Then when Max started acting all weird, I knew something was going on and I alerted Gene.'' He reached into his jacket and brought out a walkie-talkie. ''Gene had given me this just in case. He wanted to make sure there was another backup.''

''See, I told you he wasn't half bad,'' said Ferret as they reached the black Buick.

''I don't remember you saying that.''

"Picky, picky," Ferret sighed.

Kincaid gazed after Martell, remembering the man's words as he sped off in his white Camaro. *Got any ideas who was after her up there on Suicide Cliff? . . . A woman's body in a dumpster . . . Got any ideas . . . Woman's body . . . Got any . . . Woman . . .*

"Hey, Ryan, want me to drive?"

"I will."

He swung out of the lot and sped down the road where Martell had vanished. Dust flew up around the Buick. He pressed down on the accelerator, alarm slicing through his fatigue, glimmers of a new pattern shoving up against the old.

"What's your hurry, Ryan? This Buick isn't made for the autobahn, you know."

. . . woman's body in the dumpster . . . Any ideas who was after her up there on Suicide Cliff? . . . "What time does the ferry leave from Tango?"

"During the week, I don't think the first one leaves until seven. Why?"

"The night we saw Martell at the Pink Moose. How could he have possibly known it was a *woman* in the dumpster, Ferret? Even Aline didn't know then. And that night at the hospital. He slipped up when he asked if we had any ideas on who was chasing her up on the cliff. And there've been other things that—"

"Pull off up there and call Sweet Pea's place." Ferret pointed at a bait and tackle shop just ahead, and a moment later Kincaid swerved into the lot, hopped out, sprinted to the phone booth.

He reached Aline's answering machine, which she'd told him she wouldn't put on. Dread poured through him as he raced back to the Buick. "What time does the first ferry leave? That's where Whitkins was killed."

"Not until 6:30. I don't think he'd take her there, Ryan. It's got to be his sloop. Ortega must've taken her to Martell's sloop at the Cove Marina while he was here at the party. Let's try there first. Get this clunker up as high as she'll go, Ryan."

It was 5:27 A.M.

29

I

Sound was the first thing that returned to Aline's world, specifically a soft, familiar sound that made her feel safe, comfortable, sleepy. She wanted to float away in the sound, lose herself in it. But another part of her struggled to seize it, identify it, and shouted, *All right, pay attention now. Rise and shine. C'mon, upupup.*

But she didn't feel like getting up. A thick sourness coated the inside of her mouth. A terrible dryness crouched at the back of her throat. She wanted water. *That's the sound. Water purling against the sides of a boat. And an engine.*

Her eyes snapped open. The edge of a table swam into view. Then dusky light oozing through a porthole. Now, just off her feet, a door. Next to it, a small two-burner stove. She knew where she was. She knew, and as panic broke loose inside her, she gasped, struggled to sit up. But she was on her side, hands tied behind her, feet bound. Her right arm had gone to sleep from lying on it so long, and now her injured ankle woke up and screamed.

She sucked in her breath, riding the pain, willing it to stop, then rolled onto her stomach and used her toes, shoulders, and head to push herself up. She rocked back on her heels. Peered out the porthole.

Water, nothing but goddamn water and fog, so much of it she couldn't see shore.

She strained her neck, searching the sky, and there, to the east, she saw it, the first tiny bite of the Black Moon against the blaze of the rising sun.

They were moving, but where? Didn't matter. She needed to

do something. Get the ropes off. Escape. *No. First think it through. Calm down and think it through.* Yes. All right. What would Martell do?

Cover his ass.

Then he had gone to Uvanti's party after getting her onto the boat, and Hannah had come out here alone. He intended to meet her here. But since the eclipse had started, then wouldn't he already be topside?

Unless he got held up.

Unless something went haywire at Uvanti's.

Let that be what happened.

Ropes. She needed to get the ropes off.

They were loose enough at her wrists so she had some mobility in her hands. But the more she worked at them, the more the ropes burned the undersides of her wrists. *Won't work. Need a knife. Scissors. Anything sharp.*

She looked frantically around the cabin.

The stove. Fire.

Aline sat back, legs doubled beneath her, then swung them out and over the edge of the bunk. *Steady. Stand slowly.* There was enough slack in the ropes around her ankles to inch forward in baby half steps, but at this rate it would take her all day to reach the stove. She hopped a step and pain exploded in her ankle and her eyes filled with tears.

Another hop, another, each worse than the last. It felt as if a white-hot poker was pressed up against the bones and tissues in her foot, as if her skin there were being flayed. She stopped once to rest, but it was even worse when she resumed, so she didn't stop again. She kept her eyes on the stove, where the box of kitchen matches was.

She reached the stove, moved another step, tried the knob. The door was locked. No surprise.

Another turn. Her hands grappled for the box of kitchen matches. She gripped it, pulled, the damn thing wouldn't open, so she jerked and it flew open, spewing matches on the floor. She crouched, sat, picked up a couple, stood again.

She struck the match, backed up to the stove once more, realized she couldn't hold the match to the burner and switch on the gas at the same time. If she dropped the match and then turned on the gas, the match would go out and she'd have to start all over again.

Gas first, on low. Its nauseating sweetness hissed into the air.

Match.

Bingo.

Aline pulled out on the ropes as far as they would go so she wouldn't get burned when she held them to the flame. But there wasn't more than an inch or two. It would have to do. She backed up to the tiny stove again, the flame's heat uncomfortably warm before the flames had even touched the ropes.

The odor of the burning cord kissed the air, a benediction. But she couldn't hold her hands near the flame for long, and pulled them back, working at the ropes again, feeling them give a little. Again. Again. On the fourth sweep over the flames, the ropes snapped loose and she clutched her freed arms against her, licked at the undersides of her wrists, cooling them.

Drawer. Knife. Fast.

She pulled so hard on the drawer it nearly flew out of the cabinet. The silverware inside clattered, and she grabbed the edges, heart drumming, ears straining for some sign that the noise had been heard on deck.

The power had been cut back.

The boat was slowing.

The light in the cabin had dimmed.

She grabbed a knife and sliced through the ropes at her feet.

Let's not kid ourselves, Al. Over the side is your best bet. You can swim faster than you can walk.

But first she had to get out of the cabin.

Since she couldn't squeeze through the portholes and the door was locked, she picked up the knife. It wouldn't do her much good against a gun, but it was better than nothing. She reached for the skunk-shaped iron planter on the shelf above the stove, and dumped the ivy and dirt behind her. A knife and a planter, hardly the stuff that won battles.

The engine stopped.

2

The rental shop at the Cove Marina didn't open until 6:30. The only people up and about were old-timers fishing on the dock, looming in the fog like shadows. Kincaid ran out to the dock while

Ferret called the police station. He stopped alongside a gray-haired man who was baiting a hook and asked if he'd seen a sloop sail out within the last few hours. The sloop with Martell on it.

"Nope," he replied without looking up. "I just got here about five minutes ago. But maybe Luke knows. He's been here since three. Hey, Luke," he called.

"Ayuh?" said a voice in the fog.

"You seen a sloop sail outa here in the last few hours?"

"Nope. Only things that've left since three are a dinghy and an outboard, which chugged outa here about twenty minutes ago."

"Did you see who was on either one of them?"

"Nope. When the sloop left from south dock, it was still dark and I only heard the outboard. It musta left from the other side of the marina."

"Anyone here got a dinghy or a boat I can rent?"

"If we did, mister," said the gray-haired fellow, "we'd be using it ourselves."

"Right. Thanks." He raced back to the Buick and reached it almost at the same time as Ferret.

Seconds later, the Buick tore toward the lagoon three miles east, where the seaplanes were docked.

Up, up through the fog in a spray of water, up toward the strange new sun.

Once he was headed west into the Gulf at eight hundred feet, Kincaid could see nothing but a soup of fog below them. He considered radioing Tango tower of his intentions, but decided against it. They would want to know who, what and where; they would probably have to call the station. It would just waste time. He switched to the emergency frequency, advised planes in the area of his position, and dived three hundred feet, knowing that if the FAA got wind of this, his license was history.

Ferret, paralyzed in the seat beside him, groaned and slapped his hands over his eyes.

Nothing. The fog was still too thick.

He dived again. 475 feet, 450, 375, 225. No lights, no boats, and certainly no other planes.

"Palm Key," Ferret said suddenly, hands dropping away from his eyes.

"What?"

"Palm Key. That's where he's headed."

"How do you know that?"

"It's where Martell and Sweet Pea go, Ryan. Trust me. I know these things. She's mentioned it. *Si and I are sailing out to Palm Key.* Like that. Believe me."

Kincaid believed, glanced at the map open in his lap, set his heading, and took the seaplane down another hundred feet.

3

Ortega, hunkered down behind a barrier of sea oats and rocks, watched the sloop as it stopped less than ten yards offshore, a ghost ship materializing in the thin fog. He saw a figure on board, someone lowering the anchor. He peered through his binoculars and focused on the Porter woman. He had known about her and *Padrino*, but he'd thought she was just one more of his women. He'd been too blind to understand that she played any role at all.

Well, he was blind no longer, and it wasn't difficult to piece the story together. The bottom line was money. Porter's money.

They had known about Porter's affair with Rikki and had manipulated circumstances to make it look as though Porter had killed her. Mrs. Porter had even hired the private detective, Kincaid, to do research for Porter's book on *santería*, so there would be a witness to attest to her husband's interest in the subject. They had known that his arrest, even if the charges didn't stick, would humiliate him sufficiently so that he would react in a predictable way—a suicide, perhaps (or a murder that looked like suicide?), a fatal car accident on Old Post when Porter had been drinking (everyone knew he drank too much), or maybe even something more sordid, a gun to his temple (held by who? Hannah? Martell himself?).

Whatever the scenario, Ortega knew that in six months or a year Martell would marry Porter's widow and share in her considerable wealth, after convicting Uvanti—*and killing me, he intended to kill me all along*—in a well-publicized trial that would put him back in the spotlight. So Martell would get the money, the millions, his career.

But not now.

He heard the second engine before he saw it. That would be

Martell, racing the final mile from Tango, keeping his appointment with destiny. The detective was somewhere inside the
cabin, then, drugged or knocked out, and of course she would
be brought out onto the deck, to die the way Abel Whitkins had
died fifty years ago.

Except that he would stop it.

Ortega stripped down to his shorts, balled up his clothes,
threw them far enough back so the rising water wouldn't wash
them away. He would wait until *Padrino* was on board the sloop
before he started swimming.

4

The jangle of keys.

Aline pressed back against the wall, the iron planter raised
above her head. The distant whine of an outboard was probably
Martell, she thought, and she knew she wouldn't have much
time to make it up on deck and overboard before he pulled
alongside the sloop.

*If I don't hit Hannah hard enough, if my foot slows me down,
if I freak, if I*

The door creaked as it opened.

Hannah bounced down the steps.

Saw the empty bunk.

The only word she got out was, "What . . ." And then Aline
slammed the iron pot over her head and Hannah crumpled to
the floor.

Please don't be dead. Aline felt for a pulse at her neck, found
it, patted her down for a weapon. She was clean.

She dropped the knife she held and stumbled out of the cabin,
hands on the railing for support, her bum foot wailing.

On deck. The Black Moon gobbling up the sun. The air darkening, gloomy.

The whine of the second engine much closer now.

She stripped off her jeans, her blouse.

Thinning fog: maybe twenty or thirty yards to shore.

The second outboard appeared.

Aline climbed over the railing and dropped into the Gulf.

5

Kincaid saw the treetops on Palm Key, but not much else. Most of the island had been swallowed up in high tide and twilight.

"*There!*" Ferret shouted. "I see the mast!"

Kincaid turned, circling until he spotted it, dropped another fifty feet, and saw an outboard chugging toward shore. *Martell.* He swooped in lower, lower, until the altimeter registered a bare cight feet above the Gulf. The force of the propeller blew off most of the fog and churned up the water around the outboard.

"Bastard's going to shoot!" Ferret shouted.

Kincaid slammed the throttle in all the way and pulled back on the wheel. The seaplane zoomed upward fifty feet. He leveled out, banked thirty degrees, then pushed the wheel in, aiming the seaplane at the outboard, hoping to cut it off before it reached shore.

But the outboard was too close to land, speeding toward a dark something bobbing in the water, diving, surfacing again.

Aline.

Kincaid turned and headed toward the outboard from the side. Martell saw him coming, sliced sharply to the left, right, left again. The seaplane swooped in low, and Martell ducked as it zoomed over him. Lift again, Kincaid thought. Lift turn dive, lift turn dive, over and over until the plane seemed to be an extension of his body, his mind, his will. Three sweeps, four, buying Aline time.

Martell was half standing now, trying to steer the outboard and fire at the plane. The sight of him so enraged Kincaid that he slammed the wheel in and passed over the outboard within a yard of Martell's head. He ducked, and then Kincaid was past him, rising up over the sloop, already planning his next sweep. But when he played the pedals which controlled the aileron in the tail, nothing happened.

The fucker shot us.

He couldn't turn.

"We're going in, Ferret," he shouted, and pulled all the way back on the throttle.

The engine died. The seaplane hit the water.

6

Yes yes yes come to me come to me, Padrino. Come quickly. Try to outrun the plane. Very good. Closer, just a little closer.

Ortega aimed the .38 at the outboard. The weapon was firm and steady in his hands, and as his finger squeezed against the trigger, power flowed through him like an electrical current, he felt it, a power from the Black Moon, a power that should've been his from the beginning.

He fired once, twice, a third time.

Padrino's hands flew up. Ortega saw him topple to the side, into the steering mechanism on the outboard. The boat swerved and raced toward the sloop.

Just beyond it, the seaplane smacked the water.

7

Aline stumbled to her feet in the shallow water, breath erupting from her mouth in sharp, ugly gasps. She heard the high whine of the outboard, still behind her, coming for her, ready to mow her down. But when her head snapped around, she saw it careening wildly toward the sloop and the seaplane beyond it.

Kincaid's in the plane. "*Ryan!*" she shouted, waving her arms, jumping around on one foot. "*Get out of the plane!*" But a second later, the outboard crashed into the sloop and it exploded.

A fireball flew into the sky, spewing greasy smoke, momentarily obscuring the Black Moon, and then the seaplane blew up, Kincaid inside it.

Embers and debris rained down, and she threw herself into the shoals to escape it, her heart breaking up inside her.

8

Ortega charged into the trees, scooped up his clothes, and raced toward his dinghy on the north side of the tiny key. He laughed and sobbed and prayed. Thorns bit at his bare skin. He stumbled, caught himself, crashed on through the brush. *I've won, I've won.*

When he reached the dinghy, Rikki was waiting for him just as he knew she would be, Rikki who smelled of rain and summer, of the future.

I've won.

He got only six miles into the Gulf before a Coast Guard cutter picked him up.

9

Her cheek was pressed against the cool, wet sand. The smell of gasoline and oil hung in the darkening air; fire still raged on the water. Now and then a tongue of flame raced out from its source, an eager youngster intent on ruin. But it always hissed out when it reached the end of the slick that had fed it.

Aline closed her eyes, waiting for something. The end of the eclipse. A boat from Tango. Illumination. A cessation of the huge, oppressive ache inside her. The strength to get up, to move, act, do.

She heard something, shouts, voices, and lifted up. There, off to her left, rising out of the water like some sort of Neptunian being, was Kincaid, and riding piggyback was Ferret, shouting, "Hey, Sweet Pea!" And in the next instant, he said, "Oh God, Ryan, I'm gonna puke."

Kincaid fell to his knees in the sand, and Ferret rolled off him, doing exactly what he'd said he was going to do. Aline, laughing, sobbing, stumbled toward them, through the gloomy light of the Black Moon.

The Lighthouse
Late July

The lack of rain had parched the island. The lighthouse grounds were a patchwork of brown and faded green, strewn with shriveled hibiscus blossoms that had fallen from the bushes. The gardenias were dying, the zinnias had gone into shock. It was as if the place had slipped into ruin once again, Aline thought, and it wasn't even empty yet.

Kincaid drove the Saab to the end of the twisted driveway and stopped behind Porter's van. The rear doors were open. Cartons, boxes, and trunks were wedged inside, and Porter was coming down from the garage, pulling a dolly behind him with a second trunk on it.

"Most people hire moving companies for this," Kincaid called as they got out of the car.

"Most people, Ryan, don't have the junk I do. And I've only gotten as far as the garage."

Porter sounded cheerful and pleased to have company. He had never looked better. He bore so little resemblance to the man who had been arrested weeks ago, it was as if the old Porter had died with Hannah on the boat that night. He bussed Aline hello on the cheek, something the old Porter would never have done, and the three of them chatted as he and Kincaid hoisted the trunk into the rear of the van.

She leaned against the vehicle, letting her fingers glide over the cool, dark metal. This was the van that had chased her over Suicide Cliff, the van Martell had borrowed from Hannah while Porter was in jail. She expected to feel something when her fingers lingered against the metal, a connection to Martell, perhaps, to what had driven him. But she felt nothing. Most of his secrets had died with him, and only the memory of events remained.

Ortega had eagerly shared his view of some of those events. He'd traced his relationship with Martell back several years and Martell's affair with Hannah back to a meeting more than a year ago, when she'd consulted him for background information on one of Porter's books. But Ortega's perceptions were thickly colored by his obsession and hatred, by his visions, his superstitions. So she was left with her own interpretations, and in the end, it was all anyone ever had anyway.

There were some nights, though, when she lay awake in the dark, listening to the night sounds, certain she could feel Martell somewhere nearby, outside on the porch, maybe, crouched under her window. Or inside the room with her, waiting for her to acknowledge him. It was silly, of course. But still . . .

They went inside the lighthouse where it was cooler. There were empty bookshelves in the hallway, half-packed boxes on the kitchen counters. They settled at the table with fresh coffee, the magnificent view of the Gulf spread out before them.

". . . land in Auckland on the first of September and then I'm going to wing it from there," Porter was saying. "Everything's going into storage, and by tomorrow the lighthouse will be listed with a realtor."

"How much do you want for it?" Kincaid asked.

He looked around, some of his exuberance bleeding out of him. "Hell, I just want to get rid of it. I told the realtor to list it for a hundred thousand."

Aline nearly choked. "You're giving it away."

"We only paid fifty-five for the place because the county wanted to unload it. We put another twenty or thirty into it. I figured a hundred is fair."

"Well?" Aline asked when they walked outside a while later. "What do you think?"

"Whose place is worth more? Yours or mine?"

She winked an eye shut against the glare of the light. "Probably yours. It's bigger."

"Then we could sell my place and rent yours and finance half of it. Or we could sell both places and buy the lighthouse outright. No mortgage."

"Okay," she said. "That sounds good."

"Which sounds good?"

"Whichever. As long as we do it."

She stopped and looked back at the lighthouse, brilliant white against the blue Tango sky, sunlight winking against the glass in the tower.

"You sure?" he asked.

"Absolutely," she said, and smiled.

About the Author

Alison Drake lives in South Florida. She is the author of TANGO KEY and FEVERED.